THE
LONG FLIGHT
HOME

THE
LONG FLIGHT
HOME

ALAN HLAD

JOHN SCOGNAMIGLIO BOOKS
KENSINGTON BOOKS
www.kensingtonbooks.com

JOHN SCOGNAMIGLIO BOOKS are published by

Kensington Publishing Corp.
119 West 40th Street
New York, NY 10018

All Kensington titles, imprints and distributed lines are available at special quantity discounts for bulk purchases for sales promotion, premiums, fund-raising, educational or institutional use.

Special book excerpts or customized printings can also be created to fit specific needs. For details, write or phone the office of the Kensington Special Sales Manager: Kensington Publishing Corp., 119 West 40th Street, New York, NY 10018, Attn. Special Sales Department. Phone: 1-800-221-2647.

The JS and John Scognamiglio Books logo is a trademark of Kensington Publishing Corp.

Library of Congress Card Catalogue Number: 2019932232

ISBN-13: 978-1-4967-2167-9
ISBN-10: 1-4967-2167-5
First Kensington Hardcover Edition: July 2019

ISBN-13: 978-1-4967-2169-3 (e-book)
ISBN-10: 1-4967-2169-1 (e-book)
First Kensington Electronic Edition: July 2019

10 9 8 7 6 5 4 3 2 1

Printed in the United States of America

THE
LONG FLIGHT
HOME

CHAPTER 1

EPPING, ENGLAND — SEPTEMBER 7, 1940

On the day of the atrocity, Susan Shepherd was working in a pigeon loft, sprinkling feed—a mixture of sorghum, wheat, and field peas—into a long metal tray. A few sleepy squabs lifted their heads from under their wings but made no effort to leave their nests. Most of the pigeons were outside, circling the rolling green sheep pasture or decorating the bending birches of Epping Forest.

"You're going to help us save Britain," she whispered.

The loft was a twelve-foot-by-twelve-foot wooden shed lined with cubbyholes like a primary-school classroom. But instead of holding rain boots, hats, or wet gloves, the tiny compartments were the homes for more than sixty pigeons. This was the original loft, constructed by her grandfather, Bertie, before she had been born. And over the past year, a dozen new lofts had been hastily built. Except for more pigeons, her grandfather's farm hadn't changed since she'd left to study zoology at the University of London. Same musty smell: a mixture of down feathers, droppings, and grain. She hadn't expected to return home so soon, but her volunteer work for the National Pigeon Service had postponed her studies in lieu of a more important endeavor—raising war pigeons.

As Susan brushed away specks of feed from her well-worn skirt—repaired with darn and patch—her eyes were drawn to the faded pencil marks on a wall Bertie had made to record her growth as a wee child. She had pressed her back against the wall and stretched her neck like a giraffe. Desperate to grow, she had even resorted to stuffing her shoes with tissue. And six months later, Bertie only laughed when his granddaughter, who failed to remember her tissue, had shrunk an inch. During her childhood, she had grown quite fond of the pencil gracing the top of her head, the sound of scratching lead, and turning in anticipation to check her height as an audience of pigeons cooed in amusement. Susan kneeled and touched her first marking as a toddler, a date shortly after she had come to live with Bertie.

I had a little bird, its name was Enza. I opened the window, and in flew Enza.

Susan shook the childhood jump-rope rhyme from her mind, then picked up a wooden spoon and rapped the side of a can, once used to hold the paint that now peeled from the siding of her grandfather's cottage.

Pigeons flocked through a hole cut near the ceiling. One by one, they entered the loft and fluttered to the ground. The pigeons scuttled along the floor, jutting their heads and flicking their feet, while their bodies remained eloquent and steady, as if they could balance acorns on their tails. The last bird entered, stood on the grain barrel, and tilted its head.

"Hello, Duchess," Susan said.

The bird—unique with its glowing, purplish-green neck plume, more appropriate for a peacock than a pigeon—fluttered to the floor and waddled to Susan's feet.

"I'm afraid I've spoiled you." Susan poured feed into her hand and kneeled.

Duchess pecked at the grains.

The touch of the beak tickled Susan's palm. She knew she shouldn't be hand-feeding a pigeon—it wasn't the Pigeon Service's protocol, or her grandfather's—and would no doubt cause problems if Duchess were put into service. But this bird was different. All because a feral cat had managed to scratch its way under the door and take the lives of Bertie's prized racing pigeons, Skye and Islay.

Three years earlier, Susan and Bertie had found what was left of Skye behind the grain barrel. They had found Islay in her nest with a severely injured wing, sitting on an egg she had laid before her attack. They had tried to repair Islay's wing with tape and splinters of wood, but she was too weak to eat, and she sat feebly on her egg for five days before she passed. They had buried her in one of Bertie's tobacco boxes, next to Skye near the edge of Epping Forest.

When none of the other pigeons would sit on the egg, tainted from the feline tragedy, Susan insisted on incubating it, despite her grandfather's belief that the chances of the egg hatching were extraordinarily slim, especially without a calibrated incubator that they could not afford. Stubborn like her grandfather, Susan retrieved a blue ceramic bowl, once used by her grandmother to eat oatmeal. She warmed the bowl with water from the teakettle to establish a good base temperature, then delicately wrapped the egg in a lightly moistened towel and placed it inside. Setting the bowl under Bertie's desk lamp, she adjusted the distance to reach the ideal temperature by using a medical thermometer, which she had tested by sticking it under a nesting pigeon.

For two weeks and two days, Susan rotated the egg every eight hours and sprinkled drops of water onto the towel to keep the proper humidity. And despite the odds of having to bury the egg next to its parents, the egg quivered early on a Sunday morning. Susan and her grandfather skipped church, pulled up chairs, and watched for three hours as the egg slowly cracked open. As church bells rang over Epping to release their congregations, a shriveled hatchling poked its way into the world.

"Your parents and your granny would be proud of you," Bertie had said.

Susan, a heaviness in her chest, had smiled and gently caressed the hatchling.

It had been a miracle, but Susan knew that this hatchling still had a slim chance of survival without the aid of her parents' pigeon milk. Undeterred, she took to grinding seed into paste and feeding the hatchling by hand. Within a few days, the hatchling was able to stand, unfurl its wings, and peck. One week later, it was eating feed with the others in the loft. And Susan named her Duchess, despite her grandfather's fondness for naming his racing pigeons after remote Scottish land masses, none of which they had ever visited.

Duchess had grown into something extraordinary. And it wasn't just her looks, even though her neck plume shimmered like mother of pearl. It was the bird's intelligence—or odd behavior, as her grandfather believed—that made her stand out among the flock. While homing pigeons were trained by the reward of food, Duchess seemed to be driven by the need to understand the world around her, a strange sense of curiosity hidden behind her golden eyes. Instead of joining the group, Duchess was content to watch her companions eat as she stood on Susan's shoulder, cooing in response to Susan's words, as if the bird enjoyed the art of conversation. And even more impressive was Duchess's athletic ability; she was typically the first to arrive home after the pigeons were released at a distant training location. Bertie had commented that Duchess was the fastest to return only because of her desire to get a few minutes of Susan's undivided attention. Susan laughed but knew there was some truth to what he said.

As Susan stroked Duchess's back with a finger, a siren sounded. She stopped. The horn began as a low growl, then grew to an ear-piercing roar, tapering off, then repeating. Goose bumps cropped up on her arms. Pigeons fluttered. Walls vibrated. Seed in the feeding tray quivered.

The door flew open. Her grandfather, a bowlegged man wearing a tarnished tin helmet, shouted, "Luftwaffe!" He grabbed Susan's hand and pulled.

Susan saw the spring door closing behind her, Duchess standing calmly on the ground as the other pigeons scattered. "Duchess!" She broke her grandfather's grip, threw open the door, and scooped up the bird.

Susan, with Duchess tucked into the crook of her arm, ran with Bertie toward the bomb shelter, just like they had rehearsed, praying each time that this day would never come. But they knew it was merely a matter of time. As they ran across the field and past several other pigeon lofts, the siren wailed from nearby North Weald Airfield.

Bertie paused as he struggled to catch his breath. He pushed up his old military helmet that kept falling over his eyes. "Hurry!" he shouted.

Before they reached the shelter, the siren died, replaced by the buzz of mechanical bees. Susan looked up, swallowed, and pushed up the brim of Bertie's helmet. Hundreds of enemy bombers, and nearly twice as many fighters, darkened the late-afternoon sky like a swarm of black flies. Antiaircraft fire boomed. Black bursts exploded below the aerial armada.

The shelter was a broad earthen mound under the canopy of a large beech tree. Green grass now covered the embankment, blending the refuge into the rolling pasture. Except for the front door, which made it look like a home for a hobbit, the sanctuary was camouflaged. Susan had helped her grandfather build the shelter, piling up wheelbarrows of dirt and mixing concrete in buckets to line the inner walls reinforced with remnant bricks and scrap steel from a demolished cannery. And for the entrance, they used a door from an old outhouse.

As they reached the shelter, the bellies of the bombers cracked open. Instead of hunkering into the pit, they were compelled—despite their own safety—to watch scrambling Royal Air Force

Hurricane fighters soar over the trees and pitch sharply to the sky. The fighter squadron was sorely outnumbered as enemy escort fighters bearing the Iron Cross swooped down to surround them. The RAF put up a short but valiant effort. One Hurricane exploded after rounds of enemy gunfire pierced its fuel tank, sending shrapnel over Epping Forest. Another had its tail shot off, sending the Hurricane into a spinning dive and crashing into a field with no sign of the pilot bailing out. One by one, the RAF Hurricanes were shot down, and the few planes lucky enough to suffer only minor damages retreated with smoke pouring from their engines.

Susan and Bertie watched the invaders fly toward London, a mere twenty miles away, contested only by inaccurate antiaircraft fire. Seeds of destruction dropped from the bellies of the bombers and whistled to the ground.

"My God." Tears flowed down Susan's cheeks as the first bombs exploded.

As night set in, the horizon of London glowed with scores, perhaps hundreds, of great fires. And with the darkness came a second wave of bombers dropping their payloads throughout the night, using the burning fires to identify their targets. White-hot incendiary bombs flared. Echoes of explosions filled the air.

At 4:30 AM, the bombing stopped. Susan stepped to Bertie, sitting on the ground, and helped him to his feet. With weak legs, he shuffled into the shelter, then curled onto a cot with his tin helmet covering his face. Unable to rest, Susan stood outside with Duchess cradled in her arms and watched the glow on the horizon. The grinding continued as the German planes flew overhead, masking the stars and crescent moon. She closed her eyes and prayed that they would not return. But the following evening they came back. And again the night after that.

CHAPTER 2

BUXTON, MAINE — SEPTEMBER 8, 1940

Ollie Evans, lured by a squeaky porch swing and the roasted-nut aroma of chicory coffee, opened the screen door. He found his parents gently rocking, sharing a wool blanket and a cup of coffee, as an orange sun rose above the dew-glistened potato fields.

The cup in his mother's hand, Ollie noticed, was a misshapen toad-green mug he had made in industrial arts class in the seventh grade. He chuckled. "Where did you find it?"

His mother shrugged, wisps of faded brown hair resting on her shoulders. She sipped. Steam swirled in the cool air.

Ollie was no longer a little boy. He was six feet tall, give or take an inch, with wavy brown hair and caramel eyes, a gift from his mother. The dimple on his chin mirrored the one on his father. As Ollie took a seat on the porch steps, an unsettling feeling that he should be somewhere else filled his belly. It wasn't unusual to be home in the fall. After all, most of the schools would soon be on potato recess. Unfortunately, his harvest break was more permanent.

"I'm proud of you," his father said.

"For what?" Ollie asked.

"For putting family first." He accepted the mug from his wife and drank. "I'm sorry you're still home." He nudged the cane hanging from the side of the swing. "It wasn't fair that you had to stay."

"That's okay. The farm's important. And so are you."

Three years ago, his father's muddy boot slipped off the tractor's clutch while attempting to pull out a stump. The machine flipped backward, pinning his father's right leg, shattering his hip, and snapping a femur in two places. Ollie, unable to lift the tractor, dug him out with a hand trowel from the garden shed. His mother had called for an ambulance and helped by scraping earth with her bare hands, ripping off three of her fingernails. It had been a painful recovery, including two surgeries and agonizing rounds of physical therapy. And now his father, held together with screws and wire, was able to perform some of the farm duties, except for plowing and crop-dusting. He was no longer able to work the pedals, the strain too much for his brittle leg. His father didn't seem to mind moving as slowly as a tortoise, the constant ache in his joints, or the pronounced limp in his walk. It was the inability to fly that had stolen his spirit, his once-dark hair turning gray with the passing of days spent grounded, as if the lower altitude accelerated the aging process.

His mother adjusted the blanket covering their laps, took the mug from her husband, and handed him the newspaper.

Ollie's father slid the rubber band from the paper, wrapped it around his forefinger, and shot it at Ollie.

Ollie ducked, even though it whizzed two feet over his head.

The smile fell from his father's face as he unfolded the paper. "Good God."

Mother's eyes widened.

"They've bombed London," Ollie's father said, showing her the paper.

"Those poor people," Mother said.

Ollie stepped to his parents and stared at the newspaper headline: *Nazis Strike! German Planes Raid London!* He took a deep breath and exhaled.

"The Nazis took France in just over a month," Ollie's father said. "Without our help, they'll take Britain in a year. And before we know it, we'll have a regatta of U-boats in Casco Bay."

Ollie crossed his arms as another debate about the war began to dominate their conversation. It usually started with the newspaper but always ended with his father's proclamation of their British heritage.

"FDR says we're going to stay neutral," Mother said.

"We'll be in this war eventually." Ollie's father tapped his thigh. "If I didn't have a bum leg, I'd have a mind to walk to Montreal and join the Merchant Navy. At least the Canadians have the guts to stand by Britain." He lowered the paper. "Our family may have lost our accent . . ."

"But our blood is, and always will be, British," Ollie said, cutting off his father. "We know."

The porch turned silent, except for the creek of the swing and the caw of a crow in the potato field.

"I suggest that you never forget it." Ollie's father dropped the paper, retrieved his cane, and stood.

"Dad, I didn't mean to . . ."

Father raised his hand. "Your mother and I have errands to run." He turned and went inside, the screen door banging against the frame.

Mother sighed and looked at Ollie. "Have you forgotten how your father lost his brother?"

"I'm sorry," Ollie said, recalling the uncle he had never met. Uncle Henry was killed in the Great War, two years before Ollie was born. Each year on Henry's birthday, Ollie's father honored his brother's memory by going salmon fishing, their favorite childhood sport in northern England. Ollie often joined his father for the day, fly-fishing in the solitude of the Saco River's rippling waters. Although his father spoke little of the details, Ollie had managed to piece together that a cloud of chlorine gas had forced Henry to abandon his trench in exchange for machine-gun fire. Henry died, and so did a piece of his father, in a French field on the Western Front.

"You should be more respectful of your father's feelings about the war. And mine." Mother paused. "Want something to eat?"

Ollie shook his head, feeling as if his stomach was filled with clay.

"You and your father can continue this discussion when we get back from town." Mother stood. "And I expect you to apologize."

"I will."

She placed her hands on her hips.

"I promise." Ollie retrieved the rubber band and slid it onto his wrist. "I better get going. Lots of dusting to do."

"Be careful," his mother said, going inside.

Behind the barn, Ollie saw the weathered canary-yellow biplane, looking like a prehistoric bird warming its old bones in the morning sun. The plane was fully fueled and loaded with insecticide, or what his father aptly called pixie dust. He checked the tension wires strung between the upper and lower wings, stepped into the cockpit, and put on his leather cap. As he flipped the ignition, the engine coughed and the propeller turned over, sending a vibrating buzz through his body. He advanced the power, moving the plane down a bumpy earthen runway that split the potato field. The plane accelerated, and the tail began to rise. Sensing the proper speed, considering the instrument panel didn't work, he pulled back on the stick, and the plane lifted into the air. He circled their house, wondering how he would smooth things over with his father. Flying west to the farmlands, he replaced thoughts of war with his longing of someday going away to college.

The Maine potato harvest would soon be over, bringing an end to another crop-dusting season and his third year of staying home to run the family potato farm. Assuming the fall crop had a good yield and the price for potatoes didn't plummet, perhaps they'd have enough money for him to leave for college next year. He'd already been accepted at Worcester Polytechnic Institute. But before he would allow himself to leave, his father's health would need to improve. If everything went perfectly, five or six years from now, he'd have his aeronautical engineering degree, his ticket out of Buxton.

There was nothing wrong with Buxton. In many respects, a farm was a great place to grow up, and he had no regrets about staying to help his father. But most of his friends had left home years ago; many were now cutting logs for a paper mill or hoisting crustaceans from the back of a lobster boat. And the lucky ones had gone off to college, including his girlfriend, Caroline, who went to Bowdoin, where her letters had dwindled and eventually stopped. Even his high school buddies, Stan and James, had gone to the University of Maine and seldom came home on breaks. They were reveling in their life of academia and social parties, while Ollie was still living with his parents. They had taken different paths, and Ollie couldn't blame them for falling out of touch.

Caroline had been Ollie's first girlfriend. They'd dated during their senior year of high school. Caroline had been cute and popular, and her family owned one of the largest lumber mills in York County; they were wealthy by Buxton standards. And she'd been charmed, Ollie believed, by his ability to fly a plane, an attractive trait when compared to boys who were driving their parents' car. Initially, he thought Caroline might be the girl he was going to spend his life with. But things changed when Ollie's dad was injured. Caroline, who claimed that she didn't do well with hospitals, had reluctantly joined Ollie and his mother to visit Ollie's dad in the recovery ward. And Caroline had turned reticent when Ollie brought up the subject of having to defer college to take care of the family farm. In the end, Ollie had stayed home, and Caroline had gone to college, where she distanced herself from

Ollie, even making excuses on holidays for why she was too busy to see him. He'd been dejected. *She doesn't want to risk being stuck with me on a farm.* But as time passed, Ollie realized that it was best that he and Caroline had gone their separate ways. More importantly, he now knew that he wanted what his parents had in a relationship. They would always be there for each other, regardless of life's unexpected circumstances. *Someday, I'll love a woman as much as Dad loves Mom.*

Despite spending his entire life in a town where he knew everyone by their first name, he now felt out of place. In Buxton, one either farmed or fished, not a good fit for someone who preferred the speed of a plane to the crawl of a tractor. And besides, he had always been allergic to shellfish, unable to have even a nibble of lobster without breaking into hives and running for the bathroom.

With a college degree, he would certainly have options to design or build planes, taking him to new parts of the country, perhaps as far as California. But what he really wanted to do was fly. Since the first time his father had taken him crop-dusting, he was hooked. Ollie's father had placed Ollie on his lap, slid a leather flight cap on him that was several sizes too big on his son's head, and took to the sky. Ollie, a grin carved into his face, loved the way the plane angled upward to the clouds as he pulled the stick to his chest. He felt his father laugh, his back bouncing against his father's tummy. Then his father eased his hands forward to keep from pulling a loop, a dangerous maneuver considering the biplane was missing safety harnesses. By the time he was fourteen, when he had grown big enough to reach the pedals, his father acted as a copilot, gradually weaning him from instructions. Within a year, he was flying on his own, much to the chagrin of his mother, who still worried about him getting hurt playing football. To help put his mother's mind at ease, his father installed new safety harnesses, but considering Ollie's fearless acrobatics, that was about as useful as giving a tightrope walker an umbrella.

As he approached a large farm, Ollie pushed the stick forward and felt his body rise, and the nose of the biplane tipped down. The engine roared. Wind pressed against his face. Approaching the ground, he adjusted the stick, feeling the pull of gravity sink him into his seat. The plane leveled off. Five feet above a potato field, he pulled the lever. A spray of dust streamed behind the tail and fell like snow. At the end of the field, he pulled back hard on the stick, shooting the plane over a row of towering pines. He arced to the left and came around for another pass.

Ollie spent the morning dusting fields. Finishing his last farm, he checked the fuel gauge—the only instrument that seemed to work—and tipped the wings to the north. The scattered fields disappeared, and in the distance, he saw his favorite spot, Sebago Lake. There were few farmers in this area, at least none who were clients of his father's business, making it unlikely that word about Ollie's stunts would get back to his mother. Otherwise, he'd be skinned alive.

Above the lake, he did a snap roll, as if the fuselage spun on a skewer. He pulled the nose straight to the sky, flying toward the clouds until the propeller lost its battle against the pull of gravity and tipped the plane over, just before the engine stalled, into a hammerhead dive. As he fell to the lake, he pulled up and glided over the still water, feeling the urge to dip the landing gear.

A young girl in pigtails ran out of a cottage—the only home on the north side of the lake—and stood on a dock. She waved and jumped. Ollie tipped the wings, buzzed the shoreline, and performed his usual show for an audience of one. The girl, whom Ollie only knew from the air, was probably in grade school. Attracted by the roar of the plane's engine, she often came outside to watch. As the girl took a seat on the dock, Ollie swooped the plane high into the sky, pulling a barrel-roll maneuver, then leveled off. He performed a split-S, an inside loop, and a series of spins.

For the finale, he decided to perform a less practiced and more challenging maneuver, the tailslide. He did a quarter loop that sent the plane straight vertical, with full power. Wind whistled. His adrenaline rushed. The aircraft continued to climb until it lost momentum, then hung for a second before falling backward. As the nose dropped through the horizon, he pushed the stick forward and sent the plane into a dive. He pulled hard on the stick and leveled off a few feet above the lake, much too close for comfort. His pulse pounded in his ears. He saw the girl standing on the shoreline clapping her hands.

As he swooped by the cottage, he reached into his jacket and pulled out a note that was tied to a small piece of wood. He released the package. It fell gently to a grass clearing several yards from the shoreline.

The girl ran to the package, untied the string, and read the note.

Thanks for being a great audience. Ollie.

The girl waved her arms. And he flew away.

Ollie eased back the throttle and zigzagged on his way home, maximizing his time in the air before he'd have to begin his farm chores. As he neared Buxton, the thick forest of pines turned to rolling plots of corn, potatoes, and hay. As the family farm came into view, he noticed his father's truck was gone, replaced with a shiny new-model car. He swooped over and saw a man in dark clothing standing on the porch. He banked around to the runway and landed. Ollie cut the engine, got out of the cockpit, and walked to the house. As he approached, he glanced at the '39 Plymouth with an unmistakable white top and green sides. The Portland police officer stepped from the porch and removed his cap, exposing a bald head with stubbly gray sideburns.

"Oliver Evans?" the officer asked.

A knot formed in Ollie's gut. "Yes."

"There's been an accident."

Ollie opened his mouth, but nothing came out.

"It's your parents."

"Are they okay?"

The officer wiped his face with a handkerchief from his pocket. "I'm sorry."

A shock jolted Ollie. He bent over like he'd been punched in the gut. "No," he whimpered in disbelief. A bombardment of thoughts and emotions made him feel as though the ground was spinning. Numb and having difficulty walking, he was helped into the police car by the officer. As they drove away, the smell of cigar smoke embedded into the interior made Ollie's stomach churn.

"The driver had been drinking," the officer said, gripping the steering wheel. "He ran a red light, veered onto a sidewalk, and struck your parents as they were leaving Casco Hardware."

"There must be some mistake." Ollie's head throbbed, and his heart was ravaged by a mixture of anger and despair.

The officer cleared his throat. "I wish there was, son."

Ollie slumped in his seat like a marionette with its strings severed. *This can't be happening!* He had an impulse to pull the door handle and jump out, anything to escape this nightmare. Ollie, his eyes welled with tears, buried his head into his hands. He bit his lip and tasted copper.

Twenty minutes later, Ollie arrived at the Cumberland County Morgue. A scent of rubbing alcohol hung in the air. The coroner, a thin, stoic man who was washing his hands over a sink, turned off the water and then led Ollie to a wall of nickel-plated cooler drawers. The coroner wiped his hands on his lab coat, pulled two latches, and slid the bodies out.

Ollie's heart sank. His eyes watered. A flash of his father picking oxeye daisies, his mother's favorite flower. An image of Mom placing a handwritten note into Dad's lunch box. Simple gifts were symbols of their affection for each other. But there would be no more flowers for Mom to place on the kitchen table. And no more sweet notes for Dad to add to the stack that he kept in a bedside drawer.

The officer, standing in the doorway, turned his head.

The coroner finished drying his hands, using the tail of his lab coat. "Are these your parents?"

Mother was missing a shoe, her toes a pasty blue. Father's chest was sunken, and his left arm was badly broken. Unable to bring his eyes to look at their faces, Ollie touched their hands, cold and stiff. He began to weep, then nodded to the coroner. Steel casters rolled. And his parents disappeared into the chamber.

CHAPTER 3

EPPING, ENGLAND — SEPTEMBER 11, 1940

Susan woke to the smell of damp earth. She opened her eyes but saw only black, as if she had gone blind in her sleep. A rush of fear flooded her body. Her heart pounded. She shot up in her cot.

"Are you all right?" Bertie whispered.

Susan found Duchess nestled beside her leg. She touched her wings, feeling the softness of feathers beneath her fingers. "Yes."

Bertie lit a lantern, casting a glow over the shelter. He rubbed his eyes. "Are you sure?"

Susan looked up at the ceiling, a mosaic of broken bricks, stone, and mortar. She listened. No explosions. No sirens. No grinding engines. Only tweets of predawn sparrows outside the door. "Are they gone?"

"I believe so." Bertie looked at his pocket watch. "But we should wait."

Susan stroked Duchess. The pigeon cooed. Susan's heartbeat slowed, her breath gradually returning to normal. Within a few minutes, a loud, monotone siren sounded from North Weald Airfield, giving the all-clear signal.

Susan tucked Duchess into her arm, stood, and opened the

shelter door. She took in a deep breath—a mixture of fresh air, dew, and discharged gunpowder. A few remaining stars were dissolving into the sky, giving way to a rising sun. She looked toward London. Fires glowed. Streams of smoke rose from the horizon, as if the bombing had cracked open the earth, creating a gateway to hell.

Susan felt her grandfather's arm on her shoulder. She lowered her head and leaned into him.

It had been four straight nights of bombing. The ashen haze would dissipate throughout the day as fire brigades relentlessly fought raging fires. But night would bring another round of bombing and more destruction, forcing them to burrow into the shelter like moles, only to emerge each morning to learn what remained of London.

"Will they ever stop?" Susan asked, wiping her eyes.

"Eventually," Bertie said, a slight hesitation in his voice. He shifted his weight and grimaced.

"How're the knees?"

Bertie rubbed his kneecaps. "A bit dodgy, I'm afraid."

"You should be using your walking stick."

Bertie shook his head. "Saving it to break over Hitler's arse."

Susan squeezed her grandfather's hand. "Come inside, and I'll get you some ointment."

In the living room—a cozy space with a stone fireplace and timber-beam ceiling—Susan helped Bertie into his chair, rolled up his pant legs, and rubbed ointment into his knees as Duchess sat perched on the mantel. She wiped her hands with a towel, then walked to the radio in the corner of the room and flipped the switch. Static cackled. She adjusted the knob and found the signal.

They listened to news reports, which provided only vague descriptions of the destruction and no mention of fatalities.

"Why aren't they giving details?" Susan asked.

"Spies. We don't want to provide the Nazis with any intelligence on what they accomplished."

Susan shivered at the thought of spies in London. She desperately wanted to know more, and more importantly, she wanted to know what she could do to help. An hour later, she got her answers when the prime minister addressed the nation.

As Susan rubbed another round of ointment into Bertie's knees, the scent of eucalyptus filling the air, they listened to Winston Churchill's confident and unwavering voice. Churchill spoke of Hitler's goal to obtain air superiority over Britain, before the Germans commenced a land invasion. And while Churchill addressed the barbaric attacks on civilians, his broadcast was much more than about the bombings on London. His speech, Susan believed, was intended to ignite a fire in the hearts of the British people and galvanize their will to fight.

Susan's breath quickened. She noticed Bertie, his jaw dropped, staring at the radio. She imagined German troops landing on British shores and marching through Epping Forest, burning everything and slaughtering everyone in their path.

After Churchill's brief broadcast, calling every man and woman to their post, Susan stood and turned off the radio. She thought of Londoners struggling to return to a sense of normalcy. Despite the hope in Churchill's words, teachers would return to their classrooms to find that most of their students had been sent to the countryside, iron workers would return to flattened foundries, bakers would find no flour to make their rationed bread, and police officers would patrol deserted streets. But they would all go about their duty, whatever that might be. And so would she and Bertie.

"We have work to do," Susan said.

Bertie nodded, tightened the wrappings on his knees, and stood.

Susan carried Duchess outside, kissed the top of the bird's head, and tossed her into the air. Duchess circled the yard and landed on the roof of the loft. The bird tucked her head under her wing, as if to shield her eyes from London's glowing embers.

Susan looked to the apocalypse smoldering on the horizon. "It'll be over soon," she whispered to herself, unaware that the Luftwaffe would bomb London for fifty-seven consecutive nights.

CHAPTER 4

BUXTON, MAINE

The burial service for Ollie's parents was on a Tuesday. Attendance was light; he was an only child, and his closest relatives were people whom he had never met, still living in small towns dotting the English coast and Scottish Highlands. Those attending were mostly neighboring farmers, hardworking men and women who had put on their starched Sunday clothes to pay their respects. A few of his father's pilot friends stood in the back, one of them a wiry man with dark sunken eyes, proudly displaying his Great War flying wings pinned to the lapel of his sagging suit.

The ceremony was short. Ollie, his eyes fixed on the coffins, struggled to listen to the minister's words. After the service, he individually thanked those in attendance, their endless handshakes, hugs, and words of condolences unable to lift his spirits. He heard whispers about the man, now sober in the county jail, awaiting sentencing for running down his parents. But the justice of a long prison term would not bring them back.

By Thursday, the bank had requested a meeting. Ollie got up early and drove his parents' truck to Portland. He rolled down the windows, for fear that the slightest scent of his father's after-shave or his mother's perfume would make him cry again. The last thing he needed was to go in all red-eyed to meet with the banker.

A receptionist took him to the banker's office. A plump man with a bulbous nose and oiled hair sat behind a large desk, clear of any papers, except for an engraved business-card holder with the words *Sal Bronson, President.* The man did not bother to get up; instead, he gestured for Ollie to take a seat.

"Ollie," Mr. Bronson said. "This is Mr. Hood, the attorney who will help us with finalizing matters between the bank and the estate of your parents."

Ollie looked at the man with a pencil-thin mustache sitting in a chair next to him. The man tipped his hat without making eye contact and flipped open the briefcase sitting on his lap.

"Ollie, are you aware of the amount of your parents' debt?" the banker asked.

"Well, not exactly." Ollie shifted in his seat. "I'm sure they had debt. After all, we're farmers."

"It's my understanding your parents had no life insurance, correct?"

Ollie nodded.

Mr. Hood handed Ollie some papers.

The banker leaned back in his chair. "That's a list of the outstanding debt on the farm, house, equipment, and crop-dusting business. Your parents have been running behind on payments. Bottom line, the place is buried in debt, and we're foreclosing."

Ollie swallowed. "What about the harvest of the potato crop?"

The banker shook his head. "Not enough to make a dent."

"But my parents, even if they were running a little behind, always made good on their payments."

The banker raised his hand. "We've sent out a team this morning to secure the farm equipment. Mr. Hood will be handling the foreclosure proceedings."

"There must be something that can be done," Ollie said.

The banker shook his head. "It's too bad your father had been giving away crop-dusting services, not to mention using precious farmland for a landing strip." He ran his fingers, thick as sausages, through his slicked hair. "I'm afraid your father wasn't much of a businessman."

Ollie stood. His pulse pounded in his ears. "My parents may not have been financially savvy, but they were good, hardworking people who cared a lot about the farmers in Buxton." He tossed the papers, scattering them over the banker's desk, and left.

By the time he arrived home, there was already an auction sign planted at the entrance of the driveway. Ollie stopped the truck, yanked the sign out of the ground, and tossed it into the yard. Another notice was nailed to the front door. He ripped it off and crumbled it. Inside, everything seemed to be in place, but behind the barn was another matter. The tractor was gone. And the biplane was missing its propeller. The bank's repossession team, Ollie assumed, had taken the propeller until they could arrange for someone to fly it away. He felt the urge to climb into the hayloft and pull out the old propeller, as if the plane had been left naked. It had a chip in the blade but was still functional. But where would he go? What would he do after he got there? And if he stayed on the farm, how long did he have before he was evicted?

Refusing to stay and watch his parents' farm be auctioned away, Ollie went to his bedroom and packed his suitcase. He selected the few material things that were important to him: a picture of his parents, which he removed from a frame on the mantel, his flight logbook, and his acceptance letter to Worcester Polytechnic Institute. He drove away, unable to look back. His first stop was the cemetery, where he placed golden wild flowers—picked from the side of the road—on his parents' graves. He said good-bye, not knowing when he would be back. As he left their earthy mounds, he wished he had taken the time to purchase artificial flowers, something that would look nice until the grass grew.

His second stop was a small used-car dealership in Buxton. He sold the truck, needing money more than transportation. Besides, the bank would take the vehicle if he didn't sell it. He only got eighty-five dollars, but considering every panel was rusted and the engine sounded like a blender filled with coins, he believed it was a fair deal.

Ollie began the sixteen-mile walk with no regrets about not picking a car dealership closer to the Portland train station. He needed time to think. Going to Worcester was an alternative, but with eighty-five dollars and the little bit of change in his wallet, it wasn't enough to pay for college. He'd have to find a job. A place to stay. Hopefully, the walk would give him time to clear the fog from his head and figure out a plan.

He looked at his watch, then to the sun setting over the pines, and realized that he would likely miss the evening train to Boston. With no desire to return home, he continued walking, even if it meant that he'd have to spend the night at the station and catch the train in the morning.

The journey was quiet, except for the buzz of cicadas and the rustle of weeds from passing cars. As his arm tired, he switched the suitcase to the opposite hand. Step after step, he traveled on County Road 22, feeling the air turn cool as the sun began to sink. Hours passed, and he reached Congress Street, the city lights of Portland illuminating the horizon. Several hundred yards to his right, the glimmer of runway beacons drew his attention to the Portland Airport. He stopped, put down his suitcase, and rubbed his arm. Three runways spread over a large plot of land with a small, one-story brick building and two hangars. He heard twin engines choke and sputter. A few seconds later, the engines started, then abruptly stalled.

Ollie followed a service road to get a better look and found a mustached man wearing an olive military uniform with an unusual belt across the tunic, shouting to a pilot of a small passenger plane to cut the ignition. Ollie noticed the letters RCAF and a British roundel, looking like a bull's-eye target, painted on the tail. The pilot waved his hand out the window, got out of his seat, and left the plane with two other men to examine the engines. A mechanic with grease streaks across the front of his overalls came out to help them.

The mustached man noticed Ollie, took a swig from a flask in his hand, and said, "What do you want, kid?"

Ollie looked behind him and realized the man was talking to him. "Nothing," he said, squeezing the handle on his suitcase. "Sounds like the engines are flooded."

"You know something about planes?"

Ollie swallowed. "Only biplanes. And much older than this one, I'm afraid."

The man smiled, crow's-feet forming in the corners of his eyes. "In that case, care to join me for a drink?"

Ollie hesitated.

"They'll have this bird repaired in no time." The man, three rows of medals glittering across the left side of his jacket, stepped forward and extended his hand. "Name's Bishop."

"Ollie." He shook his hand, and they took a seat on a bench beside a hangar.

Bishop gave Ollie the flask. "Cheers, my good man."

Ollie took a drink, feeling a burn in his throat, and coughed. "Thanks," he wheezed.

Bishop laughed. "So, tell me what you know about biplanes."

Ollie told him about his father's biplane, the crop-dusting business, and flying since he had turned fourteen. Bishop asked a lot of questions, as if spreading fertilizer over potatoes was a glamorous business, and he was particularly interested if Ollie had more than 300 hours of certified flying time.

Ollie opened his suitcase, retrieved the flight log from under a pair of trousers, and thumbed through it. "Never really counted, but easily over a thousand."

"Impressive."

Ollie noticed Bishop looking at his suitcase. "I'm on my way to Worcester to study aeronautical engineering." He shut his suitcase and set it down, hoping he could find a way to pay for school.

Bishop took a drink from the flask and handed it back to Ollie. The second drink didn't burn as much as the first, only warming Ollie's stomach and leaving a strong peaty taste in his mouth.

"You have me beat by a full year with your first solo flight," Bishop said. "When I was fifteen, I built a plane out of shipping cardboard, crates, and twine. I flew it off the top of my parents' three-story house in Ontario or, more accurately, crashed my ostrich of a monstrosity into my mother's rose garden. My sister dug me out of the wreckage using a pruning shear. Fortunately, I was unharmed except for a bad scrape and the scolding from my parents." Bishop rolled up his sleeve, showed Ollie a long, thin scar that ran across his elbow, and took a swig from the flask.

They spent the next hour talking about flying, sharing stories of biplane maneuvers: barrel rolls, English bunts, inside loops, outside loops, lazy eights, and Immelmann turns. When the pilot came over and told Bishop that the engine was fixed, Bishop waved him off and told him to check over the plane again.

Bishop leaned back on the bench. "So, Ollie, what do you think about the war?"

He thought of his conversations with his parents and felt a sudden loss wash over him. "I don't understand why we aren't in the war yet, or at least helping."

Bishop nodded. "Ever consider joining the air corps?"

"The US Army Air Corps requires a college education, which I don't have yet."

Bishop smiled. "The Canadian and British air corps don't have that requirement, only three hundred hours of fly time, a pilot's license, and being single. In fact, you could even wear glasses." He drank more scotch from his flask. "If you change your mind about college, I can arrange for you to join the Royal Canadian Air Force."

"No offense, sir . . ."

"Call me Bish; anyone sharing a drink with me calls me Bish." He handed Ollie the flask.

Ollie took another drink, feeling his head begin to swim. "I've already delayed attending college for three years. And besides, if I were to join a foreign air corps, it would have to be the British Royal Air Force."

"RAF . . . may I ask why?"

Ollie thought of his last conversation with his father. A wave of guilt made his eyes begin to water. "My father always told me that our family may have lost our accent, but our blood is, and always will be, British."

Bishop grinned. "I like a man with pride in his roots. You have a good father, son."

Ollie swallowed. "Had."

Bishop's smile faded.

"My parents are dead."

"I'm sorry."

They sat for a moment listening to the chirps of crickets hanging onto the last few days of autumn. Then Bishop pulled a business card from his pocket, wrote something on the back with a pencil, and handed it to Ollie.

"If you should change your mind about school, here is a way to join either the Canadian or British air force," Bishop said, breaking the silence. "I happen to do a little recruiting for the Royal Canadian Air Force; the address for our headquarters in New York is printed on the front. I wrote on the back the name of a man I know in London who is working on establishing an American fighter squadron for the RAF. All you would need to do is make your way to London. No guarantees, but I'll make sure your name is on a list, Ollieeeee . . ."

"Evans."

"The rest would be up to you, Ollie Evans."

"Thanks for the offer, and the drink, but I'm leaving for Worcester in the morning."

The sound of the twin engines drowned their voices. Ollie shook Bishop's hand and accompanied him to the plane.

"Good luck to you, Ollie." Bishop climbed the steps of the plane, his crew already loaded and waiting for him.

"Bishop!" Ollie shouted, the scotch overcoming his shyness.

He turned at the top of the stairs.

"Why did you fly a cardboard plane off your parents' house?"

Bishop smiled, suddenly looking older in the shadows of night. A man, probably in his mid-forties, aged by the stress of war. "Because, my good man. I was born to fly." He entered the plane and shut the cabin door.

Ollie felt a blast of wind from the propellers. A whiff of aviation fuel filled his nostrils. He watched the plane accelerate down the runway, fly into the night, and disappear into the stars.

The mechanic who had been working on the plane approached Ollie. "Do you know who that was?" He wiped grease from his hands onto the front of his overalls.

Ollie scratched his head. "His name was Bishop."

"That was Billy Bishop, air marshal for the Royal Canadian Air Force. He was coming in from Nova Scotia. I heard the pilot say that Bishop had just met with Winston Churchill. And now he's on his way to a secret meeting with Roosevelt. Can you believe that? They're setting up a pilot recruiting office in New York; Bishop is gonna try to get the FBI to turn a blind eye to the US Neutrality Act." The mechanic nudged Ollie's arm. "What did he say to you?"

"We just talked about flying." Ollie picked up his suitcase and left.

Ollie made his way to the train station, but the gate was locked. Realizing he would have to wait until morning for the station to open, he found a park bench and sat down. As his eyes adjusted, he saw a bearded man rummaging in a garbage can. Ollie watched the man pick something out, brush it off, and put it in his mouth. He wondered if the man was just a casualty of the Depression or if he had been injured like his father and had the course of his life changed. Unable to stand by and watch him rummage through fly-infested food, Ollie reached into his pocket and took out some change. As he approached, the bearded man raised an empty milk bottle. Ollie slowly held up his hands, kneeled, and placed the change on the sidewalk.

By the time Ollie returned to his bench, the man had picked up the change and disappeared. Exhausted, Ollie curled into a ball and closed his eyes.

Minutes later, a concussive blow to the head jolted Ollie from his sleep. In a daze, he fell from the bench. Cold pavement pressed against his cheek. His head throbbed. Touching his scalp, his fingers turned wet. With blurred vision, he watched a dark figure rummage through his suitcase. He tried to stand but lost his balance and fell. As his vertigo subsided, he struggled to sit up and noticed that his attacker had fled. The contents of his suitcase were strewn like confetti over the grass. And beside him were the shards of a broken milk bottle.

CHAPTER 5

PORTLAND, MAINE

Ollie rubbed his aching head, feeling as if the man who had robbed him had also performed a lobotomy using a butter knife. He gathered his strength, stood on wobbly knees, and collected the remnants of his personal items that were spread across the grass. Ollie found most of his possessions, including his flight book and the picture of his parents. The only thing missing was his money: the proceeds from selling the car and even the couple of dollars he had stashed in his wallet. He scanned the park for the man who had robbed him, but he was nowhere to be found.

Ollie found a public restroom near Longfellow Square, and although the door was locked, he located a window that was unlatched. He crawled inside and fell to the floor, the tile cold against his hands. Pulling a string hanging from a light fixture in the ceiling, he looked in the mirror and wished he had left the light off. A large gash had split a groove into his forehead, just below the hairline. Dried blood covered the left side of his face and had dripped down his neck like hardened wax, dyeing the collar of his white shirt crimson. He turned on the water, washed his face, and scrubbed the stains from his shirt, until only a pink hue remained. He combed his hair with his fingers and thought that he could use some stitches. But he had no time and, more importantly, no money.

At the station, Ollie joined the crowd of people gathering for the train to Boston, most of whom had their heads buried in the morning newspaper. He tried to sell his watch to buy a ticket; with no interested buyers, he resorted to trying to hock his suitcase. But everyone was consumed with the paper, even annoyed when he interrupted their reading to display how well the spring latches still worked on his tattered case.

A whistle blew, and the train crawled to a stop, its wheels screeching over the rails. The engine hissed, the doors slid open, and the crowd entered, one by one, until the landing was empty. Except for Ollie.

The doors closed, the train inched forward, and Ollie watched his future disappear down the tracks. As he stood alone, trying to figure out a plan to make some money for the afternoon train, a breeze blew a crumpled newspaper to his feet. He picked it up, curious to know what had captured everyone's attention. He stared at the headline: *Bombing of London Lasts All Night! Nazis Hurl 1,000 Planes!* Each word of the article, in particular the mounting death toll, made Ollie's anger build, causing his head to throb. Dropping the paper, he reached into his pocket and removed the card Bishop had given him. It simply read *Waldorf Astoria Hotel, New York, New York*. No name. No number. And on the back, scribbled in pencil, *Charles Sweeny, London*.

Ollie rubbed his aching head and noticed the gash was sticky. He looked at the blood on his fingers and thought of his father. *Our family may have lost our accent, but our blood is, and always will be, British.* Ollie left the train station, not bothering to check the time for the next train.

The Portland shipyard was practically deserted, most ships having departed at daybreak. The few still docked were either in for repairs or headed in the wrong direction. But Ollie found a cargo ship that was going to Halifax with a load of grain. When the deck was clear, Ollie jumped onboard, lifted a canvas cover on a lifeboat, and hid inside.

The ship's horn blew. Ollie flinched, striking his head against the side of the boat. He felt something warm trickle down his face and realized he had reopened the gash in his head. He opened his suitcase and pulled out a sock, still fresh with the scent of his mother's laundry detergent. He wiped his eyes and pressed the sock against his wound. Ollie felt the boat move and wondered how many hours—or days, for that matter—it would take to get to Nova Scotia. As he rocked with the waves of the open sea, Ollie curled into the nose of the lifeboat and fell asleep.

Ollie woke with a sharp pang in his head, his tongue dried like sunbaked leather. It had been at least a day since he had last eaten, maybe more. And almost as long since he had drunk anything, except for swigs of scotch from Bish's flask, which had done nothing but suck the hydration from his body and fuel him with foolish confidence that he could safely sleep on a park bench. Fortunately, Ollie found a metal box under a pile of life jackets that was filled with survival rations, including cans of condensed milk, a jug of water, and crackers.

Unfortunately, the captain enjoyed taking his breaks behind a lifeboat that shielded the wind to light his cheap cigars. And when the captain cupped his hand over a flickering flame from his Zippo lighter, he heard the unmistakable sound of crunching saltines.

As Ollie munched into another cracker, the canvas cover ripped open. A strong hand grabbed his collar. Ollie reached for his neck to keep from choking. In an instant, he was yanked from the lifeboat and thrown onto the deck.

"Who the hell are you?" the captain shouted.

Ollie squinted from sunlight, "Ollie Evans, sir."

"What are you doing on my ship?"

Ollie's eyes adjusted, and he saw a barrel-chested man with

gray hair thick as wire. "I'm on my way to England to join the Royal Air Force." Ollie wiped crumbs from his face. "I'm a pilot."

The captain looked at the battered young man, shook his head, and laughed.

Ollie stood, then noticed the sock stuck to his head. He carefully plucked the garment from his wound and stuffed it into his pocket.

"We have two punishments for stowaways." The captain puffed on his cigar, stepped forward, and exhaled smoke into Ollie's face.

Ollie coughed.

"We can toss you overboard." The captain flicked ashes over the rail. "Considering you're a bloody mess, the sharks would get you before you drowned, even if you didn't know how to swim."

Ollie swallowed.

"Or we can put you to work."

"I'd prefer to work, sir."

"That's what I thought you'd say." The captain scratched the stubble on his face. "I normally wouldn't give you an option, but I had a deckhand quit."

Ollie hoped the captain wasn't serious about throwing him overboard, but he didn't want to find out. He retrieved his suitcase and followed the captain inside. Along the way, the captain laughed more about Ollie's plan to be a pilot for the Royal Air Force, commenting that Ollie looked more like a rodent catcher than an aviator. Ollie didn't understand the man's humor, or what exactly a rodent catcher would look like, if there was such a profession. But regardless, if the captain had decided to keep him onboard as labor, or for amusement, Ollie gratefully accepted the man's offer to work in exchange for one-way passage to Halifax.

In the galley, the captain introduced him to a cook he called Beans, a short, elderly man who was stirring a steaming pot of oatmeal. "See what you can do to fix him up, then send him topside," the captain said. "We'll give him Willie's chores." The captain puffed his cigar and left.

Beans pointed his wooden spoon, covered in clumps of oat-meal, and gestured for Ollie to take a seat. The cook put down his spoon and retrieved a bottle of alcohol and a cloth from a cabinet. "Let me guess, bar fight or running from the law."

"Neither," Ollie said.

Beans raised his eyebrows. "This will burn." He splashed alcohol on Ollie's wound and quickly covered it with the cloth.

Ollie grimaced.

"What happened?" Beans asked as he inspected the wound.

Ollie told Beans about his parents and his plans to join the Royal Air Force before realizing that Beans was referring to the gash in his head. "I believe it was a milk bottle," Ollie added.

"I'm sorry." Beans put down the cloth. "About your parents, I mean."

Ollie nodded.

Beans sewed the gash in Ollie's head with a fishing hook and some thread from the hem of his trousers. It turned out that Beans had been a tailor in his younger years, until the Depression had shut down the store where he was employed. Desperate for work, Beans accepted a position as the ship's cook. He expected the job to be temporary, but that was a decade ago.

Beans stuck the hook into Ollie's forehead.

Pain flared. "What's your real name?" Ollie asked, gritting his teeth.

"Ben." The cook tightened a stitch.

Ollie gripped the arms of his chair.

"Captain calls everyone on the ship by a nickname. I'm not sure why." Beans made several more stitches, carefully tied a knot, clipped the ends with scissors, and leaned back to admire his work. "Looks good. May not leave much of a scar."

"Thanks, Ben."

The cook nodded.

Ollie offered Ben his watch in exchange for his medical services. But Ben refused, appearing grateful to be doing something

other than stirring a pot of oatmeal or perhaps after hearing someone call him by his first name in over ten years.

Ollie spent most of the two-day voyage scrubbing decks,
cleaning the heads, greasing salt-corroded hinges, and—the
crème de la crème—catching rats. It was apparently a big deal to
control the rodent population on a cargo ship, especially one
filled with delectable grains. The rat roundups, as the captain
called them, had been one of the primary duties of the former deckhand, Willie. And Ollie understood why Willie had quit when he
found himself setting traps the size of shoe boxes, baited with green
molded cheese—more mold than cheese—and smelling of soured
milk.

Ollie collected the traps twice each day, tossing the guillotined
bodies into the sea. It was disturbing to see the rats' gaping
mouths, their sharp yellow incisors, bellies swollen with corn,
and snakelike tails. They were certainly much bigger than the
field mice back on the farm. But despite their grotesque appearance, he hoped the rats hadn't suffered. And after accidentally
snapping his fingers while placing a trap, he was assured their
end was quick and painless. The worst part was that the captain
was too cheap to buy new traps, so Ollie had to scrub the bloodied boards in a bucket of saltwater and reuse them. The captain
referred to this ritual as "doing da dishes." It was by far the least
desirable part of the job. But it kept him from thinking of his
family and that he had made the biggest mistake of his life.

When the ship reached Nova Scotia, Ollie found Ben in the
galley scrubbing a stack of dirty pots. "Thanks for the stitches,"
Ollie said, pointing to his forehead. "You could be a surgeon."

"Better get going before the captain changes his mind," Ben
said.

Ollie thought of the captain. It had turned out that the captain's surname was McCracken, and despite being a gruff seaman
who despised stowaways, he disliked US neutrality even more.
So the captain had kept his promise to allow Ollie to disembark

in Nova Scotia. Otherwise, Ollie may have found himself on another rat roundup.

Ben dropped a pot into the sink. "If I were thirty years younger, I'd quit and go with you."

The remark reminded Ollie of his father's frequent threats to walk to Montreal to join the war effort. He buried the thought and shook the cook's soapy hand.

"Take care of yourself, Ben."

Ollie picked up his suitcase, went on deck, and stared over the bow. Halifax looked similar to many of the ports in Maine—ink-blue water, rows of rickety piers, and brick warehouses cut into a land of pines. It could have been Portland, except for two distinguishing differences: Canadian flags and military ships. The docks and harbor were filled with destroyers, frigates, cruisers, patrol vessels, escort ships, and minesweepers.

Beads of sweat formed on Ollie's forehead. He wiped his brow and forced himself to step onto the gangplank, suddenly realizing he was going to war.

CHAPTER 6

EPPING, ENGLAND

A bell rang. Susan and Bertie perked their heads at the unusual sound of ringing, conditioned from several nights of explosions and roaring sirens. On the second ring, they realized it was the phone in the cottage. And even more surprising: The phone lines were working.

Susan, carrying Duchess, ran inside. She quickly placed the pigeon on the seat of a wooden chair, the bird flapping its wings to maintain her balance. "Hello," Susan said, grabbing the receiver.

"Hello, this is Jonathan Wallace of the National Pigeon Service. May I speak to Bertie Shepherd?"

"One moment." Susan looked out the window and saw her bowlegged grandfather grimacing with pain. She held the phone to her chest and shouted.

Bertie quickened his stride, biting his lower lip in response to the gravel in his knees. He reached the cottage, out of breath.

"National Pigeon Service," Susan said, cupping the receiver.

Bertie cleared his throat. "Hello," he said, trying not to sound winded. He tilted the receiver. Susan leaned in, pressing her face against her grandfather's whiskered cheek to listen.

Mr. Wallace informed them of plans for a joint meeting in London next week to include the National Pigeon Service, British Intelligence, and the Royal Air Force. Bertie, as well as several other pigeon raisers for the National Pigeon Service, were required to be in attendance. Bertie attempted to ask questions, but Mr. Wallace could only provide the date and that a Flight Lieutenant Clyde Boar from the RAF would escort him to a secret location in London.

Susan watched Bertie write the information on a piece of scrap paper, wondering if there would be anything left of London by next week, and why it had taken the British authorities so long to plan the mission.

"Good day, Jonathan," Bertie said. He hung up the receiver and looked at Susan.

"Do you know him?" she asked.

Bertie nodded. "We've raced pigeons together."

Susan picked up Duchess. "You're in no condition to travel."

"I'm fine."

Susan helped Bertie to his chair in the living room. She propped his feet on a stool and rolled his trousers above his knees. His thin legs looked like pencils, his knees swollen like melons. She pressed a finger to a kneecap.

"Ouch!"

Susan shook her head. "You can't go."

"I'll recover." He placed his hand on Susan's shoulder. "It's the running to the shelter that has flared them up."

Susan retrieved cold cloths and ointment. She gently rubbed some salve over his knees.

Duchess fluttered over and landed on the back of Bertie's chair.

"What are you looking at?" Bertie said over his shoulder.

Duchess cocked her head and watched Susan wrap cloths around Bertie's knees.

Susan tucked a loose strand of hair behind her ear. "I'm going."

Bertie shook his head. "Too dangerous."

"You can barely walk, let alone travel to London."

"I can't let you go. Your parents and Granny would never forgive me." He placed his hand on Susan's arm. "And I would never forgive myself."

Susan thought of Granny, recalling how much she missed their walks in Epping Forest to pick wild elderberries, most of which they ate before returning home. "Tell your grandfather that his pigeons have stolen all the berries," Grandmother would often say, tossing a handful into her mouth. Susan would grin, pluck a berry from a bush, and place it into her mouth, feeling a wee bit mischievous. It was their little secret. They would come home from their adventures with full bellies, empty pails, and new memories, despite always taking the same winding path. Susan could remember every detail of Granny—her wispy gray hair, a constant smile spreading the soft wrinkles in her cheeks, and the eloquent timbre of her voice, like the strings of an old violin. Granny passed away in her sleep on a warm summer night, a mere four years ago. But it seemed like a lifetime ago, the war having driven a wedge between the past and present.

Susan tried to remember her parents, casualties of the Spanish flu pandemic, but could only envision children jumping rope as they chanted. *I had a little bird, its name was Enza. I opened the window, and in flew Enza.* Susan clenched her hands, shutting the chant from her mind.

"I'm going," Susan said.

"Absolutely not," Bertie said firmly. "Besides, Wallace mentioned a Clyde Boar. The only Boar I know was the little dickens in your primary school who ate the ribbon off the parish Christmas tree. There's no way I'm letting a tinsel eater escort my granddaughter to London."

Susan shook her head. "The garland was made of popping corn. And I doubt it's the same person."

Chapter 7

Halifax, Nova Scotia

The Canadian embarkation authorities were almost nonexistent, considering most of the customs officers had left to join the war. There were only two officers working the port—one with thick spectacles who struggled to read his clipboard, and another who spent his time staring through binoculars, as if he were waiting for a German submarine to rise from the depths of Halifax Harbour. Ollie disembarked by simply walking off the ship and mingling into a crowd.

Unwilling to push his luck again as a stowaway, Ollie spent three days in Halifax trying to talk his way onto a ship headed to England. He received nothing but rejections, most of which came from crews of British or Canadian military vessels, unimpressed that a young man with a stitched forehead and a tattered suitcase had any business as a pilot for the Royal Air Force. Flashing Bish's business card and his own flight log had gotten him nowhere. And it became increasingly clear to Ollie that he was unlikely to board a military ship without paperwork.

Discouraged, Ollie walked to the end of a pier and sat down. His legs dangled over the side. He watched the tide go out, revealing pylons caked in barnacles. A briny scent filled his nostrils. With his eyes, he followed a thick rope tied to a freighter. Across the bow, painted in white lettering, was the name *Maaskerk*.

"May skurk," Ollie said, scratching his head. "Mase kirk."

A seaman who was walking along the pier stopped behind Ollie.

"Mask urk . . . Mays kerk . . ."

The seaman removed his officer's cap and shook his head. "*Maaskerk*," he said in a Dutch accent.

Ollie turned. "Maw skerk?"

"*Maaskerk*."

"*Maaskerk*," Ollie repeated.

The seaman nodded. "What are you doing here, besides butchering the name of my ship?"

"Trying to get to England," Ollie said. "I'm joining the Royal Air Force."

"You don't sound British."

"I'm American."

"Where are you from?"

"Buxton, Maine."

"Buckon?"

"Buxton."

"Booksen?"

'No, Bucks-ton." Ollie noticed the man grinning and realized that he was being made fun of. "I guess that makes us even."

The seaman replaced his cap. "Half our crew left to join the fight. Captain sent me onshore to recruit greasers. You work, and I'll arrange for your passage."

Ollie stood and extended his hand. "Thank you. Name's Ollie."

"Jansen," the officer said, shaking Ollie's hand.

Ollie picked up his suitcase, followed Jansen up the gangway, and was put to work lubricating moving engine parts and mechanical equipment. He soon smelled of oil, his hands and shirt stained the color of coffee. As Ollie lathered the teeth of a cog, he wondered what it would be like in Britain. *Where will I be stationed? What plane will I fly? What does a Nazi look like? Would Mom and Dad be proud? Will I be killed?* He smeared on more grease and buried his thoughts.

The *Maaskerk* was a Dutch freighter that was part of a convoy headed to England, seeking safe passage in the company of Canadian and British military vessels. A day into the journey, the freighter developed propeller trouble and slowed to seven knots. Unable to continue with the fourteen-knot convoy, the *Maaskerk* was forced to sail alone. Ollie heard fears from the crew that they were an easy torpedo target for a German submarine, some even placing bets on their reaching port, especially when rumors surfaced that the hull was secretly filled with ammunition, a much more dangerous cargo than grain—or rats, for that matter. But when the *Maaskerk* reached port in Liverpool, England, Ollie learned that the convoy had been attacked by a U-boat wolf pack and lost over a dozen ships. He was saddened by the loss of their crews, many of whom had waved to him from their decks as they departed Halifax. And he realized just how lucky he was to have boarded the *Maaskerk*, simply because he was intrigued by how to pronounce her name.

Ollie disembarked feeling fortunate to have made it to England, until he saw the devastation. The port was in shambles. All but a few of the docks were reduced to splintering piles of wood and crumbled concrete. To the north, an entire block of buildings was in ruins. Ollie's legs felt weak. His mouth went dry. He carried his suitcase around a large hole in the ground, no doubt caused by a bomb missing its target, and took a seat on a pile of bricks. He noticed passing shipyard workers with soiled clothes, sunken eyes, and lines of sorrow etched into their faces. And they all looked as if they had lost just as much as Ollie, if not more.

Ollie's hands were shaking. A wave of uncertainty washed over him. How was a young crop-dusting pilot from Buxton,

Maine, to make a difference? He felt incompetent. And more like a naïve farm boy than an aviator. He had thought the death of his parents was perhaps the end of his tribulation, but he now realized it was merely the beginning.

Ollie took in deep breaths to calm his nerves. He opened his suitcase and retrieved the picture of his parents, taken before the crippling tractor accident. His parents were smiling, holding hands, and dressed in their Sunday clothes. His father proudly sported a tie that Ollie had given him one year for Christmas, and Mother wore a pleated dress, her long locks of hair resting on her shoulders. Ollie wiped his eyes, overcome with guilt for the way he had disregarded his parents about their convictions to support Britain and, even more, for never having had the opportunity to apologize. His parents had sacrificed to provide him with a good life, one that until now he had taken for granted. He wished he could have even half of their spirit. Regardless of the fact that he was broke, homeless, and foolish for believing he could become a pilot for the Royal Air Force, he vowed to move on. Ollie put away the photo, buried his fear, and left his pile of bricks.

To make a little money, enough to purchase a meal of fried bread and a train ticket to London, he worked the day unloading cargo for the *Maaskerk*. As he carefully unloaded heavy wooden boxes filled with artillery shells, he noticed several burned warehouses and the Liverpool Iron Works; one wing of the structure was obliterated. Ollie asked a shipyard worker named Joseph Burke what had happened. With a quivering jaw, Joseph told Ollie that a few weeks before, the Luftwaffe had bombed the city. Joseph clasped his hands as if he were about to pray and added that his wife, Millie, and his two-year-old daughter, Christine, had taken refuge in the Cleveland Square shelter the night of the bombing. The shelter took a direct hit, killing eighteen people, including Millie and Christine.

"I was working the night shift," Joseph said. "I should have been there with them."

"I'm sorry," Ollie said.

Joseph nodded, wiped his eyes, and went back to work.

Ollie returned to unloading cargo, filled with fury at what the Nazis had done. He imagined taking to the sky in an RAF Hurricane, perhaps even a Spitfire, and ridding his parents' homeland of this evil.

After finishing his work, Ollie collected his pay and boarded a train to London, which wasn't crowded, considering many people were fleeing the cities. And he realized why when the train approached London.

Although the port of Liverpool had received heavy bombing, most of the city's residential areas had been spared. That was not the case for London. An ashen haze loomed over the great city. Ollie stuck his head out the window to get a better look. Wind blew across his face, filling his nostrils with the scent of smoke. And as the train chugged into the city limits, he saw destroyed factories, burned buildings, a church with its steeple toppled, and blocks of what used to be row houses reduced to smoldering rubble. It looked as if London was being cremated, one piece at a time.

As the train passed the first cemetery, Ollie noticed scores of fresh graves tarnishing the once-manicured grounds, with dozens of new holes being dug for those waiting to be buried or in preparation for another night of bombing. Rows of pine boxes were propped against the side of a mortuary like a macabre assembly line. And just as Ollie was becoming numb to the horror, he saw them. The small coffins.

Ollie felt as if the air had been sucked out of his body. "It's not supposed to happen this way," he whispered to himself. Children were not supposed to go before their parents. And wars were not supposed to be fought in cities. He had been taught in school that combat took place on battlefields. Gettysburg. The Western Front. Gallipoli. The Battle of the Somme. Bloodshed was in the muddy trenches, so he believed. Weren't those the rules? But that was not the case with the Nazis. The Luftwaffe had taken the war to the cities, with no regard for the killing of innocent civilians, including children.

Ollie watched the cemetery disappear in the distance and wondered if there would be enough trees in all of Britain to build the coffins.

A child whimpered. He turned and saw a mother two rows behind him attempting to console her daughter, who was perhaps five or six years old. The woman was caressing the girl's face and doing her best to distract her child from the ghastly view outside the window. "Your father is safe . . . the war will be over soon," the woman repeated, as if she were chanting affirmations. But the girl wailed harder. And the mother broke down and wept.

Ollie reached in his suitcase and found his only clean item, a sock, the twin to the one he had used for his head. He stood, rolled the garment into a ball, and walked down the aisle. The woman and her child looked up, both with tears running down their cheeks.

"I wish I had a handkerchief," Ollie said, handing the sock to the woman.

The woman accepted the gesture and dabbed her daughter's cheeks. Ollie returned to his seat and put up the window, attempting to shut out the death and destruction. He sat for the remainder of the trip with his face buried in his hands.

The London streets were filled with volunteers clearing away rubble. Surprisingly to Ollie, many shops were open. He soon learned that the Luftwaffe had bombed the city every evening for fourteen consecutive nights, and many Londoners were now spending their nights in shelters beneath the city. Ollie admired the perseverance of Londoners, going about their daily lives in spite of Hitler's bombing offensive.

Ollie was able to find the office of Charles Sweeny by asking for directions from people in the street. Apparently, Mr. Sweeny was quite a socialite and an admired businessman. A few minutes before five o'clock, Ollie entered a large office building in the heart of London, fortunate to have been spared from the bombings. He went to the top floor, where he was greeted by a gray-haired receptionist who was hastily preparing to leave.

"I'm Ollie Evans." He showed the woman the card Bishop had given him. "Bish . . . I mean Mr. Bishop . . . had told me to meet with Mr. Sweeny about joining the Royal Air Force."

The woman shook her head. "Mr. Sweeny is out of town." She threw a stack of papers into a bin. "I'm leaving."

Ollie watched the woman lock her desk and toss keys into her purse. "Please, I've come all the way from the United States."

"Come back tomorrow," she said.

A siren sounded.

The woman stepped backward. "They're coming."

The hair stood up on the back of Ollie's neck. "How much time?"

"Fifteen, perhaps twenty minutes. That siren means they've been spotted crossing the Channel." The woman threw on her coat, slung her purse over her shoulder, and turned.

"Please!" Ollie called after her. "I've got no place to go."

"Tomorrow!"

"But there may not be a tomorrow!"

The woman stopped. Then fumbled for her keys. "Name."

"Ollie."

The siren howled.

"Your last name." She jammed a key into the file cabinet and opened the lock.

"Evans."

The woman dug through a drawer. "I don't see it."

"Are you sure?"

The woman flipped through more files. She stopped. "Oliver?"

"Yes."

The woman pulled out an envelope and slammed the drawer shut. She quickly handed the envelope to Ollie. "Take a train to

Church Fenton in the morning." The woman threw her keys into her purse. "I suggest you find a shelter, Mr. Evans." She turned and left, the click of her heels echoing in the hallway.

Ollie followed the woman down the stairs. "Where should I go?"

"Follow the crowds!" the woman shouted.

Outside, Ollie lost sight of the woman in a group of people running on the sidewalk but managed to find a shelter in an underground railway station. It was crowded with Londoners who had been lining up to get in since midafternoon, but he was able to find a less desirable spot, a damp corner on a lumpy cobblestone floor. The family next to him was playing a board game, their youngest daughter holding a doll and a gas mask. When Ollie introduced himself, the young girl leaned to her mother and said, "He sounds rather odd."

Ollie smiled, perhaps for the first time in weeks, and told them that he had traveled from Maine to join the Royal Air Force.

Despite his unusual accent, the family gave Ollie some of their rationed food—dried sausage and pickled beets.

"We appreciate your sacrifice for our war effort," the father said, cutting a piece of sausage for Ollie.

"Thank you," Ollie said, taking the meat. "I wish I had something to give you in return."

"You can help give us back our sky," the man said.

Ollie nodded.

The rumble of exploding bombs began at dark. As the ground shook and dust fell from the ceiling, Ollie opened his envelope. Under the dim glow of a lantern, he found paperwork with his name on it, a train ticket, and a note.

Mr. Evans,
On behalf of the Royal Air Force and the citizens of the United Kingdom, we are gratified for your services in our hour of need. My dear friend, Billy Bishop, Air Marshal of the Royal Canadian

Air Force, sent word that you may turn up, indicating that he was "impressed with the young lad from Maine." I hope this letter finds you, and if so, the enclosed papers will lead you to the Number 71 Eagle Squadron at Church Fenton, under the command of Squadron Leader W. M. Churchill. I wish you success in our fight.

    Godspeed,

    Charles Sweeny

Ollie opened his suitcase, exchanged the papers for a sweater, and propped the garment behind his head as a pillow. Snores filled the shelter. A young boy coughed. The ground rumbled. Bits of mortar fell from the ceiling. He wiped grit from his face, rolled over, and tried to find a comfortable position on the cobblestone. Ollie thought of flying his biplane over the potato fields of Maine, and how much he missed his parents. As the thunder of German bombs fell over the city, he noticed the young girl sleeping with a gas mask clenched in her arms, her doll splayed on the floor. And Ollie vowed to do his part to give her back her sky.

CHAPTER 8

EPPING, ENGLAND

Susan's grandfather was right; Flight Lieutenant Clyde Boar was the same little dickens from her primary school. This was confirmed when the lieutenant arrived at daybreak, after another night of bombing, with orders to accompany a Bertie Shepherd of the National Pigeon Service to London. As the lieutenant prepared to knock, Bertie swung open the door and asked, "Are you the same boy who ate ribbon from the parish Christmas tree?"

Susan's face flushed hot with embarrassment.

Flight Lieutenant Boar, a six-foot, broad-shouldered RAF flight leader, slid his hands into his pockets and said, "Yes, sir. And from what I can remember, it tasted quite good."

Bertie invited him inside, seeming satisfied with the lieutenant's candidness or intrigued with the notion that eating tinsel could turn devilish boys into rugged airmen.

Bertie pointed to his bowed knees. "I'm afraid the old legs aren't up for the trip."

Susan placed a hand on her grandfather's shoulder.

"I understand," Flight Lieutenant Boar said. "After the meeting, I'll make arrangements to deliver you the orders."

"That won't be necessary," Bertie said. "Susan will be taking my place."

The lieutenant raised his brows.

Susan extended her hand. "Hello, Flight Lieutenant."

Boar looked at Bertie. "I believe the orders are for you to attend the—".

"Jonathan Wallace of the National Pigeon Service requested a representative of the Bertie Shepherd farm to attend," Bertie interrupted.

The lieutenant rubbed his jaw.

"Susan is also a member of the National Pigeon Service, and *she* will be my representative."

Susan cleared her throat, her arm still extended.

Boar shook her hand.

Bertie stepped close to the lieutenant. "I'm putting my trust in you for Susan's safety."

"The meeting is at eleven AM," Boar said. "The afternoon train will have us out of London before the bombings."

Bertie gave Susan a hug. "You're as good as they are," he whispered. "Be an egg."

Susan squeezed her grandfather.

Be an egg, Susan thought. One could be soft with fear inside, but hard as slate outside. It was her grandfather's phrase of affirmation, spoken seldom, but at the times she needed them most. Bertie had always been supportive of all her endeavors, instilling a sense of confidence that she could accomplish anything through diligence and faith. And it was this conditioning, she believed, that enabled her to attend the University of London. Susan also knew it was dreadfully painful for Bertie to let her go into the city. She wished that it had been her persistent requests that had worn her grandfather down. But in the end, it was Bertie's failing knees that were the tipping point. She prayed that she would make him proud.

"Are you sure you can take care of the pigeons?" Susan asked.

Bertie nodded, his eyes watery. "I may not be able to travel, but I can bloody well walk across this farm."

Susan kissed Bertie on the cheek and left.

Susan and Flight Lieutenant Boar got into the back of a green military vehicle. A soldier sat as a chauffeur behind the wheel. As they drove off, Susan saw Bertie hobbling across the lawn, wasting no time getting to work. And perched on top of a loft was a solitary pigeon with an unmistakable vibrant plume. From the view out the rear window, Susan watched Bertie, Duchess, and the sanctuary of her home disappear.

The driver dropped off Susan and the lieutenant at North Weald Station. They boarded the train for London and took a seat near the back.

"We attended school together," Susan said, as the train lurched forward. "I was two years behind you."

Boar raised a finger. "You were the girl that liked birds."

"Pigeons."

The lieutenant offered Susan a cigarette.

Susan shook her head.

The lieutenant lit a cigarette and inhaled. "I'm a flight leader," he said, blowing smoke. "Blenheim Bomber."

Susan nodded.

"After this mission, I expect to lead a Spitfire squadron."

"I expect to save Britain."

Boar coughed, dropping ashes onto Susan's skirt. "Excuse me." He brushed soot from her clothing, then slid down the window.

A cool breeze blew across Susan's face. *I had a little bird, its name was Enza. I opened the window, and in flew . . .* She shivered. "Would you mind putting up the window?"

The lieutenant sighed, blowing smoke through his nostrils.

Susan felt the urge to explain that it was more than the cold air but decided against it when the lieutenant flicked out his cigarette, closed the window, and leaned back to rest his eyes.

Passengers, unable to resist the urge to view the results of last night's bombings, flocked to the windows as the train approached London. Smoldering plumes rose over the city. The number of

Alan Hlad

fallen buildings increased in frequency and severity as the train
chugged toward the epicenter of London. Fire brigades battled
blazes in a futile effort to prevent flames from spreading to un-
scathed buildings.

As a child, Susan's grandparents had taken her to London each
year to celebrate her birthday. Her memory was filled with visits
to London Zoo, walks in Trafalgar Square, picnics in Hyde Park,
and dinner at Filmore Pie and Mash Shop. Unlike most patrons of
Filmore, they'd only order pudding—spotted dick with custard—
rather than the savory pies or jellied eels. She recalled how Agnes
had once attempted to wipe Bertie's custard-coated whiskers
with her napkin, only to have Bertie add a dollop of custard to his
nose, pull her into his arms, and say, "Kiss me, Agnes!"

Susan stared out the train window in disbelief. The London
she'd grown up with was nothing like this marred metropolis.
The radio reports and newspapers had done little to prepare her
for seeing this scorched, hellish ruin. Her breathing turned shallow, her chest filled with a fusion of shock and outrage.

Parades of Londoners who had spent the night in underground shelters were returning to their homes, or what was left of
them. Susan saw two children sitting on the steps of a row house
in ruins, the oldest girl consoling her baby brother by rocking
him on her lap. Susan noticed the absence of parents and wiped
tears from her eyes.

The train stopped several blocks before reaching their station
due to a bomb that had taken out the tracks, leaving a crater the
size of a bus. They stepped off the train to the wail of ambulance,
police, and fire sirens. The scent of burnt wood and petrol made
Susan want to hold her breath. A library across the street had been
converted to a makeshift hospital; stretchers of wounded were
being hauled inside by medics. Susan covered her mouth.

"There's nothing you can do," the lieutenant said, nudging
her. "We need to go."

Susan reluctantly moved on.

They walked for blocks, passing more destruction and a park where antiaircraft artillery guns were placed between a swing set and a playground merry-go-round. Once a sanctuary for playful children, the park was now a military zone, with hardened men stacking sandbags.

Sections of central London were unrecognizable. Centuries of architecture decimated. Thousands of Londoners dead. Susan's legs felt weak. She wanted to cry but continued walking through Westminster until Flight Lieutenant Boar stopped in front of the Treasury Building.

"Is this it?" Susan asked.

The lieutenant lowered his voice. "The Royal Air Force commands are moving out of London. Even British intelligence is rumored to be leaving the city. But Churchill's stubborn. He declared that he would direct the war from the bowels of this building."

"Perhaps he doesn't want to abandon our people," Susan said.

Boar ignored her comment and opened the door.

The lieutenant handed paperwork and identification to an army private, one of four armed men securing the entrance. The soldier unlocked an iron gate and led them down a set of steep stairs to a large underground complex, a concrete fortress composed of cabinet, communications, and sleeping rooms. They walked past a series of war rooms with uniformed men hovering over maps. Ringing phones and tapping typewriters filled the air. They were taken to a large room with a square conference table seating forty men. As they approached the few remaining seats, a military officer looked at Susan and said, "Could you bring me tea?"

Susan clasped her hands to keep them from shaking and said, "I'm with the National Pigeon Service."

"Pardon me," the officer said.

They took their seats. Susan scanned those in the room, a mixture of military officers, British intelligence, and members of the National Pigeon Service. The British intelligence, likely from the Government Code and Cypher School, wore suits and ties and clung together at the far corner of the table. The National Pigeon Service was a civilian organization, and even though Susan didn't recognize anyone she knew, she could spot the members by their gray hair and woolly farm attire. Susan noticed she was the only woman in the room. *Be an egg*, she thought.

A decorated military man stood at the head of the table. "I'm Air Commodore John Breen."

The room went silent.

The commodore wrote "Source Columba" on a chalkboard in large letters. "This is the code name for our mission."

Susan noticed men glancing at one another. But she knew from her studies at the university that *Columba* was the Latin word for pigeon.

"We need a hundred thousand pigeons," the commodore said, dusting chalk from his hands. "Before the war is over, we may need two hundred thousand."

Susan saw jaws drop as members of the National Pigeon Service took in this information.

"The first objective of our meeting is a commitment from each farm on the number of birds and delivery dates." The commodore wrote again on the board. *Farm . . . No. of Birds . . . Date.* "Once this is accomplished, members of the National Pigeon Service will be dismissed."

Packets were distributed. Susan selected her envelope, which was addressed to Bertie Shepherd. Inside was nothing more than a sharpened pencil and a sheet of paper on which to chart the number of pigeons and target delivery dates. Susan placed the paper facedown on the table.

The commodore quickly began obtaining commitments from pigeon raisers as though he was pressed for time or frustrated to have drawn the short straw to coordinate a mission involving pigeons. Regardless, it was obvious to Susan that the commodore was eager to get this meeting over with and move on to more important endeavors, such as the air battle over the Channel. And one by one, the old men did what the commodore requested, as if they had been conditioned by years of climbing out of muddy trenches by whistle-blowing officers.

Susan's mind raced. *What was the military going to do with all our pigeons? Where were they going? Who was going to care for them?* She raised her hand.

"Susan," Boar whispered. "Not now."

Susan hesitated, then inched her hand higher.

The commodore stopped. "Yes, Miss . . ."

"Miss Shepherd. I'm here on behalf of my grandfather, Bertie Shepherd. He was unable to come because—"

"You have a question, Miss Shepherd?" the commodore interrupted.

Susan swallowed. "May I ask what you are going to do with our pigeons?"

"It's confidential. Only a few are aware of the plans to limit potential compromise of our intelligence." The commodore turned to another pigeon raiser and requested his quota.

Susan looked around the room. The eyes of pigeon raisers were upon her. She sensed that they were all thinking the same thing but didn't have the courage to open their mouths. Susan's face began to sweat. Her palms turned sticky. Her heart pounded. And she forced herself to stand.

"Sit down, Susan," Boar whispered.

Be an egg . . . be an egg . . . be an egg. Susan stood firm.

The commodore stopped. "Yes, Miss Shepherd."

"Do you have trained pigeon handlers included in the mission?"

"Take your seat, Miss Shepherd."

"Do you plan to use our pigeons for one-way or two-way communication?"

The commodore raised his voice. "Sit down, or I'll have you removed."

"Susan," the lieutenant hissed.

"Did you know that the vast majority of the pigeons from our farms are one-way pigeons?" Susan asked.

The commodore shouted for a military private, who was stationed outside the door.

The soldier entered and saluted.

"Remove her," said the commodore.

The soldier stepped toward Susan.

Susan gripped the table. "Do you realize that most of the pigeons you take will only end up back at our lofts? We may not need to know *when* and *where* you plan to use our pigeons, but we need to know *how* they will be used if you expect Source Columba to be a success!"

A staunch man wearing a spotted bow tie stopped as he passed the door.

The military men snapped to attention. Susan turned and saw the prime minister, Winston Churchill, accompanied by two military officers.

"Has the enemy invaded my war rooms?" Churchill asked with a cigar chomped between his teeth.

Susan's eyes widened.

"Everything is under control," the commodore said.

"She's right." A thin, elderly man stood. "Name's Jonathan Wallace, National Pigeon Service. Most of the pigeons will end up back at our lofts. My apologies to everyone for not speaking."

The remaining pigeon raisers nodded their heads.

Churchill looked at Susan. "May I ask who you are?"

Susan swallowed, noticing that the prime minister looked like a bulldog wearing a suit. "I'm Susan Shepherd. I raise pigeons with my grandfather, and I'm studying zoology. Or at least I was until the war."

Churchill leaned in. "What do you think you're doing by challenging a senior military officer?"

"My duty, sir."

Jowl muscles contracted. Ash fell from his cigar. Churchill looked at the commodore and said, "I recommend we take time to listen to Mr. Wallace and members of the National Pigeon Service. Their insight may be extraordinarily valuable in the success of our mission. It's our intellect, spirit, and tough British fiber that will lead us to victory." He tipped his hat and left.

Everyone took their seats. The commodore gripped his chalk, flushness spreading over his face.

"Bloody hell, Susan," the lieutenant whispered. "I can't believe you did that."

"Nor I," Susan said, feeling as if she had come within inches of being struck by a speeding train.

The meeting lasted deep into the afternoon. Not only did Susan learn about how the pigeons were to be used, she learned everything about Source Columba and wished she had kept her mouth shut.

CHAPTER 9

LONDON, ENGLAND

Susan and Flight Lieutenant Boar missed the last train out of London by a mere ten minutes. While the lieutenant was attempting to secure a military vehicle to drive them back to North Weald, Susan searched for a telephone to call Bertie. Outside the train station, twilight cast inky shadows. *We're running out of time*, she thought. Quickly, she located a telephone box, but the lines were dead. As she placed the receiver back in its cradle, air-raid sirens sounded. Susan covered her ears. Sparse groups of Londoners looked to the sky. Paces quickened. And streets turned bare.

Susan and Flight Lieutenant Boar gave up their attempts to return home and followed a woman with her three young boys, each carrying blankets and pillows, into an underground railway station. Susan felt sick, realizing that Bertie would worry. But less than an hour later, she forgot about her grandfather, at least for the moment, when the first round of bombs exploded, shaking the shelter and dropping bits of mortar into her hair.

As she shook grit from her scalp, she noticed the woman they had followed into the shelter open a book and begin reading to her three boys. Despite the woman's best efforts to distract her children, the boys' eyes wandered to the ceiling. Susan saw another family playing a board game, taking turns rolling dice and blowing dust from the pieces. An old woman was teaching her granddaughter how to knit, a scarf slowly growing from the click of the needles. Despite the destruction of the city above them, the Londoners were doing their best to go about their lives, if not for themselves, for the children.

Eventually, the children were tucked in their blankets. Lanterns were dimmed. But the thunder of bombs continued.

Susan stared at the masonry ceiling. *Can the shelter withstand a direct hit?* Her heart thumped against her rib cage. She clenched her hands, digging her nails into her palms. The trepidation of hiding underground, while the Luftwaffe bombed London, was worse than she could ever have imagined. With each rumbling blast, Susan felt one step closer to death.

"Get some rest, Susan," Boar said, sitting next to her. "There's nothing we can do tonight."

She nodded.

The lieutenant leaned back and closed his eyes.

Susan, her gut twisted with angst, remained awake, wondering if the wings of a hundred thousand pigeons could change the course of the war.

As morning came, the last wave of explosions stopped. A siren gave the all-clear signal, a long deafening drone that stirred the occupants of the shelter. People stretched their arms; others wiped sand from their eyes. A gradual crescendo of whispers turned to normal voices as people gathered their blankets, pillows, and bags. Susan's apprehension gradually diminished. She hadn't slept but didn't feel tired, her adrenaline still pumping from the rumble of bombs, the proximity of explosions much closer than the distant echoes heard from Bertie's farm. Perhaps she would have gotten used to it if she had slept underground for weeks with the others, the deafening blasts and quaking earth becoming an expected normalcy.

As Londoners prepared to leave the shelter, Susan noticed a little girl with tangled blond hair drop a gas mask and pick up a doll. And Susan wished she could take the girl, the girl's parents, and everyone in the shelter to the safety of the countryside.

"Good morning," Flight Lieutenant Boar said. He combed his black hair with his fingers, then ran his hands over his RAF uniform, attempting to press out the wrinkles. "Did you sleep?"

Susan shook her head. She recalled waking in the night to the touch of the lieutenant's hand on her thigh, his breath across her neck. She had inched away, finding solace on the cold stone floor, but was unable to close her eyes.

The shelter door opened. People gathered their belongings and shuffled outside to the roar of fire engines and a thick acrid scent, a mixture of sulfur and burning petroleum. A block away, an apartment complex was partially destroyed. Firefighters painted with sweat and soot sprayed water on the burning building. She walked in the opposite direction, wishing she could shut out the cries of residents who had left the shelter to find their homes engulfed in flames.

To reach their train station, they had to maneuver through the maze of streets, many of which were blocked by barriers, fire brigades, or piles of rubble. The station was crowded with Londoners seeking to leave the city, to judge from the multitude of trunks lining the platform. As they boarded, people pushed to find their way into a carriage. The lieutenant claimed seats, but Susan insisted on giving them to a couple carrying a baby, so they stood in the aisle with many other passengers, all desperately seeking sanctuary outside of London.

The train whistle blew, the carriage jerked, and Susan fell back.

The lieutenant caught her.

Susan felt his fingers linger. She tried to step away, but the aisle was too crowded.

"I'd like to see you again," Boar said. He lowered a hand to her hip.

"We both have work to do," she said, inching away.

Boar leaned in. "All the more reason we should get to know each other."

Susan noticed his sour breath. "I don't think it would be a good idea, Flight Lieutenant."

"Call me Clyde."

Susan tapped her bag with her finger. "Flight Lieutenant, I can't possibly meet the demands of our orders by taking personal time, and you have your own orders that will require your full attention."

"I'm a flight leader," Boar said. "And with my rank, I'm allowed"—he paused, scanning her body with his eyes—"flexibility."

"I'm flattered. But the answer is no." Susan turned.

Boar clasped Susan's wrist.

She looked at his hand.

"I wasn't finished," he said, tightening his grip.

"Let go," came a strange voice.

Susan looked up and saw a young man with wavy brown hair holding a suitcase.

"Mind your business, Yank," Boar said.

"Let go," Ollie said.

Susan felt the lieutenant release her arm.

"What are you doing here, Yank?" Boar stepped to Ollie.

"I'm headed to Church Fenton to join the Eagle Squadron." Ollie touched the envelope sticking out of his jacket pocket.

"Impressive. I heard there was a Yank squadron being formed, but thought it was a rumor. Mind if I look?" Boar snatched the envelope.

"Give it back," Ollie said, dropping his suitcase.

The lieutenant glanced at the letter signed by Charles Sweeny, then ripped it in half and tossed it out a window. "Go home to your mum."

As the shredded paper scattered below a trestle and settled into a marsh, Susan looked at the young man who had come to her aid. She noticed ire etched into his face. And she sensed that it was more what the lieutenant had said than what he had done that had made him angry.

Ollie clenched his fist, cocked back his arm, and hit the lieutenant in the jaw.

The lieutenant's head shot to the side, but his feet remained planted.

A woman screamed. Heads turned. A few brave passengers squeezed between Ollie and the lieutenant, attempting to break up the fight.

Boar wiped his lip. Blood filled the crevices of his teeth. "You'll regret you did that, Yank." He brushed his uniform and looked calmly at Susan. "I was merely . . ."

She crossed her arms, turned, and stared out the window.

Boar glared at Ollie, then made his way through the crowd, pushing passengers aside, and entered another carriage.

"Are you okay?" Ollie asked.

"That wasn't necessary," Susan said.

"He grabbed you, threw my papers out the window, and said something about my mother."

She looked at him. "I appreciate your concern for my welfare, but I assure you that I can take care of myself."

"I was only trying to help."

She rubbed her wrist. "What's your name?"

"Ollie."

"I'm Susan," she said, trying to pinpoint the origin of his accent. "Where are you from?"

"Maine . . . United States," he said.

"Well, Ollie from Maine, I suggest that you make your way to another carriage, preferably as far to the back of the train as possible. And when the train stops in North Weald, get off quickly and take another train to where you are headed."

Ollie nodded, then extended his hand.

Susan shook his hand, noticing his grip was firm, yet gentle. As he left, she watched him work his way toward the back of the train and disappear.

Less than an hour later, the train screeched to a stop. Susan got off and saw a group of soldiers placing handcuffs on Ollie. Boar, standing next to the soldiers, barked orders. A wave of culpability struck her. Helplessly, she watched the men place Ollie in the back of a military vehicle and drive away.

Chapter 10

North Weald, England

The soldiers, led by Flight Lieutenant Boar, took Ollie to what they referred to as the Glasshouse. But to Ollie, it looked like a military jail. They held Ollie's arms, pinning his back against a stone wall. Boar hit Ollie in the stomach. Ollie's legs collapsed. He shriveled into a ball, unable to catch his breath. The soldiers lifted Ollie from the ground and slammed him into the wall.

"Not his face," Boar said. "I don't want the commander feeling sorry for him." The lieutenant cocked back his arm and gave Ollie an uppercut to his ribs.

Ollie gasped like a carp out of water—mouth open, sucking for air—but nothing came in. His lungs felt broken.

An air-raid siren sounded, sending the men scurrying out of the cell. Except for Flight Lieutenant Boar.

"You should have stayed home, Yank." He kicked Ollie in the side.

Ollie groaned, his limbs shriveled into a fetal position to protect his organs. The cell door slammed, then footsteps faded. When he was able to breathe, he crawled into the bunk, if one could call it that; it was a board covered with a mildewed blanket. Outside, antiaircraft fire boomed. He tried to stand. His head buzzed, the room spun, and it all went black.

Ollie woke when his hand fell from the bunk and landed on concrete. He tried stretching his legs, but his feet and head struck the walls of the cell. Shadows of steel bars spread across the floor. It smelled of damp stone and potato bugs, like the root cellar back on the farm.

He suspected it was now morning, even though the cell had no windows. Water trickled from a toilet. Ollie's mouth was dry. His sides flared with pain. He looked at the cracks in the ceiling and wondered if his ribs were in the same condition. Sounds of approaching footsteps echoed in the corridor. Ollie rubbed his side and prepared himself for another round of punishment.

He heard the clang of a key, the squeak of iron hinges, and the shuffling of feet beside his bunk. Ollie opened his eyes. Two men stood over him: one in uniform, and the other wearing tweed trousers with suspenders, his knees bowed outward, like he was riding an invisible pony. Ollie's suitcase hung from the man's age-spotted hand.

"Oliver from Maine," a scratchy voice said.

"Yes," Ollie said, his voice sounding dry. He coughed, feeling a sharp pain in his abdomen.

"Come with me."

Ollie slowly sat up and stood on shaky legs. He saw a soldier and was relieved to see it was not one of the men who had beaten him. The bowlegged man was short with white hair, a wrinkly face, and a pocket watch strung across his vest.

"Who are you?" Ollie asked.

"Name's Bertie. Bertie Shepherd. I'm your employer for the next three months."

Ollie scratched his head and looked at the soldier.

The soldier motioned with his head for Ollie to leave.

Ollie followed Bertie down the corridor, leaving the soldier behind. Outside, the sun struck Ollie's face. He squinted and sneezed, causing a dagger of pain to pierce his ribs.

"Bless you," Bertie said.

"Thanks." Ollie pressed his hand to his side and followed the old man to a truck.

Bertie opened the passenger door, helped Ollie in, and tossed the suitcase behind the seat. He got into the truck and took his seat behind the wheel.

"Where are we going?" Ollie asked.

Bertie put the key in the ignition, rubbed his knees, and started the engine. "To work."

"How did you get me out?"

Bertie hit the accelerator and honked the horn at a group of servicemen marching toward a hangar. "I talked to the commander and struck a deal to get you out."

"Why?"

Bertie lowered his glasses and glanced at Ollie. "Because you helped my granddaughter, Susan."

Ollie remembered the graceful woman with sandy-blond hair, the lieutenant's hand clutching her wrist. Ollie felt his face turn hot.

Bertie gripped the wheel. "If I were a young man, I'd knock some manners into that bastard." He looked at Ollie. "Thank you."

He nodded.

"What's a young man from Maine doing so far from home?"

Ollie thought of his parents, wilted flowers on their graves. "There's nothing back there for me."

The old man rubbed his knee.

Ollie pointed to a Hurricane fighter plane coming in for landing. "I'm a pilot. I need to get to Church Fenton to join the Eagle Squadron."

"You can't go for ninety days. That was the deal."

"What deal?"

"The deal I made with Commander Davies." Bertie turned the wheel sharply left, leaving North Weald Airfield and causing Ollie to brace himself against the dash.

"We agreed that you would work for me for three months. And I agreed not to file a complaint against Flight Lieutenant Clyde

Boar for his conduct, unbecoming of a Royal Air Force officer. I also told him I knew Air Vice-Marshal Keith Park and would be calling him after I left, assuming we could not reach an agreement on how to handle such a delicate situation."

"I appreciate your help with getting me out of jail, but I need to get to Church Fenton."

Bertie glanced to him. "Oliver from Maine, do you know the penalty for striking an officer?"

Ollie shook his head.

"You could spend a very long time in a military prison, until we win this damn war or we are all speaking German."

Ollie swallowed.

"I also suspect that Commander Davies didn't know what to do with you. You're American, not enlisted in the Royal Air Force—at least not yet—and he has an armada of Nazis flying over his airfield every night on their way to destroy London. Davies has lost a lot of good men; his fighters are falling like hammers out of the sky."

Bertie sighed. "He may not have been able to keep you locked up until you're old and gray, but he sure as hell could have made it very difficult for you to join the fight by making a call to Church Fenton. I suppose he welcomed my solution for an amicable agreement."

"Thanks, Bertie. I guess I owe you, and your friend, Keith Park, a bit more gratitude."

Bertie laughed and rubbed his knee. "I met the air vice-marshal at a parade in London once. And since I got close enough to shake Park's hand, I thought it couldn't hurt to use the man's name."

Hearing the man cackle made Ollie smile.

"You should have seen the commander's eyes when I mentioned Park's name. He looked like a child being called into the schoolmaster's office," Bertie continued, rubbing his knee, and laughed harder.

Ollie chuckled, something he hadn't done in weeks. He covered his ribs with his hands.

"Looks like they roughed you up a wee bit, Ollie. Ninety days of working on our mission will give you time to recover."

"What type of mission?"

"Source Columba. Commander Davies also has a vested interest in the success of this mission, probably another reason he let you out to work for me."

Ollie scratched his head. "What's Source Columbia?"

"Columba. It's top secret." Bertie's smile faded. His eyes lowered. "How can I be sure you're not a spy?"

"I'm a crop-duster." Ollie considered digging in his suitcase for his pilot's license.

Wind whistled through the open window. The truck hit a pothole, bouncing them from their seats.

Bertie laughed. "You'll know all about our mission soon enough. And you'll learn more about flying in the next few months than in a lifetime in the cockpit of a Spitfire."

Ollie watched the airfield disappear in the side mirror. And wondered what kind of mess he'd gotten himself into.

CHAPTER 11

EPPING, ENGLAND

Susan poured grain into the feeding tray, then rapped on a can with a wooden spoon. Pigeons flew into the loft and pecked at their meal. Except for Duchess. The bird, her head angled to the side, stood on the landing and stared at Susan.

"All right, Duchess," Susan said. She took a handful of grain, kneeled, and held out her palm.

Duchess fluttered to the floor, waddled to her, and cooed.

"I spoil you rotten." Susan rubbed her finger over Duchess's back.

Duchess stepped closer. And after receiving another stroke across her head, she began to peck.

After the grains disappeared from Susan's palm, either swallowed by Duchess or scattered on the floor, she brushed her hands and stood. "Now, off with you."

Duchess slowly walked to the feeding tray, stopped, and looked back at Susan.

"Go on."

Duchess lowered her head, as if her feelings had been hurt, and wedged herself into the flock of birds.

As Susan watched Duchess, she couldn't help thinking that

the bird acted more like the Shetland sheepdog, Whitby, her grandfather owned when Susan was a child. The dog had been smart as a whip and constantly seeking affection by nuzzling her or stealing her food, usually a warm elderberry scone her grandmother had made. Bertie now joked that if he had believed in reincarnation, his old dog had come back as Duchess. It was Bertie's way of trying to explain Duchess's unusual behavior; he was unable to believe, even after years of training the best breeds in Britain, that a pigeon prodigy had hatched in their loft or, more precisely, in a ceramic bowl that used to hold his wife's oatmeal.

Susan glanced one last time at Duchess, whose bright plumage stood out from that of her peers, like an Easter egg placed in a basket of ordinary brown eggs. She turned and left, the spring door slamming behind her.

As Susan took the path to another loft, she heard Bertie's truck, the unmistakable sound of missing gears as her grandfather struggled to work the clutch. The truck came into view, and she noticed a passenger. As it neared the cottage, she saw the American's head jerk as Bertie abruptly braked.

Susan straightened her skirt and noticed some droppings stuck to her shoe. She tilted her ankle and wiped her foot across the grass.

Bertie got out of the truck, followed by Ollie, his hand pressed against his ribs.

Susan stared, her mouth open.

Bertie pulled his pocket watch from his vest but didn't look at it. "Oliver from Maine will be working for us for a few months."

Susan raised her brows.

"Just until we finish the first phase of Source Columba." Bertie grimaced as he shifted his weight to the opposite foot.

"Come inside, and I'll get you something for your knees," Susan said.

Bertie nodded and went inside.

Susan looked at Ollie. "You should have left the train station like I told you."

Ollie stepped to her. "I tried."

Susan noticed Ollie holding his side. "Did they hurt you?"

"I'll be okay."

"Lovely. Just lovely. How are we to finish our mission with everyone fragile?"

Ollie shrugged and followed Susan inside.

Susan retrieved some wet towels that were stored in the icebox and wrapped them around both of Bertie's knees, his trouser rolled up to his flabby thighs.

Bertie leaned back in his tweed-upholstered chair. "Thank you, Susan. A wee rest and I'll tend to our flock."

"Use your walking stick."

Bertie shook his head. "Makes me feel old, worse than the pain."

Susan noticed Ollie looking at the walking stick propped against the fireplace. "Let's get you cleaned up."

Leading Ollie upstairs, Susan recognized that his climb was slow, a result of his kerfuffle with the RAF. She showed him to a spare room that had a small brass bed, a wash table, and a window overlooking a garden.

Susan pointed outside to a wooden shack. "There's the loo."

"The what?"

"Loo. I believe you may call it an outhouse."

"Oh, yes," Ollie said.

She gave him a towel, a bar of soap, and Bertie's spare straight razor, carefully touching the edge to make sure it was still sharp. "Come down when you're ready." She left, shutting the door behind her.

Ollie woke when there was a knock at the door. He sat up on the bed, grimaced, and placed his feet on the floor.

The door gently opened. "Ollie," Susan whispered.

"I must have fallen asleep. What time is it?"

"Dinner. You slept all day."

"I'll be right down."

As Susan descended the stairs, Ollie straightened the bed. At the wash table, he removed his shirt and noticed that his right side, from hip to armpit, was bruised the color of beets. A series of smaller marks covered his chest; the knuckles of the servicemen made him look as if he had been pounded with a meat tenderizer. He poured water in the basin, washed, then carefully shaved for the first time in weeks, using something that looked more like a machete than a safety razor.

As he buttoned his shirt, Ollie noticed a framed picture on the wall. He recognized Bertie, younger with dark hair and bowed legs, standing next to someone who appeared to be his wife. Beside them, a young couple holding a baby. Ollie suspected that the infant was Susan but couldn't tell for sure.

Coming down the stairs, Ollie was greeted by the pungent scent of cooked cabbage. His stomach ached with hunger. "Sorry," he said, stepping into the kitchen.

Susan turned to the stove and removed a lid from a pot. Steam rose to the ceiling.

Bertie, already sitting at the table, put down a newspaper. "Good evening, Oliver from Maine." He gestured to take a seat.

"Guess I overslept," Ollie said, sitting into a chair. "You're welcome to just call me Ollie."

"I prefer Oliver from Maine."

"Grandfather," Susan said.

"It sounds of royalty." Bertie raised his hands like an orchestra conductor. "Oliver from Maine."

"No royalty in Maine," Ollie said. "Just farmers and fishermen."

"And pilots?" Bertie asked.

"Crop-dusters." Ollie rubbed his aching ribs. "At the moment, I don't feel like much of a pilot."

"No worries, lad." Bertie laughed, then patted Ollie's arm. "You'll get a flying lesson in the morning."

Ollie scratched his head, not quite understanding the man's odd sense of humor.

Susan filled three bowls, placed them on the table, and then took a seat opposite Ollie. Bertie said grace, asking for the safety of Londoners and a quick end to the war, preferably with a British victory.

Ollie ate quickly. With his taste buds magnified by the lack of food, the boiled cabbage with chunks of potato and leek tasted more savory than any stew he had had in years. In fact, he couldn't remember his last decent meal. He swallowed another scoop, then sipped some tea.

"Sorry we don't have stronger tea," Susan said.

"Rationing." Bertie blew softly on his bowl.

"Thank you for sharing your food. And for taking me in." He took another spoon of cabbage.

Bertie leaned back in his chair and produced a pipe from his pocket. He packed tobacco, struck a match, and sucked on the stem, drawing the flame down. Smoke poured from his nose. The smell of burnt tobacco filled the room. "Tell me your story, Oliver from Maine."

"Do you mean why I'm here?" Ollie asked.

Bertie nodded.

"I guess I couldn't stand by and not join the fight." Ollie looked up from his bowl. He noticed Susan's blue eyes, her blond hair pulled back into a bun and held with a pin, a few loose strands falling in front of her ears.

Bertie puffed on his pipe. "Why the Royal Air Force? If you wanted to join the war, why not Canada?"

Wistful images of Ollie's parents filled his head. He took a deep breath, then said, "My father always said that we may have lost our accent, but our blood is, and always will be, British."

Bertie smiled, his pipe clasped between molars.

"Finish your stew," Susan said. "It'll be dark soon."

Ollie stuck his spoon into his bowl and hit something hard, like the shell of a walnut. He raised the spoon to his mouth and stopped. A clam. Jaws wide open, sticking out its snout-like tongue.

"Cockles are not much meat, I'm afraid," Susan said. "More for flavoring."

Ollie's mouth began to water.

"Damn rationing," Bertie said.

Ollie's mouth tingled. His lips felt swollen.

Bertie put down his pipe. "Are you all right?"

"I'm allergic to shellfish." Ollie's stomach gurgled.

Susan covered her mouth.

Ollie felt another slosh in his stomach, moving lower, as if he had chugged a gallon of pickling juice. He quickly excused himself from the table.

Through the kitchen window, Susan and Bertie watched Ollie run to the loo.

Ollie threw open the door and was greeted by the smell of earth and ammonia. He pulled at the button on his trousers. His bowels growled. He tugged harder, squeezing his bum, praying he could hold a few more seconds. The button snapped. He ripped down his trousers. And nature let loose.

"Are you all right?" Susan called from the garden.

"Yes." Ollie's voice sounded like he was sealed in a pine box.

"Are you sure?"

"Yes." He could see Susan's skirt through a small crack in the door. Even though he was certain that she could not see him, he covered himself with his hands.

"Can I get you anything?"

His intestines felt like a knotted rubber hose used in a tug-of-war contest. "No, I'll be fine."

"I'm sorry." Susan turned and went inside the cottage.

Ollie rubbed his swollen belly. His guts cramped. And then it came. First, as a low growl. Not from him. Outside. Hairs stood on his arms. A siren grew louder, higher in pitch, piercing the walls of the loo as if it were made of rice paper. The siren faded, and repeated the cycle again and again, each time growing in crescendo.

"We'll be in the shelter!" Bertie shouted. "Bastards came early!"

He saw Susan and Bertie through a crack in the wallboards, making their way to an earthen mound.

"Please hurry!" Susan shouted.

Ollie's breathing quickened. His bowels contracted. And exploding antiaircraft fire shook the ground. Ollie flinched. He braced his hands against the wall. A splinter shot into his finger. The loo rattled.

Ollie looked up. The corner of the rusted tin ceiling was peeled away, giving view to a darkening sky. He heard, in between the ground fire, the sound of mechanical drones. The buzzing grew louder. He scanned for toilet paper. Instead, he found a catalog with torn pages. He reached for a sheet, but another severe cramp had his hands clasping his belly. The roar of propellers grew. Antiaircraft fire boomed. Thousands of feet above his peephole in the loo, a bomber passed over. Then another. And another.

Ollie leaned forward, his rear angled over the hole in the floor. He cracked open the door. A squadron of Spitfires shot over the cottage, their wind shaking the loo. He looked up to see hundreds of German bombers blackening the twilight sky, accompanied by their fighters, fending off the Hurricanes and Spitfires that had scrambled from North Weald. Shells exploded. Ollie's heart pounded.

Machine-gun fire pierced the air. A Spitfire fell over Epping Forest, fire flaring from the fuselage. It rolled, then exploded, sending shrapnel through the trees.

His stomach churned. Pain shot through his abdomen and down his legs, drawing him back to his wooden seat. The spring on the door slammed shut. The war raged outside. And he was stuck in there, feeling defenseless with his pants tied to his ankles. He had traveled the ocean to fight, avoiding enemy submarines and rats the size of dogs, only to be beaten, poisoned, and have his arse glued to a loo.

The armada, followed by a few remaining RAF fighters, headed southwest toward London. The antiaircraft fire from North Weald suddenly stopped and was soon replaced by the echo of antiaircraft guns in London.

After his body had been drained and the cramps had weakened to where he could stand, he cleaned himself with a full-page advertisement for fishing equipment and left. With shaky legs, he crossed the yard. Flames flickered in the forest. The rumble of bombs filled the air. As he reached the shelter, the door swung open.

Bertie pointed to the woods, then handed Ollie a lantern.

Ollie and Susan, led by the smell of burning fuel, made their way through Epping Forest in search of the crashed Spitfire. Behind a toppled hornbeam tree, they found the mangled cockpit and what was left of the pilot.

Susan prayed. Tears fell from her cheeks.

Ollie's sour stomach turned to boiling anger. The newspaper stories back home couldn't fully describe what was happening. It was war. People died. And the United States was doing nothing, except declaring neutrality as bombs fell on London. As the countryside reverberated with explosions, Ollie realized that more men, women, and children would not see tomorrow's sunrise. He silently pledged to fly again. No matter what the cost, he would find a way to rid the heavens of Nazis.

"I wonder who he was," Susan said, her voice trembling.

Ollie glanced at the dead pilot, his mutilated arms dangling through shattered cockpit glass.

"Did he have a wife? Children?" She lowered her head.

"I wish I knew," Ollie said, hoping to comfort her. He turned the lantern away from the wreckage. "I do know that he died honorably, trying to protect his country."

"Far too young," Susan said. "Wars cause many in Britain to die prematurely, I'm afraid."

Ollie stepped to her.

She raised her head and swallowed. "You never know when you're going to die."

He looked into her eyes, glossed with tears. "That's why we need to live every day as if it were our last."

She nodded, then clasped her hands. "My parents died when I was a baby. They deserved more time together."

"I'm sorry," Ollie said.

"My grandparents raised me. I know of my parents through Grandfather's stories." She rubbed her eyes.

"My parents are dead, too," Ollie said.

"My goodness," Susan said. "What were they like?"

"The best—wonderful parents, and they cared for each other very much." He paused. A flash of his parents holding hands on a porch swing. "Someday, I want what they had."

"Me too. My grandparents had a splendid life." She glanced to the wreckage. "But with the war, I sometimes fear there will be no future."

Deep down, Ollie had the same worry but said, "Britain will survive this war." He gently touched her shoulder. "And you will have a long and happy life."

She squeezed his fingers, then lowered her hand to her side.

Ollie and Susan stood vigil by the smoldering wreckage until two servicemen, their flashlight beams flickering through the forest, found their fallen comrade. As the men worked to remove the pilot's remains, Ollie and Susan made their way back to the earthen bunker, then took seats on canvas cots. The echoes of bombs and the scent of soil filled the air. They spoke little of London being destroyed and nothing further of the dead pilot.

"How often are the bombings?" Ollie asked, breaking the silence.

"Every night," Bertie said.

Susan, her blue eyes darkened in the glow of the lantern, looked at Ollie. "They come in waves. And leave when the sun rises."

Bertie took a deep breath, then stood. "I've had enough." He threw open the bunker door and defiantly shook his fist in the air. "I will never again allow the Nazis to force me to live like a mole!"

Bertie hobbled across the lawn. Flashes of explosions lit up the sky.

"Do you want to stay or go?" Ollie asked.

"Go," Susan said.

They followed Bertie to the cottage. Inside, Susan covered the windows with blackout curtains. Bertie smoked his pipe and read a book. And Ollie went upstairs and collapsed onto his bed.

CHAPTER 12

NORTH WEALD, ENGLAND

Flight Lieutenant Clyde Boar took a drag on his cigarette, dropped the stub to the ground, and crushed it with his shoe. Night had receded to a gray sky, the sun still sunken below a smoky horizon. He watched a squadron of Hurricanes, or what was left of it, approach the runway in a line formation to land.

"How many?" Ralph asked.

"Eight." Boar looked at his copilot, a short, pudgy man with his hands stuffed into his trousers.

Ralph grimaced. "Should be twelve."

Boar lit another cigarette. Five minutes later, another squadron came in. Only six. After landing, one of the pilots was carried to a stretcher; a bullet that pierced the cockpit had torn through his calf.

Flight Lieutenant Boar watched a medic tie a tourniquet around the pilot's leg, his pants blackened with blood. The man was screaming something that sounded like "I can't lose my foot" or "They shot off my foot."

"We should have been with them," Boar said as the pilot was placed in an ambulance.

"What do you mean?" Ralph asked. "We were the only unit to score a hit last night."

Boar recalled the Luftwaffe bomber they had shot down. He had maneuvered his unit through the clouds, then swooped under the bomber, allowing a clear shot for Benny, his turret gunner. A spray of bullets pierced the fuselage. The bomber exploded, and he'd darted back to the clouds, losing two enemy Messerschmitt fighters.

The RAF's Bristol Blenheim, designed to be both a light bomber and night fighter, excelled at neither. It was a utility vehicle. Mediocre. A nocturnal predator able to find success only under the cloak of darkness. In fact, the last daylight mission Boar led against a Luftwaffe airfield near Aalborg in Denmark had resulted in disaster. Seven of the twelve Blenheim bombers in his squadron were lost. And a companion unit produced an almost 100 percent casualty rate. In the clunky armor of a Bristol Blenheim, Flight Lieutenant Boar felt like a knight sent into battle with a wooden sword.

"The Blenheim is no match against the Messerschmitt. We only have a chance with the Spitfire or the Hurricane." Boar flicked his cigarette, barely smoked. "I intend to lead a real fighter squadron and win this bloody war."

"You may be the best pilot in the RAF, but we have our orders for Source Columba," Ralph said.

Flight Lieutenant Boar had volunteered for Source Columba, believing that taking on such a dangerous mission would gain him favor with Commander Davies regarding his requests to lead a fighter squadron. And it had worked, especially when Davies had selected him to attend the meeting in London with British Intelligence. But things went sour when the American interfered.

"How was your meeting with the commander?" Ralph asked.

"Splendid."

Boar recalled his meeting with Commander Davies, who had interrogated him about his conduct with Susan and how an American, a civilian no less, had ended up in his military jail.

He calmly told the commander that he had conducted himself as a gentleman, escorting Susan to and from London, even accompanying her into a shelter when they missed the train. He had pointed out that the American would not have been arrested if he had not struck him, under the false impression that Susan was harassed. Davies had abruptly ended the meeting by ordering him to apologize to Susan Shepherd and her grandfather, Bertie. And to stay clear of the American. The commander also told him that his chances of ever flying a Spitfire rested on the success of Source Columba. Boar had saluted and left, his blood boiling at the thought of the American.

"At least you'll get to see that woman again," Ralph said.

Boar nodded.

"Too bad she doesn't fancy you."

"She will." Boar pulled another cigarette from his pocket and stuck it to his lips.

Ralph pulled his lighter from his pocket and lit Boar's cigarette. "I understand the American is working with her."

Boar took a deep drag from his cigarette.

"Seems rather unfair, don't you think?"

Boar exhaled, smoke flowing through his nostrils, and turned to leave. "I'll get even with that bloody American."

"Where are you going?" Ralph asked.

"Letters." He flicked his cigarette.

Ralph's shoulders slumped. "Bloody hell," he whispered.

Flight Lieutenant Boar went to the barracks. Many of the men had collapsed into their bunks still wearing combat clothing. Some of the bunks were empty, soon to be filled with fresh naïve pilots. He took a seat at a desk in the corner, far from the snores and smell of sweat. The wooden desktop, if one scanned it closely, contained the faint etchings of letters he had written to people he had never met, the tip of his pen pushing through paper to carve permanent grooves into the wood.

Boar recalled the fallen Blenheim in his unit, piloted by John

Simons, a soft-spoken man who dreamed of going back to Manchester and pouring pints at the family pub. The copilot, a bright young lad named William Akerman, an exceptional card player and newly married to a local woman named Elizabeth, now four months pregnant, had dreamed of someday being a flight commander and settling down to raise a family after the war. And the turret gunner, a man named Gilbert Nolan—his crew called him Gig—had long, skinny arms that shook like wire wrapped in bacon when he fired the machine guns. Gig left a wife named Samantha and three young girls, Carol, Edna, and Alice.

Boar gripped his pen. He recalled how the fallen plane had taken a direct hit to the left engine and had failed to climb to the safety of the clouds. Two enemy fighters, like pit bulls smelling blood, came in for the kill. The right engine exploded, taking off the wing. Boar and the rest of the squadron had heard their screams over the radio as the severed Blenheim fell from the sky.

It wasn't his duty, but Boar wrote letters, just like he had always done, taking time to tell their families what had happened and, more importantly, that they were beloved friends and brave, valiant men who had served their country well. Each letter was unique. John, William, and Gig would have wanted it that way. He sealed the letters and placed them in his locker to mail a few days from now, after the families had been formally notified by RAF authorities. Rather than sleep, he took a walk around the airfield, counting planes and wondering how many of his bomber squadron would be left by Christmas.

CHAPTER 13

EPPING, ENGLAND

Susan tapped on the bedroom door. "Are you awake?"

Ollie opened his eyes. Sunlight shone through the window. His arm hung off the bed, numbness spreading through his fingers.

"Yes," he said.

"Breakfast."

Ollie cleared his throat. "I'll be right down." He heard Susan's footsteps as she left.

Ollie looked down and noticed his boots, unlaced, but still on his feet. He rubbed away the tingling in his hand, then tied his boots and went downstairs. His legs felt rubbery, his body emptied of fluids.

"Good morning, Oliver from Maine," Bertie said, putting down his newspaper. "Under the weather?"

"Better," Ollie said.

Susan handed him a cup of tea. "Drink."

Ollie sipped. "Thanks."

Susan brushed strands of blond hair behind her ear and went to the stove.

"Smells good," Ollie said, taking a seat.

"Elderberry scones," Susan said, opening the oven door.

"Splendid to hear your appetite is recovering, Oliver." Bertie patted him on the shoulder. "I was worried you were trying to get out of working."

"Only if we're shucking shellfish."

Bertie laughed. "No shucking, just flying."

Ollie scratched his head. "Are we working on planes?"

Bertie grinned. "Something better, my boy."

It was obvious to Ollie that Bertie was enjoying his little secret, at least until he was put to work. And considering that Bertie had bailed him out of jail, and the fact that he was unable to join the RAF for the next few months, he saw no point in ruining Bertie's jest. So, he played along.

"Balloons?" Ollie asked.

Bertie shook his head.

"Airships?"

"Even better."

"What could be better than planes, balloons, and airships?"

"It's confidential." Bertie slapped his leg and cackled.

"Grandfather," Susan said, dropping hot scones onto a platter.

"How am I going to work if you don't tell me?" Ollie asked.

"Blindfolded."

"For three months?"

"Maybe less, assuming our mission wins the war."

"Eat," Susan said, placing the scones on the table. "We have work to do."

Ollie's appetite had shrunken, and he felt full after a few bites, but he forced himself to finish a scone. He drank three more cups of tea, feeling his strength returning with each sip.

Minutes later, Ollie found himself in Bertie's truck. Susan sat between them as Bertie drove along a farm path, a swath of tall grass running down the middle. The farm was smaller than his parents' property back home. But as far as he could see, there were no other houses in sight, just a rolling green pasture with grazing sheep. A series of wooden sheds dotted the hillside, like large outhouses or miniature barns. Ollie assumed they were shearing sheds, but why so many?

Bertie parked the truck at the first shed. "Time for work," he said, turning off the engine.

Ollie followed Bertie and Susan inside. Wings fluttered. Dozens of pigeons flew around them. Ollie shielded his face with his arm. Some pigeons landed on the floor; others retreated to their nests. As flapping wings settled into cooing, Ollie lowered his arm.

"Ready for your flying lesson?" Bertie asked.

Ollie's eyebrows raised. "Birds?"

"Pigeons," Susan said.

Ollie wrinkled his forehead. "The British government's secret mission is pigeons?"

"Source Columba," Bertie said.

"These pigeons are going to help us win the war," Susan added.

Ollie took a deep breath. "No offense, but it's going to take a lot more than birds to—"

"Pigeons," Susan interrupted.

"Okay, pigeons." Ollie noticed Susan's hands on her hips. "I was merely trying to understand why the British government would spend its efforts on pigeons when London is being bombed. It's going to take planes and pilots to fight the air war."

A pigeon, looking as if it were painted in fluorescent purple and green paint, flew to Susan's shoulder. She stroked the bird across the back with a finger. "Duchess, Ollie obviously has much to learn about pigeons."

Duchess cocked her head and stared at Ollie.

"I didn't mean to offend you. I was only . . ."

Duchess jumped, fluttered across the loft, and landed on Ollie's shoulder.

Ollie froze. Looking out of the corner of his eye, he watched the bird, its beak a few inches from his chin. He swallowed, fearing that it would peck him.

Duchess blinked, flashing her golden eyes.

Ollie exhaled. "I think he likes me."

Duchess shook her tail feathers.

Ollie felt something warm run down his arm and grimaced.

"Duchess is a she. And she didn't appreciate your comments." Susan plucked the pigeon from Ollie's shoulder.

"We have a long day ahead of us," Bertie said. "Ollie, gather the baskets behind the shed. Susan and I will load."

Ollie went outside and cleaned his sleeve with a handful of dry leaves. He gathered the baskets, which turned out to be cages, long wood-framed boxes with wire-mesh fronts, which resembled flimsy lobster traps. After stacking baskets in the shed, Bertie showed him how to place the pigeons inside by wrapping hands over their wings and tucking fingers under their bellies. Ollie was surprised that the pigeons didn't fuss, squirm, scratch, or even peck, allowing him to easily place them in baskets.

Ollie glanced at Susan.

Susan turned her head and continued loading.

After the pigeons were in baskets, except for the one that had relieved itself on his sleeve, Ollie stacked them into the bed of the truck. They drove to a second loft, where they loaded more pigeons, secured the baskets with twine to keep them from shifting, and then took their seats in the truck.

"Did you count them?" Bertie asked.

"Yes," Susan said, holding Duchess. "One hundred twenty-seven."

Bertie placed the key in the ignition and cranked the engine.

Ollie felt as if there was more room, then noticed Susan was pressed against the passenger-side door. She stared out the window, holding Duchess on her lap. Ollie felt like he had swallowed a stone. It was their mission, and he had belittled their work, even after they had taken him in. He hoped that he could think of something to say that could erase his hurtful remarks. Ollie opened his mouth but stopped when he sensed Susan inching farther away.

Bertie drove down the lane and turned north onto a paved road. Bertie shifted gears, getting the old truck up to speed. "How are the pigeons?" Bertie asked Ollie.

Ollie turned and looked through the back window. The baskets hadn't shifted. Only a trail of downy feathers. "Good," he said.

"We're headed to Clacton-on-Sea," Bertie said. "It's a remote area on the coast. The pigeons will have an opportunity to fly over water." He glanced to Ollie. "Soon they'll be flying over the English Channel."

"Where are they flying to?"

Susan interrupted. "Did you know that homing pigeons were used by the Egyptians over three thousand years ago?"

"No," Ollie said.

"Of course not. And you probably didn't know that a homing pigeon can travel distances of up to six hundred miles per day, fly at speeds of seventy miles per hour, and reach altitudes as high as thirty-five thousand feet." Susan looked at Ollie. "At that height, Ollie, the temperature would be thirty-five degrees below zero, and a pilot would need a heated suit and oxygen."

Bertie nudged Ollie. "Ever fly that high, Oliver from Maine?"

Ollie shook his head.

"For centuries, animals have been relied upon during times of war." Susan cupped Duchess in her hands. "And would you like to guess as to which animal made the most significant contributions to the Allied victory in the Great War?"

"Birds?"

Susan stared at him. Duchess perked her head.

"I meant pigeons." Ollie noticed Bertie grinning, obviously amused by the mess he had gotten himself into.

"Yes. Pigeons," Susan said.

The air felt thick. Ollie wanted to roll down a window or crawl under the seat.

"In the Great War, a pigeon named Cher Ami saved the lives of almost two hundred Allied troops trapped behind enemy lines

without food or ammunition. The day before, there had been
five hundred men."

Ollie swallowed.

"Cher Ami was the last remaining pigeon, the others shot
down by machine-gun fire. With their last desperate message for
help placed in the canister attached to Cher Ami's leg, the bird
took flight. As she flew out of the bunker, a rain of bullets shot
her down. But she somehow managed to get back in the air and
fly to headquarters." Susan lightly poked Ollie in the chest.
"Cher Ami had been shot through the breast." Susan then
pointed to Ollie's cheek. "She was also blinded in one eye."

Ollie felt Susan nudge his boot with her foot.

"And her leg was hanging by a tendon." Susan stroked
Duchess's head. "But she made it home and saved the lives of
two hundred men."

For most of the trip, Ollie listened to Susan's lecture on pigeons. And he could have sworn he saw Bertie ease his foot off
the gas pedal to prolong his torture.

When they arrived in Clacton-on-Sea, a treeless peninsula jutting into the North Sea, Ollie got to work unloading the baskets.
He felt a sense of relief, at least for the time being, to be free
from the confines of the truck. He lined the baskets in formation
per Susan's instructions, hoping his attention to detail would
help make amends for his ignorance and insensitivity.

Bertie looked at his pocket watch.

Cooing grew. Wings fluttered.

Bertie waved his hand. Susan and Ollie quickly released the
latches, and flocks of pigeons flew from their cages.

Susan picked up Duchess, perched on the truck like a hood or-
nament. She held the pigeon to her cheek and whispered, then
tossed the pigeon into the air. Duchess soared to the flock, circling the sky. After two flights around the perimeter, the pigeons
headed southwest.

Susan looked to the ocean. Waves slapped the rocks. "It seems so far."

Bertie nodded.

"How many miles to Epping?" Ollie asked.

"Sixty," Bertie said. "But Susan wasn't referring to Epping."

Ollie looked at Susan.

"France," Susan said. "Source Columba is a mission to air-drop homing pigeons in German-occupied France."

Ollie's mouth opened.

"The plan is for locals to convey information on troop movements," Bertie said.

"Most of the pigeons won't make it back," Susan said.

"I thought you said pigeons could fly hundreds of miles," Ollie said. "Surely the distance to France is within their range."

"It's not the distance," Bertie said. "It's the challenge of getting there and back."

Susan pointed to the sea. "First, the bombers need to make it to France, avoiding enemy antiaircraft fire. Those that haven't been shot down will release hundreds of small cages, each containing one pigeon. The parachutes, which have not been tested, need to open and safely deliver the pigeons to the ground."

Ollie slid his hands into his pockets.

"Many of the pigeons will be found and destroyed by the enemy," Susan said. "Others will be left unnoticed in fields or tangled high in trees, only to freeze or starve. Our hope is that some of the pigeons will land in the hands of members of the French Resistance, who will record troop movements on a piece of paper, placed into a canister attached to the pigeon's leg."

"The pigeons that remain will have a dangerous trip back," Bertie added. "The enemy, alerted to the droppings, will no doubt have snipers aiming for them."

Susan wrapped her arms around her shoulders. "We estimate that one in three will make it back."

Ollie looked at the empty cages.

"It's a high price," Bertie said. "But we have no choice. Our only chance of victory is to know what the Nazis are doing, especially when and where they will commence a land invasion."

Susan shivered. She turned and watched the pigeons, mere specks on the horizon, disappear from sight.

Ollie loaded the baskets and secured them with twine.

They got into the truck and headed home. Susan stared out the side window. Bertie grunted in pain as he shifted gears. And Ollie forgot all about joining the RAF, his thoughts on the desperate sacrifices of Susan, Bertie, and the pigeons to save Britain.

CHAPTER 14

EPPING, ENGLAND

The return trip from Clacton-on-Sea was quiet, except for the whistle of wind through empty cages in the bed of the truck. Susan sat with her arms folded, watching the English countryside pass by her window. And Ollie tried to think of the right words to ease Susan's pain.

It must be heartrending for Susan to know the fate of the pigeons, he thought.

Twice Ollie gathered the courage to speak, but each time he was interrupted by Bertie pointing out landmarks: an area of eroded coastline where he believed the Germans would invade and relics of an old mill he had once explored as a boy. Ollie harbored his words. He did his best to listen to Bertie, but his thoughts were on Susan.

They arrived back at the farm before noon. Bertie parked the truck in front of a loft; more precisely, he let his tired foot slip from the clutch and stall the engine. Their heads jerked. Ollie and Susan braced their arms against the dash.

"Perhaps I should consider driving," Susan said, rubbing her neck.

"Nonsense," Bertie said. "There's nothing wrong with my driving. I'm merely eager to check on our pigeons."

They got out of the truck. Ollie unloaded the first cage.

"Not now, Oliver," Bertie said. "We need to see who came home."

Ollie placed the cage back onto the truck and joined them in the loft. Bertie held a small notebook and pencil. Susan checked the cubbies from left to right and from top to bottom. As Susan finished counting a row, she called out a number, which Bertie tallied in his notebook. After finishing the cubbies, Susan counted a few pigeons waddling on the floor and another fluttering around the ceiling.

"How many?" Susan asked.

"Sixty-two," Bertie said.

Susan walked to the next loft. Bertie and Ollie followed. Driving the truck would have been quicker, but Ollie assumed that Susan had had enough of his bird skepticism or her grandfather's driving. He hoped that it was the latter.

Ollie watched Susan and Bertie tally the birds. The cooing grew as Susan went through the cubbies.

"How many?" Susan asked.

"Sixty-four. Our total is one hundred twenty-six. We lost one." Bertie checked his math. "Bloody hawks."

Susan pointed to Duchess, perched on a beam above her grandfather's head.

Bertie looked up. "Ah, one hundred twenty-seven."

Susan smiled. "They're all here."

"How do they do it?" Ollie asked.

"Magic," Bertie said, pretending to wave a wand.

Ollie chuckled.

Bertie put his arm around Susan. "My granddaughter's the expert. Before the war, she studied zoology at the university."

Susan glanced at a group of feeding pigeons. "Some believe they find their way home with the help of the earth's magnetic field, the sun, and the stars."

Ollie stepped to Susan. "What do you believe?"

She looked at Ollie. "Pigeons have extraordinary cognitive capabilities. I believe they have mental maps that enable them to return from unfamiliar places."

Ollie scratched his head.

"Means they're smart," Bertie said.

"They must be incredibly intelligent," Ollie said. "I would have needed a flight map and instruments to fly a plane here from Clacton-on-Sea."

"The important thing is they're all home." Bertie looked at his pocket watch. "A blessed cause for celebration. Anyone care for a wee dram?"

Susan shook her head.

"Oliver?"

"What's a wee damn?" Ollie asked.

Bertie laughed. "I see that Americans have yet to master the English language." Bertie placed a hand on Ollie's shoulder. "It's *dram*, a shot of scotch."

Ollie thought of Bishop sharing swigs from a flask that had made his head spin, and the mess he had gotten himself into by believing he could sleep in a park. Ollie rubbed the scar on his forehead. "Maybe later."

Bertie nodded and left for the cottage.

Susan picked up a broom and began sweeping droppings.

"Can I help?" Ollie asked.

She shook her head.

Ollie noticed a dustpan hanging from a rusted nail. He retrieved the dustpan and lowered it to a pile of droppings.

Susan swiftly brushed, carelessly flicking pellets.

"I didn't mean to belittle Source Columba or your work." He removed something from inside his shirt that felt like a dried pea.

"Outside in the compost," Susan said.

Ollie deposited the droppings and returned to lower the dustpan to another pile. "I guess I'm fairly inexperienced when it comes to birds."

Susan gave a hard sweep.

Ollie felt pellets sting his face. He coughed. "Pigeons."

Susan placed the broom in the corner.

Ollie dumped the few droppings that reached the dustpan into the compost pile. He returned to the loft to see Susan holding Duchess. "I'm sorry," he said.

Susan raised a hand over her mouth. Duchess turned her head.

"What?" Ollie asked.

"Your face."

Ollie brushed his cheeks.

Susan laughed. "No. You have rubbish . . ." She touched her nose.

Ollie raised his hand to find a semi-fresh dropping stuck to the tip of his nose. He flicked it with his finger. "I guess I deserved that."

"Yes, you did." She stroked Duchess. "Next time, you may want to use the shovel."

Ollie noticed a flat shovel propped in a corner.

"Dustpan is too small."

Ollie chuckled. "A little late to be telling me now, don't you think?"

"I wasn't going to tell you at all." Susan tucked a loose strand of hair behind her ear. "But it's difficult not to feel sympathetic for someone covered in rubbish, even if they can't tell a pigeon from a turkey."

Ollie noticed a softness in Susan's voice. "May I?" He held out his hands.

Susan stroked Duchess, as if to calm her, and then carefully placed her into Ollie's hands.

Ollie felt wiry feet on his palm. He gently stroked the pigeon's back with a finger. "Sorry for calling you a boy," he said to Duchess.

Duchess cooed and blinked her eyes.

"Looks like you've been forgiven," Susan said.

Ollie noticed the velvety texture of Duchess's feathers. "I

wish we could explain how noble this cause is to the pigeons." Ollie looked at Susan. "It doesn't seem fair that they can't understand why we're dropping them into battle."

Susan stepped closer. She ran her hand over Duchess's back, her fingers slightly brushing Ollie's hand.

Ollie's skin tingled. He swallowed. "You truly believe this mission can change the course of the war?"

Susan nodded.

The sound of engines caused the pigeons to flutter. Susan took Duchess from Ollie. They went outside to see a line of military vehicles rolling up the drive. A trail of dust drifted over the farm.

Two soldiers got out of one of the trucks and removed a large spool of wire. Another soldier lugged a box of tools. Several others unloaded small cages.

Susan walked toward the soldiers rolling the spool. "What are you doing?"

"Orders, miss," said one of the soldiers.

"Excuse me," Susan said.

The soldiers walked away, reeling a trail of wire.

Ollie ran ahead and stepped in front of the soldiers. "The lady asked you a question."

"We're only following our orders to secure the farm," said a soldier. The men, continuing to roll out the wire, maneuvered past Ollie and headed for a loft.

Susan and Ollie heard the sound of sawing wood. They turned to see a soldier cutting the pigeon landing on one of the lofts.

"Stop!" Susan shouted.

The soldier continued hacking.

"Put that down," Susan said, reaching the loft.

The soldier paused to examine the saw blade.

"What are you doing?" Ollie asked.

"Installing alarms."

"Alarms? No one said anything about alarms."

The soldier shrugged and resumed sawing.

Another military vehicle sped up the drive and skidded to a stop. A plume of dust drifted into a beech tree. Ollie felt his hands curl into fists when he saw an officer with coal-black hair step out of the car.

"Don't do anything foolish," Susan said.

Flight Lieutenant Boar climbed the front steps and knocked on the door. Bertie answered, clenched his hands, and quickly ducked back inside. By the time Ollie and Susan reached the cottage, Bertie was on the porch waving his walking stick like a sword.

"Bastard!" Bertie pointed the stick at Flight Lieutenant Boar's chest.

Boar raised his palms.

"Grandfather!" Susan shouted.

"I ought to knock some manners into you!" Bertie said.

Boar kept his hands raised.

Ollie stepped between the men and stared at the lieutenant.

Boar turned to Susan. "We have a change with Source Columba."

Bertie lowered his walking stick.

"It will only take a moment of your time," Boar said. "Perhaps we could go inside and I can explain."

Despite their animosity toward the lieutenant, Ollie, Susan, and Bertie found themselves sitting at the kitchen table with Flight Lieutenant Boar.

"The Cooper farm was bombed," Boar said.

Bertie swallowed. "How is William?"

Boar shook his head.

Bertie's eyes watered. "Poor William. We raced pigeons together."

Susan placed her arm over Bertie's shoulder.

"The farm was in proximity to an ammunition factory," Flight Lieutenant Boar said. "Luftwaffe missed the factory but destroyed the farm, including most, if not all of the pigeons."

"Why have you come to tell us this?" Bertie asked.

"Your delivery date has been moved," Boar said.

"When?" Susan asked.

"Tomorrow."

Bertie wiped his face. "Bloody hell, I thought we had two weeks. Do we have a choice?"

"No. The men are delivering equipment and installing alarms in the lofts. Two soldiers will be stationed here during the mission."

"Why?" Susan asked.

"Security," Boar said.

Ollie noticed Susan clutching Duchess. Bertie's face looked pasty white.

"I realize that things have not gone well between us." Flight Lieutenant Boar looked at Susan. "And I want to apologize for the misunderstanding."

Bertie interrupted. "Commander Davies order you to apologize?"

"I have orders to inform you of the change. Nothing more." Boar turned again to Susan and rubbed his hands as if he were spreading ointment. "My regrets for the misunderstanding. The train was crowded, and I was merely trying to speak with you. I meant you no harm."

Susan crossed her arms. The crack of a hammer, striking a board in a loft, caused her to flinch.

"The men will be finished in a few hours," Boar said. "A team will arrive in the morning for pickup." He paused and ran his fingers through his hair. "Again, my sincere apologies."

"Very well," Bertie said. "You've informed us of the orders and spoken your piece. I believe it's best that you leave."

Flight Lieutenant Boar stood.

Bertie struggled to get up from his chair.

"No need," Boar said. "I'll show myself out."

Susan stayed with Bertie while Ollie followed the lieutenant to his vehicle. Ollie watched Boar produce a cigarette, strike a match with his thumb, and take a deep drag.

"You're very lucky, Yank," Boar said.

Ollie watched smoke flow from the lieutenant's nose.

"If it weren't for Susan's grandfather, you'd be rotting in the Glasshouse. And with last night's bombing, your release to Church Fenton may even have accelerated. Assuming you don't do something foolish, like striking another officer, you just might join the fight."

"I plan to fly," Ollie said.

"Of course you do." The lieutenant got in his vehicle, started the engine, and rolled down the window. "I suggest you stick to shoveling pigeon shit." He flicked his cigarette.

Ollie felt the butt bounce off his chest and noticed his shirt was speckled with turds. He pressed the smoldering cigarette under his boot. As Ollie watched the lieutenant drive away, determination flared in his belly, like a fire stoked with kerosene.

CHAPTER 15

EPPING, ENGLAND

Susan and Ollie followed Bertie as he hobbled over a web of wires. From loft to loft, he examined the alarms the soldiers had installed. Thin metal rods, approximately twelve inches in length, dangled from each pigeon entrance, like a curtain of beads strung over a doorway.

"Security?" Bertie raised his arms and looked across the pasture. "Do they think this place is swarming with Nazis?" Bertie poked the curtain with his walking stick. The rods clanged together like a cheap wind chime, and a faint ringing came from a tent the soldiers had set up near the bomb shelter.

Ollie walked to the tent and peeked inside. The structure, a wooden frame covered in canvas, resembled a yurt. It held a cot, two chairs, a table, and a large switchboard with a series of numbered bells, one for each loft. Bells buzzed and abruptly stopped. When a pigeon entered a loft, it caused the rods to touch, tripping a connection and ringing the bells. He felt like a doorman for an apartment building in which guests were buzzing each of the tenants, all at the same time. The pigeons didn't seem to mind the curtains. But that was not the case for Bertie or Susan.

Ollie left the tent to find Susan and Bertie inspecting the

military-issued cages, much smaller than the ones they'd used to transport the pigeons to Clacton-on-Sea.

"How do they look?" Ollie asked.

Susan held a miniature silk parachute that was attached to a cage. "Is this large enough to work?"

"I've only flown planes. Never jumped out of them." Ollie noticed lines of tension spread across Susan's face. He felt the urge to kick himself. "But I once saw a man drop from a plane at an air show." Ollie examined the parachute. "I think it's plenty big enough."

Susan took in a deep breath and exhaled. She carefully folded the parachute.

Bertie picked up a crimson canister the size of a small prescription bottle. "They're bloody red! Are they trying to make it easy for the snipers?" He shook his head and handed the canister to Susan.

"There's nothing we can do about it now." She felt the canister's weight. "At least the Bakelite isn't heavy." She touched the metal band fastened to the tube. "I believe they should fit securely to their legs."

"Anything I can do to help?" Ollie asked.

Susan tossed the canister back into the cage. "Can you give us more time?"

"I wish I could," Ollie said.

Susan slid her arm around Bertie's elbow and helped him to the next loft.

Ollie felt horrible for them. Their pigeon farm was being turned upside down by war. He wondered how he would feel if the military had set up camp on his parents' potato farm. It was an unimaginable thought for him, an American, to comprehend. Wars were not fought on United States soil. Blood was spilled in Europe, and people back home only read about it in the newspapers. He rubbed his sore ribs, feeling a twinge of guilt for being born on the opposite side of the Atlantic.

Sensing that Susan and Bertie needed time alone, Ollie went to work. First, he stacked the military cages, making certain that they were evenly distributed at each of the lofts. For the remainder of the afternoon, he refilled water trays, carried bags of feed, and swept droppings. After tending to the last loft, he leaned his broom in the corner, near a sleeping pigeon, its head tucked under its wing.

Ollie gently stroked the pigeon. "Get some rest. Your mission is tomorrow." He left the loft hoping it would be one of the lucky ones to return.

Outside, the air was cold. Ollie rubbed the goose bumps on his arms and noticed that the leaves on an oak tree were turning the color of mustard. He looked at the sun, sinking on the horizon, and wondered if Luftwaffe pilots were stirring in their bunks, like nocturnal vampires preparing for their feast. *Too bad the Nazis aren't vampires*, Ollie thought. *At least with vampires, they could be deterred with holy water, crosses, and cloves of garlic. But with Nazis, we need antiaircraft guns, Hurricanes, and Spitfires.* Ollie glanced back at the lofts. *And maybe pigeons.*

Inside the cottage, Ollie found Bertie in his chair. He glanced at the man's knees, wrapped in cold towels. "How're the legs?" Ollie asked.

"A wee gravely," Bertie said.

"Need anything?"

Bertie shook his head.

Ollie paused, then asked, "What was your friend William like?"

"A good man. Loved racing pigeons as much as me. We used to place bets, usually a pint at the pub, on who had the fastest bird. Despite having to buy most of the ale, William never missed a race." Bertie rubbed his knees and changed the subject. "How are the lofts?"

"Cages are stacked. Lofts are cleaned."

"Splendid."

Ollie turned to a collection of old pipes displayed on the fireplace mantel.

"Antiques," Bertie said. "Agnes liked to buy them for me. More for looking than for smoking."

"Your wife?" Ollie asked, picking up a pipe.

Bertie nodded.

"What was she like?"

A smile spread across Bertie's face. "Lovely. Smart. Witty. A lot like Susan. I met Agnes as a young lad. She worked the counter at her father's bakery. Spent all my shillings on her pastries, simply to get a glimpse of her. Nearly gained enough weight to bust out of my trousers before I got up the nerve to invite her for tea." Bertie patted his tummy.

Ollie chuckled.

"She was wonderful. And there's not a day that goes by that I don't miss her."

"Sounds like you had a good life together."

"Indeed."

Ollie recalled the photo in his bedroom, the one of Bertie, Agnes, and a young couple holding a baby. "Do you mind if I ask what happened?"

Bertie lowered his glasses, a glisten of water in his eyes. "I simply outlived her, my boy."

Seeing Bertie's sadness reminded Ollie of his parents. An ache grew in his chest. He wondered how long it took to recover from losing a loved one. *One year? Ten years? A lifetime?* Ollie returned the pipe to its place on the mantel, then retrieved a cold towel from the icebox.

"Thank you, Oliver," Bertie said, changing a wrapping. "Perhaps you could check on Susan."

Ollie found Susan sitting on the porch steps. The creak of the door spring caused her to turn. He noticed Duchess on her lap.

"Mind if I sit down?" Ollie asked.

Susan slid over.

Ollie sat, wrapping his arms around his knees.

Susan stared at the dark clouds rolling over Epping Forest. "Do bombers fly in the rain?"

"Yes," Ollie said. "They can fly above the clouds, but it may be difficult to find their targets."

"Pigeons can fly in the rain." Susan ran a finger over Duchess's wing. "They have oily feathers that repel water."

Duchess turned her head, a golden eye staring at him.

"Maybe we'll get lucky and a windstorm will ground the Luftwaffe," Ollie said.

"That would be lovely," Susan said.

Ollie played with the frayed end of his bootlace. "Are you worried about Duchess?"

"Not Duchess. It's the other pigeons."

Ollie looked at Susan.

"Duchess isn't part of the mission."

"Oh," Ollie said.

"Raised her myself. She's quite the pet, even pecks at my window every morning."

"I see."

Susan stretched her back. "I should probably check on Grandfather."

"Bertie sent me to check on you."

Susan smiled.

"He was telling me about your grandmother."

"What did he say?"

"That you're a lot like her."

"I'll take that as a compliment."

"I believe it was."

A few raindrops struck their shoes. Wind rustled the birches. They moved up a step, under the canopy of the porch.

"I noticed a picture in my room. Were you the baby in the photo?"

"Yes."

"Your parents?"

Susan nodded.

The rains marched through the trees, drops striking the leaves sounding like a rolling crescendo on a snare drum.

Susan placed the pigeon to her cheek. "You need to get home, Duchess." She gently released the bird.

Duchess fluttered about the yard, then landed on a birch. Reluctant, the pigeon didn't enter her loft, despite being pelted by raindrops.

"We should go inside." Susan stood and brushed the back of her skirt. "It'll be dark soon."

Ollie watched Susan enter the cottage, feeling like he had intruded by asking about her parents. He noticed that Duchess was still perched on her branch, her head perked to the side as if she were listening. "Looks like we're both grounded," he said to the pigeon. Ollie stood and went inside, where he found Susan in the kitchen.

"Would you like some tea?" Susan asked, filling a kettle.

"Yes, please," he said, taking a seat at the table.

She placed the kettle on the stove, then opened the cupboard.

His mind toiled over what to say. There was much that he wanted to know about Susan. But he chose to start with a topic that he thought would be important to her. "What do you love most about pigeons?"

Susan turned, a smile forming on her face. "Everything."

Ollie, relieved to see her reaction, pulled a chair from the table and gestured for her to join him.

Susan sat.

"Tell me more about everything," Ollie said.

"They're remarkably clever," Susan said. "I challenge you to name another animal that can find their way home from hundreds of miles away."

Ollie rubbed his chin. "Tortoise?"

Susan chuckled.

Ollie leaned in. "What else do you love about them?"

"Affectionate—both parents raise their nestlings," Susan said. "They're exquisite, with spectacular colors and patterns. I adore their cooing, which, in my opinion, is even more soothing than a cat's purr. They walk with an endearing waddle. And their flight is quite graceful." She placed her hands on the table. "But what I admire most is their devotion to family. They'll go to great lengths to find their way home."

Ollie smiled. "What do you call someone who knows all about birds?"

"Ornithologist."

"You'll make a grand one."

"You really think so?"

He nodded.

Susan ran a finger over a scratch in the table. "What do you like most about flying?"

"I wish I had words that could describe the sense of freedom I get when I'm soaring through the clouds. It's exciting. And peaceful." Ollie pointed above his head. "Up there, I feel like a bird—even better, a pigeon."

Susan smiled and paused. "You'll make an admirable RAF pilot, Oliver from Maine."

He noticed Susan's hand, inches from his fingers. His stomach fluttered.

The kettle began to whistle.

Susan placed her hand on her lap.

"Are you preparing tea, my dear?" Bertie called from the living room.

"Yes," Susan said, looking at Ollie.

"Splendid!" Bertie said. "I'll be right in."

Ollie watched Susan leave the table, wishing the kettle would have taken hours to boil.

CHAPTER 16

EPPING, ENGLAND

The rain brought the premature arrival of darkness and, shortly thereafter, the howl of air-raid sirens. With their hunger stolen by the invading Luftwaffe, Susan, Ollie, and Bertie skipped dinner and hunkered in the living room.

Antiaircraft guns erupted. The cottage vibrated.

Susan, sitting next to Ollie on the sofa, covered her ears.

Ollie looked at Bertie, leaning back in his chair. "How long?"

Bertie shrugged. "The worst is when they pass over the guns at North Weald Airfield. They'll stop once the Luftwaffe leave for London."

Shells exploded. China rattled.

Several minutes later, the guns stopped, momentarily revealing the patter of rain. Candlelight flickered over the room. And for the next hour, they listened to the rumble of bombs on London.

As a swarm of planes buzzed overhead, Susan felt her shoulder muscles tighten. But the grinding of engines quickly disappeared. No explosion. No gunfire. Just the thrum of rain. She exhaled, then gazed at the candle. "Do you think London will burn?"

Ollie glanced at Bertie, sunk deep into his chair with his eyes closed, then turned to Susan. "The rain will help."

She looked at him. "I meant, do you think there will be anything left?"

Ollie paused, then said, "If Londoners are even half as resilient as you and Bertie, I believe there will always be a London."

"I needed to hear that." She smiled, smoothed her skirt, and returned her attention to the candle.

"Susan," Ollie said.

She turned to him, her shadow stretching over the floor.

"I was thinking about this afternoon and . . ."

Bertie snorted. A book, facedown on his chest, rose and fell as snores filled the room.

"He tires in the evenings," Susan said. She stood, walked to Bertie's chair, and touched his arm. "Perhaps you should go to bed."

Bertie snuffled and opened his eyes. "I was reading."

Susan pointed to the book.

He wiped his face. "It's difficult to see with candlelight."

"Would you like me to read to you?" Susan asked.

"I'm knackered," Bertie said. "I believe I'll go to bed." He stood, wobbled, and grunted with pain.

Ollie went to Bertie, preparing to catch him if the old man's knees gave out.

"Let us help you," Susan said.

Bertie shook his head, then placed a hand on Susan's shoulder. "Tomorrow our pigeons will change the course of this bloody war."

Susan felt her confidence reawaken, like an ember receiving oxygen. She watched him climb the stairs, taking breaks to catch his breath. As his bedroom door squeaked shut, she admired her grandfather's moxie. She had no doubt that Bertie could have been a field general in his younger years. The men in the trenches would have followed a man like Bertie, giving them faith when there was no hope at all.

"Bertie's a good man," Ollie said.

"I'm lucky to have him."

Ollie nodded. "You're welcome to go to bed."

Susan looked at the blackout curtains covering the window. "I can't sleep when they're out there." She crossed the room and retrieved a thin cardboard box from under the sofa. "I assume you can keep a secret."

Ollie joined her on the sofa, the box placed between them.

She opened the lid and placed a ball of yarn and knitting needles on her lap, then held up a piece of cream-colored fabric. "It's a sweater, a Christmas present for Grandfather."

Ollie looked at the tube of material.

"More accurately, the arm of a sweater."

"He'll love it," Ollie said.

"I didn't have any dye."

"It's perfect."

Susan tucked a strand of hair behind her ear and picked up the needles.

"Where did you learn to knit?" he asked.

"Grandmother." The needles clicked.

"Agnes?"

"You remembered." She glanced at Ollie, noticing the caramel color of his eyes.

Ollie watched Susan knit, the candlelight creating a silhouette of her slender hands on the wall. "Looks difficult."

"Only requires time and patience." Susan wrapped yarn around the needle. "My first project was a scarf when I was a little girl. In my eagerness to give it to Grandfather, it was rather short, barely enough to wrap his neck. It should have stayed in the box or had several inches added. But Grandfather insisted on wearing it clasped together with a pin." She pulled more yarn. "Better to start early so this sweater will have both sleeves."

Susan knit a row. "Earlier, you were going to say something about this afternoon."

"I was going to ask you about your parents."

An explosion rumbled like thunder. The ball of yarn fell to the floor.

Ollie retrieved the yarn and placed it on Susan's lap. "Do you mind if I ask what happened?"

Susan turned to Ollie. "When my father came home from the Great War, my parents wasted no time getting married. In fact, the day my father returned home, they summoned the minister, who had taken the day off to go fishing. My father didn't even take time to change from his uniform, and Mother was still wearing her nursing attire from the hospital." She pointed to a framed photo on the wall. "Mother served a year as a nurse on the Western Front."

Ollie stood and looked at the photo of a smiling trio: a nurse, a soldier, and a preacher disguised as a fisherman with feathered hooks strung across his vest like war medals. He took particular notice of the woman holding a bouquet of daisies. "You look like your mom."

Susan smiled. "My father promised he would marry her the day he came home. Mother wanted to get married sooner, but despite how much my father loved her, he couldn't bear the thought of potentially making her a widow. Grandfather always told me my father was a true gentleman."

Ollie returned to his seat.

"They wrote to each other every day," Susan said. "Grandfather saved the letters in a keepsake box. They're lovely." She put down her needles. "I was born less than a year from when my father came home. They—we—had our whole lives ahead of us." Susan took a deep breath, then exhaled. "Britain had thought the war was over. But when the troops came home, they brought with them an even more deadly threat than guns or mustard gas."

Ollie swallowed. "Spanish flu?"

She nodded. "Grandfather had received a call from my mother to pick me up. My parents had sore throats, and they didn't want me to catch a cold. Three days later, they were in the hospital with pneumonia. Grandfather tried to visit them, but they, as well as hundreds of others, had been quarantined." She blinked her eyes, suppressing tears. "My father died the following Sunday. Mother on Tuesday."

Ollie placed his hand on Susan's arm.

Susan made no effort to move, taking comfort in his touch. "It was a long time ago."

Ollie hesitated, then slowly returned his hand to his lap.

"As a child, I dreaded the playground. I would often hear children jumping rope and chanting the rhyme about the pandemic." Susan looked at Ollie. "Do you know the one I'm talking about?"

He shook his head.

Susan fiddled with the needles. "I had a little bird, its name was Enza. I opened the window, and in flew Enza."

"That's awful."

"Precisely why I never learned to jump rope." She completed several stitches. "I wish I could have been old enough to remember them. All I have are a few photos, letters, and Grandfather's stories, which he tells often and with endless variations to make them more interesting."

Ollie rested his arm on the box between them.

"My grandparents gave me a lovely childhood—lots of laughter and lots of birds."

"Pigeons."

Susan felt a tug in her cheeks as she attempted to contain a smile. "Yes, pigeons." She put down her needles. "So, Oliver from Maine, why are you here?"

"To join the fight. The RAF needs pilots."

"Aren't you afraid?"

"Of dying?"

Susan nodded.

"There are worse things."

"Like what?"

"Sitting idle while the Nazis attempt to conquer the world."

The explosions dwindled, like a thunderstorm losing steam.

The candle burned away to a nub; globs of melted wax covered the base.

"Maybe they're done for tonight," Ollie said.

"There'll be another wave." Susan placed her knitting into the box and slid it under the sofa. "We should rest. Lots of work to do in the morning."

Ollie nodded. He picked up the candle, the flame flickered out, and the room went dark. "I'll get another match."

"No need." Susan clasped his hand, noticing the warmth of his skin. She guided Ollie to the stairs and gently placed his palm on the rail.

Together, they climbed the stairs to the landing. The hallway was a black abyss from the blackout drapes.

"Can you find your room?" she asked.

"I think so."

Susan heard the rattle of a doorknob.

"Found it," he said.

"Ollie?"

He stopped. "Yes."

"It seems I've done far too much talking."

"I liked listening," he said.

"That's sweet. But it was impolite of me to ramble." She paused. "What happened to your parents?"

"Car accident." He stepped into the blackened hallway. The floor creaked under his feet. "With no siblings or relatives, I guess being alone made it easier for me to join the fight."

She swallowed and took a step. Her foot scraped the baseboard. "When was the accident?"

He hesitated. "Last month."

She gasped.

The hallway went silent. Then a siren sounded.

Ollie found her shoulder with his hand. "Looks like you were right about another wave." He gave a soft squeeze. "Good night, Susan."

Susan felt his hand slip away, then heard the door close. She stood alone in the hallway, until the thunder of artillery guns forced her to the sanctuary of her room.

Susan, shaken by the news of Ollie's parents, as well as the rumble of bombs, was unable to sleep. Shortly after midnight, the all-clear signal was sounded by a siren at North Weald Airfield. She slipped on a robe and slippers, then crept down the stairs, hoping a warm cup of tea would calm her mind. But as she made her way to the kitchen, she saw the front door cracked open. A sliver of moonlight illuminated the hardwood floor. She peeked outside and saw Ollie sitting on the porch steps.

"Can't sleep?" Susan whispered, stepping outside.

"No," Ollie said.

"Me neither."

"I think they're gone for the night." He patted the space beside him. "Saved you a spot."

Susan tightened her robe and sat. "I'm so sorry about your parents."

"Thanks," Ollie said. "I'm sorry about your mom and dad, too. You were far too young to lose them."

Susan nodded. "Fortunately, I had my grandparents."

He looked at her. "I bet Bertie and Agnes did a swell job filling in for your parents."

She smiled, pleased by his compliment, as well as the fact that he included her grandmother's name, a woman whom he'd never met.

Ollie adjusted the zipper on his jacket. "Did you ever miss having siblings?"

"Goodness, yes." She stretched her arms. "Someday, I'd like to have a big family."

"Same," Ollie said. "Lots of kids."

"Boys or girls?"

"Both. How about you?"

"Two girls and two boys."

"Very specific," Ollie said, nudging her leg with his knee. "What would you name them?"

Susan pondered. "For the boys, something like Peter or Ian. And for the girls, names of a flower."

"Like Iris or Rose?"

"Perhaps. Or maybe something less common, so they'd always feel unique." She blew on her hands, beginning to turn cold. "Have I said too much?"

"Not at all." Ollie removed his jacket and placed it over her shoulders.

"You'll catch a chill."

"I'll be fine."

She pulled the jacket around her body, taking in his warmth.

Ollie tucked his hands under his legs. "What does your boyfriend think about naming children after flowers?"

"I don't have a boyfriend," Susan said, her heartbeat accelerating. "I dated a little at the university, but nothing serious. And with the war, I've been focused on work for the National Pigeon Service." She wiggled her toes inside her slippers, trying to dispel the butterflies in her tummy. "And do you have a darling back home?"

"No. I had a girlfriend in high school, but it didn't work out."

"Sad ending?"

Ollie shook his head. "A good thing. We were different people."

"In what way?"

He turned to her. "Before my parents died, my dad injured his leg in a tractor accident, and I postponed college to run the family farm. Let's just say that she didn't seem to like that I was staying home to care for a parent, and she wasn't keen on being stuck with someone on a potato farm."

"It was a good thing that it ended." She crossed her feet and noticed that her knee was almost touching his leg.

Ollie leaned back. "Did you see the stars?"

Susan looked up. "Oh my." Distracted, she had failed to notice that the clouds had disappeared, revealing hundreds of twinkling stars. "It's beautiful."

"You can see constellations." Ollie traced the sky with his hand. "I think that one—"

"Look!" Susan pointed to a brief streak of light across the sky. "Quick. Make a wish."

She closed her eyes and paused.

"What did you wish for?"

"I'd rather not say," Susan said, opening her eyes. "If I tell you, it won't come true."

"In Maine, we believe in sharing wishes on shooting stars," Ollie said. "We also disclose wishes involving birthday candles, dandelions, and ladybugs. And considering you're in the company of an American for this celestial event, I think you need to tell me."

Susan felt a smile tugging at her lips.

He moved closer. "Do you want it to come true?"

"Yes."

"Then you'll want to tell me."

"Very well," she said. "I wished for the war to end."

"A perfect wish."

She paused. "Some days, I wonder if the bombs will ever stop."

"They will." Ollie looked into her eyes. "I believe in you, Susan. I have confidence in your pigeons and Source Columba. This war *will* end. And I promise to do everything I can to help make it happen."

His words comforted Susan like a blanket warmed by the sun. On an impulse, she leaned her head on his shoulder.

He placed his arm around her, pulling her close.

They sat in silence as a cold breeze rustled the birches. For the first time in weeks, Susan felt safe. His affirmations had filled her with hope. She savored the passing minutes, knowing that at any moment a blaring siren could purloin their time together.

"You should get some rest," Ollie whispered.

She hesitated. Her heart wanted to stay, but her brain reminded her that the mission was tomorrow. Reluctantly, she lifted her head from his shoulder.

Ollie rose to his feet and extended his arm.

She clasped his hand and stood. Their fingers entwined, then slipped away.

Inside, they retreated to their separate rooms. Susan crawled into bed, her skin still tingling from his touch.

CHAPTER 17

EPPING, ENGLAND

The pecking on the window caused Susan to stir. She stretched, got out of bed, and opened the blackout curtains. The glare of the morning sun made her squint. She rubbed her eyes and saw Duchess, balanced like a tightrope walker on the ledge. The pigeon gave another peck, and Susan opened the window.

Duchess fluttered to the bed.

"Good morning," Susan said.

The bird climbed over the rumpled sheets, like a child scaling a wintry hill in snowshoes.

Susan picked up Duchess and caressed her back. "How did you sleep?"

Duchess cooed.

"Better than I did, I'm afraid." Susan recalled staying up for most of the night, thinking about her time with Ollie. "He lost his parents. Just like us."

Duchess blinked her eyes.

Susan sighed. "I barely had the courtesy to ask about his family. I feel horrible."

Duchess looked toward the window.

Susan peeked outside. She saw Ollie walk across the yard and disappear into a loft. A rapping of tin. Pigeons fluttered into the loft. A slight smile pulled at the corners of her mouth. "He's feeding our pigeons," she whispered.

Duchess stretched her wings.

Susan placed Duchess on her dresser and straightened the sheets, then got dressed and stood in front of the mirror. She brushed away morning tangles and placed her hair in a bun. She pinched her cheeks to give her face some color, feeling the strange desire for makeup, something she hadn't worn since leaving the university. She reached for a perfume bottle, unscrewed the top, and applied the few remaining drops to her neck.

Duchess tilted her head.

"I know, we have work to do."

Susan placed the bottle on the dresser, carried Duchess to the window, and tossed her into the air. The bird darted to a loft. She went downstairs to find her grandfather sipping tea.

"Good morning, Susan," Bertie said. "I made breakfast."

Susan glanced at the oatmeal on the stove. She gave him a kiss on the cheek.

"In that case, I'll also make lunch." He pointed to a chair. "Have some oats. Ollie and I have already eaten."

"Not hungry."

Bertie slid over his tea. "Then drink."

Susan took a sip of tea and went to the window. No sign of Ollie, just a smoky haze looming in the west from last night's bombings.

"Ollie's parents are passed," Susan said.

"That was my assumption," he said.

Susan placed the cup on the table. "Last month."

"Good Lord." Bertie stood and wrapped his arms around Susan. "Unfortunately, we know how he feels."

Susan gave a squeeze. "You better never leave me."

"Everything's temporary, my dear." With crow's-feet protruding from the corners of his eyes, he looked at Susan. "Even this bloody war."

Susan's shoulder muscles tightened. Learning of Ollie's loss reminded her of how unfair life could be, as if people were randomly plucked from the earth, like numbers drawn from a hat. Most of her family's numbers had been drawn years ago. Londoners were being taken each night. And now their beloved pigeons were about to embark on Source Columba, a death mission.

Bertie limped across the kitchen, then placed his cup in the sink. "Let's get to work, shall we?"

"Perhaps you could take your walking stick," Susan said.

"No need, my dear. Feeling young and vigorous." Bertie flexed his flabby arms. "Today, we're going to save Britain."

Susan wrapped her arm around Bertie's elbow, buried her fear, and walked outside.

CHAPTER 18

EPPING, ENGLAND

"Hold still," Ollie said, connecting a small Bakelite canister to a pigeon's leg. The spring-clip ring snapped into place. "Now, that wasn't so bad, was it?" Ollie placed the bird into a dropping cage much smaller than the communal baskets Bertie and Susan used to transport the flock to Clacton-on-Sea. It was barely enough room for a pigeon, let alone a small packet that included paper, pencil, and instructions written in French. But despite being quarantined and having a silk parachute attached to its cage, the pigeon cooed, as if it were merely headed on a routine racing trip to the English countryside.

As Ollie stacked the cage, the door to the loft squeaked. He turned and saw Susan and Bertie.

Susan scanned the loft.

"Good work, Oliver." Bertie inspected the cages. "For a pilot, you make a good pigeon handler. Perhaps I should consider giving you a raise."

"I didn't realize I was being paid," Ollie said.

"You're not." Bertie pulled out his empty pockets, like rabbit ears protruding from his trousers. "I have nothing to give, I'm afraid. Only an opportunity to make history."

"Seems fair," Ollie said. "Maybe I should pay you."

Bertie laughed. "That's the spirit."

Susan looked at a wall of cubbies. Except for a dozen squabs and nesting mothers, the rows were empty.

"Susan, help Ollie with loading," Bertie said, fixing his pockets. "I'll inspect the other lofts." He left, the spring door cracking behind him.

Susan poked her finger through the wire of a cage. The pigeon nudged her. "How did you know which ones to leave?"

"Bertie told me."

"Why did you start so early?"

Ollie placed an empty cage near a row of nesting pigeons. "I thought it might be a rough day for you."

She looked at him. "Thank you."

He nodded, then checked a parachute.

Susan took a deep breath and exhaled. "I wish I'd asked you sooner about your family."

"It's okay."

"No, it's not. I was inconsiderate." She moved a box of canisters. "You must miss them."

"Very much."

"What were they like?"

"My parents were farmers, but if you had asked my father, he would have said he was a pilot who grew potatoes to pay the bills."

"He sounds like a man who loved to fly," Susan said.

"Taught me to fly a plane before I could drive a car."

"Sounds dangerous."

"My mother would have agreed with you."

Susan smiled. "A sensible woman."

"Mother should have been a teacher. She was incredibly smart and had a knack for making the complicated seem simple. But without a formal education, she settled for volunteering her spare time at the library, teaching adults to read." Ollie scuffed the earth beneath the heel of his boot. "And like my father, she was proud of her British roots."

"I would have liked to have met them," Susan said.

"They would have liked you."

"Do you really think so?"

"I'm sure of it."

"Because I'm British?"

"No." He hesitated. "Because you're . . . Susan."

She tucked a strand of hair behind her ear.

Ollie ran his hand over an empty cubby. "I was fortunate. They sacrificed a lot to give me a better life, saving every spare dime to send me to college."

"You went to college?"

He shook his head. "I came to join the fight."

Susan looked to the ground. "And you ended up on a pigeon farm because of me."

"I'm here because I punched a military officer." He inched closer. "And if I had it to do over again, I wouldn't change a thing." Affection swelled within him. *You're sweet, caring, and beautiful. I'm lucky to be here with you.*

She looked up at him and swallowed. "We . . . should probably finish."

Susan and Ollie loaded the remaining pigeons with the precision of an automobile assembly line. Susan plucked pigeons from their nests, whispered something into their ears, and handed them to Ollie to attach canisters and place them into cages. The stacks of cages grew. The cubbies turned bare.

As Ollie placed the last bird into its cage, Duchess fluttered into the loft and waddled over a shelf. Susan reached for the pigeon, but instead, picked up a small booklet buried under a layer of dust. She blew away soot. "I wondered what had happened to this. Haven't seen this since I was a child."

Ollie stacked the last cage and joined her. "What is it?"

"My father's codebook."

Duchess stepped along the shelf, her toenails scratching wood.

Susan thumbed through the pages. "I initially found it by rummaging through a box of my parents' keepsakes, hoping to find photos." She handed the book to Ollie.

Ollie ran his thumb over the weathered leather binding, like the skin of an old reptile. He scanned the contents, filled with intricate groupings of letters and assigned codes, then wiped the cover with his sleeve and returned it to Susan.

"My father was in the artillery. They used it to send messages along the Western Front. Supposedly, the code was unbreakable. Or at least that's what Grandfather led me to believe." Susan smiled. "When I was small, Grandfather would often attach a secret message to one of his racing pigeons, even though it likely slowed its time. I'd wait in the loft until the pigeon with the message arrived. Then I'd decipher the code." Susan slid the book into Ollie's jacket pocket. "Let's show Grandfather. He'd enjoy telling you about it."

Ollie ran his hand over the lump in his jacket. "What were Bertie's secret messages?"

"Important business. Usually where he had hidden a gift for me. A book. A piece of caramel. You should have seen my grandmother covering her ears as I clanged through her pots and pans trying to find a pack of gum."

Ollie chuckled. "I wish I could have seen that."

"Me too."

Ollie looked at her. Their eyes briefly met, causing his stomach to quiver. *Do you feel the same way?*

Susan turned and looked at the emptied rows, then to the cages. A few of the pigeons squirmed in their tight quarters, while most had their heads tucked under their wings. Susan's hands trembled.

Ollie gently clasped her hands. He struggled for the right words and simply said, "You've trained them well."

She squeezed his fingers. "I'm tired of being scared and hungry.

The constant air raids. I can't seem to get the sirens out of my head. But most of all, I hate sending our pigeons to war. I know we have no choice, but I hate it."

"Someday the war will be over," he said. "There'll be nights without bombs. Meals without rationing. Lofts without alarms. You'll finish your studies at the university."

"And you'll go home," she said, her voice dropping to a whisper.

A jolt struck Ollie. The reality of their different paths felt like a wedge coming between them. He would join the fight. She would raise pigeons. But Susan had resurrected his hope and joy, and he wasn't about to let anything drive them apart—not even a war. "I don't want to leave," he breathed.

Susan looked into his eyes.

"I want to be here—with you."

She leaned in.

Ollie wrapped his arms around Susan, feeling her warmth, chest rising and falling, soft hair brushing against his chin.

Susan raised her head and placed her palm on his neck. She slowly stood on her toes.

He felt her heart thumping against his chest. His pulse pounded faster as her lips approached his own.

A car horn sounded.

The pigeons rustled.

"They're here!" Bertie shouted from the lawn.

Their embrace faded. Susan lowered her cheek to his chest. Ollie's hands dropped from her shoulders, drifted down her arms, and rested on her waist.

Susan stepped back, space falling between them.

Ollie's arms fell to his side. His heartbeat slowed.

Susan straightened her skirt and adjusted her hair.

"Ready to win the war?" Ollie asked.

She nodded.

Outside, three military trucks rolled up the lane and then

stopped. A sergeant got out and said, "We're here for pickup." He unfolded a piece of paper. "Order for five hundred."

"The first several lofts," Bertie said, pointing. "They're in the cages."

Susan and Ollie sat on the porch and watched the soldiers load pigeons. In less than an hour, the lofts were emptied. The soldiers got into their trucks and started the engines, except for the last truck; its engine coughed as the driver turned the ignition. As the first two trucks pulled away, the driver of the stalled truck sounded the horn and waved his hand out the window. The trucks screeched to a stop.

A soldier in the lead truck stuck his head out the window. "What's the matter?"

"Won't start!" the driver shouted.

The soldiers got out of the vehicles, opened the hood of the disabled truck, and inspected the engine. After several minutes of tinkering, the truck still wouldn't start.

"We'll have to call for a mechanic or another vehicle," one of the soldiers said.

"That'll take time," the sergeant said. "We can't afford to be late." He looked at Bertie. "Is there a mechanic nearby?"

Bertie shook his head. "They've all joined the fight. Closest one is Jacob Wiseman, in Loughton."

"Too far," the sergeant said.

"Just as well," Bertie said. "Jacob makes me look like a spring squab. He's rather slow these days."

"Damn it," the sergeant said. "We'll have to call for another vehicle."

Bertie stepped toward him. "You have another option."

"What's that?" asked the sergeant.

"You can use my lorry. And *he* can drive," Bertie said, pointing to Ollie.

Ollie straightened his back.

The sergeant crossed his arms and gave a heavy exhale, his cheeks puffing.

"It'll guarantee that you'll be on time," Bertie said. "And you won't need your men to return my lorry."

The sergeant paused. He looked at Ollie, then to his watch. "Very well."

Ollie marveled at how Bertie could convince the military, or possibly anyone for that matter, to accept his suggestions. He wished he could have been in the room to hear him convince the commander to free him from jail.

The soldiers quickly moved the pigeons from the disabled vehicle onto Bertie's truck. The soldiers squeezed into their vehicles, three in each cab. Engines revved. Pigeons flapped their wings.

Bertie pulled a key from his pocket and tossed it to Ollie. "I assume pilots can drive."

Ollie nodded.

"Susan, how about a wee walk while Oliver from Maine escorts our pigeons?"

Susan looped her arm through her grandfather's arm.

Ollie got into the truck and started the engine. As he drove down the lane, he glanced at his rearview mirror and noticed Susan running toward the truck. He stopped and rolled down the window.

Susan placed her hands on the window frame and caught her breath. "Can you make sure they load them carefully?"

He touched her hand. "I'll make sure."

"Thank you." She squeezed his fingers.

Ollie felt her slip away. He pressed the gas pedal and followed the military trucks out of the farm. Through his mirror, he watched Susan disappear.

Susan watched Ollie drive away. A trail of down feathers floated from the truck and settled onto the road. It would be the last time she would see many of the pigeons, she believed. The odds of returning from France were against them. But knowing that Ollie would be with them in their final moments, before being loaded onto planes, made her fears about the mission more tolerable.

She'd never met a man like Ollie. *He's tender, handsome, and dedicated to family.* He displayed many of the qualities she cherished in a man. And he liked pigeons, something that could scare away the strongest of suitors. Her grandparents, Bertie and Agnes, had a loving marriage—continually holding hands, laughing, and kissing—something she hoped for herself someday. When the war began, her thoughts of having a relationship had turned dormant. But Ollie had awakened her heart.

Susan slowly walked to the house. *Tonight*, she thought. *We'll be together.*

CHAPTER 19

NORTH WEALD, ENGLAND

Ollie followed the trucks along Epping Road, watching downy feathers stream from their beds. He was about to drive onto an RAF air base, maybe even get a glimpse of a Hurricane or Spitfire, but all he could think about was Susan. Everything she cared about, except for Bertie and Duchess, was stuffed into the back of these trucks. The pigeons were her life's work. Her passion. They were going to war, and most would die. He felt like he was delivering prisoners to a death squad.

At the gate of North Weald Airfield, an armed guard shook his head when he learned that a civilian was attempting to drive a truck onto the base. The guard debated with the sergeant, then resorted to making a phone call before deciding to let Ollie through. Ollie wanted to believe he was allowed onto the base because he was part of the mission or, even better, because he was a future RAF pilot. But he knew it was probably because they would need to transfer the pigeons again by hand. The guard inspected Bertie's truck, checked Ollie over to make sure he carried no weapons, and let him proceed.

They drove past several hangars and turned onto a runway. Ollie's eyes widened as he saw rows of Spitfires perched along the runway like sleeping eagles. The marine-green machines looked incredibly fast. Three blade propellers. Aerodynamic frame. Sleek glass canopy. Roundels painted on the tails. Guns protruding from the wings. The planes looked as if they were forged from a single piece of metal, much different than his wood-framed bi-plane covered in weathered canvas. Ollie counted sixty planes be-fore he realized he was falling behind the other trucks. He pressed the gas pedal and followed the convoy to another runway.

They stopped in front of a squadron of Bristol Blenheim bombers. Unlike the Spitfire, the Blenheim didn't look as if it had been built for military purposes. It appeared to be a con-verted commercial aircraft. Boxy nose. Two large engines, one on each wing. A gun turret was screwed into the top of the fuselage, like an afterthought. Although the Blenheim paled in compari-son to the Spitfire, Ollie thought it still looked to be a formidable fighter, and it was unique in that it could also be used as a small bomber. And at the moment, he'd be willing to fly anything to become a pilot for the RAF, even a hot-air balloon.

Ollie parked the truck behind the other vehicles. He got out and immediately unloaded pigeons with the soldiers, hoping to catch a glimpse of the cockpit of a Blenheim. He carried cages under a fuselage, the bomb bay doors spread open. He poked his head into the plane and handed the pigeons to a soldier who was stacking cages into the tail. Ollie glanced around. Sunlight shot through the glass gun turret, illuminating the interior. The plane was small for a bomber, which appeared to be equipped for a crew of three: pilot, copilot, and gunner. Glass panels surrounded the cockpit like a miniature greenhouse, providing more than ample vision for the pilots. Dozens of flight instruments and switches covered the cockpit. Ollie suddenly felt like a novice flyer, having relied upon only one instrument in his old biplane, the fuel gauge.

"Move your arse," said the soldier in the plane. "We don't have all day."

Ollie ducked and went to retrieve more cages.

Along with three of the soldiers, Ollie carried pigeons while the remaining soldiers, like bricklayers, stacked them inside the planes. Each time Ollie lifted the birds into the plane, he twisted his head to peek into the cockpit. For the next hour, they dispersed the pigeons among the bombers.

As they were finishing unloading the last truck, a soldier—a rather large man who walked more pigeon-toed than most of the birds—tripped and almost fell. He caught the cages he was carrying, inches from the ground. The pigeons fluttered.

"You're such a lug, Angus," said one of the soldiers.

Angus adjusted the cages in his hands. "Am not."

Ollie overheard the soldiers squabbling as he shut the tailgate of the truck.

"You should have seen Angus at the lofts," said the soldier to his comrades. "The big oaf knocked over a stack of cages, and one escaped."

Ollie hesitated.

Angus lowered his brow. "But I caught him."

The soldier laughed. "You plucked another bird from its nest and strapped on a canister."

"That's not true," Angus said. "It was on a shelf. It didn't even try to get away when I picked it up."

Ollie stopped. "What did it look like?"

Angus turned his head.

"What did it look like?" Ollie repeated.

"Odd-looking fellow," Angus said. "Looked like someone splashed him with green paint."

Hairs cropped up on Ollie's neck. "Duchess."

"Who?"

"You took a bird that wasn't part of the mission."

"Way to go, Angus," said a soldier.

"A bird is a bird," Angus said.

"Pigeon." Ollie stepped to him. "It's Susan's pet. Where did you put her?"

Angus pointed to the Blenheim at the end of the row.

Ollie started walking toward the plane and felt a hand grab his arm.

"You're not going in there," the sergeant said.

Ollie's blood pressure rose. He stepped to the sergeant. "Then one of your men is going in there."

The soldier tightened his grip. "We're not unloading a plane to find one bird. Besides, we don't even know if it's the same one."

Ollie looked to Angus. "Did it have a fluorescent purplish-green neck plume, like it would glow in the dark?"

Angus nodded.

The sergeant let go of Ollie's arm. "We don't have time."

"The commander won't be happy to hear you took a pet," Ollie said.

The sergeant wiped his face.

"I understand Susan's grandfather is friends with an air vice-marshal. I believe his name starts with a P."

"Air Vice-Marshal Park?"

"That's the one," Ollie said.

The sergeant swallowed, wrinkles appearing on his forehead.

"Maybe the commander will go easy on you, and you'll only be assigned to clean pigeon lofts for the rest of the war."

"Sergeant," Angus said. "I don't want to get us in trouble."

The sergeant looked at his watch. "Pilots and crews will be here soon. Do you remember where you placed it?"

"It's in the tail," Angus said. "I put it in first."

"Bloody hell," the sergeant said. "We'd have to unload." He scratched his head, as if he were digging out a tick.

The other soldiers looked to a hangar, then to the sergeant.

"Very well," the sergeant said. "Be quick about it."

Ollie breathed a sigh of relief. Then the siren sounded.

Chapter 20

Epping, England

"**D**uchess!" Susan called from the porch. She looked at the rows of birches at the edge of the forest. The only movement was shimmering yellow leaves and a few darting sparrows.

"Duchess!"

"Did you check the lofts?" Bertie called from his chair in the living room.

Susan went inside. "All of them."

Bertie rubbed his knees, his feet propped on a stool. "She'll be back. Remember the time we took a flock to Willingham?"

Susan nodded and took a seat on the floor beside him. She recalled the training trip with a group of young pigeons. It was one of the rare occasions she had not taken Duchess along for the ride. When they arrived in Willingham to unload the pigeons, Duchess landed on the hood of the truck and angled her head, as if she were thinking, *Why would you leave without me?* It was the first and last time they failed to take her along.

"She's probably circling North Weald," Bertie said. "She'll be back before Oliver."

"How're the knees?" she asked, changing the subject.

"Same."

"We shouldn't have gone for that walk. You'll be paying for it later."

He adjusted his legs on the stool. "I needed the exercise."

"Tea?"

Bertie nodded. "That would be splendid, my dear."

Susan went to the kitchen and placed the kettle on the stove. She opened the tea jar. Only a spoonful of finely broken tea leaves remained. She glanced out the window to the garden. It looked dormant, brown stems and vines shriveling into the ground in preparation for winter. She'd have to scour the garden, or perhaps even take a hike in the forest to find something tolerable to brew. For now, she'd have to make do with weak tea.

Susan looked at a clock on the wall: 2:47 PM. The pigeons were likely inside the planes by now. She didn't know the time of the mission but assumed they would be leaving under the cover of darkness, like the Luftwaffe. She hoped the pigeons would not be frightened. After all, they had never been on a plane. Nor had she, for that matter. Perhaps they could tuck their heads under their wings and sleep. How many would make it back?

Be an egg, she thought.

She sat at the kitchen table and turned her thoughts to Ollie. She was glad he was with the pigeons and believed he would do his best to make sure they were properly cared for. Despite knowing him for only a short while, she trusted him. Perhaps it was his interest in her, her pigeons, or the way he cared for Bertie, getting him cold towels for his knees, something she deeply appreciated.

She had enjoyed sitting on the sofa with him, telling him things she had never told others. Around Ollie, she felt a sense of comfort that she had never felt around any other man. Tonight would be dreadful, her pigeons dropped into war while another round of Luftwaffe bombs were likely to fall on London. But she took comfort in knowing that Ollie would be by her side, at least for the next few months, until he was free to join the RAF. She'd worry about that when the time came. For now, she would take what time they had together.

Bertie hobbled into the kitchen.

Susan looked up. "Tea will be done soon."

Bertie pointed to the stove.

Susan noticed she had forgotten to light the burner. "I may be a trifle distracted."

"Understandable, my dear."

Susan got up and lit the burner.

Bertie took a seat. "Thinking about our pigeons?"

"Yes."

"And Ollie?"

Her face turned warm. She hesitated, then nodded.

He smiled, pulled a chair beside him, and tapped the seat.

Susan rubbed her arms and sat.

"He'll be leaving," he said.

"I'm aware," Susan said. She expected to hear a lecture, perhaps on the proper etiquette of a lady or the risks of fraternizing with a foreigner, let alone a man who would soon be going off to war. But he surprised her.

"Our Oliver from Maine has taken to the pigeons quite well." Bertie pulled his pipe from his pocket.

She hesitated. "Yes, quite well."

He packed his pipe with tobacco, struck a match, and inhaled on the stem. "We're running low on grain. Tomorrow, perhaps you and Oliver should go to the village for supplies."

Susan felt tension fade from her shoulders. "Do you need tobacco?"

Bertie shook his head. "No need for such extravagance while the country is rationing. I'll make due with something from the garden."

"It's only a little tobacco."

He smiled and touched her arm. "How about some good tea,

something we can all enjoy. Oliver must think we're quite uncivilized. It'd be nice to give him a proper cup of tea."

Susan hugged him, breathing in the scent of homemade soap and stale tobacco. She went to the stove, removed the kettle, and poured steaming water into a teapot. The afternoon sun beamed through the window, warming her face. As she watched the water slowly turn the shade of lightly baked bread, she thought of Ollie. He'd be home soon. They'd wait for the pigeons to return. Together.

As Susan carried a tray filled with a teapot and cups to the table, the siren sounded. She jumped. China shattered on the floor. Hot tea splattered her legs. She rubbed her skin and looked at her grandfather. "I'm fine," she said.

Bertie struggled to stand.

Susan helped him to his feet and they went to the porch. Sirens wailed. Antiaircraft fire blared. Looking to the west, they expected to see an armada heading to London for a surprise daylight attack. But the first explosions were not in the city. A few miles away, the thunder of bombs erupted in North Weald. Susan felt the ground quake. Her legs turned weak. She squeezed Grandfather's arm. As black smoke boiled up to the sky, all Susan could think about was Ollie.

CHAPTER 21

NORTH WEALD, ENGLAND

The low growl sent a shot of adrenaline through Ollie's body. The soldiers stopped. The siren rose to a roar.

"To your posts!" shouted the sergeant. He pointed at Ollie. "Go!"

Ollie looked at the plane. Then to the sergeant.

"Now!"

Ollie ran to Bertie's truck. He fumbled with the key and started the engine. As he pulled away, he saw the soldiers jump into their trucks and speed toward a hangar. Men scrambled across the base, several tossing on helmets and climbing into sandbag pits. Shells were stuffed into antiaircraft guns, their barrels cranked toward the sky.

At the far end of the base, men wearing flight jackets ran from their barracks. It would take the crews a minute, perhaps two at most, to reach the planes. He glanced in the rearview mirror. The Blenheim's bomb-bay doors were open. *It'll only take a second*, he thought. He slammed the brakes and veered off the runway. He threw open the door, ran to the Blenheim, and crawled inside. The tail was packed with cages and secured with a cargo net. Bronze pigeon eyes stared from behind wire. The siren wailed.

Only a narrow archway along the roof led to the tail of the plane. No aisle. No crevice to squeeze himself through. Had he paid attention to how the men had loaded, rather than taking glimpses of the cockpit, he would have known how difficult it would be to reach the tail, and maybe he'd be speeding back to the farm in Bertie's truck. He could either crawl over the top . . . or leave. Without thinking, he lifted himself onto the cages.

Pigeons flapped their wings. He crawled, spreading out his limbs to distribute his weight, like a man on a bed of nails. The cages creaked. A metal beam running along the ceiling scraped at his spine. A beak poked his finger. Sirens howled.

Reaching the back, he slid himself down to the floor, into a small gap between the cages and the plane's tail. His knees pressed into his chest. As he unhooked the cargo net, antiaircraft fire boomed. Ollie jerked and bumped his head. Pain flared. He threw open the net.

"Duchess!"

Pigeons rustled. The cages blocked most of the sunlight shining through the turret, making it difficult to see. He scanned the cages. No Duchess. He lowered himself, his palms against the cold metal floor. On the bottom, two rows in, something flashed. His eyes adjusted. And he saw her.

Duchess flapped her wings, her bright plume sparking like a lightning bug.

Shells exploded. Ollie flinched, then slid out a bottom cage, like he was removing a building block. The stack tilted but held in place. He quickly placed the cage in the corner and reached his arm into the hole. He stuck his fingers through the wire of Duchess's cage and tugged. It held firm. He pulled harder, feeling wire cut into his skin. But the cage didn't budge.

Ollie pressed his back into the tail. With his boots, he pushed the cages and made a crevice. He reached back into the hole and pulled on Duchess's cage, feeling it wiggle. He strained harder. The cage slid. He leaned down, creating more leverage. Duchess blinked her eyes. As he pulled the cage through the opening, the antiaircraft guns paused, if only for a second. But it was long enough to hear it. Whistles. Like hundreds of boiling teakettles. Hairs stood on his neck. The whistling grew, then suddenly stopped. As Ollie tucked Duchess's cage into his chest, explosions shook the ground, each approaching closer than the one before, like the feet of a giant stomping toward the plane.

Ollie climbed onto the cages. Wings beat beneath him. His foot tangled in the cargo net.

Antiaircraft guns fired.

Ollie yanked hard with his leg, freeing his foot from the netting. As he clasped Duchess's cage and crawled forward, he heard what sounded like a blast of dynamite. His back slammed the roof of the plane. He fell back into the tail, buried in a mound of cages.

Ollie opened his eyes. Pigeons flapped their wings.

"Duchess!" Ollie shouted but couldn't hear his voice because of the intense ringing in his ears. He pushed cages from his face, but several more fell onto his head. The plane vibrated. The ground quaked with more explosions. As the throbbing in his eardrums subsided, it was replaced with the sound of propellers.

CHAPTER 22

NORTH WEALD, ENGLAND

The plane lurched forward, pressing Ollie's back into the tail. The Blenheim rumbled and shimmied as it accelerated down the runway.

"Wait!" Ollie shouted, his voice drowned by exploding shells. He struggled to push away cages. Wings beat. Feathers flew. The plane rocked hard to the left, slamming his shoulder into a support beam. "I'm in here!"

The hum of spinning tires suddenly stopped. The floor seemed to slope sharply, and the plane tilted to the right. *Christ, we're in the air*, Ollie thought. Cages covered his head and chest. He grabbed the cargo net and pulled himself up. Emerging from the pile, he saw a gunner standing with his head in the turret.

The gunner leaned back, pointing the barrel skyward. His arms shook as he squeezed off rounds of machine-gun fire. Something incredibly fast buzzed over the plane. As the gunner swung his gun around, he saw Ollie emerge from the cages. "What the . . ."

Holes popped across the fuselage. Thin light beams shot over the floor. The gunner's jaw dropped. He buckled over, like a boxer who had been sucker-punched in the kidneys.

Ollie crawled over the cages. He reached the gunner, slumped against a box of ammunition.

The gunner coughed, blood spraying his flight jacket.

"Hold on," Ollie said, pressing his hands over the gunner's abdomen.

"Benny!" someone shouted from the cockpit.

The gunner's larynx gurgled as he tried to speak.

"He's hit!" Ollie shouted.

Heads jerked in the cockpit.

Shots opened more holes in the fuselage. Sparks flew.

The plane banked hard to the left. G-force pressed the gunner against the fuselage, causing him to moan.

Ollie turned the man over and propped his head. He applied pressure to the gunner's abdomen, noticing that the leather flight jacket was warm and sticky.

The gunner grunted and mouthed words but was unable to speak, as if his vocal cords had been cut.

Ollie scanned the plane and spotted a first-aid kit mounted on the fuselage. He grabbed the kit, but bullets whizzing up through the floor caused him to jump into the turret. Through the glass dome, he saw a swarm of enemy fighters surrounding their unit. The Blenheim bombers dodged left and right but held their formation. The sky was filled with the phosphorous glare of tracers. High above, Luftwaffe bombers were headed west, dropping what appeared to be endless payloads. Ollie swung the turret and saw a diving Messerschmitt targeting the Blenheim behind them. The enemy fighter fired its guns. The Blenheim's cockpit glass shattered, causing the nose to drop. And the plane spiraled toward the ground.

The Messerschmitt swooped left, then right, and zeroed in on their plane. Ollie's heart pounded. He dropped the first-aid kit and grabbed the machine gun, his hands slick with blood. He pointed the barrel as best he could, never having aimed anything more powerful than a peashooter, and pulled the trigger. His arms shook like he was wielding a jackhammer. Bullets flared, missing its target. But the Messerschmitt veered away.

Ollie swung the gun around its turret, looking for the enemy, but the Messerschmitt fighters left to escort their Luftwaffe bombers. Gunfire trickled to a stop, leaving the drone of the Blenheim engines. He felt the plane climb. Within seconds, they were hidden in the clouds.

Ollie returned to the gunner, the man's eyes closed, bloodied spit oozing from his mouth. He checked the gunner's pulse. A weak beat. Ripping open the first-aid kit, he pulled out the largest bandages. He unzipped the man's flight jacket to a strong copper smell and immediately realized that things were worse than he expected. The bullet had pierced the abdomen and come out his side, leaving a hole the size of a peach. He placed bandages on the man's torso, desperately trying to contain the loss of blood. Ollie briefly thought of his father trapped under the tractor, leg snapped, hip crushed. His mother's bloodied fingers, nails ripped away as she frantically scraped the earth to free her husband. He shook the vision from his head and applied the last of the bandages. The gauze instantly became saturated with blood.

Glancing toward the cockpit, he saw the captain using the radio. The copilot was in control, pushing the wheel forward to level off the plane. Ollie turned his attention back to the fallen gunner, pressing his hands on the man's wound. The gunner let out a frail whimper, like a fevered child too ill to wake.

The captain left the cockpit and went to his fallen gunner. He removed his cap, revealing a crop of black hair.

Ollie cringed, immediately recognizing the captain. "He's bad," Ollie said.

Flight Lieutenant Boar grabbed Ollie's jacket. "What the hell are you doing here?"

Ollie looked at him. "I was retrieving a pigeon your men mistakenly loaded when we were attacked."

Boar looked at his gunner. "Bastard. You got him killed."

Ollie pushed Boar's hand away. "Luftwaffe shot him." He pressed the gunner's abdomen. "And he's not dead."

Boar glanced at the holes in the fuselage, then kneeled and placed his hands on the gunner's cheeks. "Benny!"

The gunner moaned.

"Benny!"

The gunner slid open his eyes.

Boar squeezed the man's face. "Hold on, Benny!"

The gunner blinked.

"He needs a hospital," Ollie said, pressing the man's wound.

"We're not going back," Boar said.

A jolt shot through Ollie's body.

"The mission has commenced." Boar ground his teeth. "Keep him comfortable." He stood and returned to the cockpit.

Ollie pressed harder on Benny's wound, trying to slow the bleeding. But the hole, caused by a high-caliber bullet that could pierce steel, was far too big. Blood dribbled down the man's leg to form a puddle. His face turned white. The floor turned red. As the plane flew high above the English Channel, the gunner gave a final gasp, desperately trying to suck in air. Then his chest deflated, like a partially filled balloon snipped with scissors.

With shaking hands, Ollie zipped the man's flight jacket, then brushed over Benny's face to close his eyes.

CHAPTER 23

10,000 FEET ABOVE THE ENGLISH CHANNEL

"He's dead," Ollie said, standing behind the cockpit. Thick clouds masked the window, as if they were flying through milk.

Flight Lieutenant Boar tightened his grip on the controls, veins protruding over the back of his hands.

"Bloody hell," said the copilot. He adjusted his cap, wiped perspiration from his forehead, and turned to get a good look at the American. His eyebrows raised.

Ollie noticed the man staring at his blood-stained hands and slid them behind his back.

The copilot reached inside his jacket and removed a bronze St. Christopher medallion. He rubbed it feverishly with his thumb, as if he were trying to erase the engraving or absorb its saintly protection.

"You'll pay for what you've done, Yank," Boar said. "But for now, I need you to do exactly what you are told." His jaw muscles flexed as he glanced at his watch. "Secure Benny. We'll be over our target in forty-eight minutes. I don't want to lose him when we open the doors."

Ollie nodded.

The copilot swallowed again, as if he were about to become sick.

"Who was he?" Ollie asked.

"Our gunner," Boar said.

"No, I mean *who* was he?"

Boar stared at his instrument panel. "Benny Sullivan, a miner from South Wales." He shook his head. "Bloody fool believed the air war was less dangerous than the coal fields."

The copilot slid open his side window. Air rushed in, pushing back a growing metallic smell.

Ollie returned to the gunner, propped near the cargo doors, and scanned the fuselage for a place to move him. But the plane was small and packed with pigeons. The only places to stand were in the turret and over the cargo doors, both not an option. So Ollie moved several cages into the base of the gunner's turret, making sure there was enough room to swivel the gun. He placed several more cages on an empty bomb shelf mounted to the side of the fuselage.

Standing over the gunner, Ollie placed his hands under the man's armpits, the left side warm and sticky. He suddenly felt weak and out of breath, but forced himself to slide Benny to the back, his soaked body painting the floor. Using the cargo net, he covered the gunner, an arm and leg woven through the webbing to ensure he wouldn't slide. The pigeons closest to the gunner had closed their eyes or stuffed their heads under their wings.

He sat in the gunner's turret, in the mounted chair that Benny once used, and pressed his head against the gun. The steel felt cold. A man was dead. He was on his way to France. And this would be his last flight. He'd screwed up. Even if Bertie was best friends with Air Vice-Marshal Park, Winston Churchill, FDR, or God, for that matter, there was no talking his way out of this mess. But most of all, his body ached with the thought that he might never see Susan again. *They'll lock me up. I'll never be with her again.* He struggled to fully grasp the impact of his blunder.

He'd never hear the sweet timbre of her voice, nor would he hold her in his arms again. His heart sank. *We could have had a future together.*

As the drone of propellers filled the cabin, he wondered what his parents would have thought of his choices. Would they approve of him trying to join the fight? Surely, yes. But not with how he had handled things—stowing away on a ship, punching a lieutenant, getting thrown in jail, and being sentenced to a pigeon farm. And now, being caught onboard an RAF mission, no doubt a serious offense that would likely have him spending the rest of the war behind bars.

He exhaled and saw his breath, the temperature plummeting from the altitude. As he went to blow on his hands, he noticed his blood-stained fingers and stopped. With nothing to clean himself, he untucked the tail of his shirt and rubbed until his skin turned raw.

For the next forty minutes, Ollie sat in silence until heavy turbulence made him peek his head into the turret. The camouflage of clouds was dissipating. He counted bombers. One missing—a miracle considering the surprise attack. Suddenly, the plane tilted its wings, causing him to brace himself against the machine gun. He watched the Blenheim bombers fall out of formation. Through breaks in the clouds, he saw the French coastline, Earth's crust rising from the depths of the English Channel. The planes spanned out, each taking solo routes to drop their pigeons along the French countryside.

Ollie felt a hand touch his shoulder. He turned and saw the copilot.

"We're approaching the coast," the copilot said. "I'll be unloading."

"I can do it," Ollie said.

The copilot shook his head. "Flight Lieutenant wants it done right." He glanced to the tail and saw the body wrapped in a cargo net shroud.

Ollie saw the color drain from the man's face. "How about I hand you the pigeons?"

The copilot rubbed the medallion inside his jacket and said, "Fine, but stay clear of the doors."

With the other planes having gone their separate ways, the buzzing of two engines seemed comparably soft. Ollie stepped from the turret, making room for the copilot, and found a cramped space next to the gunner. He looked at the pigeons. Most had their heads under the folds of their wings. Somewhere deep in the tail of the plane was Duchess. He thought of Susan and silently promised to make sure her pigeon was returned.

"Prepare for drop!" Flight Lieutenant Boar shouted from the cockpit.

The copilot gripped a hand brace mounted near the bomb doors. He looked around for a safety cord to attach to himself but found nothing but ammunition.

The doors cracked open. Freezing wind gushed into the fuselage.

"Where's Benny's safety cord?" The copilot frantically looked around the cabin.

Ollie pointed to Benny, a wrapped wire cord strapped to his belt. "You looking for that?"

The copilot bit his lip. "Yes."

Ollie retrieved the cord, having to unbuckle the gunner's belt, then handed it to the copilot.

The copilot quickly fastened one end of the wire to his belt, the other to a hook near the bomb doors. Wind blasted his face, making fleshy waves over his jowls. "We'll drop them one at a time. Every twenty seconds. To spread them out."

Ollie nodded.

"Hold tight." He pointed to a leather strap mounted on the fuselage. "We're likely to have company."

Ollie gripped the strap. Far below, the water turned to earth. They flew over a small cluster of houses and a stone church. An empty road snaked through the village and into the countryside. No guns. No tanks. No Nazis. Only dried-up fields intertwined with clusters of forest. The place looked deserted, as if the French had waded into the Channel and drowned, rather than live with Nazi occupation.

"Drop!" Boar shouted.

Ollie handed the copilot a cage. The pigeon perked its head, suddenly becoming alert. The copilot released the package. The pigeon attempted to fly, its instincts taking over, wings beating against the sides of the cage. The chute shot open. And the cage floated toward a field.

In the distance, Ollie heard the crack of Nazi antiaircraft fire. His heart rate spiked. He quickly handed the copilot another cage.

Cage after cage, Ollie transferred them to the copilot. The pile dwindled. Pigeons floated like dandelion clocks to the fields.

Reaching the tail, Ollie saw Duchess in her cage, her head jutting side to side as if she were trying to understand why her companions were individually exiled from the plane. He placed Duchess in the corner and handed the last two cages to the copilot.

The copilot dropped the birds, scanned the fuselage, and noticed the glowing pigeon. "There's one more," he said, pointing.

Ollie shook his head. "She's not part of the mission."

"Give it to me."

Ollie stepped to the copilot. Wind flapped his pant legs. "If this bird goes," he said, pointing to France thousands of feet below, "so do you."

The copilot swallowed. "Are you serious?"

"Yes," Ollie lied.

"Finished?" Boar shouted from the cockpit.

The copilot rubbed the medallion inside his jacket, then glanced over his shoulder, as if somehow the lieutenant would could come to his aid.

"Your choice," Ollie said.

"You'll rot in the bloody Glasshouse." He unhooked the safety wire from his belt and shouted, "Done!"

Ollie felt as though his life had been thrown away, like the pigeons. He'd be watching the sun rise behind iron bars for many years. But at least he'd live knowing he had done his best to return Duchess to Susan.

The copilot brushed his hands, as if the pigeons carried disease. He peeked down to the French countryside as the doors inched closed.

A pepper of explosions rocked the plane, knocking the copilot to the floor. The nose of the Blenheim shot up. The copilot slid toward the bomb doors, his hands slapping the floor in desperation for something to hold on to.

Ollie reached him just as the man's legs slid out of the plane. He grabbed the copilot's jacket.

The copilot clawed at Ollie's arm. "Don't let go! Don't let go!"

Ollie wedged a boot into the frame of the fuselage and pulled. Black puffs of exploding shells filled the sky as the bomb doors closed on the copilot's legs like a vice.

The copilot kicked against the air. He dug his fingers into Ollie's arm.

Ollie strained. His muscles burned. He gave a hard tug and pulled the man into the plane just as the doors slammed shut.

The explosions suddenly died. The wind gusts were replaced by the panting copilot.

"Everything all right?" Boar called.

The copilot dropped the back of his head against the floor. He stuck his hand into his jacket and squeezed the medallion. "Yes."

"We're heading home," Boar said.

The copilot turned to Ollie. "I owe you one, Yank."

"I believe you do." He pointed to the tail of the plane. "You can repay me by getting that pigeon safely back to Susan Shepherd."

The copilot nodded. He stood, the color drained from his face, and returned to the cockpit.

Ollie leaned back and closed his eyes. Light streamed through the turret but did little to warm his body. He struggled to come to terms with the fact that this would be his last flight. He'd never join the fight. And he'd never see Susan again. Instead of being allowed to return to Epping, he'd be imprisoned or deported from Britain. The possibility of being with her after the war was gone. He yearned for a second chance. A pang of sadness wrenched at his core.

As the copilot buckled into his seat, a shell exploded. Ollie heard what sounded like rocks striking an oil drum. The plane rattled. He stood in the turret. Black smoke poured from the left engine, the propeller seized, blades bent like tines of an old fork. The right engine coughed and sputtered. His gut floated into his chest as the plane lost altitude. He waited for the weight of gravity as the plane attempted to pull up, but it never came.

CHAPTER 24

EPPING, ENGLAND

Susan watched a wall of black smoke rise in the east, as if the runways at North Weald Airfield had been doused with petrol and set ablaze. A squadron of Messerschmitt fighters swooped over the forest, then climbed toward the clouds. High above, an armada flew toward London. The German fighters swarmed their bombers, like hornets protecting their nest. There were no Hurricanes. No Spitfires. Only Luftwaffe. She feared everyone and everything in North Weald had been destroyed. Her legs shook. Her breath turned to short gasps. She grabbed the porch rail to keep from falling.

"Bastards!" Bertie glared at the invaders.

The sirens died, and the antiaircraft guns suddenly stopped, as if the RAF had run out of ammunition, revealing the grinding of German engines. Susan looked up and shuddered. The Luftwaffe looked unstoppable, their pilots immortal, their planes indestructible.

She turned to Bertie and said, "Ollie."

The color drained from his face.

Susan's jaw quivered.

He hobbled inside the cottage and went to the telephone.

Susan heard him feverishly crank the phone, briefly pause, then slam the earpiece to its cradle.

"Lines are dead," he said, returning to the porch.

Susan stepped into the yard, shielding her eyes from the setting sun, and watched the Luftwaffe fly west. Soon she heard echoes of antiaircraft fire. Black bursts peppered the horizon. Then came the thunder of bombs on London.

She turned to Bertie. Over the cottage, a veil of soot scarred the clouds. "We must do something."

Bertie shook his head and limped off the porch. "There'll be another attack."

"Is he all right?" Her hands trembled. "Our pigeons? Duchess?"

His mouth opened but didn't speak.

"I need to know."

Bertie looked at his pocket watch, then glanced at the sun, using his thumb to estimate its distance from the horizon. "There's not much daylight left. One hour, maybe two. And we have no bloody car."

"We can borrow the McCrearys' lorry," she said.

"We won't be permitted near the airfield."

"We must try."

Bertie hesitated. "I'll go."

"I'll go with you."

"Absolutely not." He stuffed his watch into his pocket.

"Your knees. It'll be dark by the time you reach the Mc-Crearys' farm. It'll only take me a few minutes."

"It's too dangerous," he said.

"I can do this." She noticed a weakening in her grandfather's eyes, a slight drop in his shoulders. "Be on the porch with your walking stick."

Before Bertie could argue, she turned and ran down the drive. Gravel and mud clumped to her shoes. Her heart pounded as she passed the lofts, a third of which were empty, either on their way to France or facing an inferno at North Weald. The sheep huddled inside the barn preparing for rain, fooled by the rumble of human thunder. A few lambs lay in the field nibbling grass, their legs tucked feebly under their bellies. Their ears twitched at the beat of Susan's footsteps.

Her legs ached. Her lungs burned. But she didn't stop until reaching the McCreary farm. Running up the stone path that led to the house, she slipped because of the mud on her shoes and fell, scraping the palms of her hands. Pain shot through her forearms. Quickly brushing away bits of gravel embedded in her skin, she stood and knocked on the door. Seconds passed. Her eardrums pounded with the pulse of her blood. She sucked in air, a rasping attempt to catch her breath. A jolt of fear shocked her body as she realized that the McCrearys may have left for a shelter. Scanning the farm, she noticed the lorry parked near a shed. She knocked harder, bruising her knuckles.

Rustling came from inside the house. A lock clicked, and the door creaked open to reveal old man McCreary holding a lantern, like he had emerged from a cave.

"Who is it?" Mrs. McCreary said, coming up from the cellar.

Before Mr. McCreary could answer, Susan said, "It's Susan Shepherd. May I borrow your lorry?"

Mr. McCreary started to speak, his eyes widened as he realized that he had forgotten to put in his dentures, and quickly covered his mouth.

"Everything all right, dear?" Mrs. McCreary said, stepping in front of her husband. Her scraggly white hair sprouted from a poorly tied bun.

"No," Susan said, catching her breath. She pressed her hand to her side, trying to suppress a cramp.

"Bertie?" Mrs. McCreary asked.

"He's fine." She sucked in gulps of air. "We don't have our lorry. It's an emergency."

"It's bloody raining bombs," Mr. McCreary said.

"Albert!" Mrs. McCreary snapped.

The old man clamped his gums, making his cheeks sag.

"Please," Susan said. "I'll explain later." Susan thought of Ollie and her pigeons. Her eyes watered.

Mrs. McCreary nodded. "Would you like Albert to drive you?"

The old man's toothless jaw dropped.

"No," Susan said.

Mr. McCreary breathed a sigh of relief, then retrieved a key from a hook in the foyer and handed it to Susan.

"Thank you." She took the key and ran.

"Be careful, dear," Mrs. McCreary called after her.

The McCreary truck, used to haul hay and livestock, was larger and much older than Bertie's vehicle. It took several tries to start the engine, the acceleration was poor, the cabin smelled of exhaust fumes, and she could see the ground through a hole in the rusted floorboard. But it ran. Otherwise, she would have resorted to using her old bicycle.

As she approached the cottage, she saw Bertie hobbling, carrying his walking stick, its tip never touching the ground. Susan slammed on the brakes. The truck skidded to a stop.

Bertie tossed the stick into the back of the truck, opened the door, and grimaced as he climbed into his seat.

You're supposed to use your walking stick, Susan thought. She pressed the accelerator and popped the clutch.

Bertie's head jerked. "Would you like me to drive?"

Susan shook her head. She struggled to turn the truck around, its large steering wheel feeling like a ship's helm. The truck bounced as the tires rolled onto the main road. She slammed the accelerator to the floor.

The village of Epping was deserted. Cars were haphazardly parked on the street, abandoned during the surprise daylight attack. Drapes covered most of the windows, the residents preparing early for the blackout or shutting out the view of destruction left by the Luftwaffe. All of the businesses in the market were closed. The only sign of life was a speeding ambulance headed toward the hospital. Susan felt sick. She suppressed her fear and aimed the truck toward the smoke over North Weald Airfield.

Less than a mile from the airfield, a military vehicle blocked the road, with two soldiers standing guard. Susan glanced at Bertie and slid her foot from the accelerator. The truck coasted to a stop.

Susan rolled down her window. The air smelled of expelled gunpowder. She gripped the wheel to keep from shaking.

"You need to turn around, miss," the soldier said.

Bertie leaned in. "Our employee was making a delivery to the airfield."

"I'm sorry," the soldier said. He glanced toward the rumble of explosions in London, then gripped his rifle. "Road is closed."

"Please," Susan begged.

"Orders. Go home, miss." The soldier waved for her to leave.

Susan turned the truck around, struggling to remove the stick from reverse. After finding the correct gear, she popped the clutch and pulled away. Through the rearview mirror, she stared at the smoky haze covering the airfield, then sniffed and wiped her face. "We tried."

"There may be another way," Bertie said.

Susan looked at him.

"Yes," he said, scratching his head. "It may just work."

"What?"

"Turn on Woodside." He pointed. "There!"

Susan turned the wheel sharply, pressing Bertie into her shoulder.

He straightened himself in his seat.

"Where are we going?" she asked.

"We can't get in, but we can get a better look."

Susan drove north. To the left was Wintry Wood. Thick groves of virgin trees covered the ground, their fallen leaves pasted to the damp road like a carpet. To the right lay pastures overgrown with dormant weeds. No sheep. No crops. Only thorny bramble.

Beyond the fields, a long wire fence ran parallel to the neglected farms. *North Weald Airfield?* She struggled to get a better look, felt the tires rumble on the berm, and quickly adjusted the wheel.

"Focus, my dear," Bertie said. "It's not far."

A few hundred yards ahead, she followed Bertie's instructions and turned into a farm. She slowed as she approached a brick farmhouse. Brown vines slithered over the front door, their progress stopped shy of the second-story windows by approaching winter. She briefly wondered if the entire English countryside would soon be deserted, fearing the inevitable German invasion.

"The Jamisons moved to Shrewsbury when the war started," Bertie said. "Several years ago, Mr. Jamison had fallen ill during lambing season. I tended to his sheep while he recovered. The barn overlooks North Weald." He pointed. "Drive around back."

Susan drove to the back of the house and parked in front of the barn. She helped Bertie out of the truck. As she expected, he refused to use his walking stick but accepted the crook of her arm. Together, they pried open the barn door, its hinges squeaking from rust. The inside, despite being empty, still smelled of old manure and straw.

"Up there." He pointed to a ladder leading to a hayloft. "I'll follow."

"Your knees."

"I'll be fine."

Susan climbed the ladder, the rungs worn smooth from decades of soiled boots and sweaty hands. Faint afternoon sun sprayed through cracks in the boards. Reaching the top, she heard Bertie grunting as he labored to climb the ladder. She lowered herself to her knees, took his hands, and helped him to the landing. As she brushed straw from her clothes, Bertie stood and swung open the doors. Light illuminated the hayloft.

He looked outside and squinted. "Too far for me."

Susan joined him. The elevation from the hayloft gave a distant, but clear view of North Weald Airfield. Her heart raced.

"What do you see?" he asked.

She scanned the airfield looking for Grandfather's truck or any sign of Ollie and the pigeons. But smoke, drifting in thick black billows, clouded much of the view. "There's a burning hangar. A fire brigade is fighting the flames. Men are filling holes in a runway." Her legs felt brittle. She leaned on the door to steady herself. "I don't see him."

"How many planes?"

She noticed what appeared to be the charred skeletal remains of two planes. She bit her lip, fighting back tears. "I see a couple of burned planes."

"Bombers or fighters?"

She squinted. "I can't tell."

He raised his chin. "They're on their way."

"How do you know?"

"The runways are usually lined with planes, except during flight missions. They must have scrambled them all into the air during the attack." He placed his arm over her shoulder. "Our pigeons, at least the majority of them, are likely on their way to France."

"What now?"

"We go home and wait for Ollie and our pigeons to return."

Susan looked one last time at the ravaged airfield, but the distance, smoke, and fading sunlight prevented her from seeing any sign of Ollie. She clasped her hands and prayed he was safe, then helped Bertie down from the hayloft and drove home.

As she pulled the lorry into their farm, an overwhelming sense of helplessness caused her heart to palpitate. She hoped to see Bertie's truck parked at the cottage, Duchess pacing her window ledge, and Ollie waiting on the porch. But there was only the intrusive military tent, its canvas flapping in the wind.

"They'll be all right," Bertie said unconvincingly.

Susan noticed a slight change in the tone of his voice. "It's getting dark. Go inside, and I'll check on the pigeons."

He nodded, then limped into the cottage.

Susan rapped on the grain can much harder than usual, hoping the noise could somehow draw Duchess home. Between lofts, she glanced down the lane, praying that she'd see Ollie returning in Bertie's truck. It was the setting sun, and knowing that the Luftwaffe would likely return, that forced her inside.

She retrieved cold towels for Bertie's knees to control the swelling. But the damage was done. His kneecaps were red and the size of melons. He grimaced as the towels touched his skin.

Susan tried to make a call to get information about the attack, but the telephone lines were still dead. She checked the radio and found nothing but static, typical during blackouts. After lighting a candle and closing the curtains, she sat on the sofa and noticed the indentation where Ollie had sat beside her the night before. She ran her hand over the cushion and wanted to cry. She barely knew him, but there had been an instant connection. She trusted him. Her heart had never felt this way about another man. And she believed—despite a war and being from different continents—that they could have a life together. She prayed that he was unharmed. *Where are you, Ollie?*

"Don't give up hope, my dear." Bertie rubbed his knees. "We must believe Oliver is safe."

Susan nodded, then lowered her head.

"And Duchess, too."

Susan buried her head in her hands.

"I never told you this, Susan," Bertie said, adjusting a towel over his leg and leaning forward. "When you tried to hatch a pigeon egg in your grandmother's bowl, I had all but given up hope. In fact, I had bought another box of tobacco, just so I could be prepared to bury the egg."

Susan raised her head and looked at him. The candlelight flickered over his gray whiskers.

"You never gave up. You kept the egg warm and rotated it like clockwork for weeks. Even after Duchess hatched, you fed her homemade pigeon milk until she could join the squabs." He gave a slight smile. "It wasn't a miracle. You believed. And made it happen."

She stood and went to his chair.

"Have faith." He took her hand and squeezed.

Susan nodded, then went to the icebox to fetch another cold towel. She appreciated her grandfather's words and, even more, his continuous efforts to fill the void of a missing father and mother. But deep down, she knew something was wrong.

As night approached, Bertie fell asleep in his chair, not making the effort to climb the stairs with his aching knees. His head slowly bobbed with the rhythm of his snores.

Susan quietly put on her coat, slipped outside, and took a seat on the porch. In the distance, a red glow of fires surrounded London as dozens of searchlights scanned the sky for Luftwaffe. A mix of desperation and guilt filled her soul. *Why did I let him leave? Why did I let her out of my sight?* She struggled to convince herself that Ollie would return. A pang of loneliness tugged at her heart. She rubbed her hand over the porch step, where Ollie had sat with her the night before, and she began to fear that she might have lost the love of her life. She wiped water from her eyes and prayed that Ollie would drive up the lane and Duchess would flutter from the birches. But by morning, neither had come.

CHAPTER 25

EPPING, ENGLAND

The predawn chirping of sparrows caused Susan to raise her head from her lap. She rubbed her eyes and saw the McCrearys' lorry parked in front of the lofts, sending a jolt through her body. *Ollie. Duchess.* She stood, her joints stiff from the cold, and blew warm air over her fingers. *How long did I sleep? A few minutes? An hour?*

The farm was eerily calm, the sky clear of searchlights and Luftwaffe. But the echoes of war remained etched into her consciousness like the grooves of a phonograph record. A pang in her eardrums. A vibration under her feet. A looming sense of doom. She wondered if she would spend her life, whatever might remain of it, reliving memories of exploding bombs.

A soft cooing joined the choir of wild birds in the forest. She went to a loft and found many of the pigeons, the fortunate ones that had not yet been drafted for a mission, flocked on the earthen floor. They jutted their heads and circled the feeding tray. She hoped to see Duchess perched on the grain barrel, but there was only the rusted feeding can and wooden spoon. She picked up a pigeon and stroked its wings. It blinked and cooed. Gently returning the pigeon to the floor, she scooped grains into the feeding tray. The pigeons flooded the floor and pecked.

The other lofts were the same. No Duchess. And the sight of all the empty cubbies made her eyes water. *Be an egg*, she thought. She tended to the hatchlings, squabs, and nursing parents, and went inside to check on Bertie.

The squeak of the door caused Bertie to sit up and rub sand from his eyes.

She unbuttoned her coat, hoping her grandfather wouldn't realize she had spent most of the night on the porch.

"You're up early," he said, yawning.

She hung her coat on a rack and went to his chair. "How're the knees?"

He removed the towels and pressed his kneecaps. "Splendid."

"They're still swollen," Susan said, noticing that one knee was bigger than the other. "Stay off your feet today."

"I'll be fine." He slowly stood, leaning most of his weight on the chair. "Did you sleep?"

Susan shook her head.

"I'll make us some tea." He hobbled to the kitchen.

"I'll do it."

"I need to get these old bones moving." His feet shuffled over the floor. Before making it to the stove, he stopped at the sound of an approaching engine.

Susan jerked when she heard the unmistakable sound of Bertie's truck—slipping gears and the metallic ping of pistons. She threw open the door and ran outside. A flash of hope washed over her as she saw their truck, followed by a military vehicle, coming up the lane. The truck slowed to a stop in front of the cottage. She jumped down from the porch and ran to the driver's door. Her heart sank when a soldier stepped out.

"Where's Ollie?" she asked, not recognizing the soldier.

The soldier slipped his cap from his head and squeezed it in his hands like he was ringing out a washrag. "I don't know, miss."

Bertie emerged from the cottage and said, "He was with the soldiers delivering the pigeons."

The soldier looked at the old man and shrugged.

A soldier driving the accompanying military vehicle joined his comrade. He glanced at Susan, then looked at Bertie and said, "We don't know where he is. We were ordered to return the lorry." He pointed to the tent. "We've been assigned here for the duration of the mission."

Bertie gingerly stepped down from the porch and hobbled, his legs bowed like the forearms of an old bulldog. "You must have been told something," he said, approaching the men.

"Only that the lorry was left at the airfield and that its driver was presumed to have fled during the attack." He handed the key to Bertie.

"Presumed?" Susan asked. "Something's wrong. He didn't come home."

"That's all we know, I'm afraid." The soldier returned the cap to his head. "If you'll excuse us, we need to set up and check the alarms." The soldiers retrieved olive-green canvas bags from their vehicle and disappeared into the tent.

Bertie put his arm around Susan and walked her inside.

She watched him check the telephone line, which was still not working, but it likely didn't matter. She knew there would be no use in contacting North Weald Airfield. The RAF had more important things to do than search for a missing American or a pet pigeon.

"Come on," he said, reaching for his coat.

"Where are we going?"

"To check the hospital."

The words stung her. She quickly retrieved his walking stick and followed him out the door.

After returning the McCrearys' lorry, which they simply left in the drive with the key under the seat, they drove to St. Margaret's Hospital in Epping. The parking lot of the small brick community hospital was filled, so she resorted to parking along the street. She got out, removed Grandfather's walking stick from the back of the truck, and found him already standing on the curb.

"I'd rather use your arm, my dear," Bertie said.

Susan returned the stick and looped her arm around his elbow. She knew he should be off his feet or at the very least using a cane. But selfishly, she felt comforted to help him. And it briefly occurred to her that Bertie knew this as well.

As they approached the entrance, an ambulance, followed by a civilian truck with three men sitting in the bed, pulled to the front of the building. Medics ran to the rear of the ambulance, flung open the door, and slid out a stretcher. Although the body was completely covered, it was the rounded belly protruding from under the gray wool blanket that made Susan freeze. She gripped Bertie's arm.

"Bloody hell," he whispered.

Susan wanted to turn her head but felt compelled to watch the men leap from the back of the truck and remove another woman wearing a soiled nightgown. Thin legs covered in deep cuts and scratches dangled from the stretcher. The woman, clearly pregnant and in labor, hugged her swollen stomach and cried, "No! It's too early!"

The injured women were rushed inside. The vehicles raced off, the ambulance leading the way with its blaring siren. Susan desperately wanted to go home. But she forced herself to take one step, then another, and another, until they reached the door.

Inside, the doctors and nurses were in a frenzy treating survivors from Sprigg's Oak Maternity Home. They overheard that a parachute mine had struck a wing where staff and expectant mothers who had no air-raid shelter were taking refuge.

"How many?" Bertie asked a gray-haired orderly retrieving a gurney.

The orderly stopped, his eyes dark and sunken from lack of sleep. "At least a dozen. More, counting the babies." He sniffed and cleared his throat. "They're still digging them out."

Susan cupped her mouth.

"Good Lord," Bertie said.

"Is there anything we can do?" Susan asked.

The orderly wiped his face. "Pray for them."

Bertie placed his hand on the orderly's shoulder. "Was anyone brought in from North Weald Airfield?"

He shook his head. "They were sent to RAF Hospital Ely."

Susan watched the orderly grab the gurney and push it down the hallway. The squeaking wheels sent shivers up her spine.

She left St. Margaret's Hospital, realizing the war had come to Epping. As they drove in silence to RAF Hospital Ely, she couldn't stop thinking about the expectant mothers who had come to Sprigg's Oak from London, seeking a safe place to deliver their babies. They were bringing life into a world of war. And the Luftwaffe had found them. Not only had someone lost a mother, a daughter, or a wife, they had also lost an unborn baby. She turned to ask Bertie for his handkerchief and saw that he was using it to dry his eyes.

They arrived at RAF Hospital Ely before noon. Even in the waiting area, the smell of ether and antiseptic made Susan want to hold her breath. They stood in a long line waiting for a receptionist, fielding questions from relatives desperately trying to learn about a son or husband. As they inched forward in line, the thought of Ollie possibly being injured turned her body weak. Goose bumps rose on her skin. Her legs felt like twigs about to snap. She clasped Bertie's arm to keep her hands from trembling. When they reached the front of the line, the receptionist scanned her papers and said, "We have no civilians here, in particular an American brought in from North Weald."

"Are you certain?" Susan asked. "His name is Ollie Evans."

"Oliver," Bertie added.

The receptionist looked again through her papers and shook her head. "I'm afraid we have no one by those names."

A nurse overhearing the conversation approached the receptionist and said, "What about the burn patient?"

Susan's heart palpitated.

"I thought he was an airman," the receptionist said.

"He was recovered near a plane with no identification." The nurse adjusted the cuffs on her long-sleeved uniform and approached Bertie. "Is he a relative?"

"My grandson," Bertie said. "He's come from Maine to help us with our farm. He was making a delivery at North Weald at the time of the attack."

Susan looked at Bertie, his eyes remaining focused on the nurse.

"Would you be willing to identify a patient?" the nurse asked. "You should know that he's badly burned, heavily sedated, and can't speak."

Susan's body shuddered. She struggled to breathe.

Bertie swallowed, then nodded.

"Follow me," the nurse said.

Susan took her grandfather's hand. "I'll come with you."

"No, my dear."

"Please."

He shook his head.

Susan took a seat in a waiting area as Bertie followed the nurse. The tapping of their shoes against the tile floor faded, and Susan became aware of moans and whimpers filtering the hallways. Young men, their bodies battered, broken, burned, and severed. Their lives cut short or, at best, changed forever. She closed her eyes, slipped her fingers into her ears, and tried to pray.

After several minutes, Bertie returned, his feet slowly shuffling over the floor. Susan noticed the lines on his face seemed deeper, as if he had aged from the visit to the ward. Her hands trembled. She looked into her grandfather's weary eyes and spoke, her voice able to produce only a whisper. "Ollie?"

CHAPTER 26

GERMAN-OCCUPIED FRANCE

Ollie opened his eyes to a setting sun that painted the clouds a beautiful hue of pink. *Am I dead?* Any notion that he had passed and was ascending, or descending, to an afterlife, were quickly eliminated by the acrid scent of aviation fuel filling his nostrils. Something dripped, then hissed, like a water droplet hitting a hot skillet. *I gotta get out of here.*

He twisted his neck, stiff from the impact, and noticed that the fuselage roof had been sheared away. Jagged metal teeth loomed over him. His foot throbbed. A heavy metal box pressed against his side, cutting off the circulation to his arm and turning his hand numb. With his good arm, he pushed over the box, spilling ribbons of ammunition onto the floor.

The returning blood flow burned like a hot poker shoved into his shoulder socket. His wrist protruded from the cuff of his jacket, as if his arm had grown. He touched his sunken shoulder and immediately realized it was dislocated, or worse. He sat up, trying to avoid moving his arm, and examined the rest of his body. A large bump protruded from the back of his head. His nose was bleeding. And his foot, twisted in the machine-gun turret, was badly swollen. But he was alive. A miracle, considering the rate of the descent.

He scanned the plane or, more precisely, what was left of it. The tail was cracked and partially separated from the fuselage. The gunner's body lay tangled in the cargo net, like a fly spun in a spider's cocoon. A flash of applying bandages to the man's punctured abdomen, the helplessness of watching him bleed out, no matter how hard he pressed. The hole was too big, his hands too small. Ollie shook away the image and turned his attention to his shoulder.

He clasped his clavicle and tried popping his shoulder into place but could only manage to raise his arm a few inches before spasms tore into his shoulder blade. His arm burned, like his nerves had been set on fire. He clenched his teeth. *I can't just leave my shoulder like this*. Before he could change his mind, he wrapped his wrist in the cargo net and gripped the webbing. The dead gunner dangled above him. Ollie's heart pounded. His ears thumped with rushing blood. He bit his lip and leaned back. His arm stretched. Tendons strained. He braced his legs against the fuselage and pulled harder. Excruciating pain ravaged his shoulder. But his arm didn't pop into place.

He eased off his weight, untangled his wrist, and fell back. He sucked in gulps of air until the pain subsided to a dull pang. Wiping sweat from his brow, he looked to the cockpit. Limbs of a large oak tree had pierced the cockpit glass and sprouted toward the gunner's turret. His heart sank. *They couldn't have survived that*. But he heard something faint, masked by whistling wind over shards of metal. He listened. Moaning.

Ollie got to his knees and crawled toward the cockpit, his useless arm hanging at his side. Another spasm spiked into his shoulder. With one hand, he struggled to break away branches and thick limbs, and realized it would take him too long to reach the pilots at this pace, especially with the growing smell of fuel. So he wriggled through the crack in the fuselage and slid to the ground. As he stood, pain shot through his ankle.

He steadied himself against a broken wing, its engine ripped away and sitting in the field like a fallen meteorite. A deep rut ran through the field from the skidding Blenheim, abruptly stopped by trees bordering a forest. He limped to the front of the plane, feeling his swelling ankle press against his boot.

The Blenheim had severed a tree, most of which was gouged into the cockpit. He climbed onto the nose, taking several attempts to find his footing, and cleared away chunks of glass. He stuck his head inside and immediately realized there was nothing he could do for the copilot. A sharp limb, launched like a wooden javelin, protruded from the man's neck. A St. Christopher medallion dangled over his jacket. Ollie winced and turned to the pilot.

Flight Lieutenant Boar was slumped to the side, his face and neck covered in blood from a deep vertical gash across his right eye, and he didn't seem to be breathing. He appeared dead, until Ollie grabbed his flight jacket.

Boar grunted and cracked open his good eye, if one could call it that, the socket red and bulbous, his eyelid swelled shut. "Ralph?"

"Dead," Ollie said.

"Bloody hell." He coughed and extended a hand toward his copilot but stopped short of touching him.

Ollie unbuckled the lieutenant's harness.

Boar grimaced.

"Can you move?" Ollie asked.

Boar struggled to wipe blood from his eyes. "It seems I don't have a choice, Yank."

Realizing that he would have to remove the lieutenant through the windshield, Ollie cleared away the rest of the glass using the sleeve of his jacket. He wedged a hand under Boar's arm and pulled. Boar rolled forward. Ollie's shoulder flared. He maneuvered Boar onto the nose of the plane, then slid him to the ground.

Boar fell to his back. He struggled to stand, then sat back down.

Ollie slid down from the cockpit and examined Boar, but there wasn't much he could see because of all the blood covering his face. He ripped away the tail of his shirt and placed it over Boar's eye. "Keep pressure on it."

Boar cupped the fabric to his face. "You hurt?"

"Ankle." Ollie touched his shoulder. "And my arm's hanging loose."

"Broken?"

"Not sure." Ollie looked around. To the west, the sun was sinking below a large field, dotted with mounds of straw. Beyond a hill, a thin stream of rising smoke, possibly from a farmhouse chimney or another downed Blenheim. To the east, thick woods. It'd be dark soon. Twenty, perhaps thirty minutes. "Where are we?"

Before Boar could respond, a distant shout echoed over the hill.

"*Beeilung!*"

Adrenaline shot through Ollie.

"France." Boar unzipped his jacket and fumbled to unsnap a pistol from its holster. "Somewhere between Amiens and Abbeville."

Ollie got to his feet, most of his weight on one leg.

"Where you gonna run, Yank?"

"Who you gonna shoot?" Ollie pulled Boar to his feet. "You can't see."

Boar gripped his pistol, his breath in heavy gasps.

"Your legs work?"

Boar nodded.

Ollie looked for someplace to run. But there were no houses. No roads. Only a dirt trail that led from the far end of the field to a hill where the voice came from. And in the opposite direction, the forest.

"*Beeilung!*" The shout was louder. Closer.

Ollie's heart pounded against his rib cage. His first instincts were to run into the trees, the logical place to hide. But something deep down inside him caused him stop, if only for a second. *Where will they search first? Second?* He scanned a ravaged wheat field, which made him think the farmer was in hiding or had fled from the German invasion. Many of the stalks appeared to be randomly ripped out, likely from hungry French citizens scavenging for food, leaving behind piles of rotting stalks. Before he could change his mind, he pulled Boar with him.

Ollie led Boar into the field. He gathered clumps of straw. It was getting dark, but not soon enough. They'd likely see them if they were close, but he had few choices. He grabbed more stalks.

"Why are we stopping?" Boar gripped his pistol.

Ollie quickly scraped at a groove in the earth with his hand. "Lie down in this plow run."

"You're mad, Yank." He pointed his pistol toward the hill. "You'll get us killed."

Ollie gathered more straw. "They won't look for us here."

"We haven't bloody left." He wiped his eyes.

"You can't see, and I can't outrun them." Ollie threw a pile of straw at Boar's feet. "You'll have to trust me."

Boar hesitated, then slipped his pistol into its holster and blindly scraped together straw.

They fell into a plow run no deeper than several inches and covered themselves as best they could. As Ollie shoveled a pile of straw onto his chest, he noticed the broken plane and stopped. *Duchess.* In his panic to leave the Blenheim, he had completely forgotten about Susan's pigeon.

The silence was broken by the sound of an approaching engine.

He peeked through the straw to the hill. No movement. His mouth went dry. He thought of Susan, her pigeon somewhere in the Blenheim. *Damn it.*

Vehicle brakes screeched. Guttural voices. The metallic clack of cartridges stuffed into weapons. Through cracks in the straw, he noticed movement, what first appeared to be gray turtles cresting the hill. First, one turtle. Then another turtle. And another. Within seconds, a platoon of German soldiers, wearing shell-like helmets, stood on the hill.

"*Dort Druben!*" A soldier pointed to the plane. The platoon raised their weapons.

Ollie squeezed his shoulder and counted. *One, two, three, four, five.*

Another German soldier crested the hill carrying a machine gun.

Six. Damn it. Ollie watched the soldiers spread out into two flanks. He heard the click of Boar removing the safety on his pistol. "Wait," Ollie whispered.

The soldiers, their weapons raised, cautiously crept toward the plane. Eyes peered through rifle sights.

The crunch of German boots grew closer. The path of the platoon would place them in the middle of both flanks. Ollie suddenly regretted his decision to hide. Every fiber in his body ached to run.

The German soldier with the machine gun, holding it like a guitar from a leather strap over his shoulder, passed within a few yards of their nest and stopped.

Ollie held his breath. His lungs felt like balloons about to burst.

The soldier, a fair-skinned, blond-haired man, about the same age as Ollie, gripped the trigger. He nodded to his comrades, and the soldiers moved forward, all eyes fixed on the plane.

Ollie's instincts had been right. As the soldiers passed, they remained focused on the smoldering plane, giving little, if any, notice to the strange bunches of straw among the many rotting piles covering the field.

Ollie quietly exhaled, then slowly sucked in air.

As the flanks reached the plane, the soldier with the machine gun fired into the fuselage, sending off a spray of sparks. He then emptied the rest of his bullets into the cockpit.

Ollie squeezed a handful of straw, feeling powerless as bullets riddled the plane. *I'm sorry, Susan.*

Three of the soldiers crawled inside the Blenheim while the others examined the wings, like hunters making sure their prey was dead. After several minutes, the soldiers emerged from the plane. The man carrying the machine gun held up a finger, then motioned to search the woods.

Ollie watched the soldiers disappear into the trees. When he could no longer hear the snap of sticks beneath their boots, he sprang from the pile and hopped toward the plane. "I'll be back."

"Get back," Boar said, reaching for Ollie's leg but missing.

Ollie limped to the plane and crawled into the fuselage to the smell of fuel and blood. The shelf where Duchess had been placed was empty, crinkled like a baking sheet beaten with a hammer. He overturned pieces of wreckage. No Duchess. In the tail, behind the body of the gunner, he saw a green flash. The thud of beating wings. A wave of relief washed over him, then quickly disappeared. The soldiers would return. Time was running out. He worked his way back, doing his best not to touch the gunner, but he had no choice but to push aside the man's legs, cold and stiff, to reach the tail. Stretching his arm as far as he could reach, he grabbed the cage and fled the plane, not taking time to check Duchess.

As he limped across the field, sweat dripped down his back. His shoulder throbbed. Duchess flapped her wings. The wire from the cage cut his fingers. He pushed to run on both legs, sending flares of pain into his ankle. As he reached the hiding spot, Boar rose from the straw pile.

"I hope you got a weapon," Boar whispered.

Duchess cooed.

"Shhhhh," Ollie said, covering the cage with his arms.

"Bloody fool," Boar said.

The next sound Ollie expected to hear was Boar firing his pistol into his chest. Instead, it was the hum of approaching vehicles. Without speaking, they crept away, Ollie limping and carrying Duchess, Flight Lieutenant Boar blindly pointing his pistol.

Ollie led them out of the field and over the hill. Avoiding the road, they followed a stream that flowed away from the fields. The ripple of water over stones masked the sound of their sloshing boots. As they waded calf-deep through cold water, Ollie's ankle went numb, making it easier to walk. He lowered the zipper on his jacket to use as a sling, tucked in his useless arm, and quickened the pace.

They continued their aqueous march well into the night, using the glow of a rising moon to guide their way. No speaking. No stopping. Following the stream, they wandered deep into the French countryside.

It was the drone of Luftwaffe flying overhead that eventually caused them to pause. The Nazis were no doubt on their way to bomb London. Again. The engines sounded louder. More aggressive, like the roar of iron lions. Perhaps it was the lack of antiaircraft fire that made the Luftwaffe seem mighty, or perhaps it was the solitude of the French countryside under German occupation. Either way, Ollie sensed that there might be no stopping Hitler.

He looked down at the cage in his hand. Duchess's fluorescent green feathers shimmered in the moonlight. The pigeon cocked her head skyward and blinked. Ollie pressed the cage to his side and sloshed forward.

For two more hours, they followed the stream, over eroded

rocks and muddy holes, until they reached a shallow pond. Ollie's feet were cold and numb; his shoulder ached. They waded to the bank and worked their way up a hill, their boots filled with silt and muck, then made their way through a patch of thorns. Emerging from the thistle, their hands scraped and bleeding, they arrived at a farmhouse. In the distance, a silhouette of a village, a church steeple pointed to the stars.

The lieutenant pressed the bandage on his lacerated eye, then strained to look through his swollen one. "What do you see?"

"A farm. A town a few miles away." Ollie glanced around. "There's a barn where we can hide."

Boar nodded.

They crawled under a gap between the barn siding and the ground, rather than risk opening a squeaky door and alerting the owner. Inside, Boar rummaged through his jacket pocket, then struck a match. The phosphorous flash caused a sleeping hog to shoot up its head. It stood on stocky hooves and snorted. Boar reached for his pistol.

Ollie gripped his arm. "It's only a pig."

Boar lowered his hand.

Fortunately, the hog didn't squeal. It gave a couple of snorts, then fell back onto its side to rest. As Boar's match burned away, they found an empty stall and collapsed to the ground. No straw, only chunks of what felt like mushy apples, but Ollie immediately recognized the musky smell. Molded potatoes. Feed for the hog.

As the temperature in his feet rose, the throbbing in his ankle returned. He wanted to take off his boot but feared the swelling would prevent him from getting it back on. The pang in his shoulder worsened, the flares synchronized with his heartbeat. To distract himself from the pain, he placed Duchess's cage beside him and poked his finger through the wire. The pigeon lightly pecked. He thought of Susan and hoped she and Bertie were safe, and that the Luftwaffe attack on North Weald Airfield had stayed clear of Epping. He'd likely never make it out of France alive. But Duchess would. He'd release her in the morning. It was his only comfort, knowing one of them would make it home. He lowered his head. Exhausted, he fell asleep.

CHAPTER 27

AIRAINES, FRANCE

Ollie woke to a snorting hog and a rifle pointed at his face. *It's over*, he thought.

He slowly raised a hand. With his eyes, he followed a steel barrel. He expected to see one of the turtle-headed German soldiers or perhaps an Aryan, steel-jawed Nazi. Instead, he saw a toothpick-thin woman with a sagging green sweater covering her trigger hand. Salt-and-pepper hair sprouted from under a weathered felt hat.

He glanced at Flight Lieutenant Boar, sleeping in the corner, then felt the cold tip of the gun press against his cheek.

"*Qui êtes-vous?*"

Boar shot up and pointed his pistol.

The hog squealed. The woman turned the rifle on Boar.

"Wait!" Ollie shouted.

Boar struggled to see through the crack in his swollen eye, the other covered with a bloodied shirttail.

"British," Ollie said. He tried to say something in French, but it sounded like gibberish.

"Your French is terrible," the woman said in English. "And your accent isn't British."

"American."

The woman raised an eyebrow. Her hog snorted, then twitched its triangle-shaped ears.

"Where are we?" Boar asked, still aiming his pistol.

"My farm." Her rifle remained steady. "Who are you?"

"Flight Lieutenant Boar, Royal Air Force."

"Shot down?"

Boar nodded.

The woman glanced at Ollie, then returned her attention to the lieutenant. "He doesn't look like a pilot."

"He's not," Boar said.

Ollie slowly stood, clutched his sunken shoulder, and stepped between them. "The Nazis are the enemy. Not us."

She looked at him, then lowered her rifle.

"You can put that away," Ollie said to Boar.

The lieutenant hesitated, then placed the pistol in its holster.

"Name's Ollie," he said, extending his hand.

The woman kept her hands on her rifle. "Madeleine."

Ollie lowered his hand, then adjusted his footing, his ankle stiff and swollen. "Madeleine, we need medical supplies. Alcohol, bandages, anything you can spare."

She looked at the lieutenant, his face crusted with dried blood.

"We also need a place to hide," Ollie said. "If you can't help us, we'll leave and won't put you at risk."

Madeleine reached down and scratched the hog's bristly brown fur, as if it were a dog. The hog grunted and wiggled its curled tail. "Wait here." She turned and left the barn, the hog trotting close behind.

"Where's she going?" Boar asked.

Ollie looked outside and saw the woman enter her house, then emerge a moment later without her rifle. She proceeded down a dirt road with her hog by her side. "Headed to the village."

"We should leave," Boar said.

"And go where?" Ollie tried walking, but each step shot pain into his leg, as though his ankle was filled with broken glass. His shoulder began to throb. He exhaled and leaned against the barn door. "The sun is up. The place will be swarming with Germans searching for a missing pilot."

"She could be helping them, on her way to the Nazis right now." Boar adjusted the bandage over his eye.

"I don't think so. She would have gone to them instead of waking us."

Boar cleared his throat and spat on the ground. "Let's get this straight, Yank. I don't take orders from you. I give them."

Ollie looked at the battered lieutenant. "You're right."

Boar turned his head, as if his ears had also been injured in the crash.

"I'm American. We're supposed to be neutral." He stepped to the lieutenant. "Maybe I should just leave. Let you fight your bloody war."

The lieutenant laughed. "They'll find you."

"I could claim I was traveling and got stuck in France during the invasion."

"They'd still shoot you."

"Possibly," Ollie said. "But I'm not the one wearing the RAF flight suit."

Boar's jaw muscles flexed.

"The fact is, you need me more than I need you. If you want to go, go. I'm waiting for Madeleine."

Boar tapped his pistol. "If she returns with Germans, the first shot I fire will be for you."

Duchess fluttered in her cage.

Ollie limped over to Duchess. He noticed that she looked impatient, scratching her feet and turning in her tight quarters. Opening the cage, he reached in and stroked her back. She made no effort to escape, seeming content to receive a bit of attention. After brushing her wings with his thumb, he retrieved the paper and small pencil that was stored inside. Placing the paper on his lap, he began to write.

The scratching of lead caused Boar to turn his head. "What are you doing?"

"Gonna send Susan's pigeon home," Ollie said, writing. "I'm including a note to tell them where we are."

"Brilliant, Yank. The bird could be shot down, then the Nazis will have a map to find us."

"She's a pigeon."

"Same thing. Can't believe we wasted the lives of airmen on a bloody bird mission."

Boar's words caused Ollie to stop. He recalled his last morning with Susan and ran his hand over the lump inside his jacket. "I won't be able to sleep during the mission," Susan had said as the soldiers were loading pigeons onto their trucks. "Will you stay up with me again tonight?" He'd looked into her eyes and said, "There's no place I'd rather be." But now he was behind enemy lines. *She probably thinks I'm dead*. A wretched ache burrowed into his chest, dwarfing the pain in his shoulder.

"Save it for later, Yank," Boar said. "We'll need that bird to send back intelligence, assuming we find anything worth reporting."

Ollie put away the paper and pencil, then took Duchess from her cage. He placed her at his feet. She made no effort to fly, only stretched her wings and waddled in a circle. As he waited for either Madeleine or the Nazis to return, he passed the time by watching Duchess peck at his bootlaces.

In less than an hour, Madeleine returned with her hog and an old man carrying a black leather bag. He was bald, except for a mustache and white bushy eyebrows that looked like twin albino caterpillars crawling over his brow. "*Médecin*," Madeleine said, stepping into the barn.

The man, whom Ollie believed to be a doctor, stared at the injured lieutenant. He glanced at Ollie's dropped shoulder, nervously twisted the tip of his mustache, and said something in French to Madeleine.

"We go inside," Madeleine said.

She led them to her house, a small stucco cottage with a thatched roof. The doctor guided the lieutenant by the arm as Ollie limped. Reaching the door, Madeleine patted her hog on the head and said, "*Reste, Louis. Nous travaillons bientôt.*" The hog snorted, then nestled into a worn patch of earth next to a shrub.

Inside, the doctor sat Boar on a wooden stool and motioned for Ollie to remove his jacket.

Ollie carefully took off his jacket, wincing as it slid over his shoulder.

The doctor ran his hand over Ollie's back and shoulder blade, then slowly raised Ollie's arm.

Ollie groaned. His shoulder felt like it was being stretched in a torture rack, ligaments and tendons about to snap.

The doctor lowered Ollie's arm. "*Disloqué,*" he mumbled, then spoke to Madeleine.

Madeleine looked at Ollie. "Your shoulder is dislocated. It's badly swollen, and he doesn't think he's strong enough to reset it."

Ollie swallowed and looked at the frail doctor, his arms like pipe cleaners. "Then I'll do it myself."

Madeleine shook her head. "He'd like for him to set it," she said, pointing to Boar.

Ollie groaned. He glanced at the lieutenant and noticed a sense of satisfaction on his battered face.

Ollie found himself on the floor listening to the doctor give instructions, interpreted through Madeleine. The last thing he wanted was for someone to tug on his arm, especially Flight Lieutenant Boar. But what choice did he have? He couldn't leave his arm a dangling mess. "Okay," he said. "Let's get this over with."

Boar sat on the floor next to Ollie. The doctor placed Boar's hands on Ollie's wrist, then positioned the lieutenant's boot into Ollie's armpit.

Ollie felt Boar's sweaty grip. His shoulder throbbed.

"On three, Yank," Boar said, applying pressure.

He's going to rip my arm off, Ollie thought.

"One . . ."

A hard jerk. A surge of pain. A loud pop, like a cork exploding from a champagne bottle.

Boar released his grip.

"Damn you," Ollie said, grabbing his shoulder. He carefully rotated his arm to make sure it still worked. Although he could barely lift his elbow, everything seemed to be in the right place, and most importantly, he noticed an immediate relief in pain. "Thanks."

Boar cracked his knuckles. "My pleasure, Yank."

The doctor produced a roll of gauze from his bag and made a sling for Ollie's arm. He then proceeded to swiftly remove Boar's bandage, as if he were running behind with a line of patients waiting to be examined. He looked at the lieutenant's eye using a small flashlight, shook his head, and then whispered to Madeleine.

The woman opened the kitchen window and began clearing off a large table.

"What'd he say?" Flight Lieutenant Boar asked.

"*Chirurgie.*" She glanced at the doctor. "He needs to repair your eye."

"No," Boar said. "Tell him to just stitch me up."

Madeleine shook her head. "He said you'll lose your sight if he doesn't try to fix it."

Boar cupped a hand over his eye. "Can he save it?"

Madeleine spoke again with the doctor. He looked at Boar and said something in French.

"Perhaps," Madeleine said.

"Bloody hell," Boar said. "Is he qualified to perform eye surgery?"

"He can be trusted." Madeleine pushed chairs away from the table. "He's putting his life at risk. The Nazis have no tolerance for anyone aiding their enemy."

The lieutenant hesitated, then said, "Very well."

The doctor pulled out a small brown bottle and gauze and placed them on the table, then began setting out sharp metal instruments, including a needle and surgical string.

Ollie helped Boar onto the table. Dried mud fell from the lieutenant's boots and scattered over the wood floor. The doctor turned to Ollie and said something he didn't understand. But he soon realized what the doctor was referring to when he extracted a bit of the mixture from the bottle with a dropper and squeezed the solution onto the gauze.

"He wants you to assist with administering the anesthesia," Madeleine said, taking a hand-rolled cigarette from her pocket. She lit the end with a match and took a deep inhale, accentuating the wrinkles around her lips.

Boar sniffed. "Could I have a cigarette?"

Madeleine handed him the one in her hand.

Boar took a deep drag. The tip glowed. He held his breath, then blew smoke through his nose. "Don't kill me, Yank." He handed the cigarette back to Madeleine.

"I'll leave that for the Nazis," Ollie said.

"Fair enough," Boar said, lying down on the table.

The doctor placed the anesthetic-soaked gauze over the lieutenant's nose. Boar inhaled. Coughed. Then inhaled again. Within seconds, the lieutenant's head tilted to the side, his hands limp. The doctor handed the gauze to Ollie.

Madeleine puffed on her cigarette and went to the door.

"Aren't you going to help?" Ollie asked. The gauze felt cold and wet in his hand.

She took a worn leather satchel that was hanging on a hook and placed it over her shoulder. "He's your friend."

Ollie looked at the unconscious pilot. *He's not my friend.*

She opened the door. "Louis." The hog got to its feet and raised its snout, as if it were sniffing Madeleine's tobacco smoke. She stepped outside and shut the door, her voice fading as she carried on a conversation with her hog.

Ollie didn't blame her for leaving. The last thing he wanted to see was this doctor operate, especially on someone who had threatened to shoot him. But he had no choice. He couldn't run, let alone walk. He spoke only a few words of French. And at the moment, he had no other place to hide. Besides, the countryside was probably swarming with Nazis searching for a missing RAF pilot. So he adjusted his weight onto his good leg and pretended to understand the doctor's instructions.

First, the doctor cleaned the lieutenant's facial wounds with alcohol and a rag. Then he poured a saline solution into the eyes, clearing away dried blood and yellow discharge.

Ollie grimaced and turned his head.

Boar started to moan.

"*Anesthésie*," the doctor said.

Ollie placed the gauze over the lieutenant's face until he went silent.

"*Assez*," the doctor said, pushing Ollie's hand away. He then swabbed the laceration above Boar's eye.

Ollie lowered the gauze to his side. The smell was slightly nauseating, like that of overcooked sweet cabbage, and made him feel groggy. It was a good thing there was a breeze flowing through the room from the open windows; otherwise, he might have succumbed to the fumes. But the doctor didn't seem to mind, as if he had grown tolerant of anesthetic.

For the next two hours, the doctor cleaned, probed, poked, swabbed, and stitched. Every several minutes, the lieutenant would begin to twitch, causing the doctor to speak; then Ollie would apply more anesthetic. After a while, Ollie could time when to place the gauze over Boar's nose, allowing the doctor to focus on repairing the damage. To Ollie, the left eye didn't look too bad, mostly swollen and badly bruised. But the right eye was another matter. The vertical laceration ran deep through the brow, splitting the eyelid and into the cheekbone. Most of the doctor's time was spent on the eye itself, delicately maneuvering the cornea with a pair of tweezers. Ollie felt nauseous. Suddenly, he forgot all about his injured shoulder and ankle.

As the doctor finished the last suture, they heard Madeleine approach, the sound of the hog's hooves tamping the ground. She came inside and hung up her satchel but kept her distance from the table; obviously, she had no desire to see what was being done.

The doctor made a makeshift patch out of cotton and gauze, then taped it over the lieutenant's eyes.

"Ask him how it went," Ollie said to Madeleine.

She spoke to the doctor. He responded, then quickly wiped off his medical instruments and tossed them into his bag.

"Time will tell." She looked at the body on her kitchen table, then lit a cigarette. "The bandages need to stay on for ten days." She took a deep inhale and blew smoke over the room.

Ollie helped the doctor move the lieutenant to the floor, though Ollie—wedging his good arm under Boar's torso—did most of the lifting. The lieutenant remained unconscious. He briefly wondered if he had killed him with an overdose of anesthesia, until he saw the lieutenant's chest rise and fall.

The doctor tapped Ollie's boot.

Realizing that he wanted to check his ankle, Ollie loosened the lacing and carefully pulled off his boot.

The doctor squeezed Ollie's swollen ankle like he was checking a piece of ripened fruit. He pushed the foot backward, forward, then rotated it in a circle.

Ollie clenched his fists and grimaced.

The doctor placed Ollie's foot on the floor, stood, and said something to Madeleine.

Before Ollie could ask, Madeleine said, "He doesn't think it's broken." She took a drag on her cigarette, then retrieved something from her satchel and handed it to the doctor.

Ollie watched the doctor examine what looked like a black piece of fungus coated in soil.

"*Merci*," Madeleine said.

He sniffed the fungus, slipped it into his coat pocket, and left.

Madeleine looked at Ollie. "When he wakes, you can hide in the barn."

Ollie nodded, then laced up his boot. He stood and limped over to the woman.

"Thank you," Ollie said.

Madeleine nodded. Ashes from her cigarette dropped to the floor.

Waiting for the lieutenant to wake, Ollie retrieved Duchess from the barn and brought her into the kitchen. He asked Madeleine about troop movements, locations, numbers, and equipment. But Madeleine was unable to provide any meaningful intelligence, other than that the Luftwaffe was using a local airfield.

"The Wehrmacht is everywhere," Madeleine said, rolling a cigarette. "They've taken over many of the homes in the village. They loot our food, making us wait in line to receive nothing but scraps." She twisted the tips of the paper and stuck the cigarette to her lips. "Our men have not returned from the front. They've either been killed or sent off to prison camps. It's only women, children, and old men."

Ollie nodded. From his jacket, he took out the codebook, once used by Susan's father in the Great War. The cover was warped and crimpled, but the pages were in relatively good condition for having been stored in a pigeon loft. He thumbed through it, gathering an understanding of the sequencing and codes. He quickly wrote a message and slipped it into the canister attached to Duchess's leg.

The pigeon cooed. "Good girl, Duchess," Ollie said.

"Your pigeon has a name?" Madeleine asked.

Ollie nodded.

She puffed her cigarette.

"So does my Louis."

Ollie looked at the woman. "Louis is a fine name for a pig."

She gave a slim smile. "Truffle hog."

Ollie pretended to understand what a truffle was by nodding his head, then hobbled outside with Duchess tucked into his arm. The lieutenant would be pissed, maybe even try and shoot him. But he didn't care. He only wanted to return Susan's pigeon. And with each wasted moment, he felt opportunity slipping away.

"You're going home," Ollie said.

Duchess tilted her head.

He stroked her back. "Fly high and stay clear of bullets."

The pigeon blinked.

He tossed Duchess into the air. She flapped her wings and soared above the barn. She circled the perimeter twice to gain her bearings, just like the pigeons had done during the trip to Clacton-on-Sea, then flew west. As she disappeared from sight, he heard Boar gag and cough. The anesthesia had worn off.

CHAPTER 28

EPPING, ENGLAND

Bertie's shoes shuffled over the disinfected floor of RAF Hospital Ely. Slowly, he stepped to Susan and cleared his throat. "No," he said. "It's not Oliver."

Susan exhaled. "Are you certain?"

He nodded, pulled a handkerchief from his pocket, and wiped his eyes. "He wore a wedding ring."

She swallowed, then searched for the right words. "Will he recover?"

Bertie shook his head.

A wave of shame washed over her. She had prayed, her silent request shouted to the heavens, for the misfortune to be with someone else. Anyone but Ollie. And her wish had been granted. Now a husband, perhaps even a father, was burned. Dying. She told herself that destiny's card had already been played and that her prayer had little to do with who was lying in that hospital bed. But she still wanted to cry. Before she did, she took Bertie's arm, and together they left the hospital.

Reaching the truck, Bertie opened the passenger door and said, "My dear, would you mind terribly if I drive?"

Susan noticed a weariness in his eyes. Normally, she'd insist on driving. His legs didn't need the extra stress. But she didn't argue, sensing her grandfather needed to distract himself from what he'd seen at RAF Hospital Ely. So she slid into the passenger seat, tucked her skirt under her legs, and shut the door. Through the windshield, she watched him labor around the truck and get into the driver's seat.

Bertie's hand trembled as he tried to insert the key into the ignition. The tip scratched the insert, but never found its destination.

"I believe the key is swollen," Bertie said. "Like my knees."

Susan steadied his hand.

Bertie slipped the key into the ignition and started the engine. "Thank you, my dear."

Susan took one last glance at RAF Hospital Ely and wished she hadn't. Two orderlies emerged from the side of the building carrying something wrapped in what looked to be a soiled mattress cover. A woman wailed, causing the hairs to stand up on the back of Susan's neck. And it was then that she noticed the line of funeral cars. Family members gathering on the lawn watched with somber eyes as the orderlies placed the body into a hearse. It appeared to Susan that the entire left wing of the hospital was being used as a morgue. Her hands trembled. A hospital was supposed to be a place of hope. A place of healing. But not today. Or tomorrow. Not while bombs were still falling. As the truck pulled away, she closed her eyes and hoped she'd never see a hospital again.

Susan didn't speak for much of the drive home, distracting herself by watching Bertie shift gears and maneuver the truck around gaping pits in the road. The maintenance crews had enlisted and were now shooting bullets instead of filling potholes, and the roadways were quickly becoming a crumbled mess.

She noticed an abandoned vehicle left on the berm with its doors wide open and thought of Ollie. "Where can he be?" she asked, cracking open her window. Cold air filled the cabin.

Bertie sighed. "Perhaps he went home."

Susan looked at him.

"It's not his war."

"Do you really believe that?"

Bertie scratched the whiskers on his chin.

"Something happened," she said. "He'd never desert us."

Bertie nodded, then adjusted his hands on the steering wheel.

She wondered where Ollie could be. As a civilian or, more precisely, a foreigner, he wouldn't have been permitted to remain on North Weald Airfield. And it'd be difficult not to draw attention with an American accent. It was as if he had vanished, like a down feather in the wind.

Part of her wished Bertie was right. If he had deserted and left for home, maybe he'd be safe, away from the rationing, bombs, and death. But the selfish part of her wanted him by her side. Her pigeons had gone to war. London was being destroyed by the Luftwaffe. Inevitably, the Germans would invade. More than anything, she needed him. She longed for his support and affection. He'd given her hope. And during the darkest of days, he'd stirred her heart.

As they drove through Epping, she closed her eyes, trying to avoid catching a glimpse of St. Margaret's Hospital. She couldn't bear the sight of another expectant mother dug out of the debris at Sprigg's Oak Maternity Home.

The tires rolled over large ruts. Susan pressed her cheek against the window and looked up. The clouds were thick and strewn with streaks of navy—a sign of approaching winter. High above, she saw a speck. She strained to focus. A bird. The unique stroke of its wings made her shoot up in her seat. She quickly cranked down the window.

"What's wrong?" Bertie asked.

Susan pointed. "Pigeon."

He looked up through the windshield. "Duchess?"

Susan stuck her head out the window. Cold wind blasted her

face. The pigeon was too high to see the colors, but she knew the effortless grace of Duchess's flight, and this pigeon was flapping its wings too fast.

"No," she said, pushing hair from her eyes.

"One of ours?" He squinted.

She leaned farther out the window. The pigeon veered to the west. Her heart raced. "I think so."

Bertie pulled Susan to her seat and slammed the accelerator to the floor.

"There!" Susan pointed. "It's headed home!"

Bertie downshifted and rounded a turn. The bald tires squealed. The truck gathered speed. The engine howled. Pistons banged against their casings. He drove like a young British racer trying to qualify for a grand prix.

Gusting wind unraveled the bun from Susan's hair. She pushed flying strands from her face and struggled to spot the pigeon.

Making little effort to slow down, Bertie spun the truck into their dirt lane. They bounced from a rut and almost hit their heads on the roof of the cabin. Only then did he resort to using the brake. The tires splashed through puddles, spraying mud onto the windshield. Bertie flipped on the wipers. The worn blades did nothing but spread brown goop. It was like looking through a fishbowl filled with cake batter. So they drove the rest of the way with their heads stuck out the side windows.

A soldier stationed on the farm for the mission emerged from his tent. As he zipped up his jacket, the pigeon shot over a horn-beam tree.

Bertie braked hard, grunting from the strain to his knees. The truck slid to a stop. Susan flung open her door.

Another soldier emerged from the tent, and as he did, the pigeon fluttered to a loft. It paused on the landing for a moment, as if to catch its breath, then waddled inside, triggering the alarm that had been installed.

A buzzer sounded. The soldiers jerked. They looked to the tent.

Susan ran to the loft.

A soldier poked his head inside the tent. The alarm buzzed. "Loft one!"

Susan was the first to reach the loft, having had a good head start on the soldiers. She threw open the door, and high above on the landing stood a pigeon. It jutted its head, scanning the emptied cubbies. The pigeon blinked and then fluttered to the floor.

Susan plucked the pigeon from the ground and cradled it. She felt its pulse against her hands. The bird cooed. Susan's eyes watered. "You made it."

The door opened, and a soldier approached her. "You'll need to step aside, miss," he said, extending his hands.

Susan noticed the Bakelite canister attached to the pigeon's leg. She kissed the bird on the head, then reluctantly handed it to the soldier.

The second soldier appeared in the doorway, followed by Bertie, out of breath and pressing his hands to his knees.

Susan watched the soldier place the pigeon on the floor, then carefully remove the canister from its leg. He held up the Bakelite canister, exposing the outline of a note inside. Instead of unscrewing the top, he quickly handed the canister to his partner.

"You'll need to leave, miss," the soldier said.

Susan looked at the pigeon on the floor. "It needs food and water."

"Finish your duty, then stay clear of the lofts," the soldier said.

Susan nodded, then sprinkled seed into the feeding tray and refilled a water bowl. The loft was barren. Instead of a flock of pigeons parading at her feet, a solitary bird, one that had made a journey all the way from France, pecked at the feeding tray. As she stood beside the grain barrel, a buzz came from the tent. She looked to the landing. Another pigeon waddled through the metal curtain.

"Bloody hell," the soldier said.

Susan turned to Bertie.

He smiled. Crow's-feet formed at the corners of his eyes.

Susan took a seat on the porch with her grandfather. For the remainder of the afternoon, they watched the return of their pigeons. Over the next hour, a total of seven pigeons returned. The following hour, twelve. The hour after that, sixteen. Each time a pigeon would appear on the horizon, Bertie would stand on shaky knees, point a flabby arm, and shout, "There's another!" Soon after, the returning pigeon would land and enter the loft, setting off the alarm. The place buzzed like a beehive.

"Those bells make a beautiful racket," Bertie said.

Susan nodded and watched another pigeon appear on the horizon.

A stream of military vehicles, acting as couriers, came through the farm. The stationed soldiers gave the couriers the canisters, which they locked into metal boxes. The couriers ran the boxes to their vehicles and sped off. They could have waited to collect more arriving messages, but it was obvious to Susan that the couriers had orders to transport the intelligence immediately upon arrival. She suspected that the messages were not going to North Weald Airfield. They were likely going to London, to the heart of British military command.

By sunset, a total of forty-eight pigeons had returned. Four hundred and fifty-two were missing. Before going inside to prepare for the blackout, Susan watched an orange sun sink below the birch trees. She imagined the Luftwaffe was already in flight, the bellies of their bombers filled with tons of explosives, preparing to destroy what was left of London. Then they'd invade. She prayed that one of the returning pigeons could provide something, anything that could give Britain an edge to survive.

"We'll know when you're coming, you ruddy Nazis," Bertie said, shaking his fist in the air. "And we'll be ready for you."

A soldier, handing over a canister to a courier, overheard Bertie's comment and said, "Jolly good work, sir."

Bertie pointed to Susan. "You can thank my granddaughter. She's the brains behind the mission."

The soldier tipped his cap. "Congratulations, miss."

Susan forced a smile. Part of her was relieved that the pigeons were returning. But only a fraction of the flock had made it back. And Ollie and Duchess were missing. Soon the sirens would howl. Bombs would fall. She feared she would never see them again.

Chapter 29

Epping, England

The attack on London began shortly after dark. The couriers had left when the flow of returning pigeons trickled to a stop. But the two soldiers remained, hunkered into their tent and likely to find their way to Bertie's homemade bomb shelter if another air raid struck Epping.

Susan made a dinner of stale rationed bread. She toasted it, sliced it in quarters, even slathered it with the last of the gooseberry jam, but it still tasted like the flour had been replaced with sawdust. As usual, Bertie didn't mind, even complimenting her on the weak tea that had been brewed so many times it barely colored the water. She spent the evening talking to him about the returning pigeons, a brief period of light in what felt like endless days of despair. All the while, her heart and mind were on Ollie.

As the tremor of bomb blasts escalated, she washed the dishes and then helped Bertie onto his chair. He fell asleep with his swollen knees propped on a stool. She covered him with a quilt, blew out the candle, and went off to bed, shutting out the thought that she might never see him climb the stairs again.

Susan layered mounds of pillows over her head, even packed

her ears with cotton from a bottle of Bertie's aspirin, but couldn't shut out the rumble of explosions. The bombing was relentless. The Luftwaffe seemed to have upped their arsenal, the unnerving silence between explosions less frequent. There were rumors that 30,000 bombs had dropped on London in a single night. Nazi propaganda. If true, German factories were pumping out massive amounts of weaponry. There would need to be miles of assembly lines filling shells with explosives, not to mention ruthless conditioning of Luftwaffe pilots. After all, what human, unless brainwashed, would knowingly drop bombs on women and children? She hoped the British would never resort to such atrocities, no matter how bad things got.

As Susan rolled over in bed, the plug slipped from her ear. She slid her hand under her pillow, searching for the missing cotton, and heard it.

Peck.

She shot up, dug out the remaining plug from her ear, and looked toward the window. The blackout curtain had turned her room into a sightless void, like she had been dropped into an inkwell. Her hands trembled. She waited. Nothing. Only the echo of bombs. *I must be going mad*, she thought, lowering her head to her pillow.

Peck.

Her heart skipped.

Peck . . . peck.

Susan threw off the covers and ran to the window.

Peck . . . peck . . . peck.

She ripped back the curtain and looked outside. A bomb flash lit up the sky, illuminating the fluorescent feathers of an unmistakable pigeon.

"Duchess!"

The bird angled its head, then tapped the glass with its beak.

Peck . . . peck.

Susan struggled with the latch, chipping two fingernails, then threw open the window. Another flash lit up the sky. And there she was. Duchess. Perched on the ledge with her head tilted, appearing surprised at how long it had taken Susan to open the window.

Susan plucked Duchess from the ledge and squeezed the pigeon to her chest. "Duchess! Where have you been?"

The pigeon cooed.

"Susan," Bertie called. "Are you all right, my dear?"

Susan sprinted from her room. Her shoulder bumped the wall. She searched for the banister. "It's Duchess! She's come home!"

"Good Lord!"

Susan scrambled down the stairs. As she adjusted Duchess in her hands, she noticed the Bakelite canister attached to the pigeon's leg and almost tripped. She tucked Duchess into her arm, then descended the remaining steps using the handrail. She stepped into the blackened living room and heard the cracking of Bertie's joints as he stood from his chair.

Bertie struck a match, lit a candle, and hobbled to Susan. A soft glow covered the room.

Duchess blinked.

"By George," Bertie said, rubbing his eyes. "It is Duchess."

Susan kissed her pigeon on the head.

"Where've you been?" Bertie stroked the pigeon with his finger.

Susan lifted Duchess, exposing the red canister.

"Bloody hell." He looked at Susan. "Is there a message?"

"I didn't check."

Bertie gently clasped Duchess's leg. With his thumbnail, he unclipped the metal band. He held the canister to his ear and shook it.

"Anything?" She stroked Duchess.

He nodded, then began to unscrew the top.

"We mustn't." She touched Bertie's hand. "We're not permitted."

Bertie looked at her. "This is your pigeon. She wasn't part of the mission. And since it appears our military snatched her away,

I believe that permits us to have a wee look." He pointed to the table next to his chair. "My dear, could you get my eyeglasses?"

Susan hesitated, then retrieved his eyeglasses.

Bertie slipped on his glasses, unscrewed the canister cap, and slid a note into his hand. With arthritic fingers, he carefully unrolled the paper. As he scanned the writing, his eyes widened.

"What does it say?"

He took a deep breath, exhaled, and handed her the paper.

Susan placed Duchess on the table and held up the note. She expected to see something written in French, or perhaps an attempt at English. But it was neither.

```
ALKFQ  NPTMI  HLCXP  QNMVX  PUTXJ  GQZKE
HIQAN  SYAEF  AMVXQ  PLWTR  OSJWL  IWLNF
QLKDF  SLIEF  SOEVC  PLEFV  AMEFL  YELFP
JSPFD  SKEAF  RHBVC  WYGHI  OPAEF  HUVQA
URPXY  QOSDM  OPZQR  TWNVI  BZITE  OPNCT
IGBVM  WPORL  QBVXI  OLKSE  JGBMV  PIXSW
TZCOP  VQWEM  KWLKV  YSLEK  OPAVE  CXPTY
FJGLE  KPQCX  MBKSQ  PEOJS  TYAWM  ZYRTP
```

Susan struggled to breathe. Her legs quivered. She looked up to see her grandfather hobbling to the bookshelf.

Bertie dug through the shelves. He flipped book after book to the floor. The pile grew. He stopped when he reached a copy of *Rob Roy* by Sir Walter Scott. Behind it, pressed against the back of the bookshelf, he retrieved a small leather-bound book. He worked his way over to Susan.

She took the book, wiping a layer of dust from a companion copy of her father's artillery codebook. She glanced at the note. Garbled codes. It was if she were eight years old, preparing to decipher one of Bertie's playful messages, which had sent her rummaging through the cottage in search of a hidden piece of caramel. But this wasn't a game. And she was no longer a child. Besides her and Bertie, there was only one other person who had seen her father's codebook. Deep down, she knew something dreadful was on that piece of paper.

They sat at the kitchen table. Duchess pecked at a piece of bread crust, then dipped her beak into a teacup filled with water. Susan shuddered as she opened the codebook.

Bertie leaned over her shoulder. "It's all right, my dear."

Susan flipped pages and scribbled onto the stationery. Barely through the first sentence, she stopped and reread the words. Her heart pounded. She dropped the pencil.

"What is it?" Bertie said.

"It's from him."

"Who?"

"Ollie."

Bertie clasped the table. "Jesus wept!"

Susan picked up the pencil and pressed it to the paper. The tip snapped. She continued writing with the broken piece of lead rather than take time to sharpen it. As she continued to decipher codes, her brief sense of relief turned to despair. Her hands shook as she examined the message. "It can't be," she said.

"What's it say?" Bertie asked.

Susan closed the codebook. She took a moment to gather her courage, then read the message to her grandfather.

> Susan,
> Duchess was taken.

Susan looked up to see her pigeon waddle across the table. She felt her grandfather place his arm over her shoulder. She wiped her eyes and continued reading.

> I attempted to retrieve her, but we were attacked. The plane scrambled, with Duchess and me onboard. Mission complete. Plane shot down in France.

Her hands trembled. She swallowed, preparing herself to read further.

> *Gunner and copilot killed. Flight Lieutenant Boar and I are hiding. Wehrmacht everywhere. Luftwaffe using nearby airfield. I'll try to send more intelligence, if I find another pigeon.*
>
> *Ollie*
>
> *P.S. Your pigeons were brave. Wish I could have been with you to see them return.*

A warm drop rolled down Susan's cheek. She made no effort to wipe it away.

"He's alive, my dear."

Duchess waddled to Susan.

"Can he make it back?" She caressed Duchess and sniffed back tears.

"He bloody well made it to France. He'll bloody well make it home." Bertie stood and peeked behind the blackout curtains. "Luftwaffe is gone. Go to the lofts and retrieve some paper from the dropping cages."

Susan looked at him.

"Quickly, before the soldiers wake."

Susan put on her wool winter coat, covering all but the lower fringes of her nightgown, and threw on a pair of wellies. She crept to a loft and collected a piece of paper from an unused cage. Returning inside, she saw Bertie searching through a cabinet to retrieve a pencil sharpener.

She handed him the paper.

Bertie placed the paper on the table and twisted the pencil into the sharpener. Woodchips and lead dust coated the table.

"What are you going to do?"

"Rewrite the message." He blew on the pencil tip and pressed it to the paper.

"We must turn this over to the RAF," Susan said.

Bertie stopped. "The bloody RAF. Bollocks. How are we to win the war with such incompetence? If they hadn't placed Duchess on a plane, Ollie would be with us right now."

Bertie's words stung Susan. A wave of guilt followed. "I should have kept Duchess with me."

"It wasn't your fault." He reached and held her hand. "Our military will get their intelligence. But they will not see what is meant for you."

Susan watched Bertie carefully rewrite the message, much shorter than the one she had deciphered, and finished by signing, Flight Lieutenant Clyde Boar, RAF.

"Grandfather!"

Bertie placed his pencil on the table. "Our Oliver from Maine has had enough trouble with the RAF. Being viewed as a stowaway could create trouble for him when he returns." He clasped her hands. "And he *will* return, my dear."

Susan squeezed his fingers.

"Trust me," he said.

"Very well."

Bertie rolled up his note, slid it into the canister, and screwed on the top. "Let's wake the soldiers."

Susan followed Bertie outside and almost ran into him when he suddenly stopped.

"God help us," he said.

His words sent shivers up her spine. She looked toward the London skyline. In the ashen haze of daybreak, the fires gave the appearance of a monstrous sun rising over the city.

She lowered her head, regretting that she had chosen to look up, and helped Bertie down the porch steps. At this hour, the world was at its worst. After waves of sirens, whistles, and explosions, the sudden silence was unnerving. Even the birds, stunned by the bombardment, had delayed their chirping. She squeezed her grandfather's arm and pressed forward.

As they approached the tent, a soldier stepped outside and zipped up his jacket.

"We have something for you," Bertie said.

The soldier blew on his hands, then rubbed them together.

Bertie handed him the canister. "A pigeon returned to our cottage."

The soldier glanced to the fires in London, then turned his attention to Bertie. "Why didn't it return to the lofts?"

Bertie shrugged.

"Where's the pigeon?" the soldier asked.

Susan stepped forward and showed him Duchess. The pigeon tucked its head under its wing.

"If another bird returns to the house, bring it directly to us," the soldier said. "Understood?"

Bertie and Susan nodded.

The soldier slipped the canister inside his jacket and returned to the tent.

Susan cradled Duchess and walked with Bertie toward the lofts. "Are you sure we did the right thing?"

"Absolutely, my dear." He stroked Duchess's head with a finger. "She must be hungry. Perhaps you could feed the pigeons early. I'm sure the others will be happy to see her."

Susan nodded and opened the loft door. The squeak of the hinge caused the pigeons to flutter from their cubbies. She gently tossed Duchess toward her favorite perch, a beam above the grain barrel.

Duchess flapped her wings. Instead of landing on her perch, she swooped around.

Susan felt the breeze from Duchess's wings across her face. As the spring door was about to close, Duchess darted outside. The door slammed shut.

She threw open the door and ran outside. Looking up, she watched Duchess soar above a hornbeam tree.

"Duchess!" she shouted.

Bertie turned, just shy of reaching the cottage. The soldiers sprang from their tent.

Susan watched Duchess circle high over Epping Forest. As the pigeon looped around the perimeter for a second time, Susan's heart skipped a beat. *She's gaining her bearings, like she's preparing to fly home. But she's already home!*

The pigeon finished her circumference and flew east.

"No!" Susan ran across the yard. She tripped and fell, then struggled to her feet. "Duchess!"

The pigeon continued her flight.

Susan fell to her knees. Her muscles turned weak. Helplessly, she watched Duchess fly toward the English Channel, until her pigeon disappeared from sight.

CHAPTER 30

AIRAINES, FRANCE

Ollie stepped into the cottage and saw Flight Lieutenant Boar sitting on the floor, lightly touching the gauze over his eyes. Madeleine, standing over Boar, pushed away her truffle hog as he insistently sniffed at the lieutenant's boots.

The creak of Ollie's weight on the floorboards caused Boar to raise his head. "Did the doctor fix my eyes?"

Ollie recalled the sickening scent of anesthetic, the doctor manipulating the severed cornea with a pair of tweezers. A brownish discharge now blotched the lieutenant's bandages. "Yes," Ollie said.

Boar exhaled, then picked at the tape on his bandage.

Madeleine pushed Boar's hand away. "No. Ten days."

Boar dropped his hand and licked his lips, crusted with dried saliva.

Madeleine placed her hog outside, then poured a glass of water from a ceramic pitcher. "Drink," she said, placing the glass to Boar's lips.

Boar gulped the water, spilling much of it down his flight jacket.

"Take him to the barn, then come back," Madeleine said. "We've got work to do."

Ollie helped the lieutenant to his feet and guided him to the barn. The lieutenant's legs were still weak from the anesthesia, causing Ollie to support much of the man's weight. Ollie's arm joggled inside his sling, no matter how hard he tried to isolate his lifting, sending hot flares into his shoulder socket. The additional stress of Boar's weight made his swollen ankle throb. He desperately wanted to rest but feared that a Wehrmacht platoon could arrive at any moment and spot him in the open. So he buried his pain and pressed on.

Reaching the barn, he placed Boar on the ground and cleared away an area of molded feed potatoes. The place reeked of manure and rotting vegetables. Last night, he had paid little attention to the smell, distracted by the overwhelming pain in his shoulder, dislocated like a chicken wing that had been snapped by a butcher. He noticed that Boar, still groggy, didn't seem to mind the stench. The lieutenant rested his hand on his holstered pistol, leaned back, and immediately fell asleep.

As Ollie returned to the house, he saw Louis nestled beside a shrub, his head lowered on his front hooves. Ollie glanced around the farm to make certain there were no approaching vehicles, then reached down and petted the hog on the head. Louis twitched his tail and snorted.

"You can come in now," Madeleine said, standing in the doorway.

Ollie thought the woman was speaking to him, until the hog sprang up and trotted inside. Its hooves tapped across the wood floor.

"He's smart," Ollie said, entering the cottage. "I've never seen a tuffle hog before."

Madeleine laughed and produced a cigarette from her pocket. "Truffle."

"Truffle?"

"You don't know what a truffle is, do you?"

Ollie noticed a hoarseness in her throat, as if years of smoke over her vocal cords had lowered her voice a full octave. "No," he said.

Madeleine sucked on her cigarette. Wrinkled skin stretched over her sharp cheekbones. "I'll teach you about truffles," she said, exhaling smoke. "But first, we have work to do." She retrieved a wooden toolbox from a doorless cabinet, concealed by curtains made from a burlap bag. She placed the box on the counter and retrieved a hammer and a small pry bar. "Move the table."

Ollie slid the table to the side of the room. His shoulder ached.

"Remove them." Madeleine tapped her foot on a floorboard. "But don't scar the wood."

Ollie looked at her, suddenly realizing what they were about to do. "Are you sure you want to do this?"

Madeleine took a deep drag on her cigarette, then exhaled. "The Wehrmacht stop here. One of their officers is quite fond of requisitioning my truffles." She scratched her hog behind the ears. "They'd find you if they searched the barn."

Ollie took the hammer and pry bar, then hesitated. "If we stay in the barn and we're caught, you could pretend that you didn't know we were there."

"Wouldn't matter. They'd shoot me either way. When the Germans invaded, there were British soldiers that didn't make it out of Dunkirk. They hid in basements, attics, and barns. Many were captured. French residents were shot, regardless if they knew the soldiers were there." Ashes dropped from her cigarette. "The Nazis have no tolerance for those in the company of their enemy."

Guilt swelled in Ollie's head. He hated placing this woman at risk. But considering his physical condition, he didn't have much choice.

She looked at him. Dark bags sagged under her eyes. "The Nazis have pillaged our country. They've killed most of our soldiers, and the ones lucky enough to only be captured were sent away to prison camps. We're starving, waiting in endless lines for morsels of bread while they eat our meat, drink our wine. Even our police have become cowards, preferring to collaborate rather than fight." She tapped out her cigarette in a clay ashtray and took another from her pocket. "Nazi flags hang from our streets, even our schools."

Ollie adjusted the sling around his neck. The air turned thick. He couldn't imagine what Madeleine must be going through. A prisoner in her own country.

Madeleine pulled up the sleeves of her sweater, exposing her bony wrists, and lit her cigarette. "You remind me of my twin boys, Marius and Marcel."

"How's that?" Ollie asked.

"Committed to fight for a belief, despite the cost." Smoke rose from her cigarette and spread over the ceiling. "They were good boys."

Ollie pushed aside the tools and took a seat next to Madeleine.

"Marius liked to read and dreamed of becoming a professor. Those are his books," she said, pointing to a bookcase.

Ollie eyed the rows of books, looking out of place in the rustic cottage, like fine china on a picnic table.

"Don't look so surprised," Madeleine said.

"I'm not surprised."

She tapped him lightly on his hand. "Yes, you are."

"Well, maybe a little."

The woman smiled. "My family was well educated. But we chose a simpler life." She stood and retrieved a photo from the bookcase. "Marcel wanted to be a truffle hunter like Guillaume, his father. These were my boys," she said, handing Ollie the photo.

Ollie looked at the picture of two young boys wearing pressed school uniforms. The identical twins were mirror images of each other. Standing beside the boys, a man and woman. "Is this you, Madeleine?"

"Yes." She tucked gray hairs behind her ear. "I was once beautiful."

"You're still lovely," Ollie said.

"Sweet boy," she said, staring at the photo. "I regret I have few pictures to show you. They were handsome, strong, and, most of all, they were gentlemen." She closed her eyes. "Marius and Marcel were killed in battle."

"I'm so sorry," Ollie said, sympathetically.

She nodded, returned the photo to its spot on the bookcase, and then took a seat. "My boys were born on the same day; they died on the same day. Together." She inhaled on her cigarette and glanced at her fingernails, stained brown with nicotine. "It was hard to move on, especially for Guillaume. He would have gone off to war, despite being too old to fight, if I would have let him."

Ollie noticed a man's hat hanging on a rack near the front door.

"Guillaume's," Madeleine said.

"Where is he?" Ollie asked.

She took a deep breath and exhaled. "Guillaume was delivering truffles in Arras when the Germans invaded. He hasn't returned home."

Ollie noticed a gloss in the woman's eyes. The lines in her face appeared deeper.

"My heart still believes that Guillaume will someday walk through that door. But my head thinks otherwise." She coughed, then wiped her eyes with the back of her hand. "There's a rumor that hundreds of the French Resistance have been executed in Arras. Despite being an old man, I fear my husband would have tried to fight."

Louis stood and walked to Madeleine's side. The hog nuzzled her leg. She scratched him behind the ears. "Until Guillaume comes home, we'll hunt truffles. Yes, Louis?"

The hog snorted.

She sniffed, wiped her nose with her sleeve, and changed the subject. "So, Ollie, why would an American be on an RAF plane? Has the United States joined the war?"

"As far as I know, the United States plans to remain neutral," he said.

"Then how did you end up here?"

"It's a long story."

"I've got time." Madeleine tapped the floor with her shoe. "You can tell me while you pry up those boards."

Ollie kneeled and began work on the floorboards, but he quickly realized it would be tough to extract nails using only one arm. In fact, it was damn near impossible to slide the claw of the pry bar under the nail heads. Chipping out chunks of wood could expose the nails, but marring the boards was not an option. So Madeleine helped by holding the pry bar in place as he tapped it with the hammer. It worked. Although slow and tedious, the claw wedged under the nail head. He pried, causing the board to screech. He tried to keep one side of his body steady, but it was of no use. Pain flared into his shoulder socket. He managed to loosen two nails before having to take a break.

"Hurt?" Madeleine asked.

Ollie nodded and leaned against the wall. He was sweating, despite the temperature in the cottage being cold enough to store meat.

The sound of a motorcar caused Madeleine to glance out the window. She squeezed the crowbar. The hum of the engine faded as the vehicle passed.

"Best we get this finished," Ollie said, picking up the hammer.

For the afternoon, they worked on removing floorboards. To distract himself from the pangs radiating into his shoulder, he told Madeleine about his family. His journey to Britain. And his dream to fly for the RAF, only to end up working on a mission for the National Pigeon Service. But most of all he talked about Susan, and for the first time since plummeting into German-occupied France, he didn't notice the pain.

"Pigeons are smart, like Louis," Ollie said, placing a board to the side. "Susan's a remarkable trainer. She's gonna help us win the war."

Madeleine smiled and adjusted the cigarette in her mouth.

Ollie removed the last board, making a three-foot-diameter opening, big enough for him to crawl through. He stuck his head into the hole. A dirt floor. Cobwebs. The smell of earth and stagnant air. The cottage, or at least the area under the kitchen, had been built without a basement. It was a simple cobblestone foundation. No more than two feet of space lay between the earth and floorboards.

With pieces of canvas that Madeleine retrieved from a shed, Ollie lined the floor of the crawl space. He replaced the boards, like pieces of a puzzle, and noticed the glaring holes left by the missing nails. So he removed the nail heads with a pair of thick pruning shears, then glued them over the holes using paste they made from flour and water. It had taken them all day. Except for a few scratches, the loose boards were almost unnoticeable.

As Ollie admired their work, he heard a sizzle. The scent of sautéing onions. His mouth watered. He made his way over to Madeleine, hovering over a wood-fired stove, stirring the contents of an iron skillet with a wooden spoon.

Madeleine tossed in a handful of limp carrots, including the withered tops. "Hungry?"

"Yes," Ollie said. The aroma of caramelized onions was intoxicating. He couldn't recall the last time he had eaten.

"Get your friend," she said, pointing her spoon.

Ollie found the lieutenant just as he had left him. Sleeping. It took several attempts to wake him, and he had to resort to kicking his boots.

Boar slowly sat up and rubbed the stubble on his jowl. "How long was I out?"

"All day," Ollie said.

"You gave me too much anesthesia, Yank." He took a few deep breaths.

Ollie gave the lieutenant a moment to get to his feet, then led him into the cottage, where Madeleine was spooning browned vegetables onto plates. He helped Boar into a chair as Madeleine set the table. A buttery scent of steaming vegetables filled Ollie's nose. His belly gurgled.

Madeleine placed a fork in the lieutenant's hand.

Boar blindly stabbed at his plate. Metal tines clicked against the pottery. After forking a hunk of carrot, he stuck it in his mouth, chewed, then gagged. He spit the food into his palm and placed it on the side of his plate. "Take me back to the barn, Yank." Boar lowered his head onto the table. "I need to rest."

"We're sleeping inside," Ollie said, standing up from the table.

Ollie removed the floorboards and helped Boar into the hole. The lieutenant hunkered into the crawl space, like a bear entering a cave for hibernation.

When Ollie returned to the table, Madeleine leaned over his plate and rubbed something over a grate. Black snow dusted his meal.

"May need a little something," Madeleine said.

"Truffles?"

She nodded.

Ollie didn't know if it was the truffles, or if it was because he hadn't eaten in the past two days, but this simple meal of onions and withered carrots was extraordinary. The truffle, although ugly, like a shriveled potato, gave a slightly garlicky and earthy taste to the food. It was one of the best meals he could remember. The last time he had tasted something this good was when he had eaten Susan's soup, laced with shellfish that had sent him running to the loo. He felt a tug at the corners of his mouth and realized he was smiling.

"You like, yes?" Madeleine asked.

"Yes," Ollie said. He ate his food, then finished it off with a glass of cold water. He looked over at the hog, sleeping in the corner of the room. "Nice work, Louis."

The hog twitched its ears but continued sleeping.

Madeleine grinned, then continued eating her meal.

Ollie sat with Madeleine until she finished eating, realizing how rude he had been to devour his food so quickly. He helped her clean the table, then took Louis out to the barn for the night. He was surprised that the hog followed him, but the animal obviously knew it was dinnertime. Per Madeleine's request, he tossed a handful of potatoes into the hog's trough. The potatoes, if one could call them that, were in nasty condition: molded black, covered in hairy sprouts, and wriggling with grubs. By all accounts, the potatoes were spoiled. Inedible. But Ollie quickly found out that Louis was not a tuber connoisseur. The hog ate his potatoes, meaty grubs and all, then flopped on his side to rest. Ollie glanced at the empty trough and wondered what the coming winter would do to the French. *Would they starve? Or resort to eating rotten potatoes? Grubs? Or worse?* He shook the thought from his mind and left the barn.

When he returned, Madeleine lit a candle and closed the drapes. She placed two tattered woolen blankets into the hiding place. Ollie lowered himself into the hole in the floor, careful not to step on the lieutenant. He lay down, feeling thankful to have a piece of canvas under his back, and watched Madeleine place the boards over them. Board by board, the hole above him grew smaller.

He looked up through the slit in the floor. "Madeleine," he said.

"*Oui?*"

"Thank you."

The woman nodded. She lowered the last board and sealed the hole.

Everything went black. Wood scraped as Madeleine slid the table above him. Her footsteps faded. Then silence. If it weren't for the snores of an RAF lieutenant, he would have believed he had been sealed inside a coffin.

He balled up the blanket and used it to elevate his arm. He tried to sleep but couldn't rest, despite his exhaustion. It wasn't the constant ache in his shoulder nor the throb in his ankle each time he moved his toes. It was regret. His mind roiled with mistakes and missed opportunities. *Why did I leave Epping? How could I have gotten stuck in a Blenheim? Will I ever see Susan again? Why didn't I say more?*

He thought of Susan. The enchanting resonance of her voice. The way her sandy-blond hair gracefully rested on her shoulders. The subtle lavender scent of her perfume. How his skin tingled when she leaned over him to pour tea. The silhouette of her delicate hands, cast by candlelight as she knitted Bertie a sweater. Her passion for saving Britain, and her belief that pigeons could win the war. He adored her. Missed her. *God, I wish things could have been different*, he thought.

Time was running out. A day, perhaps a week. He couldn't live under the floorboards forever. They'd have to come out, and when they did, the Nazis would eventually find them. There was no future. Only the past and present. So he spent the night reliving his brief time with Susan, over and over again, until he could no longer keep his eyes open.

CHAPTER 31

AIRAINES, FRANCE

A tickling on Ollie's neck caused him to stir. He took a deep breath, taking in the scent of damp soil and old wood. He opened his eyes, but everything remained black. *Is it night? Morning?*

Something brushed his clavicle. Groggy, he reached to scratch under his collar and touched something. Long. Thin. Hairy. Adrenaline rushed into his body. He tried to grab it, but whatever it was quickly scuttled under his shirt. He jerked, bumping his head on a floor joist.

"Christ, Yank!" Boar said, waking up. "What the bloody hell are you doing?"

"Bug," Ollie said, reaching into his shirt.

Boar kicked Ollie's leg. "Go back to sleep."

The bug scurried toward Ollie's armpit. Shivers shot up his spine. Hundreds, perhaps thousands, of hairlike legs crept over his skin. A centipede? Millipede? He slid his hand under his injured arm, bit his lip to shield back the pain that was now flaring into his shoulder socket, and pulled out the bristly intruder. It wriggled in his hand, like a worm about to be set on a fishing hook. Bugs, especially ones he couldn't see, gave him the willies.

He tossed it and immediately realized he had thrown it in the wrong direction when he heard what sounded like the lieutenant having a seizure.

"Wanker!" Boar brushed over his flight suit as if he were covered in bees.

Ollie heard him flick something from his clothes, the ping of the bug landing somewhere in the bowels of the crawl space.

Boar gave Ollie a kick to the shin. "I should have shot you back in the field."

Ollie elbowed the lieutenant in the ribs. "I'm all you got."

"That's what I'm afraid of."

Ollie had expected the lieutenant to pull out his pistol, or at the very least throw another punch. After all, the anesthetic had worn off. Other than the lieutenant's eyes, Boar was in better physical shape. Ollie, on the other hand, was a wreck. In the tight confinement of the crawl space, the lieutenant could have beaten the hell out of him if he had wanted to. The only thing stopping Boar, Ollie believed, was that he couldn't see. And that maybe the lieutenant temporarily needed him. Unfortunately, considering Ollie's lack of military training or knowledge of escape routes, he needed the lieutenant, too. As the sting in his shin faded, it suddenly occurred to him that Boar might not be the fearless RAF pilot he thought he was. After all, the man was more afraid of bugs than he was—a thought that made Ollie chuckle.

"What's so funny?" Boar asked.

"You." Ollie gave another chuckle.

"You're a bloody lunatic, Yank."

Ollie's laugh faded, and he suddenly realized that if it were not for his choices—or, more accurately, countless errors in judgment—he could have been waking up in a neutral country. Instead, he was hunkered in a hole in German-occupied France with an ill-tempered lieutenant. "You may be right," he said.

Ollie heard the scraping of wood above him as the table

inched over the floor. A moment later, Madeleine removed the boards. Sunlight flooded the hole. He squinted and shielded his eyes.

"Too loud," Madeleine said. "Do you want the Wehrmacht to find you?"

As Ollie's eyes adjusted, he saw Louis's pink snout. The hog's nostrils twitched as he sniffed over the hole. Ollie reached up and scratched the hog's chin.

Louis grunted.

"What time is it?" Ollie asked.

"It's morning," Madeleine said. She struck a match and lit a cigarette.

Ollie crawled out of the hole, then carefully adjusted the sling holding his arm. He rubbed his fingers, which had turned cold from lack of circulation.

Boar stood, then took a seat on the floor, his legs dangling into the crawl space. He rubbed the bandages over his eyes and sniffed. "Do you have another cigarette?"

Madeleine blew smoke threw her nostrils, then gave her cigarette to Boar.

Ollie sat patiently as Madeleine and Boar smoked, passing the cigarette back and forth until a thin haze filled the cottage. He spent the time by scratching Louis behind the ears.

Madeleine tapped out the cigarette in a clay ashtray, filled with cindered remnants of hand-rolled paper. She stepped to the kitchen and prepared breakfast—grayish bread and yellowish coffee.

Sitting at the table, Ollie bit into the hardened bread and almost cracked a tooth. He looked at Boar, gnawing on his hunk of crust, like a dog chewing rawhide.

"*Tremper*." Madeleine shook her head, then dunked her bread into her coffee.

Ollie followed suit and sank his bread into the yellow mixture, a coffee brewed from what he believed to be roasted barley. The bread softened nicely but tasted like ground straw. He washed it down with the coffee, polluted with bits of gray matter. Despite the taste and texture of the bread, it felt good to have something warm in his belly. Sleeping on the ground had lowered his body temperature. He felt like a reptile in desperate need of the sun.

"Well," Madeleine said, lighting another cigarette. "What shall we do with you?"

"As soon as I can see, we'll leave," Boar said. He gulped his coffee, then set the cup on the table. "In the meantime, we'll get word to the RAF on where we are, assuming that bloody bird can fly across the Channel."

Ollie looked up from his empty cup and saw Madeleine staring at him. His mind raced. *Did Duchess make it home to Susan? Would Boar shoot me for releasing the pigeon?* Ollie gripped the table and said, "About the pigeon—"

"Would you like more coffee, Flight Lieutenant?" Madeleine interrupted.

Boar nodded.

Ollie appreciated Madeleine's attempt to delay the fact that he had released Duchess. But sooner or later, he'd have to tell the lieutenant. And when he did, he'd likely have hell to pay.

"Where will you go?" Madeleine asked, refilling Boar's cup. She placed the pot in the center of the table. Steam rose from the spout.

"I'll figure it out." Boar sipped his coffee.

Ollie looked at the lieutenant. In the air, Boar had no doubt been a fearless flying ace. But now he was grounded, without a squadron to lead into battle and, for the moment, blind. Strangely, the battered pilot appeared both formidable and harmless, like a king cobra with its fangs clipped.

"The only unoccupied area is *zone libre*, far to the south," Madeleine said. "Unless you plan to steal a plane or swim the Channel."

"Then we'll go to *zone libre*," Ollie said.

Boar rubbed the edge of his cup with his thumb. "Who's going to help us get there, the French Army?" He looked in Ollie's direction. "In case you haven't heard, they've been wiped out."

Ollie glanced at Madeleine. The woman's shoulders slumped. Her eyes turned glossy. Ollie's face turned hot. Before he could stop himself, he reached over the table and grabbed the lieutenant's jacket.

Boar jerked, but Ollie's grip held firm.

"Madeleine lost her sons in this war." Ollie loosened his grip, then lowered his hand. "And her husband has been missing since the invasion."

Boar straightened his jacket and looked in Madeleine's direction. "If I had known, Madeleine, I wouldn't have made such a remark." He gripped his pistol holster. "You touch me again, Yank, and you'll wish the Nazis had found you."

"Enough." Madeleine inhaled her cigarette and blew smoke over the table, creating a cloud barrier between Ollie and the lieutenant. "We have much planning to do, if you want any chance of returning home."

"Madeleine," Boar said, "with all due respect, there's little chance of us getting back to Britain. Once my eyes are healed, I plan to use my bullets on the Wehrmacht, assuming I don't use them on this Yank."

"You're of more use as a pilot to fight the Luftwaffe. Yes?"

"Perhaps." Boar drank the last of his coffee and looked in Madeleine's direction. "My condolences."

"*Merci*," she said.

Boar's words surprised Ollie. He had believed the pilot to be an insensitive bastard and wondered if the shake he had given him had temporarily unveiled a trace of human consciousness, buried under thick layers of war calluses.

Madeleine cleared her throat, then placed her cigarette in Boar's hand.

As Madeleine and the lieutenant shared another cigarette,

Louis trotted to the door. He sniffed and scratched his hooves over the floor. Madeleine began to get up and stopped when Ollie placed his hand on her shoulder.

"I'll let him out," Ollie said. "Thanks for breakfast."

Madeleine smiled.

Ollie looked forward to spending a brief moment outside. After all, it appeared quite clear that he'd be spending his days, at least until his body recovered, breathing stagnant crawl-space air and burnt tobacco. As he opened the door, a bird shot over his head. He ducked. The hog squealed. The lieutenant jumped and ripped out his pistol.

Ollie looked up and saw the bird flutter to the counter.

"What the hell is it?" Boar said, gripping his pistol.

"Pigeon," Madeleine said, placing a hand on Boar's arm.

Boar gave a heavy exhale, then returned his pistol to its holster. "Keep that bloody bird locked in its cage, Yank."

At first, Ollie thought his eyes had failed him. *It can't be Duchess. I sent her home. She flew away.*

The bird perked its head, then ruffled its luminescent feathers.

Ollie plucked Duchess from the counter.

The pigeon cooed.

The first thing Ollie noticed was that her feathers were cold. Then he noticed that her canister was missing.

CHAPTER 32

EPPING, ENGLAND

Susan scanned the loft. Empty cubbies. Of the 500 pigeons dropped into France, only 104 had returned, barely one in five. And only two had returned this morning. Neither was Duchess. *Why had she flown away? Shell shock?* Deep down, Susan wished she could fly away herself. Go someplace safe. A land where food was plentiful and not acquired through ration books. A place without sirens and bombs. But she couldn't leave Bertie, her pigeons, and the belief that Ollie would someday come home.

She reached into her coat pocket and pulled out the note. She'd read it countless times, each glimpse with a pang of guilt in her chest. And now Ollie was a casualty of Source Columba, dropped like one of her pigeons into war.

She slipped the note back into her pocket, tended to the remaining lofts, and went inside. She saw Bertie, a paleness in his face, hanging up the phone. "What's wrong?"

"I made you tea," Bertie said, dodging her question. He took a seat at the kitchen table and tapped the chair beside him.

She sat. A wave of anxiety turned her skin warm. "Who was it?"

He slid a cup of tea to her. "National Pigeon Service. Order for five hundred more pigeons."

"When?"

"A week."

Susan shook her head. "We only have three hundred ready."

"We'll have to prepare more." Bertie sighed. "And if necessary, use the pigeons that have just returned."

"It's not enough time."

"We don't have a choice, my dear."

"Tell them to call another farm."

"Susan," Bertie said, "the military has specifically asked for our pigeons."

She clasped her cup. Lukewarm tea spilled over her fingers. "Why?"

"They must have returned something important; otherwise, they would have simply requisitioned pigeons from the next farm on the list." Bertie grinned. "They're doing it, my dear. Our pigeons are carrying French intelligence. And they're bloody well informing our military where Hitler is moving his forces."

Susan tried to smile, but she had already lost far too much. It's what she had wanted, for Source Columba to be a success. But not at Ollie's expense. She stood from her chair.

"Where are you going?" Bertie asked.

She retrieved her coat. "I have five hundred pigeons to prepare."

"I'll help." Bertie stood, hobbled toward the door, and grabbed his jacket from the coatrack.

The cracking of Bertie's knees caused Susan to stop. "You should rest."

"I'll holiday when we defeat that barbaric German führer," Bertie said. "Until then, I'll be even more relentless than his Luftwaffe."

Susan took her grandfather's arm and helped him to the lofts. They began packing pigeons into baskets to prepare for a training flight. As she loaded baskets into the bed of the truck, she noticed her grandfather hobble over to one of the soldiers, standing outside of his tent smoking a cigarette.

"Could you help us?" Bertie asked.

"We have our orders, sir. And you have yours." The soldier flicked his cigarette and returned to his tent.

"Plonker," Bertie said, returning to Susan. "They squat on our land, even eat our food, but they won't lift a finger to help us."

Susan noticed Bertie's cheeks had turned red.

"Orders, my arse," Bertie said. "They just sit in their tent, waiting for the bloody bells to sound. I can tell you this, my dear. In the Great War, our military were not such lazy sods."

Susan watched Bertie pick up a basket and hobble to the truck. The fact that the soldiers were sitting in their tent, likely playing cards or napping, made her furious. An old man, one who could barely walk, was laboring right under their noses. And they did nothing. So before she lost her nerve, she marched to the tent and threw open the canvas door.

A soldier, reading a magazine, slapped the cover shut. His comrade shot up from lying on a cot.

"Get off your bahookies!" Susan's pulse pounded in her ears.

Their faces flushed, as if a woman had just stepped into their shower room.

"Outside and help!" She pointed. "Otherwise, I will call your commander and report that you are sleeping on the job."

The soldier, the one who had been reading the magazine, said, "You'll do no such thing."

"Yes, I will." Susan placed her hands on her hips. "Or would you prefer me to make a call to Air Vice-Marshal Keith Park?"

The soldier's jaws dropped. They glanced to each other, then scuttled outside.

Bertie, carrying a basket of pigeons, stopped and grinned. He watched the soldiers pick up baskets and walk toward the truck. "Nicely done," he said, stepping to Susan.

"Can't believe I did that." She pulled in a lungful of air, attempting to calm her racing heart.

"The name-dropping was a nice touch, something I should

have done. But I think it was your cussing that got the blokes moving."

Susan's shoulders relaxed. "Heard Granny use it once, or twice."

"Always worked on me." He smiled at Susan and returned to work. "Bahookie," he chuckled to himself.

For the remainder of the morning, she and Bertie placed pigeons into baskets, while the soldiers, muttering occasional profanities, loaded them onto the truck. While the assembly line worked efficiently, Susan knew that the training runs would be the least of her worries. The big problem was the quota of an additional 500 pigeons. Inside the lofts, she selected every bird that was old enough and strong enough to fly the Channel, even though many of them had limited training. So, to ensure their guidance on the training run, she mixed in thirty or so veteran birds, fatigued from their return from France. By the time she was finished, the lofts were left with nothing but squabs and nesting mothers.

She insisted that Bertie stay behind to keep an eye out for returning pigeons. He argued, but finally relented when she pointed out that the soldiers, hunkered back inside their tent, were now in a foul mood and that someone should stay behind to ensure things went smoothly. Before leaving, he packed her a lunch, a piece of bread toasted to hide its staleness and a bit of cheese. As she drove away, she noticed Bertie sitting on the porch waiting for another pigeon to emerge on the horizon.

The drive through Essex was uneventful; there were few cars on the road and fewer people outside. It seemed as if all of England was hunkered inside, preparing for a long winter or another round of bombing, until she neared Clacton-on-Sea. On the side of the road, she noticed three members of the Home Guard, volunteers too old or physically unable to join the fight, digging out a signpost. Their coats covered most of their uniforms but were easily recognizable by their olive-green military caps. Their weapons—an assortment of old hunting rifles—were propped like kindling wood against a beech tree. She slowed to a stop and rolled down her window.

"What are you doing?" Susan asked.

A gray-mustached man with swollen jowls, like a chipmunk hiding acorns, dropped his shovel and stepped to the truck. "Preparing for the invasion."

Susan's knuckles turned white as she gripped the steering wheel.

The man adjusted his cap and placed his hands, covered with soil, on the door. "What's your business?"

"National Pigeon Service." She hesitated, then retrieved an NPS badge, a metallic pin that she preferred to keep inside her purse rather than wear on a lapel, and handed it to him.

He looked at the badge, then to the pigeons in the back of the truck.

Susan noticed the man's eyes soften.

"My son, Andrew, when he was a wee lad, loved to feed pigeons in the park." He cleared his throat and returned the badge. "He was fond of giving them the crust from his sandwiches."

Susan smiled and placed the badge back into her purse.

The man exhaled, his breath forming a mist in the cold air. "Andrew hasn't returned from Calais."

His words surprised her. But Susan knew, from what she and Bertie had read in the papers, that a few thousand British soldiers in Calais had held their ground against the German invasion. They fought to the end, creating time to evacuate troops from France. In all, over 300,000 soldiers had fled Dunkirk Harbor on an argosy of military vessels and rickety fishing boats. It was the miracle at Dunkirk. And the men in Calais were gone. They were what Bertie had believed to be sacrificial lambs.

"He'd be proud of his father, working hard to protect his home." She made eye contact with the man. "I'll add Andrew to our prayer board."

"Thank you." The man sniffed, then straightened his back. "I suggest you finish your business and go home. They've been coming early the past few nights."

Susan nodded and pulled away, humbled that the sight of a pigeon could resurrect fond memories for the man. And saddened by the cost of so many young men, with likely many more to follow.

Along the route, she noticed more Home Guard and soon realized that they were blacking out what appeared to be every road sign on the peninsula. The signs, too sturdy to rip out with mere garden tools, were painted over. The Essex coast was a labyrinth of winding roads, and it appeared that the military, or at least the Home Guard, didn't want to make it easy for the Germans to find their way. *Would creating a few wrong turns really slow Hitler's army?*

She arrived at the coast by afternoon. It had changed or, more accurately, had been transformed into a military outpost since her last visit. Instead of unloading or taking a moment to eat the lunch that Bertie had packed for her, she was compelled by her curiosity to see what had been done. So she parked the truck on the side of the road and stepped outside.

The ridge above the shoreline was littered with pillboxes, reinforced concrete structures with rectangular slits for windows. The once-pristine beach was now covered in what appeared to be miles of concertina wire, large coils covered in razors. Huge guns, their barrels angled to the sky, had been erected on the cliffs above the shoreline. Soldiers, one stationed by each of the pillboxes, stood vigil over the Channel.

The reality that the invasion was coming made her legs quiver. Britain was preparing for war on *its* shores. And somewhere, far across those slate-gray waters, was Ollie. She clasped her hands and prayed that he'd somehow make it home. But home to what? A German-occupied Britain?

She had expected to hear military commanders barking orders, soldiers moving shells and boxes of ammunition. But the peninsula was eerily quiet. *A calm before the Nazi storm*, she thought.

Just crying gulls, floating like kites over crashing waves. Glancing at a pillbox, she noticed the soldier hadn't moved. Disciplined. Stoic. Doing his duty. But seconds later, a gull, apparently tired from coasting the winds, glided over and landed on the man's helmet.

She expected the soldier to shoo away the bird, but he remained at attention, staring toward the sea. Hairs prickled the back of her neck. "Hello," Susan called, her voice seemingly drowned by the surf. The soldier remained steadfast. She shouted again. But neither the soldier nor the others made any effort to acknowledge her.

She gathered her courage and crept to the pillbox. As she approached, the gull flew off, causing the man's helmet to tilt awkwardly on his head. The soldier, unruffled, continued his watch over the Channel. A few steps farther and she realized that the soldier—if one could call him that—was nothing more than a mannequin dressed in a military uniform. The helmet was specked with gull droppings. A shock shuddered her body. On closer inspection, she found not just a mannequin, but a dummy pillbox constructed of loose brick, painted in dove-colored paint. The guns, erected to protect the coast, were drainpipes, their barrels doing nothing more than collecting rainwater. The entire beach fortification was a deception. All of the pillboxes, guns, and soldiers were fake. The only thing that was real, it appeared, was the razor wire. *God help us*, she thought.

Where was the British military? The Germans needed nothing more than a cheap pair of wire cutters and they'd run through Essex. The Home Guard, armed with hunting rifles, knives strapped to poles as bayonets, and Molotov cocktails, would barely slow them down. They'd march through Epping, then take London. Susan wanted to cry. Give up. Instead, she forced herself to return to the truck.

Daunted by the fictitious fortification, it took her more than an hour to unload the pigeons. As she placed the last basket in the dormant grass, the pigeons, sensing the start of their journey, began to rustle. One by one, Susan flipped open the doors. Pigeons flapped into the sky. As they circled the perimeter, a wave of sadness caused her shoulders to droop, realizing that it was their last training flight. And considering the survival rate of the mission, the last time she would see them fly as a flock again.

Susan packed up the empty baskets and drove away. A few miles down the road, she missed the turn, due to either the absent road sign or the fact that she was distracted by the British Army resorting to recruiting mannequins. Regardless, she found herself at the far end of the peninsula before realizing what she had done.

The sun was sinking over the trees. It had taken far too long, and she'd be lucky to make it back before dark. So she whipped the truck around. The sandwich Bertie had packed for her spilled to the floor. She slammed the accelerator. The engine roared. Wind whistled through the empty cages. Trying to save time, she decided to take what she believed to be a shortcut and got lost again. She'd been to Clacton-on-Sea dozens of times, but without the road signs, everything looked different, yet the same; it was like being dropped into a garden maze. She struggled to find her way out. Unfortunately, it was dark by the time she reached the main road out of Clacton-on-Sea.

Adhering to the blackout, she kept the headlights off. The road, barely visible, required her to drive slowly. The countryside was barren. Everyone, it appeared to Susan, was hunkered into shelters. Before she reached Epping, sirens howled. Dozens of searchlights near North Weald Airfield scanned the atmosphere. White beams crisscrossed the clouds. She gripped the wheel. Within moments, the antiaircraft guns fired. Concussive blasts pounded her ears. Flashes of aerial explosions lit up the sky. She drove faster, struggling to keep the truck on the road.

She reached home as the first bombs struck London. Through the windshield, she watched white-hot flares illuminate the horizon. Seconds later, the sound waves hit. Rumbling blasts. The ground, truck, and even her bones seemed to vibrate. She got out, leaving the key in the ignition, and ran to the cottage. The scent of expelled gunpowder filled her lungs. She threw open the door and shouted, "Grandfather!"

Bertie stood from a kitchen chair—placed near a front window—and threw his arms around her.

Susan felt a huge squeeze. "Sorry."

Bertie looked at her. "Are you all right, my dear?"

She nodded.

"I tried to get the soldiers to help me look for you, but they bloody wouldn't leave their posts. Cowards."

"Did the pigeons make it back?" she asked.

"All of them."

"Any from Source Columba?"

He shook his head, then leaned his weight against the chair. "What happened?"

Susan heard a loud explosion and hesitated. "They blacked out all the road signs."

Bertie raised his eyebrows. "Why?"

Susan swallowed. "Preparation for the invasion." She didn't have the courage to tell him that the coastline was being protected by department-store mannequins.

CHAPTER 33

EPPING, ENGLAND

Susan stared at her bowl of porridge. Despite her hunger pangs, and the fact that her ribs had begun to protrude like those of a stray dog, she couldn't bring herself to lift the spoon. She hadn't slept. The bombing had been extraordinarily heavy. So fierce that she thought there would be nothing left of London, except a hole all the way to Earth's core.

For much of the night, sirens howled. Guns fired. The earth quaked. With her blanket, Susan curled into a cocoon and prayed, until her knuckles ached—for the safety of Londoners, for Britain to survive, for Ollie to return home. And this morning, she woke to find that only one additional pigeon had returned from France. One out of almost 400 that were still missing. It wasn't Duchess.

"You must eat something," Bertie said.

"I can't."

"Try," he said. "We must keep up our strength to win the war."

Susan thought of Clacton-on-Sea. The fake pillboxes. Mannequin soldiers. For the first time, her hope of winning the war had not just faded; it had been snuffed out. At best, the British would need to find a way to live under Hitler's rule.

Bertie nudged her bowl. "Be an egg, my dear."

Her eyes watered. She wiped her cheeks and picked up her spoon, then ate every bit of her porridge, bland from the lack of milk, spice, or sugar. Dropping her spoon into the bowl, she believed that Source Columba would need a miracle, the revelation of a weakness in the Nazi armor, if Britain were to survive.

The morning was spent caring for the pigeons. While she cleaned the lofts, Susan looked to the sky, hoping to see Duchess circle the birches. But the trees were empty, except for cheeky squirrels scrambling to collect nuts for winter. As she was disposing of droppings into the rubbish bin, she heard a military truck rumble up the lane. The soldiers, alerted by the sound of the engine, came out of their tent. Bertie stepped from the cottage and zipped up his coat.

Susan quickly learned that the military was dropping off parachute cages for the next wave of pigeons. But this time, the cages were nothing like the ones used for the previous mission. These weren't cages, nor were they baskets. They were tubes. Nothing more than cardboard, reminiscent of mailing tubes for posters, with small attached parachutes. No screen. Only holes poked in the endcaps for air. A pigeon would be sealed inside what appeared to be a tubular sarcophagus.

"It's inhumane!" Bertie said, inspecting a tube.

The delivery soldier, a man with a square jaw, freckled skin, and hair the color of a phone box, stepped to Bertie and said, "It's a new design."

"New design, my arse," Bertie said. "It's a mail tube."

"They won't be able to move," Susan added. "Or see."

"The cages took up too much room in a Blenheim." The soldier blew on his fingers to warm them, then stuffed his hands into his jacket. "With these, it'll take fewer planes, risking fewer pilots."

Susan couldn't imagine her pigeons being stuffed like blueprints into tubes. They weren't pieces of paper to protect from being wrinkled. They were pigeons. Her beautiful, intelligent, loyal pigeons. These devoted animals could possibly be Britain's only insight into what the enemy was doing across the Channel, and they were being treated like second-class mail. She wanted to stomp on the tubes, rip them apart, and burn them in her grandfather's fireplace.

As she stared at a stack of tubes, her mind raced. *Had the soldier been told everything? Did the cages work? Had some of the parachutes failed to open?* Susan shuddered. She wished Ollie were here, recalling how he had reassured her that the parachutes would safely float the pigeons to the ground.

She watched the soldiers unload the last of the tubes and drive away, their tires digging deep grooves into the mud. She turned to Bertie and noticed that his face was red, his hands clenched.

"Are you all right?" she asked.

"The military is turning the mission all to pot," he said, hobbling from the yard.

"Where are you going?"

"To stretch my legs," he said.

"Take your walking stick."

He shook his head and shuffled toward the field.

Susan suspected he was headed to the barn. Bertie cherished his sheep, which he used solely for shearing their woolen fleece. Bleating sheep, although not as soothing as cooing pigeons, always seemed to comfort him. And since the lofts were now filled with cardboard tubes and parachutes that would send his blood pressure rising, spending time with the sheep would be a good way for him to forget about Source Columba, if only for a short while.

She went about her duties, caring for the pigeons for the remainder of the morning. She poured feed. Refilled water bowls. Examined squabs. Even repaired loose boards that separated the cubbies. Anything to keep her mind occupied.

After Susan finished sweeping, she went inside and made lunch, albeit it was nothing but leftover oatmeal mixed with withered bits of turnip. As she placed the food on the table, she noticed it was almost two o'clock, rather late to be having lunch considering the sun would be setting in a few hours. So she went to retrieve Bertie, hoping he was enjoying his brief time of solace. As she crossed the field, a herd of sheep, huddled in one of the few remaining sections of green grass, began to disperse. What she saw took her breath away.

A shoe. A calf. A scream boiled in her throat. She tripped and fell. She struggled to get up, stepped on her skirt, and dropped to her knees. Sheep scattered. And there he was, facedown in clover, surrounded by crying lambs.

CHAPTER 34

AIRAINES, FRANCE

"The flight lieutenant doesn't like you," Madeleine said, walking with Ollie to the barn. Louis trotted along behind them.

Ollie glanced at the cottage.

Madeleine rubbed Louis's snout, causing the hog to snort. "Is he angry with you for getting stuck inside his plane?"

Ollie opened the barn door. "Let's just say he's not fond of Americans." He carefully removed Duchess, tucked inside his sling, and then placed her into the cage, which he had hidden under a pile of straw. Duchess closed her eyes, as if she were sleepy, then curled her head under her wings. He stood, his ankle stiff and sore, and looked at Madeleine. "Especially ones that strike an officer."

Madeleine laughed. A rasp rattled in her lungs. "Over a woman?"

He nodded.

"Susan?"

"You could be a palm reader, Madeleine." Ollie poked a finger into the cage and examined Duchess's leg, wondering how he could have failed to properly secure the canister. *What can I use to attach a message with now? String? Wire? Tape?* "I don't suppose you could tell me where I could find a pigeon canister, could you?"

She paused, then glanced outside. "*Oui.*"

Ollie adjusted his weight. His swollen ankle pressed against his boot. "Where?"

"An hour, through the woods," Madeleine said. "Louis and I were returning from collecting truffles when your parachutes dropped from the sky."

"How do I get there?"

"Too dangerous," Madeleine said. "The Wehrmacht have patrols. And the Luftwaffe have an airfield. They'd spot you."

"I'll blend in," Ollie said, pointing to his clothing.

"Your English will get you shot."

He swallowed. "I must try. We need another canister. And if there are more pigeons, we could use them to send intelligence to Britain."

Madeleine hesitated, then said, "Best to go at night."

Ollie shook his head. "The chances of finding a basket in the dark, especially when I can't use a flashlight, would be almost nonexistent. Besides, the pigeons, if they haven't already been found, won't last long. It's cold, and they have no water."

Madeleine picked at a loose thread on her sweater.

"Tell Boar that you tried to stop me," Ollie said, "but I insisted on taking a look around."

She crossed her arms and lowered her head.

Ollie placed his hand on her shoulder. "I don't plan on being caught. But if I were captured, I'd never tell them that you helped me."

"Follow the stream," she said reluctantly. After providing him details of where she'd seen the falling parachutes, she gave a ragged sigh. "Be careful."

He nodded and zipped up his jacket.

If Ollie had known how much his ankle would hurt, he wouldn't have left. Fifteen minutes into his trek through the forest, his foot began to ache. And like a falling line of dominoes, the pain worked its way up his leg and triggered a spasm in his shoulder. Soon his foot was throbbing, forcing him to waste precious time to find a wishbone-shaped branch to use as a crutch. Ollie labored on, limping through the underbrush. He climbed moss-covered logs and waded through shallow streams, using his recollection of Madeleine's directions to guide his way.

In less than an hour, he reached a rolling field, similar to what Madeleine had described. Sitting down to rest, he tightened his sling to keep his shoulder from shifting in its socket, then he loosened his boot laces. Instantly, he felt a relief in pressure. He slid up his pant leg and peeked inside his boot. His ankle, nearly twice its normal size, was the color of an eggplant. He grimaced. If not broken, like the French doctor had said, he'd swear his ligaments had been stretched in a taffy puller.

As he contemplated applying cold mud to reduce the swelling, he scanned the terrain. The field was bare. Whatever had been planted had been harvested. Dead plant stubs pricked up through the soil, as though the field had been given a crew cut. At the far end of the field, movement caught his attention: a creamy speck, as if a pillow had been tossed into the field. He squinted. Wind whistled. And the silky parachute flapped, exposing a wooden cage. He got to his feet and limped ahead.

Several paces into the field, he heard what sounded like a lawnmower. He froze. Held his breath. Listened. The engine grew. He turned and ran. Pain shot through his foot. The crutch gouged his armpit, sending a fiery flare into his shoulder. He hopped on one foot. The engine whined. He dove into the underbrush, just as three Wehrmacht soldiers, two on a motorcycle, the third in a sidecar with a mounted machine gun, crested a hill. Ollie's chest pounded. He prayed he hadn't been spotted.

The soldier in the sidecar pointed. The motorcycle screeched to a stop. The soldiers got out, slung their weapons over their shoulders, and walked into the field.

Damn it. He wanted to cover himself with dirt and fallen leaves but feared any movement would draw their attention.

As the first soldier reached the cage, he lifted the parachute with the tip of his rifle. "*Taube,*" he said. The others gathered.

The soldier, a tall, lanky man who had been driving the motorcycle, raised his rifle and slammed the butt of his weapon into the cage. A crack echoed over the field. A flock of starlings shot from the trees, causing the soldiers to glance in Ollie's direction.

Ollie lowered his head, chin pressed into the earth.

The soldiers' attention returned to the cage. And the tall one reached in and ripped off the canister, producing a crisp snap, like a pencil breaking.

Ollie clenched his hands.

The soldier unscrewed the top and looked inside the canister. A severed leg hung from the clasp. "*Nichts,*" he said, tossing the canister into the broken cage. He ground his boot into the debris, as if he were extinguishing a cigarette.

The soldiers, appearing satisfied that there were no more cages in the vicinity, returned to their vehicle. The driver kick-started the engine and revved the throttle. Smoke spewed from the exhaust. As they drove away, Ollie heard, under the whine of the motorcycle, what he thought was laughter.

Once Ollie was certain they were not coming back, he stood and limped into the field. With each step, the base of his crutch sank into the soil. Dried leaves clung to his jacket; he made no effort to brush them off. Acrid gas fumes hung in the air. He pressed on until he reached the remains.

The pigeon's torso was flattened, its wings crumpled like origami fans. As Ollie reached into the cage to retrieve the canister, his hand brushed the bird, and he noticed that its body was still warm. The pigeon's head was twisted. Bloodied feathers clung to the cage. He carefully removed its leg from the clasp. As he placed the canister into his pocket, he thought of Susan and regretted he hadn't arrived sooner.

The return trip took longer, since Ollie had to make several stops to rest, prop up his leg, and ease the blood flow to his ankle. When he reached a railroad track, he feared he had gotten lost, until he noticed, in the distance, the church steeple of Madeleine's village, Airaines. As he turned to adjust his direction, the sound of aircraft engines caught his attention. He ducked under a pine tree. The buzzing grew. Moments later, a Messerschmitt squadron swooped over the forest. Instead of gaining altitude, the fighters formed a line. Their landing gear lowered. And they disappeared beneath the trees on the opposite side of the tracks.

Choices flooded his head. He could go back to Madeleine's. After all, he had gotten the canister he needed. His ankle, not to mention his shoulder, hurt like hell. But how could he pass up the opportunity to gather useful information? For now, the only thing he could send back to Susan—and the RAF, for that matter—was that he and Boar were hiding like rats under floorboards. Before he could change his mind, he crossed the tracks and worked his way through the pines.

Fallen needles created a soft blanket under his feet. He crept forward. In minutes, he reached the edge of an airfield. Under a canopy of branches, he lowered himself to the ground. He slithered on his belly. His heart rate quickened. Four runways had been created by the Germans, who had commandeered several farms and leveled them with bulldozers, now parked along a barbed-wire fence. Where crops once grew was now a port for a Luftwaffe armada.

Along the side of a field were dozens of Messerschmitt fighters, their black noses and sleek, shark-gray bodies giving them a ferocious appearance, even on the ground. There were over forty Heinkel bombers, each big enough to hold enough explosives to pulverize a city block. There were numerous Stukas, ugly mechanical mosquitoes with a reputation for precision dive-bombing, and several other aircraft Ollie didn't recognize. He'd read about Germany's growing air superiority at the Buxton Library. He'd seen their planes over Epping and the English Channel. But nothing prepared him for the ominous sight of the resting Luftwaffe, as though he had walked into a den of sleeping lions.

Near a hangar, soldiers were loading bombs and boxes of ammunition onto a truck, likely in preparation for another night of raids. Beside a runway, there were hundreds of oil drums.

Ollie inched forward, then stopped. At the far corner of the airfield, a sentry was walking the perimeter. A machine gun hung from his shoulder. His hand was tethered to a German shepherd.

Oh, brother.

He scanned the area. At the corner of the field, the ground sloped sharply upward to a group of sagging pines. If he could get there, he'd have an elevated view of the runways, enabling him to get an accurate inventory of the aircraft. But he'd be right next to the fence and likely to be seen when the sentry rounded the corner. At the very least, the dog would pick up his scent. After all, he reeked of sweat, and it was a good thing the wind was blowing toward him; otherwise, he might have already been detected.

As he was about to crawl back into the woods, he heard a shout. The sentry snapped to attention and extended his arm in a salute. An officer, given the curved shape of his cap, approached the sentry. The dog sat on its haunches like a garden statue.

Ollie hesitated. The officer conversed with the sentry. A minute passed. He glanced at the spot at the corner of the field—twenty, perhaps thirty yards away. Rather than waste another second, Ollie crawled forward. He buried the pain in his shoulder and ankle, and he reached his destination. When he looked up, he saw that the officer had departed. And the sentry was rounding the fence.

He quickly counted aircraft on the first runway. Then the second.

The sentry pressed forward. The dog sniffed the ground, its shoulder blades flexed under its thick brown coat.

He counted the remaining aircraft, hoping he had an accurate inventory of the airfield. And as he crept into the forest, the dog barked.

Shit. He tripped and caught himself with his crutch. A spasm shot through his ankle.

Another bark. Louder.

Ollie imagined the sentry releasing the dog, now galloping toward him with sharp canine teeth. At any moment, he expected the dog to pounce on his back. Chew the skin from his arms. Maul his face. His respiration surged. He hobbled forward, the pressure torturing his leg.

An airplane engine sputtered. Propeller blades buzzed, muting the crackle of pine needles beneath his feet. As he reached the railroad tracks, he noticed that the dog had stopped barking. He hoped that it had only been irritated by the plane preparing to take off. But he wasn't sticking around to find out. He crept through the woods, determined to get the intelligence to Susan.

CHAPTER 35

AIRAINES, FRANCE

"Where've you been, Yank?" Boar said, as Ollie entered the cottage.

Ollie placed Duchess, curled into a feathery ball inside her cage, onto the table. He fell into a chair and wiped sweat from his face.

Madeleine, stirring a pot of boiled cabbage, put down her spoon and exchanged it for a cigarette.

"I didn't give you permission to leave." Boar adjusted the bandage covering his eyes.

Ollie loosened his bootlaces and propped his aching foot onto a chair. "I'm not in the RAF."

"Don't care, Yank." Boar touched his holster. "I won't tolerate you placing us at risk."

Ollie looked at Boar. He suspected that the lieutenant, despite being unable to see, was near enough that he'd have no trouble putting a bullet in him. But after his close encounters with the Wehrmacht and the Luftwaffe, Boar seemed almost harmless in comparison. He removed the canister from his pocket and placed it on the table.

Hearing the sound, Boar jerked his head. "What's that?"

"Got intelligence to send home," Ollie said.

Madeleine sucked on her cigarette. The tip glowed and crackled. She glanced at Louis, resting on the floor.

Boar looked in Ollie's direction. "What did you see?"

Ollie told them about the Wehrmacht patrol and how he had stumbled upon the Luftwaffe airfield. He described the precise location of the airfield, including the type and quantity of planes, then retrieved a pencil and paper stored in Duchess's military-issue cage. As he began to document his findings, the sound of a car engine made him freeze.

Boar clenched his hands. "Were you followed?"

Ollie thought of the sentry. *Did the dog follow my scent?*

"Hurry." Madeleine tossed her cigarette into the sink.

The engine growled. Louis grunted.

They pushed aside the table and quickly plucked out the boards.

Brakes screeched. The engine sputtered, then stopped.

Boar slid into the hole. Ollie followed. Madeleine reached for a board.

"Wait," Ollie said. "Duchess."

A car door slammed.

Madeleine plucked the cage from the table, causing Duchess to flap her wings. She lowered the pigeon. Boards slapped into place. As she slid the table over the floor, there was a hard knock. Louis snorted. She rubbed the hog's head, then went to the door.

"Herr Dietrich," Madeleine said, opening the door.

Through a crack in the floor, Ollie saw what he believed to be a Nazi SS officer. The man wore a gray uniform with a swastika patch on his left sleeve. His visor cap was gilded with silver skull-and-eagle insignias. Polished jackboots shined like volcanic glass. Ollie's pulse pounded.

The Nazi had waxen skin and pink eyelids that appeared almost translucent. And even more distinguishable, a chunk was missing from his left ear, like a moth wing that had been clipped in half. The absence of cartilage caused his cap to sit cockeyed.

The officer glanced at Louis and wrinkled his nose. "*Schweine-stall.*"

Madeleine retrieved her leather satchel and gave him a handful of truffles.

The Nazi felt the weight in his hand and shook his head. He grabbed Madeleine's bag.

Louis snorted.

Ollie sensed Duchess moving in her cage. He braced himself, ready to leap from the hole.

The Nazi emptied Madeleine's satchel. Truffles plopped onto the table. And one small truffle, the size of a blackberry, fell to the floor, rolled, and settled next to Ollie's peephole.

Ollie stared at the truffle, which partially blocked his view. He prepared for the Nazi to snatch the fallen fungus and notice the crack, the loose boards. Perhaps Boar could get off a shot, but considering his lack of vision, he'd be lucky to land a lethal hit. Then the Nazi would unload his pistol. Ollie imagined bullets shattering the boards, his body punctured with lead. This crawl space would be his grave. Helplessness roiled in his gut. He struggled to control his breath.

The Nazi scooped truffles from the table and placed them inside his cap, using it as a basket. He lifted a fungus to his nose and sniffed.

Ollie saw Madeleine's hand pass by the peephole. The truffle vanished. He squinted and saw her brush off the fungus and place it into the Nazi's cap.

"*Sie finden mehr,*" the Nazi said, admiring his truffle treasure.

Madeleine lowered her head.

The Nazi turned to leave and found Louis blocking his way. He swung back his leg and sunk his jackboot into the hog's ribs.

Louis squealed. The hog shot over the floor, knocking over a chair.

Ollie's skin turned hot. He wanted to shoot the Nazi. While he contemplated snatching Boar's pistol, he heard the door open as the officer left.

Soon an engine started. Tires spit gravel. And the car drove away. A moment later, the table scraped over the floor, and Madeleine plucked out the floorboards.

"You okay?" Ollie crawled from the hole.

Madeleine nodded.

"Louis?" Ollie asked.

She rubbed the hog's ribs, causing its tail to twitch. "*Oui.*"

"Bloody Nazi," Boar said, taking a seat on the floor.

Duchess flapped her wings. Ollie retrieved the cage from the crawl space and placed it on the table.

Boar pressed his hands over his bandaged eyes. "Think your bird can get a message to the RAF?"

"I know she can," Ollie said.

Ollie finished writing a message, then removed Duchess from her cage. He attached the canister, inserted the note, and carried the pigeon outside.

"Let's try this again," Ollie whispered to Duchess. "The canister is on better this time."

Duchess cooed.

Ollie tossed Duchess into the air. As the pigeon circled the perimeter, he thought of Susan and their trip to Clacton-on-Sea. An image of her sandy-blond hair, dancing in the North Sea wind. Her eyes, the color of sapphire, gazing to the sky as her pigeons flew away. The stacks of empty cages. And his growing sense of foreboding as Susan told him that most of the pigeons would not return from France.

Ollie watched Duchess disappear over the trees. He returned to the cottage, hoping that in just a few hours Susan would be reading his message.

CHAPTER 36

EPPING, ENGLAND

Susan crawled to Bertie, facedown in the field. His limbs were splayed, like a fallen scarecrow. The lambs scattered; their wavering cries grew. She touched his shoulder. No movement. Her breath accelerated, spawning cloudy puffs in the cold air. She rolled him over to find his eyes closed. Mud covered his cheeks. Coagulated blood clung to his forehead.

Susan trembled. Quickly, she placed her ear to his chest. A pulse. Then another. His chest slowly rose, then fell.

"Grandfather!"

He moaned. His eyelids quivered but didn't open.

Tears welled in her eyes.

Bertie swallowed. "Susan," he whispered.

"I'm here." She touched his face.

"I fell." His hand lifted, then settled to the ground.

She tried to lift him, but his limp body was too heavy. "I need to find help," she said, glancing across the field. The cottage was a mere speck in the distance. With no other choice, she quickly ripped off her coat, tearing off two buttons, and placed it over her grandfather's chest.

Bertie slowly opened his eyes. "Give me a moment, my dear."

"I'll be back," she said, squeezing his hand. Before he could argue, she stood and ran, sprinting over the sheep pasture. Her pulse pounded in her ears. Cold air stung her skin. Her boots sank into the wet soil, causing her to lose one of her wellies. She retrieved her boot and put it on, then dashed towards home.

As she neared the cottage, she released a deep howling yawp that tore at her vocal cords. She shouted again. Louder. And the soldiers fled their tent.

"What is it?" a soldier asked, rubbing his eyes, as if woken from a nap.

"Grand . . ." Susan sucked in air and pointed. "Grandfather collapsed. I need help."

He paused, then said, "We can't leave our post. I'll ring for an ambulance."

"There's no time!"

The soldier straightened his back. He glanced at his comrade. Susan grabbed the soldier's sleeve. "Now!"

Perhaps it was her shouts or her recent meltdown with the soldiers that created the misconception that she had a smidge of authority. Either way, she didn't care. She needed help. Anyone's help. Finally, after a hard tug on the man's arm, the soldiers disregarded their strict instructions to man their posts and came to her aid.

When they reached Bertie, he was sitting up and rubbing a large goose egg on his forehead. He tried to stand and fell. His legs were weak, like sticks holding up a piano. Susan requested that the soldiers carry him, despite Bertie's refusal for help.

"Put me down," Bertie said.

The soldiers ignored him and pushed on, marching through the muddy field.

"Put me down, I say," Bertie repeated.

The soldiers carried him, arms clasped under Bertie's legs and back, like a human sedan chair. When they finally reached the cottage, the soldiers placed him on the sofa. Susan called for the doctor. The soldiers glanced at each other and slipped outside, driven by Bertie's reprimands for carrying him against his will or, more likely, when he somehow mustered the strength to snatch his walking stick and attempted to give them a swat. By the time Doctor Collins arrived, Bertie was insisting that he needed to get back to work, despite his inability to stand on his own.

Doctor Collins, a plump man with thick spectacles and small, childlike hands, cleaned the cut on Bertie's head with a swab and alcohol. He plucked a stethoscope from his bag and listened to Bertie's chest.

"The bump is here," Bertie said, pointing to the protuberance on his forehead.

Doctor Collins continued listening to Bertie's chest, front and back, then removed the stethoscope from his ears. "You may have a concussion." He coiled up his instrument and looked at Bertie. "And your heart sounds enlarged."

Susan took a deep breath.

"Nonsense," Bertie said. "I merely fell and hit my noggin."

Susan looked at Bertie, his skin still pallid, his clothes stiff with dried mud.

"Were you dizzy before you fell?" the doctor asked.

"No," he said.

"Light-headed?"

Bertie shook his head.

"I want you to rest," the doctor said.

"I've got work to do," Bertie said.

Susan stepped to her grandfather. She looked at the doctor, the same physician who had delivered her into the world. When she was a child, he had mended her back to health from an acute case of the whooping cough. "Shouldn't we go to the hospital?"

Doctor Collins sighed. "Recovering at St. Margaret's isn't an option, I'm afraid. The beds are full. More casualties are coming from London every day."

"I don't need to go to the bloody hospital," Bertie said.

The doctor retrieved a bottle from his bag and set it on a stand beside the sofa. "I want you to place one of these under your tongue if you have any chest pain."

"My heart's fine." He tapped the doctor's leather bag. "But if you have anything in there for dodgy knees, I'll take it."

The doctor looked at him. "Hope our boys in the fight have as much tenacity as you, Bertie."

Susan glanced at the brown bottle with a cork top. It contained minuscule white tablets, like aspirin cut in quarters.

"Nitroglycerin," Dr. Collins said. "It's for angina."

Susan nodded.

"I don't have angina," Bertie said. "Nor do I have an enlarged heart. I stepped in a bloody rabbit hole, for God's sake. If anything, I have wonky legs and a blasted headache from that psychopathic dictator dropping his bombs."

Doctor Collins placed a hand on Bertie's shoulder. "Rest."

"I'll rest when we win the war." Bertie took a deep breath and straightened his back.

Doctor Collins looked at Susan as he put on his coat. "I'll check in with you tomorrow." He tipped his cap and left.

Susan followed the doctor to his car. She looked down at her wellies, covered with mud. "Will he be all right?"

The doctor tossed his bag into the passenger seat. "Bertie overexerted himself."

Susan crossed her arms and bit her lip. *What did he hear through that stethoscope?*

The doctor hesitated, then glanced at the military tent in the yard. "There's a rumor in Epping that your pigeons have gone off to war."

Susan ignored his comment. She slipped her hand into her pocket and gripped Ollie's note.

"You'll need to pick up Bertie's duty," the doctor said, taking a seat behind the wheel. "Until he recovers," he added.

Susan watched the doctor drive away, the underside of his car scraping the deep ruts left by the convoy of military vehicles. Then she returned to Bertie, who was already asleep on the sofa. He looked exhausted. Mud still crusted his cheeks and clothes. *I'll clean him up later*, she decided. Retrieving a worn patchwork quilt her grandmother had sewn together from scrap material, she gently covered him. Many of the other blankets were thicker, softer, and no doubt warmer. But this tattered piece was his favorite.

Bertie opened his eyes and forced a smile. "A wee rest, my dear, and I'll get back to work."

Susan tucked the quilt over his shoulders. She glanced at the bottle of pills and wondered if the medicine would collect dust, just like his walking stick. But deep down, she already knew the answer.

CHAPTER 37

EPPING, ENGLAND

Bertie slept for most of the day. Each hour, Susan checked on him only to find that he hadn't moved. She'd pause, wait to see his chest rise, then quietly leave. It was quite unnerving for Susan to see her grandfather, always a diligent man, sleeping through the afternoon, even though she knew he needed the rest.

When Bertie finally woke, Susan washed the grime from his face, then gathered a clean set of clothes. While he changed in the living room, given privacy by the curtain strung across the kitchen door, she prepared him broth made from boiled cabbage. As she ladled the watery mixture into a bowl, she wondered if he had told her everything. *Had he been dizzy? Did his chest hurt? And if so, would he even tell me? Of course not.*

She retrieved a spoon and carried the bowl to Bertie. As she entered the living room, she saw that he had somehow managed to maneuver himself into his living room chair. A pile of soiled clothes lay at his feet. He looked exhausted. Chin dropped. Eyes closed. She glanced at the bowl of broth. The tiny amount of nutrients from withered cabbage was barely enough to tame one's hunger, let alone nurse an elderly man back to health. As she placed the bowl on the stand next to his chair, Bertie stirred.

"Thank you, Susan," Bertie said. "But I insist on sitting at the table."

"Feeling better?" she asked.

He nodded and tried to stand, then fell back into his chair. He grunted, then reached out his hand.

Susan helped him to his feet. The crackle of his knees reverberated through his bones and into her hands. Slowly, she helped him shuffle to the table.

"I don't want you worrying about me," he said, taking a seat.

"Eat, then rest." She retrieved his broth and placed it in front of him, noticing that the crow's-feet in the corners of his eyes appeared deeper.

He tapped Susan's hand. "Merely a fall, my dear. I'll be better tomorrow." He picked up his spoon and tasted his broth. "Splendid. Never knew soup could taste so rich."

Susan watched him eat his broth, his hand shaking as he raised the spoon to his mouth. "How about you keep a lookout for returning pigeons," she said, as he finished, "while I tend to the lofts."

Bertie lowered his spoon.

"I could put your chair on the porch," she said.

He nodded.

She had expected him to put up a fuss. The fact that he didn't caused the knot in her belly to tighten. "Merely for this afternoon," she added, immediately realizing that she was reassuring herself.

"Perhaps it's a good idea that one of us keeps watch," Bertie said. "The soldiers are daft eggs."

Susan washed the dishes, then moved Bertie's living room chair to the porch. It took some effort to squeeze the oversized upholstered piece through the door frame; she had to flop it on its side and wiggle it through. As he settled into his chair, she noticed the fabric had been torn.

"I'm sorry," she said, tucking the stuffing under the ripped flap of fabric. "I'll mend it."

"Gives it character, my dear," he said, patting her arm.

She covered him with layers of blankets. Beside him, she placed his walking stick and the bottle of pills, even though she knew full well he'd never touch either one. Then she went to work.

For the remainder of the afternoon, she forced herself to go about her duties. She dreaded leaving Bertie, but she had no choice. Five hundred pigeons needed to be prepared for the next mission, which was less than a week away, and by her standards, they weren't ready. Not even close. They needed several more training flights, but she'd only have time for one, perhaps two at most. Normally, she'd select only the strongest pigeons. However, to meet the deadline, she'd have to rely on any pigeon that was capable of making a three-hour flight. Then the canisters would need to be attached to their legs, a task that would take the better part of a day. The worst part would be placing the pigeons into those god-awful tubes. She was determined not to expose Bertie to seeing their pigeons stuffed into the containers like mail. That job she'd do herself.

She had a quota to fill. The survival of Britain rested on the wings of these birds, she believed. But she struggled to focus, the image of her grandfather, facedown in a field, continued to flash in her brain. To distract herself, she scraped droppings with a shovel, despite the floor being fairly clean. She shoveled until the plywood floor splintered and blisters began to bubble on her fingers. Then she sat in the corner of the loft, wrapped her arms around her knees, and cried.

It's my fault. There must've been something I could've done. In the privacy of the loft, only the pigeons witnessed her vulnerability. And she knew full well that once she stepped outside, she'd shed her weak skin. She had no choice, she believed, but to be strong. Resilient. She wiped away her tears, then peeked through a crack in the door, preparing herself for what lay ahead. She was relieved to see Bertie, alert and scanning the skies. But his walking stick and bottle of pills, at least from a distance, appeared to have moved farther from his chair.

Susan went to work, examining and counting pigeons. But a few minutes later, as she was plucking a squab from its nest, she heard Bertie shout.

"Susan!"

Her heart palpitated. A flash of her grandfather, collapsed on the porch. She placed the squab into its cubby and dashed outside to find him leaning forward in his chair. She exhaled, relieved to see that he wasn't in distress.

Bertie forced himself to stand, using the porch rail as a crutch, and pointed.

As her heartbeat began to settle into a normal rhythm, she looked up. High above the forest, a pigeon. The smooth, unmistakable stroke of its wings caused her pulse to race again. *Duchess!*

"There!" Bertie shouted.

Susan watched Duchess swoop to the loft. And as she did, the soldiers, alerted by Bertie's ruckus, emerged from their tent.

Duchess fluttered to the landing board mounted to the top of the loft. Instead of entering the loft through the alarm curtain, she cocked her head and watched the soldiers approach.

As Susan stepped to the landing, she noticed the red canister attached to the pigeon's leg and stopped.

"Why won't it go inside?" a soldier asked as he reached Susan.

She hesitated, believing it had to be a mistake. *It can't be Duchess. She didn't have a canister when she flew away.* But as she stared up at the pigeon, its feathers like bloomed garden flowers, she knew it could be no other.

The soldier, appearing to become impatient, approached the landing.

"Don't touch her," Susan said. "She'll go in on her own."

The soldier turned his back to her and stood on his toes. He reached, his fingers like claws, and grazed the bird's wing.

Duchess tilted her head, then gave a hard peck.

"Ouch!" He pulled back his hand. "Bloody bird bit me."

"Leave her alone!" Susan shouted.

The second soldier maneuvered to the opposite side of the landing. Working as a team, they closed in. Duchess ruffled her feathers.

Susan struggled with what to do. She wanted to retrieve Bertie's walking stick to fend them off. Instead, she stepped behind the soldiers and waved her arms. *Shoo!*

Duchess fluffed up her feathers. Blinked. As a soldier's hand swiped toward her legs, she stretched her wings and flew.

"Bollocks!" the soldier said.

Duchess darted. She swooped left, then right, and disappeared behind the cottage.

"Now look what you've done." Susan pressed her hands to her waist. "You scared her off."

The soldiers looked at each other, then ran toward the cottage.

Bertie shook his head as the soldiers passed by the porch.

The soldiers disappeared around the corner, near a row of dormant rosebushes. Seconds later, Duchess soared over the roof, dove sharply, and landed on the porch rail.

Bertie tried to shuffle toward the pigeon. But his knees wobbled and gave out. He clung to the porch rail, as if it were a life preserver.

Susan ran. She was only twenty yards from the cottage, but she already heard the soldiers approaching. They had cut through the garden and were barreling toward the front. They'd reach Duchess first. The thought of them touching her pigeon sent off a flare of anger. She lowered her head and forced her legs to move faster, all the while hoping the soldiers would stumble.

She reached the porch at precisely the same moment as the soldiers. But it didn't matter. Duchess was gone. And Bertie, strained from standing, had fallen into his chair.

"Where'd it go?" a soldier asked, wiping sweat from his brow.

"Tweedledee and Tweedledum," Bertie muttered.

"Sorry?" The soldier removed his cap.

"I said, it's a wee scared. And a wee tired." Bertie leaned forward and adjusted his blanket over his knees. "You've frightened her into the woods. It may be hours before she returns."

"Blasted bird," the soldier said. "Why didn't it just go inside the loft?"

Susan's face turned hot. "She was merely resting! How would you feel after hours of flapping your arms?"

The soldier cleared his throat, then spat in the grass.

"I suggest you stay in your tent until the alarm sounds," Bertie said.

The soldier puffed his chest. "Do I have to remind you that we're in charge?"

"No," Bertie said. "But if you continue to behave like children chasing butterflies, that pigeon will never come home."

The soldiers glanced at each other, then walked to their tent and slipped inside.

"Our military has clearly assigned their most incompetent to our mission," Bertie said.

Susan scanned the forest. "Which way did she fly?"

"Here."

She turned.

Bertie lifted the blanket on his lap to expose Duchess, tucked onto his belly.

Susan covered her mouth.

He wrapped Duchess inside the blanket. "Let's go inside. Shall we?"

Susan helped him inside and quickly shut the blackout curtains, all the while trying to imagine how he had managed to reach Duchess. She unwrapped the blanket that hid her pigeon.

"She flew to me as the soldiers were approaching." He coughed and cleared his throat. "I merely covered her with my blanket."

Susan held Duchess. She caressed her wings.

The pigeon cooed.

Bertie pointed. "Where did the canister come from?"

Susan unclipped the canister and gently placed Duchess on the table. This time she didn't need her grandfather's prodding to inspect what was inside. She unscrewed the top and slid out the paper.

```
ALKFQ  NPTMI  HLCXP  QNMVX  PUTXJ  GQZKE
HIQAN  SYAEF  AMVXQ  PLWTR  OSJWL  IWLNF
QLKDF  SLIEF  SOEVC  PLEFV  AMEFL  YELFP
JSPFD  SKEAF  RHBVC  WYGHI  OPAEF  HUVQA
URPXY  QOSDM  OPZQR  TWNVI  BZITE  OPNCT
IGBVM  WPORL  QBVXI  OLKSE  JGBMV  PIXSW
TZCOP  VQWEM  KWLKV  YSLEK  OPAVE  CXPTY
FJGLE  KPQCX  MBKSQ  PEOJS  TYAWM  ZYRTP
```

She retrieved the codebook and began deciphering the message. As she wrote, a sense of déjà vu turned her legs weak. She finished and handed the paper to Bertie.

"Don't have my reading glasses."

Susan paused, then read the note.

Susan,
Duchess taken. Attempted to retrieve her,
but airfield attacked. Plane scrambled with
Duchess and me onboard. Mission complete.
Shot down in France. Gunner and copilot
killed. Flight Lieutenant Boar and I are
hiding.

"It's the same message," Bertie said.

Susan shook her head. "There's more."

Wehrmacht everywhere. Luftwaffe using
nearby airfield, two miles south of Airaines.

46 Heinkel bombers, 60 Messerschmitt fight-
ers, 23 Stukas, 16 unknown aircraft, many
oil drums, 3 hangars of bombs.
Ollie
P.S. Susan, your pigeons were brave. Wish I
could have been with you to see them
return.

Susan slipped her hand inside her coat pocket and produced the previous note, softened like cotton from numerous readings. She placed both pieces of paper on the table.

"Good Lord," Bertie said, rubbing the bump on his head. "She flew back to France."

"But she's a one-way racing pigeon," Susan said. "She hasn't been trained for two-way flight."

"Pigeons aren't supposed to hatch from breakfast bowls either." He stroked Duchess with a finger. "But this one did."

Susan looked at the note again, making certain her eyes were not deceiving her. "Ollie must think that his first message never reached us."

Bertie paused and scratched his whiskers. "Our Oliver likely believes that the original canister had fallen off, and Duchess simply returned to him. He must have tried again, using a canister from another pigeon."

The thought of Ollie desperately trying to relay a message made her head throb. She ran her hand over Duchess's wings. "Do you think it's possible she could carry a message back to him?"

"She's already proven that she can, my dear."

"But it will place her at risk."

"Yes," Bertie said. "But she may fly back anyway. After all, she returned to Oliver on her own."

Susan recalled Duchess flying away, her desperate pleas to her pigeon ignored. She shook away the thought and went to the kitchen, filled a teacup with water, then placed it in front of Duchess.

The bird dipped its beak into the cup. Water droplets covered the table.

Rather than risk alerting the soldiers by going to a loft to retrieve grain, Susan scraped together a handful of stale crumbs from the bottom of a pie rack that hadn't been used for almost a year. She sprinkled the morsels onto the table. As Duchess pecked at her food, Susan retrieved paper and a pencil, then began to scribble.

"Are you going to try and send her back?" Bertie asked.

Susan shook her head. "I can't bear the thought of forcing her to leave. But if she flies away again, she'll at least have a message."

She took several minutes to code a note. Halfway through her writing, she looked up to see Bertie transposing Ollie's message onto another piece of paper, just as he had done before. *Our Oliver from Maine has had enough trouble with the RAF*, she recalled her grandfather saying. *Being viewed as a stowaway could create trouble for him when he returns . . . And he will return, my dear.* She so needed to hear those words again. The military would get their intelligence, but they'd keep Ollie out of the picture. So, just like before, Bertie signed the altered message *Flight Lieutenant Clyde Boar, RAF*.

Susan finished her coded note and placed it inside the canister. After Duchess had finished pecking at her crumbs, she attached the canister to the pigeon's leg.

Duchess shook her tail feathers. She waddled, as if she were testing the weight of the package.

Bertie patted Duchess, then slouched in his chair.

Susan picked up Duchess and carried her to the window. Peeking through the curtain, she made sure that the soldiers were not outside of their tent. She glanced at Bertie, too weak to stand. "If she flies to the loft, I'll reach her before the soldiers. And I'll replace my note with your message."

"You always were rather fast," Bertie said, sliding his paper to the edge of the table.

She forced a smile and pressed Duchess to her cheek. Feathers caressed her face. "I won't force you to go," she whispered.

Duchess blinked.

She kissed the pigeon's head.

Before she lost her nerve, she opened the curtains and quietly raised the window. Duchess squirmed. Talons scraped Susan's palms. She tossed her pigeon into the air.

Duchess beat her wings. She fluttered, then gained altitude.

Susan gripped the windowsill.

Duchess circled the birches. Instead of descending to her loft, she flew east. Toward the Channel.

Susan, unable to bear seeing her pigeon fly away again, lowered her head. The odds were against Duchess. The empty cubbies were all the statistics that Susan needed; it'd be difficult for her to make it to France, let alone return home. As she closed the window, a wave of guilt engulfed her body.

CHAPTER 38

AIRAINES, FRANCE

Ollie, Madeleine, and Boar sat down for a dinner of stale gray bread and turnips fried in hot fat. A dust-coated glass jug, reminiscent of a vessel containing vinegar, sat in the center of the table. At the bottom of the jug was a thick layer of dead yeast.

Madeleine poured the tan liquid, careful not to disturb the sediment, into cups and slid them to Ollie and Boar. "I waited in line for three hours at the butcher for a minuscule strip of fat." She sighed, then poured herself a drink. "Bartered the last of my truffles for this inedible baguette and what's in this bottle. I believe it used to be apple brandy."

Ollie sniffed his glass. Oaky fumes filled his nose. He took a bite of turnip, then washed it down with a sip. It didn't taste anything like apples or any other fruit. The alcohol content was high, burning his throat and searing his empty stomach, as though he had swallowed a hot coal.

Boar scratched the bandage over his eyes, then ran his hands over the table as he found his cup. He gulped his brandy.

Madeleine refilled the lieutenant's cup, then reached down to pat Louis on the head. "Tomorrow we'll search for more truffles. And then get better food."

The hog grunted.

As Ollie chewed stale bread, he watched the lieutenant drain his second cup of brandy, as if it were spring water. No grimace. No clearing of his throat. Boar, it appeared to Ollie, was self-absorbed, counting the days until he could remove the bandages. And as each moment passed, the man's irritability grew. It would be another week before the bandages would be removed. And by then, Ollie suspected, the lieutenant would be a demon, if not the devil himself, to live with.

Although Boar had been civil with Madeleine, even making cordial conversation while sharing cigarettes, the same could not be said for his attitude toward Ollie. In the evenings, hunkered under the floorboards in proximity to Ollie, Boar's disposition turned sour. Perhaps Madeleine, sensing the lieutenant's growing irritability, had intended to acquire the brandy to soften Boar's temperament. Or to enable Ollie's tolerance. But Ollie learned the real reason for Madeleine's trip to the village when she excused herself from the table and returned with a weathered map.

"I've arranged for your passage," Madeleine said, taking her seat.

Ollie looked at her.

"Bloody hell," Boar said, dropping his fork. A bit of turnip fell to the floor, which Louis gobbled up.

Madeleine ignored the comment and slid the map to the center of the table. "I've spoken with—"

"You were to keep your mouth shut." Boar gripped his cup.

Madeleine calmly refilled the lieutenant's brandy. "Do you speak French?"

"That has nothing to do with it," Boar said.

"It has everything to do with it."

Boar rubbed his jowl. "You should have consulted me first. You'll cock up our escape."

"It doesn't matter," Ollie said. "It's done."

The lieutenant turned his head toward Ollie's voice, then took a gulp of brandy.

Madeleine lit a cigarette. She took a deep drag, then blew smoke through her nose. "You'll be taken south." She drew her finger over the map. "To Spain."

"Who's taking us?" Boar asked.

She paused and drew a breath. "A friend of my husband."

"Guillaume," Ollie said.

She nodded, seeming pleased to hear her husband's name.

"French Resistance?" Boar asked.

"No," she said.

"Splendid," Boar scoffed. "How do we know he won't go to the Nazis?"

She puffed her cigarette and handed it to Boar, as if it were a peace offering. "Trust me. He won't tell a soul."

Boar placed the cigarette to his lips. Smoke swirled past his bandaged eyes.

Ollie looked at the map. He focused on what lay between France and Spain. The Pyrenees. Even on paper, the jagged lines that depicted the mountain range appeared formidable, much steeper than the eroded Appalachian range that ran through Mount Katahdin in Maine. He wondered if he would physically be able to make a 500-mile trek through France, let alone avoid the enemy, and then climb a mountain on a bum leg.

"You leave in a week," Madeleine said. "When the lieutenant's bandages come off and your ankle has had time to heal."

Ollie stretched his foot. Pain shot through his tendons. *May need longer than that.*

As Ollie rubbed his ankle, Boar questioned Madeleine. The lieutenant attempted to gain details about their guide and the escape route. But Madeleine held firm, refusing to break her confidentiality, like a priest who had heard confession.

"I won't burden my husband's friend with more risk," she

said, retrieving her cigarette from Boar. "If the Nazis find you before you leave, they'll torture you. No matter how strong you think you may be, you'll talk. Then they'll kill you." Ash fell from her cigarette. "No need for another to be shot."

Ollie's mouth turned dry. He knew that if he or Boar were caught during their escape attempt, and Madeleine's name was revealed, she'd be executed. He ran his fingers through his hair. And promised himself that if he were captured, he'd take Madeleine's name to his grave.

"Very well." Boar slid his hand over the table and found the bottle. He refilled his cup, using his finger to sense the rising brandy.

Ollie ate the rest of his turnips, despite losing his appetite, then said to Madeleine, "I'll take Louis to the barn and feed him."

Madeleine nodded.

Ollie stood and went to the window. He peeked through the curtain to make certain the area was clear. Only rustling leaves. It was dusk, and the sky was painted in hues of orange and blue. He opened the door and froze. On the doorstep, peering up at him, was Duchess.

"No," Ollie said.

The pigeon blinked.

"What is it?" Boar asked from the table.

"Duchess." Ollie picked her up and noticed the canister was still strapped to her leg. *At least you didn't lose the message again.*

The pigeon cooed.

"Go home," Ollie said, as if he were giving orders to a stray dog.

Duchess tilted her head.

Ollie stepped outside and tossed the pigeon into the air. She fluttered to the barn, then swooped back to the cottage and landed at his feet.

Boar stood. He stepped blindly, stretching his arms, until he found the doorway.

Ollie picked up Duchess, then tossed her again. "Home."

Duchess glided to the ground. She waddled, like a duck, back to Ollie.

"Your pigeon is rubbish," Boar said.

"Susan's pet," Ollie said. "She wasn't part of the mission."

Madeleine stepped outside. She looked down at the pigeon and asked, "Has she returned?"

Ollie shook his head. "Never left."

Madeleine pointed to the canister. "Have you checked?"

Ollie hesitated, then removed the canister from Duchess's leg. The pigeon jutted its head as it waddled in a figure-eight pattern. He unscrewed the top, expecting to find his note. But what he found was a rolled piece of yellow stationery, quite different from the military-issued paper in the drop cages. His eyes widened. He looked at Madeleine. "Inside."

Ollie placed Duchess on the table and took a seat. Madeleine sat next to him while Boar remained standing.

"What does it say?" Boar asked, as Ollie unrolled the paper.

Ollie scanned the message, a series of five-letter words. His heartbeat accelerated. "It's coded." He retrieved the book from his jacket and began to decipher.

Madeleine leaned over Ollie's shoulder.

"Hurry up, Yank," Boar said.

After a few minutes, Ollie finished decoding. He took a deep breath, then read the message out loud.

Ollie,
Intelligence relayed to RAF. Not sure Duchess will reach you. Don't feed her. Only water. Increases odds of returning home.

Ollie glanced down at Duchess, pecking at a speck of gray bread. "Sorry," he said, removing the crumb.

The pigeon angled its head, then sat, like a hen nesting an egg.

"That's it?" Boar asked.

"There's more." Ollie continued reading.

Preparing second wave of Source Columba. Bertie ill. War taking toll on him. Bombs falling. I think of you often and pray for your return. Susan.

"What about the RAF?" Boar asked.

"Nothing." Ollie folded the message and placed it in his pocket.

"Bloody hell," Boar said. He ran his hand over the table and found his cup, then took a swig of brandy. "The message should have come from the RAF, not from her."

Ollie noticed a tone of jealousy in Boar's voice. "Duchess isn't a military pigeon."

"Bollocks," Boar said. "Get some paper. I'll tell you what to write."

For the next several minutes, Boar dictated a note to the RAF. Ollie scribbled, but he ignored the lieutenant's commands. Instead, he coded his own message. By the time Boar was finished, he had begun to slur his words. Fortunately for Ollie, he hadn't drunk his brandy and was able to recite Boar's message from memory.

The lieutenant, seeming satisfied, slouched into a chair.

Ollie slid the note into the canister. He looked at the lieutenant, drunk and bandaged, and asked what had been on his mind since Boar had beaten the hell out of him in the Glasshouse. "Why do you hate Americans?"

Boar lowered his cup. "You're all bloody cowards."

"You know nothing about us," Ollie said, tightening the canister lid.

"I know far more than you think, Yank." He looked in Ollie's direction. "You join the party late, screw our women, and then go home."

Madeleine crossed her arms.

Ollie placed the canister on the table. "What are you talking about?"

Boar stood and stumbled. "My father was American."

Ollie stared at the lieutenant.

"Bastard maker was stationed near Epping." Boar grabbed the table to steady himself. "Like the other bloody Americans, he arrived three years after the Great War began. Coward never saw combat, so he found time to get his way with my mother. Got her pregnant, and when his regiment was sent home, promised to come back for her. But my mother never heard from him again. No telegram. No letter." He paused, attempting to keep his body from swaying. "The woman named me after my father, and she was reminded of that son of a bitch every time she looked at me."

"What he did was horrible," Ollie said. "But we're not all like your father."

Boar reached back, as if he was about to take a swing, then lost his balance. He fell into the table, causing a plate to shatter on the floor.

Madeleine took Boar's arm and helped him to the sofa. The lieutenant leaned his head back and mumbled something neither Ollie nor Madeleine could understand. Seconds later, the lieutenant began to snore.

"Jeez," Ollie said, "no wonder he hates me."

"What should we do?" Madeleine asked.

"Let him sleep it off. I'll get him under the floor later."

She pointed to Duchess. "And what about her?"

"I'll release her in the morning." He picked up Duchess and fastened the canister to her leg. She squirmed, then fluttered to the door.

"She wants to leave," Madeleine said.

Duchess pecked the door.

"I don't think pigeons fly at night."

"How do you know?"

"Just a guess." He kneeled to Duchess, then stroked her back. "You need to rest."

Duchess blinked, then pecked.

"Okay." He peeked through the curtain, then opened the door.

Duchess waddled over the threshold, flapped her wings, and disappeared into the night.

CHAPTER 39

AIRAINES, FRANCE

Ollie sat in the barn with the decoded messages on his lap. He blew on his fingers, numb from the cold, and read the words again. And again.

For the past five days, he had corresponded with Susan. Each afternoon, Duchess swooped down from the sky and gracefully landed on Madeleine's doorstep. And considering that the pigeon's flights had become keenly accurate, like the arrival times at a train depot, Ollie was often already peeking through the curtains, prepared to snatch her inside.

After removing Duchess's canister, he'd stroke her wings and give her fresh water, while his pulse quickened with anticipation. Then he'd open the canister to retrieve the note. And there, on a small piece of rolled yellow stationery, were Susan's words, hidden under a plethora of codes.

Susan's messages, which Flight Lieutenant Boar had demanded be read out loud, confirmed that the intelligence on the airfield was being relayed to the RAF. But there was nothing directly from the RAF, which rankled Boar. It didn't surprise Ollie that the RAF wasn't communicating with them. After all, Duchess was Susan's pet, and the British military had recently fled France and were occupied with Luftwaffe bombings, not to mention preparation for their own German invasion. Besides, there was nothing the military could do for them. Behind enemy lines, they were on their own.

Mostly, Susan's notes contained bits of news and words of hope that were directed toward Ollie, which he purposely left out during his readings to Boar. It wasn't that he feared the lieutenant, although he'd have to admit, the man was intimidating, even blindfolded. The fact was, some of what was in the messages was none of Boar's business.

He leaned against a barn stall and read the deciphered messages, focusing on Susan's closing words. Whispering somewhere deep inside his head was the sweet sound of her voice.

Miss you. Wish you were sitting next to me.

Ollie gently touched the paper, then retrieved another message.

I hope the war will soon be over and we'll be together.

I wish I could be with you. Hold you. And never let you go. But he couldn't say that. Any of it. After all, the chances of him making it out of France were slim at best. He couldn't imagine causing her any further sorrow. She'd already lost too much. And now, he learned, Bertie's health was in decline. As much as he wanted to say more, the most he could do was journal his emotions, which he kept tucked inside the codebook.

He read through Susan's messages a second time, then took out a piece of paper and began to write. Hopefully, Duchess had made it to Epping. He'd have another message, which included the recent sighting of a dozen Panzer tanks, ready to send when Duchess arrived. As he wrote, he debated whether to tell Susan about the pigeons.

He'd learned from Madeleine, returning home after standing

for over four hours in a bread line, that some of the starving French had resorted to eating Source Columba pigeons. Dropped across the ravaged countryside, some of the pigeons, depending on when the person finding them had had his or her last meal, were viewed as food packages. Rather than send what they may have viewed as a futile message to Britain, along with what could be a meal for malnourished children, the French were smuggling pigeons into their homes and eating them. He hoped that Madeleine's stories were exceptional instances of survival. But considering the rationed scraps she was permitted to bring home from the market, he feared that the situation would only get worse. Much worse.

To complicate matters, the Wehrmacht had enlisted falcons. During Ollie's last reconnaissance at the airfield, he had witnessed a German soldier at the far edge of the field with a raptor perched on his arm. Ollie had expected to count only planes, their numbers seeming to multiply like rodents in a corn silo. But as he peered through the underbrush, his eyes were drawn away from the rows of Messerschmitt fighters to that soldier.

The soldier had dropped his binoculars, raised his arm, and slipped off the falcon's leather blindfold. The raptor awakened. It flapped its large wings and surged skyward. Ollie saw its target. A bird, high above a row of pines, less than a hundred yards away. And he knew, from his brief time with Susan, that it was a pigeon. The falcon closed in. The pigeon, unaware of the predator, continued its westerly flight toward the Channel. Within seconds, the falcon had shot out its talons and snagged the pigeon in midair flight. It glided to the ground with its prey in its grasp. As the falcon ripped away flesh with its beak, Ollie hoped that Duchess wouldn't fly near the airfield. Despite being an agile pigeon, she'd be no match for a falcon.

Ollie pressed his pencil against the paper. The air inside the barn was thick with the smell of manure. He struggled between truth and faith, whether he should include details about the fate of the pigeons or believe that the mission, despite its losses, would eventually be successful. In the end, he omitted news on the pigeon casualties.

He finished his note and slid it into his pocket, then rubbed the ache in his foot. The past few days had done him some good. The swelling had receded. Although he had trouble raising his elbow, he was able to remove the sling and walk with his arm at his side. He was feeling better, perhaps even enough to make the escape attempt. But he couldn't say as much for the lieutenant.

Boar's eyes were still bandaged. It'd be two more days until the doctor returned to examine him. Over the past week, Boar and Ollie had stayed away from each other, as much as two men sleeping in the confinement of a crawl space could. It was clear, at least to Ollie, that there was no changing Boar's dislike toward him, an American corresponding with an Englishwoman. And the daily messages from Susan only seemed to fuel Boar's envy.

As Ollie was about to leave the barn, he heard an engine. The ping of pistons grew. He stopped. Crouched. The engine stopped. He peeked through a crack in the siding. A Nazi officer got out of his vehicle and adjusted his cap over his partially missing ear. In contrast to his dark uniform, his waxen skin appeared to glow.

Dietrich. Ollie froze. His mind raced. *Would Madeleine have time to hide Boar?*

The Nazi's jackboots crunched over gravel. He stepped to the door and knocked.

Shivers shot up Ollie's spine.

Dietrich slipped off his leather gloves and knocked harder.

Ollie scanned for a place to hide. A minuscule pile of hay. A mound of rotten potatoes.

The cottage door opened.

"Herr Dietrich," Madeleine said.

The Nazi pushed her aside. He stepped inside and shut the door.

Choices flooded Ollie's head. *Stay? Hide? Run?* He struggled to clear his thoughts. Despite his instincts to flee, he stayed. Waited. Minutes passed. His skin turned cold. As he was second-guessing his decision not to hide in the woods, he heard a crack, like a chair falling over. Squeals. Shouts. Hairs stood on the back of his neck.

Ollie stared through the crack. He expected to hear shots. Instead, the cottage door flung open. Dietrich, holding Louis by the hind leg, dragged the hog outside. Adrenaline flooded Ollie's veins.

Louis squealed and wriggled, frantically attempting to dig his front hooves into the earth. But the tiny truffle hog, no bigger than a dwarf-sized bulldog, was no match for the Nazi.

"*Arrêtez!*" Madeleine screamed, as she ran from the cottage.

Dietrich pulled the hog into the yard and unfastened his pistol strap.

Louis, desperately trying to escape, twisted and arched his head toward Madeleine.

Ollie clenched his fists.

In one fluid move, Dietrich removed his pistol and aimed at the squirming hog.

Madeleine, reaching Dietrich, pounded her hands against the Nazi's chest.

Dietrich snarled. He cocked back his arm and struck Madeleine with his pistol, snapping the woman's head back and tumbling her to the ground.

Ollie scanned the barn. A rake. Mushy potato piles. Broken boards. Above him, hanging from an iron hook, a broken scythe missing its handle, the blade chipped and rusted. He grabbed it anyway.

Madeleine slowly raised her head. Dry leaves clung to her hair. A wad of saliva hung from her lower lip. Her chest heaved as she sucked in air. Somehow, she managed to get to her feet. She wavered, as if she were about to fall, then approached Dietrich.

The Nazi shook his head. The hog wriggled in his grasp.

Madeleine, her hair wicked with blood, stepped to him. "*S'il vous plaît. Libérez-le.*"

Dietrich pointed the pistol at her face.

She closed her eyes. Her hands trembled. But she held her ground.

If it weren't for Louis's squeals, and the fact that Dietrich had his back turned to him, Ollie couldn't have approached without being detected. For the moment, a squirming hog and a bold Frenchwoman had Dietrich's full attention. At least until he pulled the trigger. And it would all be over—Louis's squeals, Madeleine's cries. Ollie limped faster. His pulse pounded in his ears. Ten yards. Five yards. Then gravel crunched under his boots.

Dietrich jerked. Pupils widened. A scowl flared. He turned his weapon.

Ollie swung back. He lurched forward and brought the rusted blade down over the man's hand. He expected a discharge of gunpowder and braced for a bullet to pierce his rib cage. Instead, a loud snap, like a hickory branch that had been swung against the base of a tree.

Dietrich howled. The pistol fell.

Ollie glanced at the Nazi's hand, a thumb cocked at an obtuse angle, as if he had suddenly grown an extra joint. He expected Dietrich to run. Retreat. At the very least, raise his hands to surrender. Because, Ollie believed, that is what a typical human would do. But he quickly realized that the Nazi was no ordinary man when the German came at him like a Greco-Roman wrestler. Hands extended. A bone, resembling a bloodied piece of chalk, protruded from his thumb.

Okay. It's you or me. Ollie swung. As the blade cut through the air, a sick feeling flooded his gut. He had underestimated Dietrich's quickness. And aimed too high.

Dietrich ducked, shot forward, and landed his shoulder into Ollie's leg.

Ollie's knee buckled. His ankle gave out, and he toppled to the ground with Dietrich pouncing on his chest. His ligaments strained, and his injured shoulder was about to pop from its socket. He struggled to use the blade. But Dietrich, like a rabid dog, bit into Ollie's coat sleeve. Incisors ground into his flesh. Pain flooded his arm. And he dropped the blade.

Ollie's jaw snapped back as Dietrich, with his one good arm, landed a punch. Dazed, he clawed for the blade.

Madeleine screamed. She pounded her fists against Dietrich's back.

The Nazi jammed his elbow into Madeleine's torso. Her high-pitched cries were gagged as air rushed from her lungs. She collapsed, clutching her stomach.

Dietrich rolled off of Ollie's chest. Initially, Ollie thought the Nazi had found the blade and was preparing to sink it into his skull. Instead, he saw Dietrich scrambling like a crab. A few feet away, the pistol.

Ollie dove. He seized Dietrich's leg.

The Nazi stretched his arm. His fingers inched toward the weapon.

A jackboot smashed into Ollie's cheek. His vision turned black. He struggled to clear the fog in his head and realized that Dietrich was out of his grasp. *It's over*, he thought. A few seconds was all the Nazi needed. He expected to hear shots ring out. Instead, a high-pitched yelp. He raised his head and saw a trail of gauze in the yard. And Dietrich with the blade protruding from his back. Standing over him was Flight Lieutenant Boar.

Dietrich flung his arms. Twisted. Turned. But couldn't reach the blade, placed like a harpoon between his shoulder blades.

Boar tackled Dietrich onto his back, sinking the blade deep into his body. The Nazi screeched.

Boar gripped Dietrich's neck. His forearm muscles flexed as he cut off the man's air.

Dietrich kicked. His legs weakened. A foot twitched. Then his body went still.

Ollie crawled to Madeleine. "You okay?"

She nodded; blood and dirt smeared her face. Louis nuzzled her side.

Boar released his grip on Dietrich's neck, then stood over the body. "Fools," he said with his back to Ollie. "You risked our lives for a bloody pig."

"He was gonna shoot her," Ollie said.

The lieutenant turned.

The first thing Ollie noticed was Boar's missing bandages. The second, the lieutenant's eyes. One clear and alert. The other dead, like unpolished alabaster.

CHAPTER 40

EPPING, ENGLAND

Susan attached the canister to the pigeon's leg, caressed its wings, and gently slid the bird into the cardboard tube. She felt the weight of the pigeon sink to the bottom. Sealing on the cap, perforated with holes to allow in air, she placed the tube with the others in the corner of the loft. She stacked them in a pyramid, careful not to rotate the pigeons upside down, realizing that in a few hours the military would load them onto planes like airmail.

She lifted a parachute and rubbed the silky material between her fingers. The parachute appeared to be terribly small, more suitable for floating a child's toy soldier from a second-story window than dropping a pigeon from a plane. Also, the cardboard tubes looked flimsy in comparison to the former RAF baskets. She understood the reasons why the military had made the changes. *Smaller packages equals fewer planes equals fewer dead pilots.* But she loathed them anyway. The tubes were far too dark and restrictive, not to mention coffin-like. No way to treat a pigeon, especially one that was risking its life to save Britain. She dropped the parachute and continued loading. And with each pigeon she removed from its cubby, anxiety swelled inside her chest.

She started preparing the last of the pigeons for the mission before dawn, waking well before Bertie. He'd barely slept last night—or the past several days, for that matter—kept awake by his rounds of coughing. The only times she didn't hear him wheezing or blowing his nose, it seemed, was during deafening bursts of antiaircraft fire.

Grandfather was right, she thought. There was likely nothing wrong with his heart. Just his dodgy knees and an ordinary cold that had progressed to the brink of pneumonia, given the rattle in his chest. Still, Dr. Collins had insisted that Bertie remain on nitroglycerin, as well as begin taking sulfa pills. But the medication, and hours spent with his head draped in a towel over a steaming pot of water, had done little to loosen his congestion.

"There's no room at St. Margaret's. The beds are filled with casualties from London," Dr. Collins had said. "He'll receive better care at home." But the infection continued to grow in his chest. Armed with nothing more than sulfa pills, measly rations, weak tea, and old eucalyptus oil that had lost its scent, she questioned if her ministrations had done him any good.

Susan placed the last pigeon into a canister, sealed the cap, and carefully placed it on the stack. Her mind raced. Her body ached with doubt. To reassure herself, if only for a moment, she reached into her coat and removed Ollie's recent decoded message. And read it for the fourth time.

> *Susan,*
> *I'm grateful for your messages. You once told me that your mission was going to win the war. Now, more than ever, I believe in you.*

She glanced at the stack of dropping tubes. The loft, once filled with cooing pigeons, was silent, except for the muted scratching of talons on cardboard.

Wish Bertie a swift recovery. He's in good care with you by his side.

Your letters give me strength. I hear your voice when I read the words. I'll escape. Promise to return to Epping.

Ollie

Susan folded the note and placed it inside her coat. Gathering her strength, she left the loft.

The past few nights, the battles in the skies had been fierce. Antiaircraft guns boomed. The earth quaked. China fell from shelves. And now the sheep pasture was speckled with shrapnel, like ugly black hailstones. As she walked across the yard, she noticed a dull shimmer among the bits of shrapnel. She stopped. A brass bullet casing, the length of a stick of gum. She imagined that the casing came from either an RAF fighter or a Luftwaffe bomber. She picked it up. The cold metal made her skin crawl. Rather than check for markings, she threw it toward the forest; it landed several yards short of a bordering beech tree.

"I hate war!" she shouted.

A rustle came from the RAF tent still erected in the yard. A soldier poked out his head.

Susan glared at him. "You heard me."

The soldier, like a startled gopher, ducked his head back inside.

As she approached the cottage door, she heard a wheeze. Hacking. A wet cough. She glanced up at her bedroom window, which was now left partway open for Duchess. A gust of frigid wind caused the blackout curtain to sway.

I had a little bird, its name was Enza. I opened the window, and in flew Enza.

She shivered. Pulling her coat around her body, she stepped inside.

Chapter 41

Epping, England

Susan entered the cottage to a wave of deep rasping coughs. The air was dank from steaming pots that had been left on the stove to loosen Bertie's congestion. Mist covered the windows. Upholstery had turned damp. The first floor of the cottage, it seemed, had been turned into a croup tent. She hung up her coat and went to Bertie, slumped in his chair under layers of wool blankets.

"You're up early," Bertie said, opening his eyes.

Susan nodded, noticing the hoarseness in his voice. "A military lorry will be here in an hour."

He coughed and spat into a tattered piece of fabric. "I'm afraid I've soiled all our handkerchiefs."

She touched his arm. "That's why we have them."

Bertie folded his handkerchief and leaned back.

"How are you feeling?"

He struggled to clear phlegm from his throat.

Susan picked up his cup, half filled with tepid tea, from the side table and raised it to his lips.

He sipped. Winced. Swallowed.

She set down the cup. "Something to eat?"

He shook his head.

"Eucalyptus oil?"

He pressed his handkerchief over his mouth to muffle a cough, then lowered his hand. "We need to talk."

"You need to rest."

He forced himself to sit up. Blankets slumped to his lap. "Pigeons ready?"

"Yes." She stared at him. Lacking the energy to shave, he had allowed white whiskers to sprout on his face. Dark bags sagged under his eyes, and his breath was sour from the infection in his lungs.

He reached his hand and lightly squeezed her fingers.

Susan forced a smile.

He released her hand, then adjusted his blankets. "You're making a difference in this war, Susan. Despite the losses, our pigeons are gathering intelligence on Hitler's military."

She thought of the empty cubbies, the hundreds of missing pigeons. "We need more to train."

"We won't receive more." He blew his nose but produced nothing but a thick gurgle.

"How do you know?"

"I've already spoken to Jonathan Wallace of the National Pigeon Service."

"That's not fair," Susan said. "Just because you're feeling poorly doesn't mean that we can't continue with Source Columba. I'll talk to Mr. Wallace, tell him that I'm perfectly capable of taking on the extra work until you recover." She stepped to the telephone.

"It's not my condition, my dear." He labored to inhale. "It's our location."

Susan stopped. She turned and looked at him.

"Our farm is near an RAF airfield, a target for the Luftwaffe." He coughed, then picked up his cup and drank. "We're also directly under their bloody flight path to bomb London. It's not safe."

"What can we do?" she asked.

"The National Pigeon Service is setting up training farms in Northampton, away from the bombings." He cleared his throat. "Jonathan is saving a position for you."

"I'm not leaving."

"Britain needs you." He paused, then tucked his dirty handkerchief under his blanket, as if to hide the evidence of his worsening condition. "We'll soon have no pigeons. Unless you go to Northampton, you'll no longer be part of Source Columba."

She stepped to his chair. "I won't leave you."

"I'll join you later, my dear." He glanced at the bottle of sulfa pills on the side table. "The McCrearys can check in on me until I've recovered."

"Nonsense." Susan crossed her arms. Mrs. McCreary was a sweet woman who would no doubt go out of her way to care for Bertie. But her husband, a meek man who spent much of the day hiding in his root cellar, would be of little, if any, help. Regardless, she'd never leave Bertie. Ever. Rather than argue, she leaned over him and retrieved his cup. "We'll talk of this later."

In the kitchen, she prepared tea. As the leaves steeped, she heard him cough, struggling to expel mucus from his lungs. A sudden sense of helplessness washed over her. She wanted to cry. Give up. Instead, she bit her lip and buried her tears. *Be an egg.*

As she carried his tea into the living room, a flutter came from upstairs. She placed the cup on Bertie's side table, spilling tea on the floor. She turned to see Duchess swoop down the stairs and land on the sofa.

Susan rushed to Duchess and swept her into her arms. Cold feathers pressed against her skin.

"Your open bedroom window works splendidly to avoid the soldiers," Bertie said.

Susan kissed Duchess on the head. As she removed the canister from the pigeon's leg, a tail feather fell to the floor. She stopped, noticing that Duchess's once-shimmering fluorescent colors now appeared dull, as if bleached by the sun. Along with the bird's rapid heart rate, Susan realized that Duchess wasn't cooing. She blew warm air over her frigid wings. After a few minutes, Duchess began to produce a soft murmur. Susan exhaled. She retrieved a jar of grain that she had stored in the kitchen and sprinkled the feed onto the table. Gently, she placed her pigeon in front of the food.

Duchess gave a few pecks, then sat down and closed her eyes.

Susan pushed grain to her.

The pigeon made no effort to eat.

"She can't keep up the pace," Susan said to Bertie. "It's too much."

Duchess tucked her head under her wing.

Bertie leaned forward, attempting to get a better view from his chair. "She's doing what she believes to be her duty."

Susan hesitated, then opened the canister and slid out the note.

"No need to read it all to me," Bertie said. "Merely tell me the intelligence, and I'll scribble it on paper for the soldiers."

Susan nodded.

Bertie removed a sulfa pill from the bottle on his table and swallowed it with a gulp of tea. He looked at Susan. "You'll see him again, my dear."

She stepped to him and gave him a hug.

"Not so close. Don't want you ill."

"Don't care." She squeezed him tight, noticing that he'd lost weight. Bones protruded under his pajamas.

Duchess raised her head, stretched her wings, and fluttered to Bertie's chair.

He stroked a wing with his finger.

Susan retrieved a note that she had already written for Ollie. She began to place it in the canister and hesitated. She grabbed a pencil and the codebook, then added to her message.

May need to leave for Northampton. Come back to me. I'll be waiting.

She rolled the paper, placed it inside the canister, and attached it to Duchess's leg.

Duchess flew to the window. She pecked against the glass.

"No," Susan said. "You need to rest."

Duchess tilted her head and ruffled her feathers. She pecked at the glass.

Susan picked up Duchess and stroked her back.

Duchess squirmed, then fluttered from Susan's hands. The pigeon returned to the window and pecked harder.

Bertie coughed. "She wants to leave."

"Too soon."

For several minutes, Duchess incessantly tapped on the glass. Each time Susan tried to touch Duchess, the pigeon flapped away and then waddled along the baseboard. After Susan's sixth attempt to calm her, Duchess fluttered around the living room.

A breeze brushed Susan's face. She turned to see Duchess land on the mantel.

"Please," Susan said. Slowly, she stepped to the fireplace and gently rubbed the soft tuff on Duchess's head. "A wee rest."

Duchess waddled. Her talons scratched over the wood.

Susan glanced at Bertie and noticed that he was pointing to the ceiling.

A jolt hit her. *My bedroom window*. She looked up.

Bertie nodded.

As Susan turned to go to her room, Duchess leaped into the air and swooped upstairs. Susan's heart raced. She ran, her wellies feeling like deep-sea diving shoes as she scaled the steps. Reaching her room, she found Duchess perched on the windowsill.

"Wait!"

Duchess dove from the ledge.

Susan stuck her head out the window. Cold wind bit at her cheeks. She watched Duchess flap her wings, using more effort than usual, as if her canister were filled with sand. As her tired pigeon slowly gained altitude, Susan shuddered. *There's no place to rest over the Channel*.

CHAPTER 42

AIRAINES, FRANCE

"Bury him in the woods," Boar said, standing over the body. "And hide the car in the barn."

Ollie looked at Dietrich, his mouth gaped. Blood oozed from his shattered hand. "No."

"Do it," Boar barked.

Ollie glanced at Madeleine, sitting next to him on the ground and pressing a hand to the cut on her scalp. "We can't leave any evidence. The Nazis will know his routine. They'll search this place and blame Madeleine."

Boar stepped to them.

Madeleine looked up and gasped. "Your eye!"

Boar touched his face, as if he were expecting to find one of his eyes still bandaged. Instead, he found a shriveled cornea. His face turned pale.

Madeleine reached for the lieutenant.

Boar turned. He stormed into the cottage, leaving the door open.

"Let me see." Ollie kneeled next to Madeleine and examined her head. Near her temple was a quarter-inch-deep gash. And a protrusion the size of a small river stone. He plucked a dead leaf from her hair, then pulled a handkerchief from his pocket and carefully pressed it to her wound.

"*Merci*," Madeleine said.

"What happened?"

"Herr Dietrich had come for his truffles. He wasn't due to arrive for a few days." She rubbed Louis's head.

The hog snorted.

"When I told him that I had no truffles, he became angry and said he was going to shoot my *schwein*."

"Jesus," Ollie said. "That's it?"

"The Nazis have little tolerance." She took the handkerchief from Ollie and glanced at the bloodied fabric. "Even for a woman who's neglected her truffle hunting."

Ollie helped Madeleine to her feet. "You've been busy helping us. I'm sorry we've put you in this mess." He looked at the Nazi's car; its shiny grille and bug-eye headlights appeared to stare back at him. He paused, then slipped off his jacket.

"What are you doing?" she asked.

"I'm gonna take care of this." He removed his shirt.

"But the flight lieutenant—"

"I know what Boar said, but I'm not leaving this Nazi or his car on your farm for the Germans to find." Cold wind whipped through his undershirt, causing goose bumps to crop up on his arms. He handed the clothing to Madeleine, then stepped to Dietrich and began to unbutton his tunic.

"No," Madeleine said.

Ollie finished unbuttoning Dietrich's tunic, noticing that the man's body temperature was already beginning to cool. He slid the Nazi's arms from the sleeves. As he attempted to pull off the tunic, the clothing remained stuck to Dietrich's back. He swallowed, rolled the body over, and lifted the tunic over the scythe that protruded from his spine. Burying a wave of nausea, he slipped on the tunic, then retrieved Dietrich's cap and pistol.

Madeleine grabbed his arm. "You must not do this."

Ollie pulled away, then opened the trunk of the car, only to find that it was barely big enough to fit a small bag, let alone a Nazi. With no other option, he grabbed Dietrich by his jackboots and dragged him to the car. Struggling to lift the weight with his bad shoulder, Ollie flopped the body onto the floor of the back seat. He covered the Nazi with a black leather trench coat that had been neatly folded on the passenger seat.

Ollie looked at Madeleine as he fastened the top of the tunic. The collar tightened against his neck. "I need you to trust me."

Madeleine squeezed her handkerchief. Louis pressed against her leg.

"Make sure Boar doesn't do anything stupid." He placed a hand on her shoulder. "He'll listen to you."

Reluctantly, she nodded.

"Find Guillaume's friend. Tell him that we leave tomorrow. If I'm not back by morning, have them go without me." Before Madeleine could respond, he got into the car and shut the door. As he reached for the ignition, he noticed the key was missing. He found it by leaning into the back seat and searching Dietrich's pants pockets. His hand shook as he inserted the key into the ignition.

CHAPTER 43

AIRAINES, FRANCE

Flight Lieutenant Boar tried using the back of a spoon to see his reflection, but the pewter was too tarnished. He threw the utensil back into the sink and went to Madeleine's bedroom. Although he rarely left the confinement of the kitchen, other than sleeping under the floorboards, he knew exactly where her room was located by the creak of her footsteps. He found what he was looking for above a washbasin—a chipped gilt-framed mirror. He stepped toward his reflection. And saw a monster.

The left eye worked properly, although his brow was bulbous and the sclera was completely bloodshot. But the right eye was gruesome. A disfigured eyelid was pieced together with stitches. Lashes gone. And the cornea was sunken and clouded, like a spoiled fish. He touched his eye, shriveled and broken. His socket contained what appeared to be a hunk of gristle.

Boar slammed his fist into the mirror, sending shards of glass over the floor. He pressed his hands to his face. *I'll never fly again.* His breath quickened. He adjusted his weight. Under the crunch of broken glass beneath his boots, he heard a mechanical cough. A rev of an engine. He ripped his pistol from the holster and ran to the door. On the porch, he saw the Nazi's car driving away, the

Yank behind the wheel. Rage boiled. *It's your fault.* He raised his weapon.

"*Arrêtez!*" Madeleine shouted from the yard.

Boar aimed at the rear window. The only reason he hadn't used his pistol to kill the Nazi was that the shots would have alerted the Wehrmacht. But now he didn't care. His finger tightened on the trigger.

Madeleine scrambled toward the porch. Her hog squealed. She waved her arms. "Please . . . no!"

Boar squinted. His depth perception, with one eye, was gone. As he narrowed his sight on the silhouette behind the wheel, Madeleine grabbed his arm, causing him to lose his target.

"He's trying to help," Madeleine said.

"Idiot." He lowered his pistol and watched the car disappear.

Louis brushed Madeleine's leg. She patted her hog on the head. It snorted and nestled under a bush.

Madeleine paused to catch her breath, then retrieved Ollie's jacket and shirt from the yard and went inside the cottage.

Boar, noticing that a patch of Madeleine's hair was soaked with blood, slipped the pistol into his holster. He followed her inside and helped her into a chair. Taking her handkerchief, he dipped the end in a pitcher of water and softly dabbed her scalp.

"*Merci.*" She looked at him.

Boar cleared his throat. "I'm blind in my right eye."

"I'll call the *docteur.*"

Boar shook his head. "It's gone."

"I'm sorry."

He continued examining her wound. "Broke your mirror, I'm afraid."

She sighed. "Just as well. I haven't had a reason to look at myself in quite some time."

Boar pressed on her cut until the bleeding stopped. He cleaned her hair, leaving a section of gray roots dyed red.

Madeleine took the handkerchief from Boar and placed it on

the table. She rummaged through an ashtray and plucked the remnant tail of a cigarette. She dusted it with a finger, lit it, and handed it to him.

He took a drag and tasted ash. A tiny amount of burnt tobacco filled his lungs.

Madeleine stood and grabbed her coat.

"You should lie down." Boar dropped the smoldering nub of paper into the ashtray.

She ignored him and retrieved a hat hanging on a hook next to her truffle bag and placed it on her head. She adjusted the brim to cover the protrusion on her temple. "The Nazis will notice a missing officer." She buttoned her coat and opened the door. "They'll retrace Dietrich's steps, including his visits to requisition my truffles."

A gust of cold air brushed Boar's face. "Where are you going?"

"To talk with my friend." Madeleine looked at him. "You leave tomorrow." She stepped outside and shut the door.

He thought about stopping her. But it didn't matter. In fact, nothing mattered anymore. Although his heart beat, his lungs held air, and his limbs worked, he was broken. Worthless. Every fiber in his body wanted to fight. But now, even if he did make it back to Britain, he'd never command a squadron. Nor would he be allowed to fight with one eye. At best, he'd be assigned to work behind a desk. *Bloody hell.* He pulled out his pistol and took inventory of his ammunition, including the bullets in the extra clip that was attached to his belt. Consumed with resentment, he resolved to kill as many Nazis as he could and save one bullet for himself. And perhaps another for the Yank.

An hour later, as he sat in a chair waiting for Madeleine or Ollie to return, a faint scrape on the porch caused him to raise his pistol. He listened, then crept to the window. Inching back the curtain, he peeked outside. Nothing.

Peck. Peck.

Recognizing the sound, he exhaled and opened the door. On

the porch, he saw what had to be the Yank's pigeon, considering its vibrant plume. "You look like a bloody peacock." He shook his head. "Surprised you haven't been shot down."

Duchess looked up and ruffled her feathers.

Boar stepped toward the bird.

Duchess waddled away. She stretched her wings, preparing to take flight.

He stopped. Slowly, he slipped his weapon into the holster.

Duchess fluttered into the yard.

Boar ground his teeth. He paused, then turned toward the cottage and said, "Yank, your bird is back. Come and get it before it flies away."

He went inside, leaving the door open. Pressing his back against the wall, out of view of the pigeon, he waited. Several minutes passed. As he was about to give up, he heard a flutter, then scratching. A moment later, the bird waddled inside.

Boar slammed the door. A crack shot through the cottage.

Duchess leaped and flapped her wings.

He watched the Yank's bird fly about the cottage, banging against a curtain and knocking a cup off the table. Realizing it'd be difficult to catch a bird with his bare hands, even in a small room, he retrieved a blanket from his hole under the floorboards. He tossed the blanket, like a net, into the air.

Duchess swooped. The blanket grazed her tail and fell to the floor. She darted to a bookshelf.

Boar picked up the blanket, and holding it like a matador, he closed in on the bird.

Duchess, her body aslant, clung to a shelf with her talons.

Boar threw the blanket. The bird and several books fell to the floor. Beneath the wool fabric, a small wriggling bulge. He slid his hand inside, wrapped his fingers over its wings, and pulled out the bird.

Duchess pecked. She flexed her wiry legs.

Boar tightened his grip and noticed the Bakelite canister. Turning the pigeon over, he unclasped the tube from its leg. He bundled the bird inside the blanket, tying the ends to keep it from escaping.

He unscrewed the cap, slid out the note, and stared at the jumbled lettering. "Bollocks," he muttered. As he was about to slip the note back into the canister, he noticed the Yank's jacket hanging on the coatrack. He rummaged through the jacket and found the codebook tucked inside the breast pocket. Opening the cover, several notes fell out. He picked them up from the floor. As he read the messages, a much different variation from what the Yank had read to him, his skin turned hot.

Duchess squirmed. The blanket twitched.

Boar stepped to the blanket and placed his boot over the bulge. As he began to lower his foot, he stopped.

Despite the urge to crush the Yank's pigeon, he sat down at the table and deciphered the message. An acidic bile burned behind his breastbone. He crumpled the paper, tossed it into the woodstove, and watched it ignite. Then he retrieved a pencil and paper. And using the codebook, he began to write.

CHAPTER 44

AIRAINES, FRANCE

Ollie's heart pounded as he turned onto the road heading away from the village. The cabin of the car, although empty, smelled of cheese and cured meats, as if Dietrich had been spending his time requisitioning food from starving villagers. Madeleine, Ollie realized, was not the only exploited person in Airaines.

He ground the gears, attempting to figure out the foreign stick shift. *Where do I go? How far will I get?* Fearing that the roads would be controlled by the Wehrmacht, he always hiked through the woods on his attempts to obtain intelligence on the airfield. Three miles down the road, he found that his assumptions were correct.

As Ollie rounded a curve, he saw a Wehrmacht soldier blocking the road with what looked like a wooden sawhorse. The soldier picked up his rifle.

Dread flooded Ollie's body, causing his foot to slip from the gas pedal. His pulse increased as the car decelerated. He grabbed the pistol from the passenger seat and tucked it under his leg.

The soldier, his weapon propped on his shoulder, stepped into the road.

Ollie's mind raced. *Turn around? Run the roadblock?* He adjusted his cap, then gripped the wheel. As he was about to slam the accelerator, the soldier grabbed the sawhorse. Ollie hesitated and noticed the small Nazi flags mounted on each of the sloped fenders. Red cloth emblazoned with black swastikas thrashed in the wind.

The soldier pulled the roadblock aside, then snapped to attention. He shot up his arm, stiff and straight in a Nazi salute.

Ollie stared ahead, avoiding eye contact. As he approached, he raised his arm, mirroring the soldier, and saw blood on his cuff. His breath stalled in his lungs. Quickly, he lowered his hand as he passed by. He shifted gears and accelerated. In the rearview mirror, he expected to see the soldier raise his rifle. Instead, the sawhorse was slid back into the road.

For two, maybe three minutes, the road remained clear, until a convoy of Wehrmacht trucks approached from the opposite direction. Soldiers packed into the back of the trucks looked down at him as he passed.

Ollie lowered the cap on his head, hoping they wouldn't recognize a farm boy from Maine disguised as a Nazi officer or detect the peculiar mass in the back of the car. Wind from the trucks blasted the automobile. He steadied the wheel and noticed sweat growing on his back, quickly realizing it was blood from Dietrich's tunic seeping through his undershirt. When the last truck passed, he rolled down the window and sucked in air.

A few miles farther, he turned into a barren field. The car bounced from the ruts. Dietrich's body pressed against the back of his seat.

He drove to the edge of the woods and wedged the vehicle under a row of pines. Flooring the accelerator, Ollie propelled the car deep into the canopy, until the tires sank into the mud. He turned off the ignition and got out. Scanning the area, he saw the remains of a burned farmhouse fifty yards away. The roof was missing, windows were broken, and the siding was streaked with char marks. He pulled Dietrich's body, which was beginning to stiffen with rigor mortis, from the back seat. Unable to straighten the Nazi's legs, knees scrunched to the torso, Ollie placed Dietrich on the trench coat and used it to drag him across the field.

As he neared the farmhouse, he saw a stone well surrounded by tall weeds. He tugged harder. His shoulder throbbed. Reaching the well, he fell to the ground as the sound of a vehicle approached. He closed his eyes and listened to the engine whine closer, then fade away.

He took in deep breaths to gather his strength, then propped Dietrich against the well. Refusing to look at the man's face, he covered him with the coat. His back strained as he lifted the body. With one huge heave, he rolled Dietrich, trench coat and all, into the well. He expected to hear a splash. Instead, he heard a revolting thud.

He tossed Dietrich's cap, along with the tunic, into the well. Frigid air bit at his exposed skin, making him regret that he hadn't brought his jacket. He returned to the car, then ripped branches from a pine to cover the vehicle. In time, the car and Dietrich would be discovered. Hopefully, it would look like the work of the French Resistance, not a sweet woman who collected truffles. He removed the pistol from the car and placed it in the back of his trousers. As daylight faded, he worked his way through the forest, hoping he was headed in the right direction.

Returning to Airaines was far more difficult than any of Ollie's previous nocturnal excursions. Shortly after disposing of Dietrich's body, it began to rain. What started as a light drizzle turned to sleet. Without a coat, he struggled to keep his teeth from chattering. Storm clouds hid the moon and stars. With no markers to guide him, Ollie was forced to travel near the road. As headlights appeared, he hunkered on his belly in the underbrush. Ice pellets stung his neck. After each vehicle passed, he stood and continued his trek, knowing that, within a few minutes, he'd likely be back on his stomach.

The road swarmed with military traffic. Either the Nazis were searching for their missing officer or the Wehrmacht were adamant about maintaining their strict nightly curfews, regardless of the inclement weather. And high above the storm clouds, Luftwaffe bombers droned as they continued their nightly efforts to pulverize Britain.

What should have taken a couple of hours took almost four. It was late in the evening by the time Ollie reached Madeleine's cottage. He shivered. Wet clothes clung to his skin. He knocked, unable to feel his frozen knuckles rapping on the door. A moment later, a blackout curtain moved, exposing a flicker of candlelight.

The door swung open. Madeleine helped him inside and placed a blanket over his shoulders.

"Were you spotted?" Boar asked, sitting at the table.

Ollie shook his head. He tightened the blanket around his body and looked at Madeleine, a patch of her hair crusted with dried blood. "How's your head?"

She shrugged, then poured him a cup of warm water from a kettle.

Ollie gripped the cup, allowing the warmth to thaw his fingers. He sipped, then noticed Madeleine, her head lowered and staring at the floor. "What's wrong?"

Madeleine's lip quivered.

"Your bird came back while you were gone," Boar said.

Ollie placed his cup on the table. The blanket fell from his shoulders. "Where is she?"

Boar picked at a cigarette stub in an ashtray. "I sent it back with a message informing the RAF of our escape."

A cramp formed in Ollie's abdomen. "Was she carrying a message?"

Madeleine drew in a choppy breath. She retrieved a piece of paper from the kitchen counter and handed it to Ollie.

On first glance, Ollie noticed that the message was written on Source Columba stationery. But it wasn't coded. And it wasn't

Susan's handwriting. As he read the words, a shock jolted his core. He looked at Boar. His bad eye appeared as if its socket was filled with smoke. "You did this."

Boar scowled "Go to hell, Yank."

Anger flared. Ollie dropped the message, then stood and grabbed the lieutenant's collar.

Boar leapt to his feet, toppling his chair.

"No!" Madeleine screamed.

Ollie cocked back his arm and heard a click, then felt something hard against his torso. He looked down to see the lieutenant's pistol.

"The bird wouldn't let me get close." Boar pressed his weapon into Ollie's chest. "Madeleine caught it."

Ollie lowered his arm and slid his hand behind his back to grip the Nazi's pistol tucked against his belt.

"Enough!" Madeleine wedged herself between them, like a boxing referee breaking up a fight.

Boar lowered his pistol.

Madeleine, with watery eyes, looked at Ollie. "I returned from the village to find the flight lieutenant trying to catch Duchess. She wouldn't go near him." Gently, she placed her hands on Ollie's shoulders. "She came to me."

Ollie's body went numb. He picked up the message. Unable to read it again, he slid the paper into his pocket. In a fog of disbelief, he left the cottage and walked into the freezing rain.

CHAPTER 45

EPPING, ENGLAND

The earth quaked, knocking one of Bertie's smoking pipes off the mantel. Susan, desensitized from the nightly bombings, picked up the pipe, dusted it against her skirt, and returned it to its proper place. Then she kneeled beside Bertie, slumped in his chair. She picked up a washcloth from a small ceramic water basin and wiped his face.

Bertie opened his languid eyes.

"You must drink something," she said.

"Later," Bertie said.

As she moistened the cloth in the basin, a concussive detonation shook the cottage. Bits of plaster dropped from the ceiling.

Bertie coughed phlegm from his lungs. "I want you to sleep in the bomb shelter."

Susan noticed the rattle in Bertie's chest. Despite the sulfa pills, eucalyptus oil, Dr. Collins's daily visits, and hours of sitting over a steaming bowl of hot water with a towel draped over his head, her grandfather's condition was worsening. As days passed and his congestion thickened, she disguised her fear with a façade of optimism, hoping that he wouldn't notice the tremor in her voice. "No," she said, placing the cloth on his forehead. "We agreed we'd never go back there."

"It's getting worse," he said.

Susan thought of the bombings. The Luftwaffe had attacked Britain each night for well over a month, but she'd stopped counting. London was crumbling. People were dying. And the enemy was showing no sign of letting up. In fact, the attacks had only escalated, in both frequency and intensity, as if the Luftwaffe had limitless numbers of planes and explosives. They kept coming. Every night. The bombs bigger. The destruction greater. She had stopped reading the newspaper, dreading the reports of fatalities, many of whom were civilians. She also made it a point to step outside when Bertie listened to the daily radio broadcast. The words over the airways were depressing, speaking often of war atrocities and reminding her that Ollie was stuck in the midst of Nazi occupation. Hitler would likely bomb Britain into submission by spring. Life, as she knew it, would be changed forever. "I won't allow them to make us sleep in holes."

Bertie removed the washcloth from his head and dropped it into the basin. "I want you to go to Northampton," he said, taking her hand.

His weak grip caused a lump to form in Susan's throat.

"I've always been proud of you," he said. "I can't imagine a better granddaughter."

Her eyes welled with tears.

"Source Columba needs you, my dear. You're of greater help to Britain by training pigeons than caring for an old man with a wee cold."

"I'm not leaving you."

"I'm not asking you, Susan." He looked at her, his eyelids swollen with fever. "I'm telling you."

Susan felt his fingers relax. She watched his frail hand, covered with dark, bulbous veins, drop to his lap.

He coughed and pulled his blanket to his chest. "You got your stubbornness from me, I'm afraid."

Discreetly, she wiped her eyes. He'd brought up the subject of her going to Northampton more than once over the past two days. And knowing Bertie, he'd continue his endeavor to keep her safe. But how could she leave him? Who would care for him? Although she'd sent word with Duchess to inform Ollie about Northampton, she wasn't ready to leave. This was her home. Her grandfather. Her pigeons. Deep down, she knew she'd have to go. But not today. Or tomorrow. The most she could do, at least for the moment, was to delay the inevitable.

Susan retrieved the washcloth, squeezed out the excess water, and returned it to Bertie's forehead, noticing that his skin was hot to the touch. "All right," she said. "I'll go to Northampton, when you've recovered."

She had expected him to argue. Instead, he leaned back in his chair and said, "Have I told you the story about how your parents met?"

Susan smiled. "Yes," she said, "but I'm fond of how you tell it."

Amid coughs, sniffles, and the muted scent of eucalyptus, Susan listened to a much-shortened version of Bertie's story. She'd heard the tale perhaps a hundred times, but tonight was different. His words were precious to her, as she realized that the times she would hear his beautiful stories were numbered.

CHAPTER 46

EPPING, ENGLAND

Susan looked at Bertie, asleep in his chair. A candle, burned to a nub, flickered a dull amber glow over the room. His chest rose, then fell. She exhaled. Refusing to leave his side, she'd spent the night on the sofa rather than her bed. After an evening during which he coughed frightfully, she was glad he was finally able to rest. And she hoped that the worst of tonight's bombardment was over.

As she tried to sleep, a rustling, like a chipmunk had gotten into the attic, caused her to sit up. A cushion she had been using for her head fell to the floor.

Bertie opened his eyes and cleared his throat. "All right, my dear?"

She nodded, lit another candle, and then listened. The rumble of distant explosions. A gust of wind caused the cottage to creak. Seconds later, a flutter. And Duchess swooped downstairs.

Susan shot up, wanting to hold her pigeon, caress her wings, and warm her feathers. But she didn't want to make the same mistake of leaving her bedroom window open. So she ran upstairs and closed the sash to prevent Duchess from prematurely flying away. Running down the hallway, thoughts of Ollie's message filled her with hope. Her heart raced. She dashed downstairs and froze.

She found Duchess perched on Bertie's lap. Her once-exquisite feathers, which had shimmered with fluorescent green and purple, now appeared dull, tarnished like old silver. Despite being in the prime of her pigeon years, she looked haggard. Perhaps it was the candlelight. Or maybe Duchess's wan appearance was compounded by Bertie's condition—unshaven, oily hair, shoulder bones protruding under his nightclothes.

"She's knackered," Bertie said, staring at Duchess. He coughed into his handkerchief.

Duchess blinked.

"I'm under the weather," Bertie said to the pigeon.

Susan carefully picked up Duchess, untangling a toenail that had gotten stuck in Bertie's blanket. She kissed her pigeon on the head, then caressed her wings.

Duchess closed her eyes.

"She's freezing," Susan said. She blew warm air over her feathers. After a few minutes of warming her, she noticed that Duchess had fallen asleep. Rather than disturb her rest by unstrapping the canister from her leg, she carefully removed the message and returned the cap. Gently, she placed Duchess on Bertie's lap.

"It's too much for her," Susan said.

Bertie rubbed a finger over Duchess's back.

Susan stared at her exhausted pigeon and frail grandfather. Determined to mend them back to health, she'd begin by grounding Duchess for at least several days before allowing her to fly again. As for Bertie, she'd continue with his sulfa pills and vapor treatments until his infected lungs were clear.

She squeezed the rolled piece of paper. More than ever, she needed Ollie. She longed for his words, which would give her hope that everything would be all right. As she unfolded the note, a strange penmanship shocked her. Quickly, she retrieved the codebook and began to decipher the message.

> *Susan,*
> *Regret writing this. Encountered enemy.*
> *Ollie fled and failed to return.*

"No!" Susan shouted.

"What's wrong?" Bertie coughed.

Susan shook her head and continued decoding. She struggled to concentrate as she translated the message.

> *Assume he's been captured. Found*
> *codebook in belongings. Write no further.*
> *Inform RAF I attempt my escape tomorrow.*
> *Flight Lieutenant Clyde Boar, RAF*

"It can't be . . ." She labored to breathe. Her legs swayed.

Bertie slipped on his glasses.

Susan handed him the paper, then picked up Duchess and pressed the pigeon to her chest. As Bertie read the message, she prayed that her brain, shaken like a snow globe by the shock waves of exploding bombs, was not interpreting the words correctly. But she knew what she had read. And what it meant. There was no denying that whatever had happened in France had had tragic consequences.

No! Not Ollie! Dread gathered into a lump in the back of her throat, producing the urge to vomit. A cold sweat formed on her neck. *He's alive*, she struggled to convince herself. *He'll make it home.* But the revelation on that piece of paper was clear. Her hope of him returning to her was lost. Ollie was gone. A spasm of loneliness twisted her heart. Her mind and body gutted, she began to weep.

Bertie lowered the message and removed his glasses. He extended his arms.

Susan released Duchess and buried her head in Bertie's chest.

"We must have faith that he's all right," he said.

Duchess waddled in a circle on the floor.

Susan felt Bertie's chest heave as he struggled to contain a cough. "What are we to do?"

"First, we relay the message to the RAF."

She sat up and wiped her eyes. "Then what?"

"We wait."

"We must do something."

"At this point, we only know that our Oliver from Maine is missing."

Hearing the word *missing* caused Susan to lower her head into her hands.

Duchess perked her head. She waddled across the floor and poked Susan's ankle with her beak.

She looked at her pigeon. Duchess scratched the floor. Susan reached down to pick up Duchess, but she fluttered to the window and began pecking at the blackout curtain.

"She wants to leave," Bertie said.

Ollie's not there to receive a message. She clasped her hands to keep them from trembling.

Duchess stretched her wings and took flight. She circled the living room and darted upstairs.

A moment later, Susan heard pecking on her bedroom window. She glanced at the ceiling. When the noise stopped, she thought Duchess had given up, until she saw her swoop into the living room. Instead of landing, Duchess flew headfirst into the blackout curtain.

Susan gasped.

Duchess dropped to the floor.

"Good Lord!" Bertie said.

Susan went to pick up Duchess, but she shot up and fluttered.

The pigeon darted again for the window. The thud of Duchess's body striking the curtain caused Susan to scream.

Stunned, Duchess flapped one of her wings, propelling her sideways into the wall.

Susan scooped her pigeon into her arms. She stroked her back. But her touch only seemed to make things worse. Her wiry legs wriggled. Her talons scraped Susan's forearm. "What wrong?"

Duchess jutted her head.

For the next hour, Susan tried to calm Duchess. She rubbed her wings, tempted her with food, which she didn't eat, and blew warm air over her plume. And each time she thought her pigeon had calmed down, she released her grip only to see Duchess dart into the curtain and fall to the floor, now covered with a blanket to protect her from being injured. She'd even tried placing her in a basket she'd retrieved from a loft. But the confinement only made Duchess beat her wings against the cage. With few other options, Susan resorted to wrapping her pigeon in a towel.

Bertie struggled to stand from his chair. His weak knees wobbled. He grabbed his walking stick, dust-covered and propped against the fireplace, and hobbled to Susan.

Susan, swaddling Duchess, looked up from her seat on the floor. The sight of Bertie, relenting to use his walking stick, caused her eyes to water. "She's gone mad."

"We must let her go," he said.

"But she'll fly away. She doesn't have the strength."

Bertie coughed, then took a moment to catch his breath. "If she stays, she'll hurt herself."

Susan sensed Duchess fidgeting. The mission, it seemed, had turned her pet into a wild bird. Through tear-filled eyes, she looked at Bertie and knew they had no other choice.

Bertie worked his way across the living room, having to stop twice to rest. Reaching the window, he pulled back the blackout curtain and undid the latch. The window screeched open.

The cold air seemed to settle Duchess. Carefully, Susan unwrapped the towel to find that a tail feather had fallen out.

Duchess looked up, her golden eyes shimmered with candlelight.

"Please, don't go." Susan caressed her pigeon.

Duchess blinked. She leapt, flapped her wings, and flew into the night.

CHAPTER 47

AIRAINES, FRANCE

The staccato rhythm of rain on the barn roof slowed to a stop. Ollie's breath, penetrating the cold air, produced a puffy mist. Morning sunlight spilled through cracks in the boards.

He'd spent the night alone in the barn, with the exception of Madeleine stopping in at one point. Without speaking, she'd placed his jacket over his shoulders, set a blanket at his feet, and returned to the cottage. And for the next several hours, he deliberated over the note. *Boar wrote the message*, he repeated to himself. But a voice deep inside his head continued to remind him that Madeleine, not Boar, had been the first to retrieve Duchess.

Ollie's body shuddered with anguish. He shook away images of the message and thought of Susan—her eloquent stature, the exquisite curvature of her cheekbones. A flash of their trip to Clacton-on-Sea and the way she had enlightened him on the history of pigeons in war, making him realize how little pilots, especially crop-dusters, knew about flying. The way their knees slightly touched as they sat on the sofa together, sending a tingle up his spine and making him forget, at least for the moment, about the loss of his family. He admired her bravery as bombs fell on London, her unwavering belief that her mission would enable Britain to win the war. And her tenacity to carry on, no matter how bad things got.

Ollie struggled to maintain his faith. As he reached into his jacket to reexamine the message, he heard the plodding of hooves. He stepped to the barn door and peeked outside to see a large wagon being pulled by a pair of bristly mules, vapor spewing from their nostrils. Holding the reins was a priest, Ollie assumed, considering the man was wearing a dark-brown clergy robe with a hood pulled over his head.

The cottage door opened. "Lieutenant," Madeleine called.

The priest pulled on the reins. The mules brayed, and the wagon stopped.

Ollie, realizing that this must be the guide Madeleine had arranged, left the barn. As he approached, the priest turned and removed his hood, causing Ollie to slow his pace.

A mask covered half the priest's face, below the eyes. What appeared to be a molded piece of copper was painted a bright flesh tone, a shade or two lighter than the exposed skin on the man's forehead. Hair clippings, the same dark brown as his side-burns, were glued to form a mustache.

Boar stepped to the doorway and stopped. He glanced at the priest, then turned to Madeleine. "Is this our man?"

Madeleine nodded and walked to the wagon. "Lucien Bellamy, my husband's friend."

Boar cleared his throat. "I didn't expect a priest."

"He's a monk, not a priest," Madeleine said.

Lucien dropped the reins, stepped down from the wagon, and greeted Madeleine by placing a hand on her shoulder.

Ollie stepped to Lucien. "Ollie," he said, extending his hand.

The monk hesitated, then shook his hand.

Ollie noticed thick scaly scars on Lucien's forearm. "Did you serve in the Great War with Guillaume?"

Lucien nodded.

"What's your plan?" Boar asked, keeping his distance.

The monk produced a piece of slate, the size of a postcard, that was hanging from a string around his neck, then scribbled with a piece of chalk.

"He's taken a vow of silence," Madeleine said.

"Splendid," Boar groaned.

Lucien flipped the piece of slate to read, *Monastères*.

"He plans to smuggle you through monasteries," Madeleine said. "Until you reach *zone libre* and eventually Spain."

"Does he understand English?" Boar asked.

Madeleine nodded.

Boar walked to Lucien. "How do you plan to get us to Spain?"

Lucien pointed to the wagon.

Boar shook his head. "Even if we fill it with straw, the Wehrmacht will search the wagon." He glanced at the masked monk, then looked at Madeleine. "No disrespect, but he looks like he's going to a bloody masquerade. He'll do nothing but draw attention to us."

"His name is Lucien," Ollie said. "And he's risking his life to help us."

"He'll get us shot at the first checkpoint." Boar rubbed his broken eye, as if he were trying to get it to work.

Lucien climbed into the back of the wagon and worked his way to the front of the bed. He gripped a panel and tugged. A false wall opened, revealing a small space of less than two feet in depth, running the width of the wagon under the driver's bench.

"Clever," Ollie said. He looked at the hidden compartment, split in half with a horizontal board. The space was far smaller than their hole under the floorboards, but it appeared that there would be enough room for two men. He climbed into the wagon and wriggled into the lower half of the compartment, having to scrunch his limbs.

"It's ludicrous," Boar said.

Ollie squeezed out of the compartment, then stepped down from the wagon. "It'll work." He took the pistol from his jacket and slid it next to his belt, making certain that the lieutenant could see it. Speaking softly, so only Boar could hear, he said, "Madeleine will be shot if we're found here. She's done enough."

Boar paused, then said, "Sorry about your news, Yank."

Ollie's face turned hot. He inched closer and stared into Boar's lifeless eye. "Take Lucien and the wagon to the barn. Fill the back with manure."

"Fucking rotter," Boar hissed. "I don't take orders from you."

"I've got something to do before we leave." Before Boar could respond, Ollie walked into the cottage.

Inside, he retrieved a hammer and nails, then began securing the floorboards. The sound of Madeleine's footsteps, accompanied by the patter of Louis's hooves, caused him to look up. "If the Nazis show up, I don't want them to find the hole," he said, adjusting a board.

Madeleine nodded. She scratched her hog behind the ears, causing him to twitch his tail.

Ollie quickly pounded in the nails. After securing the last of the floorboards, he slid the table back into place.

"*N'abandonnez jamais*," Madeleine said.

Ollie turned.

"It means, Never give up," she added.

He nodded, realizing how much Madeleine reminded him of his own mother. "You could come with us, pretend to be Lucien's interpreter. It'd be safer for you in the free zone."

Madeleine shook her head.

"Please," Ollie said. "Join us."

She rubbed Louis's head. "I must wait for my Guillaume."

No matter how hard Ollie tried to convince Madeleine to leave, she refused. It was clear to him that she was determined to wait for her missing husband, despite the likelihood that the Nazis, retracing Dietrich's routine, would eventually return to her cottage. As he walked her to the door, he knew there would be no changing her mind. And he hoped that his efforts to dispose of Dietrich's body would eventually lead the Nazis far away from Madeleine.

Outside, to his surprise, he found that Boar and Lucien had

loaded the back of the wagon with manure and some of the rotten potatoes, too far gone for even Louis to eat.

Boar brushed his hands on his pants and stepped to Madeleine. "This is it, I'm afraid."

Madeleine, having to stand on her toes, kissed Boar on both cheeks, then watched him climb into the back of the wagon.

As Ollie prepared to say good-bye, a flutter caused him to stop. He turned to see Duchess land at his feet.

The pigeon looked up and blinked.

Boar stared from the back of the wagon. He pressed his boot into a rotten potato.

Ollie picked up Duchess and stroked her wings. Then, like he always had, he opened the canister attached to the pigeon's leg. His heart sank. "It's empty."

Boar crossed his arms. "I think you owe me an apology, Yank."

Ollie ignored the lieutenant. He caressed Duchess, noticing that she'd lost weight. Her feathers, once lustrous, now seemed tattered. Ollie believed he was to blame for her condition. She'd selflessly risked her life carrying his messages. He wished he could tuck her into his jacket and carry her safely out of France. But he'd likely never make it to the free zone, let alone Britain. Her best chance for survival was to fly out of here, just as she had done before. "I can't take you with me," he said to the pigeon.

Duchess's chest pulsed as she took in air.

As Ollie caressed Duchess, he thought of Susan. A wave of regret flooded his head. He reached into his jacket and removed the codebook. Taking out a piece of paper, he quickly coded a message, then slid it into the canister and sealed the cap. "I want you to rest with Madeleine. Then fly home and stay."

Duchess lowered her head.

Ollie stepped to Madeleine. "She's weak. Two-way pigeons are not supposed to have food and water at the second location, but she needs time to recover."

"Come on, Yank," Boar called from the wagon.

"I'll take good care of her," Madeleine said.

"I know you will." As Ollie handed Duchess to Madeleine, the pigeon leapt. He reached, but it was too late. His fingers graced her tail. Her wings brushed his face. Helplessly, he watched the pigeon shoot over the wagon.

Duchess circled the cottage and slowly gained altitude.

"It's my fault," Madeleine said.

"No," Ollie said. "If she wants to fly, there's nothing we can do."

"Will she come back?" she asked.

"I don't know." He watched Duchess disappear over the trees, then stepped to Madeleine. He hugged her, then kissed her cheek.

"*Adieu.*" Madeleine wiped her eyes.

"I'll never forget you." Ollie climbed into the wagon, then slid into the hiding compartment. Boar wedged into the bunk above him. Ollie watched Lucien seal the panel, turning the compartment black, except for a small crack of light near his knee. The wagon rocked as Lucien took his seat. A snap of leather. The mules brayed. And the wagon rolled forward.

CHAPTER 48

ROUEN, FRANCE

It was no more than an hour before the wagon stopped. Without a breeze, the hidden compartment began to reek of manure and rotted potatoes. Guttural German dialect made Ollie's hair stand on the back of his neck. *Roadblock? Wehrmacht?* The wagon shook as Lucien shifted in the seat above him.

Someone, Ollie presumed a soldier, said something that made his companions laugh. Ollie heard a hand gripping the side of the wagon several inches from his head. He held his breath. At any moment, he expected the Wehrmacht to notice that the dimensions of the wagon bed were slightly off, leading them to inspect the area beneath Lucien's seat. Instead, the wagon jerked. The mules clopped at a slow pace. And they continued on their journey.

Ollie felt a large bump as the wagon rolled over a hole. He closed his eyes and listened to plodding hooves. Several minutes later, he was startled when the lieutenant spoke.

"My father's army had good aim," Boar muttered.

Ollie shifted. "What?"

"I understand a little German," Boar whispered. "Keep quiet, Yank."

Ollie thought of Lucien. He imagined that the monk's mask,

no doubt hiding war wounds, was the target of the soldier's comments. But over the next several hours, as they successfully navigated through two more roadblocks, he questioned if it was more than just the man's mask that was helping them pass. Each time they were forced to stop, Ollie heard German voices. A pause. Then a jerk, as the mules plodded on. Only once did he hear a soldier inspecting the bed of the wagon. And from what sounded like a metal rod hitting wood, Ollie suspected the soldier had merely tapped the outside of the wagon with his rifle, rather than get his weapon, or his boots, covered in excrement.

After traveling for what Ollie believed to be most of the day, the wagon stopped. Instead of German commands, he heard Lucien climb into the back of the wagon. The panel popped open. Ollie rubbed his eyes, though the sun had already set, and crawled from his crevice. Although his shoulder had partially healed, it still ached. He suspected his ankle would also begin to hurt once circulation returned to his legs.

Ollie stepped down from the wagon and almost fell. His legs were wonky, as if numbed with procaine. He rubbed his thighs, trying to expedite the flow of blood, and noticed a large three-story stone building, which he presumed to be a monastery. To the rear, a small cemetery with crooked tombstones. Ollie, with nerves tingling in his legs, followed Lucien and Boar to the monastery.

Lucien approached the entrance, a large arched door of ancient boards, held together with bands of rusted iron. He knocked, then glanced toward the road.

Ollie turned. Bordering the road, a dusk sky outlined a row of trees, their branches bare of leaves. He noticed movement. A gust of wind carrying a putrid scent of decomposition, far more revolting than the smell of manure and rotted potatoes, brought his eyes into focus. Two men and a woman, their bodies bloated and mutilated, hung from the branches of a large oak. Nooses taut. Necks snapped.

"Oh no," Ollie whispered.

A breeze caused the bodies to sway. The branches creaked.

Boar turned to Lucien. "Resistance?"

Lucien nodded. As he prepared to knock again, a metal slat in the center of the door slid open.

A spectacled man peered through the peephole. Ollie assumed the man recognized Lucien, no doubt by his copper mask, because the slat abruptly shut. A second later, the bolt clicked, and the door swung open.

A monk, dressed similarly to Lucien, although he was much older judging from his gray hair and wrinkled face, led them inside and bolted the door. Without speaking, they followed the monk down narrow stone stairs barely wide enough to fit Boar's broad shoulders. Once in the basement, the monk lit a lantern using the candle he was carrying. The room, which was probably once a root cellar, was empty, except for a pile of barren burlap sacks.

The monk glanced at Lucien, then quickly ascended the stairs.

Lucien took out his piece of slate and chalked a drawing.

"You need to tend to the mules?" Ollie asked.

Lucien nodded. He tucked away his slate and left.

Boar picked up the lantern, scanned the cellar, and walked to the far end of the room.

They had barely spoken all day. But that suited Ollie. And judging by the way Boar had selected a spot in the opposite corner, he suspected the man had no desire to be near him as well. So Ollie layered pieces of burlap and sat down to rest.

An hour later, Lucien returned, carrying a small baguette and a clay pitcher of water.

Boar took the pitcher and gulped, then placed it on the floor.

Ollie picked up the pitcher and drank, the water cold and laced with minerals. As he finished, he noticed that Lucien had broken the bread into thirds.

"Where are we?" Boar asked.

Lucien shook his head.

"Best we don't know?" Boar asked.

Lucien nodded.

"Fair enough." Boar bit into his bread.

As Ollie chewed his meal, he noticed that Lucien wasn't eating. Instead, the monk placed his food into his pocket, then prepared a bed of leftover burlap. Ollie had expected that Lucien would sleep upstairs, but perhaps the swinging corpses, within a stone's throw of the monastery, were a daily reminder of how the Nazis dealt with resistance fighters. It was probably safer, Ollie believed, for the inhabitants of this abbey to isolate themselves from Lucien as much as possible or require him to keep close tabs on the smuggled guests.

Boar finished his bread, took a spot on the floor, leaned back, and closed his eyes.

Lucien extinguished the lantern. The room turned black.

Ollie curled up on the floor and tried to sleep, but as he lay on his side, the book containing Susan's messages pressed against his ribs, resurrecting thoughts of what might have been. He spent the next few hours deliberating whether there was anything he could have done to change the course of events.

Late in the evening, the scratch of a match caused Ollie to stir. He opened his eyes to see Lucien light the lantern, then quickly lower its wick to a dull glow. The monk pulled out his piece of bread, soaked it with water from the pitcher, and mushed it in his palm. Ollie thought it was rather late to be eating, not to mention that this was an odd way to prepare one's food. As he was about to roll over, Lucien removed his mask, sending a shock through Ollie's body.

Lucien's lower jaw was not merely disfigured, it was missing. Shot off. At the place where his mouth should have been was a gaping hole. No tongue. A few useless teeth dangled from his upper jaw.

Ollie watched Lucien place a bit of bread into the hole, pick up the pitcher of water, and tilt back his head. Water gurgled into Lucien's esophagus.

Ollie knew, from the copper mask, that Lucien was hiding injuries from the Great War. Perhaps burns. A maimed face. But he had never expected that someone could live with such horrific injuries. And suddenly, he realized that Lucien was likely removing his mask at the roadblocks, using his mangled face as a distraction. He recalled the soldier's comment at the roadblock. *My father's army had good aim.* Anger burned in Ollie's belly.

Lucien inserted more bread paste. Wet burbles filled the cellar.

He quietly rolled over to allow Lucien his privacy and noticed Boar was awake, staring, his brow contorted in disbelief.

CHAPTER 49

EPPING, ENGLAND

Susan placed her palm on Bertie's forehead. The heat emanating from his skin caused her legs to weaken. *I had a little bird, its name was Enza.* She fumbled to open his medicine bottle, spilling sulfa pills on the floor.

Bertie, too frail to cover his mouth, expelled a wet cough. His handkerchief, like a soiled doily, lay on the side table.

I opened the window, and . . . Susan bit her lip, battling to mute the indelible chant inside her head. She scooped up the pills and placed one in his mouth. Her hand trembled as she lifted a glass of water to his lips.

Bertie gagged. Water dribbled down his chin. On his second attempt, he swallowed the medicine.

Susan stared at Bertie, too ill to sit up and confined to a makeshift bed on the sofa. She wished that more could be done. A miracle pill. Divine intervention. Something other than Dr. Collins's daily visits to listen to Bertie's chest. Each time Collins removed his stethoscope, he'd comment that the hospital beds were filled to capacity with trauma patients from London and that Bertie was better off at home to receive the individual care that he needed. The doctor's intentions were good. But seeing

Bertie's declining state, she questioned his judgment. And she regretted that she hadn't done more.

"Soldiers?" Bertie whispered.

Susan noticed the feebleness of his voice. "They packed up this afternoon." She took a cloth and dipped it into a ceramic water basin. As she wiped his face, she recalled the soldiers loading up their tent and equipment, then driving away. They were assigned to another duty. And she wasn't surprised. After all, there was nothing for them to do, considering the lofts were barren and a pigeon had not returned from France in over a week, including Duchess.

"She's not coming back, is she?" Susan asked, unable to control her thought.

Bertie slid his hand from under his blanket.

She squeezed his fingers. It had been nine days since Duchess had left. And Susan knew, from years of racing pigeons with Bertie, that a pigeon, more than a day or two unaccounted for, never returned.

"Northampton," he whispered, almost inaudible.

"I'm not leaving you," she said. "The National Pigeon Service can wait."

He blinked, his eyes swollen and bloodshot. "I'm not getting better."

Susan's skin turned cold.

"Promise me you'll go." He paused to catch his breath, then licked his lips, crinkled and chapped.

"First, we're going to make you well."

He coughed, then feebly shook his head.

Susan's eyes watered. She caressed his arm, thin and fragile, like the branch of a willow.

Bertie took in a labored breath. "Be an egg, my dear."

CHAPTER 50

EPPING, ENGLAND

Susan went to the phone and found that the lines were still dead, as they had been for the past three days. Through the curtains, the sun had set, turning the sky indigo. A fading glow of amber traced the horizon. The blackout had commenced. It was too late to venture outside, but she didn't care. Bertie's condition had worsened, and she decided to take matters into her own hands.

"I'm going to prepare the lorry," she said, grabbing her coat. "We're going to St. Margaret's."

Bertie cracked open his eyes. He tried to speak but produced a wheeze.

As she buttoned her coat, the sirens sounded. The horrid howl sent chills up Susan's spine. She ran outside, not bothering to close the door. Reaching the truck, she lowered the tailgate, knowing Bertie would be too infirm to sit in the cabin.

The sirens roared. She glanced up to see searchlights criss-cross the sky, then turned her attention to the truck. Her mind raced on how she'd make a bed in the back. *Blankets? Cushions?* Suddenly, she remembered the cots that were in the bomb shelter. As she turned, antiaircraft guns fired. She flinched and covered her ears.

Booming guns shook the ground. She looked up. Flashes lit up the sky, revealing approaching Luftwaffe bombers. The metallic grind of German engines intensified. She swallowed, then ran toward the shelter.

Shells exploded. Her eardrums pounded. She ran faster.

Reaching the shelter, she threw open the door and shot inside. In the darkness, she tripped over something on the floor and fell, jamming her fingers into the ground. She rummaged over the dirt floor and found the wooden leg of a cot, last used months ago when the Luftwaffe began their nightly bombings. She dragged the cot outside and froze.

Fifteen thousand feet above Epping, a Luftwaffe pilot struggled to steady the yoke of his Heinkel bomber. Six months ago, he had completed his flight training at Fürstenfeldbruck Air Base. A mere six minutes earlier, he had assumed the position of squadron leader after the lead bomber took a direct hit and exploded into pieces as they crossed the coastline.

Rounds of explosions shook his plane. Shrapnel pelted the wings. A search beam shot through the cockpit glass. Cold sweat clung to his forehead. The pilot, frightened and confused, either believed that the antiaircraft guns were coming from London or he was anxious to drop his bombs and flee. Regardless, he gave the order. Bombs fell from his plane. The rest of the squadron released their payloads. Twenty-two tons of explosives plunged toward the earth.

It was a sharp shrill above the menacing chorus of antiaircraft guns that compelled Susan to stop. Hundreds of screaming whistles. She'd heard them before, but always at a distance. The tone was different. Louder. Closer. Her body turned weak. Powerless, she dropped the cot and fell to her knees. In that fleeting moment, her mind flashed with thoughts of a future that would never be. She clasped her hands and prepared for the impact.

CHAPTER 51

ASCAIN, FRANCE

Ollie awakened. He took in a deep breath, then exhaled and glanced around his sleeping cell. Silvery moonlight spilled through a crack in the curtains, illuminating bare plaster walls. A small wooden desk, void of any objects, sat in the corner. His feet dangled from the bottom of the small bed. The scent of ancient timbers and candle wax filled the air. Somewhere down the hall of the church dormitory, Boar and Lucien were sleeping. He closed his eyes and tried to rest, but a strange uneasiness stirred within him.

They had traveled for two weeks and three days. By day, he and Boar hid, crammed like contortionists, behind the false wall of the wagon. At night, Lucien smuggled them, their bodies stiff and sore, into a monastery, church, or abbey. Most evenings, they slept in a barn or cellar. However, tonight was a rare occasion when Ollie had the luxury of a bed, as well as a room to himself. But despite having a warm place to sleep, he was restless. Perhaps it was the rumble of German patrols in the village or that he was about to embark on the last and most dangerous leg of the journey. But deep down, he knew the reason he couldn't sleep. So he sat up, put on his boots, and crept from his room.

Quietly, he walked down the darkened hall, careful not to disturb the clergy tucked away in their sleeping cells. He stopped when he reached the glimmer of the cloister hall connecting the dormitory to the church sanctuary. A medieval ceiling arched high above his head; a wall of stained-glass windows glowed with luminescence. He sat on the stone floor and stared at the glass mural encrusted with red, green, gold, and purple glass. It depicted the scene of a garden paradise. He supposed the angelic figures and lush garden served as a daily reminder for the priests and monks—a promise of paradise at the end of their earthly lives.

"The world is falling apart." Ollie's voice resonated through the hall. "And you do nothing."

He stared at the angels, their eyes looking away, as if ignoring him or offended by his words. Lowering his head onto his knees, he ran his hands through his oily hair. He sat in the cloister for over an hour, hoping to receive a revelation. But nothing came. Returning to the dormitory, he found Lucien and Boar awake.

"We're leaving, Yank," Boar said, standing outside his door. "Best to get started before sunrise."

Ollie retrieved his coat from his room and returned to the hallway. He stepped to Lucien, who was holding up his slate to show a chalked map. A jagged line depicted the mountain border between France and Spain. A winding band, which Ollie believed to be a river, was marked Bidasoa. There were two dots: Ascain, the village of their current location; and Ergoien, Spain, where Lucien had presumably arranged to hide them in another church until they could be smuggled to a British consulate or, in Ollie's case, a United States embassy. Ollie nodded, letting the monk know that he understood.

"You've done well, Lucien," Boar said.

Eyes blinked behind the copper mask. Lucien erased the chalk with his sleeve, then tucked his slate inside his cloak.

As they left, Ollie noticed that the church remained silent.

When they had arrived yesterday evening, the monks, although willing to harbor them, had scattered like mice. He envisioned the clergy creeping from their rooms and going about their daily routine once they left. *Best to pretend that they hadn't collaborated with Germany's enemy.*

Outside, cold air stung Ollie's face. He blew on his hands and glanced at the unhitched wagon. The mules had done their duty and were now tucked inside a barn. From here, they'd walk. He looked to the south and saw a silhouette of mountain peaks, traced by a spattering of stars. The Pyrenees.

As they crept from the village, Ollie recalled their travel. Lucien had gone to great lengths to avoid roadblocks by traveling on back roads. But as their path took them closer to the coastline, the presence of German troops escalated, giving rise to the clack of tanks and the buzz of planes. They had maneuvered south, smuggled within Lucien's Catholic network, going through Tours, Poitiers, Bordeaux, Dax, Anglet, and, most recently, the village of Ascain. And now the protection of the Church was gone. Ahead, a grueling seventeen-hour climb through the Pyrenees lay between them and freedom, assuming they could avoid Spanish patrols, which, according to Boar, would throw them in prison for illegally crossing the border.

By the time they reached the base of the mountain, the air had turned damp. Thick clouds had moved in, blocking out the moon. They began their ascent by marching upward through thick pines. The scent of crushed needles beneath Ollie's feet reminded him of Maine, giving him a brief surge in energy. They continued their climb into a dense fog. Lucien, leading the way, disappeared and reappeared from the mist, as if he were an apparition.

Two hours into the trek, it began to rain. The pines disappeared, leaving little protection from the wind. Wet gusts beat against Ollie's face. Water seeped through his coat. He began to shiver. Heavy clumps of mud stuck to his boots. As the air

thinned, he labored to lift his feet. He struggled to keep pace
with Boar and Lucien. The weeks of being confined to the interior of a wagon, not to mention an ankle that hadn't fully recovered, had taken their toll.

"Pick it up, Yank," Boar said, looking back.

Ollie stopped and sucked in air, then continued his climb.

Within minutes, the mountain turned to steep inclines. The
once-wide path became narrow. His ankle began to swell, pressing against his boot. As daylight came, so did heavy rain. Huge
drops stung his exposed skin. With no trees for protection, Lucien stopped under a rocky overhang and removed the pack he
was carrying.

Boar took a seat on the ground and wiped rain from his face.

Ollie sat and looked down to the valley. They'd traveled for
hours, winding up the slopes, but they'd made it only halfway up
the mountain. He squeezed his swollen ankle, attempting to dispel his trepidation. *I'll tolerate the pain. Or I'll crawl if I have to. Either way, I'm gonna make it home.*

Lucien unpacked his sack, opened a canteen, and handed it to
Ollie.

Ollie took a gulp of water and gave the canteen to Boar.

Lucien removed a wrapped hunk of meat from his sack. He
placed it on a rock and cut it in thirds with a small flip knife. He
handed chunks to Ollie and Boar.

Ollie looked at what appeared to be a piece of boiled mutton,
the wool still attached. He assumed that the clergy in Ascain, or
perhaps in Dax, given the deteriorated, gray, fleshy color, had
abruptly prepared it. Despite the repulsiveness of the food, he
needed to eat it if he were to have the energy to hike the next
dozen hours. As he prepared to bite into his woolly mutton, he
noticed Lucien had slipped away, as he always did, to eat in solace.

Boar sighed, put down his food, and stepped into the rain. He
approached Lucien, sitting on a rock with his hood pulled over
his head. "Join us."

Lucien looked up.

"You going to make me eat alone again with the Yank?" Rain pelted Boar's face. "You're much better company."

Water dripped from Lucien's copper mask.

"It doesn't bother me." Boar rubbed his broken eye.

Lucien hesitated, then stood and followed Boar.

Ollie looked up to see Boar and Lucien return to the shelter.

"I've asked Lucien to join us," Boar said.

Ollie nodded. Two weeks ago, Boar's gesture would have surprised him. The travel with Lucien had softened Boar, Ollie believed, making the lieutenant aware that a blind eye, although career ending for a pilot, paled in comparison to a missing jaw. More importantly, Lucien had shown Boar—and Ollie, for that matter—that one could join the fight despite one's physical limitations.

Boar plucked a hair from his mutton and took a bite.

Lucien, his back to the others, removed his mask. With his knife, he cut his mutton into tiny bits, then placed a piece into what remained of his mouth and washed it down with water. Long after Ollie and Boar had eaten, Lucien labored to ingest his meal in small increments, like a patient swallowing a platter of pills.

Finishing his mutton, Lucien retrieved his mask.

"You don't need to wear that," Ollie said. "Unless it's keeping you warm."

Lucien glanced over his shoulder.

"There's no need," Boar said.

Lucien paused, then slipped his mask into his pack.

They collected the remains of the meal, including the chewed mutton hide, and tossed it into Lucien's sack. It was clear, at least to Ollie, that Lucien had no plans of leaving any trace of their travel.

They climbed for an hour. To Ollie, the incline seemed to grow steeper with each step. His thigh muscles burned. His foot throbbed. Despite the pain, he pushed on. Step by step, he forced himself upward. As the rain slowed and the fog began to dissipate, Ollie was relieved to see Lucien stop to rest prior to scaling a steep trek.

Boar, ahead of Ollie, stopped to catch his breath.

Lucien looked down at Ollie, then raised a hand.

Ollie rubbed his legs and looked up. He noticed what he thought was a sense of peace in Lucien, free from the burden of hiding his war wounds. The squint of the man's eyes gave the illusion of a victory smile, despite the fact that he had no jaw. Ollie inhaled. He nodded and raised his arm to Lucien.

A loud crack exploded.

Ollie flinched.

Lucien clasped his chest. Blood spurted through his fingers.

Ollie climbed toward Lucien, but another gunshot forced him to the ground. The discharge echoed through the valley.

Boar, already on his back, ripped open his coat and pulled out his pistol.

Lucien collapsed.

A bullet ricocheted near Ollie's face, sending limestone shrapnel into his cheek. He scrambled to Lucien.

Boar fired two shots into the valley.

Ollie dragged Lucien, his body limp, down the embankment. As he placed him behind a large boulder, he saw a Wehrmacht patrol, perhaps six or seven soldiers, less than a hundred yards below. He pulled the Nazi's pistol from his pocket, stood, and pulled the trigger, only to find the safety was on. A bullet whizzed by his ear. His pulse pounded. He flipped the safety, fired, and missed.

Boar rushed down the embankment, bringing with him chunks of rock. He fired a shot. Then another. A bullet shattered his kneecap. He howled as his right leg buckled.

A German soldier scaled the slope forty yards below. Ollie aimed and fired. The soldier's back arched, then fell. German helmets turned as their comrade tumbled down the embankment.

Ollie raced to Boar. As he dragged him by the coat, a bullet pierced the lieutenant's thigh.

Boar yowled.

They fell behind the boulder. Ollie fired shots, sending the patrol for cover. He rolled Lucien over, already knowing there was nothing he could do. His pupils were dilated. A hole, the size of a plum, had opened his sternum.

"Bastards," Boar grunted. He gripped Lucien's cloak.

Ollie noticed blood spilling from Boar's knee.

"How many?" Boar gasped.

Ollie peeked around the boulder. Shots skipped over stone. He snapped back. "Six or seven."

Boar, his fingers covered in blood, checked the bullets in his weapon. He pulled another clip from his belt.

Ollie ripped a piece of cloth from the lining of Lucien's cloak. As he wrapped it around Boar's leg, he noticed bloodied bits of bone on the lieutenant's trousers.

Boar grabbed the cloth. He winced as he tightened the tourniquet.

Ollie crawled to the side of the boulder, and as he did, he heard German commands. He scanned below, finding another patrol making their way up the mountain. His adrenaline surged. "There's more."

"How many?" Boar pulled himself toward the edge of their rock.

"Ten." Ollie looked at his pistol, regretting he hadn't searched Dietrich's vehicle for ammunition.

Boar looked below. "Bloody hell."

Ollie glanced to the snowcapped summit. "The only way out of here is up and over."

Boar struggled to stand on one leg and fired two shots.

Ollie heard a yelp. Machine-gun fire battered their rock.

Boar flopped down. He gasped for air and pointed at Ollie with a bloodied finger. "Give me your weapon."

"No," Ollie said. "I only have a few bullets. And I plan to use them." He scanned around the boulder to see Wehrmacht flanking them. Closer. Thirty yards at most.

"I don't think you understand, Yank." Boar took in short breaths, like a panting dog.

Ollie prepared for another shot.

"Ollie."

The sound of the lieutenant using his name caused him to hesitate. He looked at Boar, his trousers soaked with blood.

"I'm offering you a chance to get out of here." Boar tightened the tourniquet.

"I'll fight." Ollie turned, preparing to target the enemy, and heard a metallic click.

"Give me your weapon," Boar said, pressing his pistol to Ollie's temple.

Ollie froze. Machine-gun fire sprayed the boulder, sending bits of rock into his hair.

"You and I both know that I'm not getting out of here," Boar said. "If you choose to stay, I'll pull the trigger. You'll be dead anyway when the ammunition is gone."

"Why are you doing this?"

Boar leaned forward and ripped the weapon from Ollie's hand. He checked the clip and slammed it back into the pistol. "I need to set something straight."

Ollie heard rocks falling as the Wehrmacht climbed the slope. "What are you talking about?"

Boar grimaced as he propped himself against the boulder. "You'll understand, if you make it out of here."

"This isn't right."

The lieutenant removed his identification discs, strung on a cord around his neck, and tossed them to Ollie. "Go, before I change my mind."

Stunned, Ollie watched Boar lean over the boulder and fire. A soldier let out an agonizing scream. Realizing this was his only opportunity, Ollie shook away his indecisiveness and scrambled up the embankment. Pain shot through his ankle. His boots slipped on rubble. Bullets ripped over limestone. He climbed, tearing skin from his palms.

Boar fired another shot. Then there was a spattering of gunfire as the Wehrmacht closed in.

Ollie dove behind a large slab, sucked in air, then sprang upward. Each time Boar fired a shot, he was given a few seconds to ascend. He did this four times until he reached a steep trail, turning out of view from the Wehrmacht. Continuing his climb, he stumbled and fell. He fought to catch his breath in the thinning air. His lungs heaved. The temperature began to plummet. Unwavering, he continued his ascent until the rain turned to sleet, then, eventually, snow.

Reaching the summit, Ollie collapsed. Ice scraped his face. As he rolled over, he heard a pistol shot, followed by a long blast of machine-gun fire, and then silence.

Chapter 52

The Pyrenees

The descent was far more difficult than the climb. Believing the Wehrmacht patrol would continue their pursuit, Ollie disregarded caution as he clambered down the mountain. Stepping onto a limestone shelf, he slipped on ice and fell. His wet clothes, like a lubricant, plunged him down the sleet-covered slope. Kicking his legs, he rolled onto his stomach and frantically clawed for a handhold. But the slide accelerated. Loose scree gouged his hands. He dug in his toes, feeling his bootlaces snap. His body skidded to a stop. He gasped for air and stood on shaky legs inches from the edge of a cliff. His pulse hammered in his eardrums. As he peered down the ridge, he noticed that two of his fingers were crooked. With numb hands, he snapped them back into place, sending a sharp twinge through his arm.

Unable to find a trail, Ollie traversed through rock fields and steep grades. With the lower altitude, he gained oxygen, allowing him to breathe better. But his body was a wreck. His muscles, atrophied from weeks of confinement, flared with pain. Forced to rest, he leaned his back against a boulder. As he took in air, he glanced at the summit and noticed movement. He strained to focus and saw two Wehrmacht soldiers scaling down the ridge.

They were several hundred yards away, well out range for an accurate shot. But their pace was fast, nearly twice the speed of his own descent. He crouched, hoping he hadn't been spotted. Seconds later, a gunshot echoed through the valley, sending him to his feet.

For the next two hours, Ollie struggled to stay out of range of the enemy. As the Wehrmacht narrowed their gap, gunfire turned from distant echoes to crisp cracks. Bullets ricocheted over rocks. Dashing over gravel, he twisted his bum ankle and toppled to the ground. Pain flared through his foot. He stood and tried again to run, but his body could only produce a hobbled jaunt. And he realized that it was only a matter of time before the soldiers would overtake him.

The stony terrain turned to scraggly trees, then eventually a thick forest, temporarily placing him out of sight of the soldiers. The warming temperature returned feeling to his hands, causing his fingers to throb. Exhausted, he hid in the cavity of a rotted log and hoped the soldiers would pass him by. He struggled to control his breathing, expecting at any moment the thud of German boots. Instead, he heard rippling water. *Bidasoa River*, he thought, recalling Lucien's map. Sensing the divide between France and Spain was within reach, a decision ravaged his gut. His head told him to stay hidden. But a deep-seated desire to return home caused him to crawl from his hiding spot.

A shot rang out. The branch near his head splintered. His heart rate soared. He turned. Fifty yards away were the Wehrmacht soldiers, one kneeling with his pointed rifle, the other with a machine gun propped on his hip. Ollie dove behind a tree. Bullets sprayed the forest.

He struggled to run. His ankle throbbed. As he staggered through the pines, more shots rang out. A sharp pain stung his arm, his sleeve turning warm and sticky. He barreled through thornbushes. Needles scratched his face. He pressed on, drawn by the crescendo of gushing water. The soldiers closed in. He reached the river and stopped.

The water raged, brown and thick with debris. The heavy rains had caused the river to overflow its banks. He scanned the area. No bridge. No place to hide. He stared into the muddy abyss. Blood dripped from his fingers.

A branch snapped. *"Dort!"*

Ollie saw the soldiers emerge from the pines. Brows lowered. Faces scowled. They raised their weapons. With no other choice, he jumped.

The icy water shocked him. He surfaced and sucked in air, taking in a mouthful of silty muck. He choked. Shots rang out. Bullets split the air near his head. He dove under and kicked his legs. The force of the current twisted his limbs. He struggled to swim, his soaked coat like a lead blanket. His chest heaved, recycling used air in his lungs. As he was forced to surface, more shots exploded. He gulped air and went under.

As he came up again, he saw a soldier running along the shoreline with his machine gun raised. Ollie sank. The German squeezed off his ammunition. Bullets rippled the water.

He kicked harder, attempting to propel himself farther into the river. Unable to hold his breath any longer, he surfaced and saw the soldier shove another clip into his weapon. Too exhausted to dive under again, he watched the riverbank rush by, a blur of mud and brush. The soldier sprinted and pointed his weapon, and the current swept Ollie around a bend.

He heard the soldier shout, then fire his weapon into the air. The water gushed. As the river took him out of range of the Wehrmacht, he labored to swim. His body, overrun with fatigue and cold, weakened with each stroke. He made it to the middle of the Bidasoa and wrapped an arm around a floating log.

His teeth chattered uncontrollably; his frigid joints were like seized pistons. He strained to keep his head afloat. The chances of crossing the Bidasoa, let alone making it home, dwindled with each breath. Before hyperthermia stole what remained of his body's warmth, he managed to slip his hand inside his coat. With numb and broken fingers, he found the pocket. Amid his pain and regret, one vision held steady. *Susan*. His eyelids grew heavy. And the river swept him away.

CHAPTER 53

EPPING, ENGLAND

Grit blurred Susan's vision; her tear ducts were clogged with soot. The weight of bricks pressed on her torso. She labored to inhale, taking in thick dust mixed with the sour scent of cordite.

"Grandfather," she said, coughing, her voice muted from the high-pitched ringing in her ears.

She struggled to push debris from her body, then rolled onto her knees. Her ribs ached, as if she had been struck with a club. Large bumps protruded from her scalp. From the strong copper taste in her mouth, she sensed that her tongue was bleeding or that her nose had been broken. Using the lining of her coat, she wiped dirt from her eyes. Her vision slowly returned. As her head began to clear, she realized that the force of the explosion had hurled her into the bomb shelter. The ceiling, partially collapsed, exposed billows of smoke rising toward evening stars. Beyond the shelter door, which was hanging askew on twisted hinges, she saw an amber flicker.

She crawled to the doorway. The first thing she noticed was the festering crater. A huge hole, the size of a pond, had replaced what used to be a dense thicket.

"No!" Using the doorknob as a brace, she struggled to stand, then stepped outside, dreading what she was about to see.

Where the cottage once stood was now a smoldering pit. Bestrewed flames, a mixture of explosive residue and shredded timbers, surrounded the hole. The chimney was toppled, like stones of a broken cairn.

"Grandfather!" She limped, her left foot missing its shoe. A nail from a broken board punctured her heel, and she fell. Ignoring the pain shooting up her calf, she kicked away the board, wrenching the nail from her foot, then crawled over scorched grass. She prayed, her hands pressed against the hot soil, that he had been blown clear of the blast.

She reached the hole, a deep cone in the earth. Below, mounds of charred wood. A broken chair leg. And what used to be the stove, its door ripped from the hinges.

"No!" Susan screamed, her vocal cords about to rupture. She dropped into the hole and dug through rubble. Jagged splinters ripped skin from her hands. Dirt clung to her bloodied heel. She dredged debris, crying his name, again and again.

She found him under what used to be a dresser. Prying off the broken furniture, she fell to her knees and caressed his cheeks. Carefully, she wiped dirt from the crevices of his eyelids.

"Wake up," she sobbed. She dug out his limp legs, buried in a mixture of stone, plaster, and broken wood. "Wake!"

The distinct sound of a fire-engine bell approached but was turned away by the roar of another air-raid siren. She lowered her head to Bertie's still chest and wailed.

CHAPTER 54

EPPING, ENGLAND — MARCH 21, 1941

Spring rain dripped onto the earthen floor. Susan looked up at the tarp covering a large hole in the roof of the bomb shelter and noticed a corner was loose. She retrieved a spool of string from under her cot and cut off a strip, using a rusted paring knife that had been salvaged from the rubble. She stepped outside. The string wriggled in the wet wind. As she began to secure the tarp, she glanced at the spot that was once her lovely cottage.

The debris had been removed, and the hole filled in, now distinctly marked by newly sprouted grass—thin, wispy, and two shades lighter than the rest of the yard. Although the flower beds had been either destroyed in the blast or trampled by village volunteers during a hasty demolition, sparse patches of resurrected crocuses and daffodils now decorated the lawn. Scarring the grounds was a pile of stone and lumber that had been placed next to the loo.

It had been some months since Bertie's funeral and over six months since the Luftwaffe began their aerial raids, which continued almost nightly. The passing of time had done little to ease her pain. And solitude, she believed, only exacerbated her regret, the horror of that dreadful night seared deep within her soul.

Refusing to leave Epping—and her family's farm, for that matter—she'd chosen to temporarily live in the bomb shelter, surviving on cold rations: bread, boiled eggs, turnips, and wilted cabbage. She collected her water, for both drinking and washing, from a rain barrel. She slept on a cot buried under mounds of musty blankets, which did little to keep her warm or muffle the nocturnal war that raged in the skies. She stayed in the shelter, except for the coldest of nights, when she accepted an occasional bed and a warm bath at the McCrearys. Although Mrs. McCreary had offered for Susan to move in, Susan had politely declined by saying, *It's only temporary.* But a day turned into a week, which turned into a month. And winter turned to spring.

Susan finished tying down the tarp, then scanned the empty green pasture. The sheep, and even the lambs, had been requisitioned by the government to clothe and feed the military. Her grandfather had adored his sheep and had only sheared the flock for wool. And it saddened her to think that, although it was necessary for Britain's survival, Bertie's beloved lambs were now canned meat.

She made her way to a pigeon loft. Along with the cottage, most of the lofts had been destroyed. With only a few pigeons remaining, Susan consolidated them into a single loft. As she opened the door, she glanced at the grain barrel, which had been Duchess's favorite perch. Her hopes of Duchess returning had been snuffed out months ago. All she had left of her pet pigeon were memories. And Ollie's messages that she had so bravely carried out of occupied France.

Each morning, Susan read Ollie's messages. Before meals and sleeping, she prayed that he was alive. But as months passed, her belief that he would someday return slowly faded. Now, several months since Ollie's last note, she'd become resigned to the fact that she'd never see him again. And that everyone she loved had been taken by war.

Susan poured grain into the feeding tray. The pigeons swarmed and pecked. Less than fifty pigeons remained, a fraction of the nearly 1,000 that had once filled their lofts. Most were old pigeons or squabs, unsuitable for service. But she didn't care that these birds were of no use to the National Pigeon Service. They were alive. And for the moment, that's all that mattered.

Leaving the loft, Susan picked a handful of daffodils and placed them in the basket on her bicycle. Having no use for the truck, she'd sold it to buy an old woodstove and pigeon feed. She pedaled to the village with cold rain pelting her coat. As she turned into Epping Cemetery, the bicycle's tires bounced on chunks of gravel, causing her arms to rattle. She braked near a patch of upturned soil and leaned her bicycle against an alder tree adorned with long brown cones. She gathered the contents of her basket and walked to a newly chiseled hunk of limestone. She kneeled, rain seeping through her skirt, and stared at Bertie's headstone. A twin marker a few feet away bore her grandmother's name, Agnes Shepherd. Her parents, casualties of the Spanish flu pandemic, were buried on the opposite side of the cemetery.

Susan placed half of the flowers on her grandparents' graves, keeping the remainder for her parents when she finished her rounds. As she stared at the etched stone, her guilt swelled, crashing like waves in a storm.

"I'm sorry," she said, her words muffled by the pattering rain. "I should have insisted that we sleep in the shelter. I'd much rather live like a mole than carry on without you." She pressed her fingers to the headstone. "I miss you terribly."

Carefully, Susan adjusted the flowers between the graves, making sure they were evenly distributed. And after visiting her parents' graves, she got on her bicycle, wiped a mixture of rain and tears from her face, and then pedaled away.

By the time Susan returned to the farm, the rain had become

heavy, transforming the lane into a marsh. Unable to ride, she pushed her bicycle through soupy ruts until she reached the shelter. Inside, she tossed scrap wood lath, once sealed inside the plaster walls of the cottage, into a rusted iron woodstove to stoke a fire. As the scent of burning wood filled her nose, she removed the notes from her pocket, then draped her coat over a makeshift clothesline strung above the stove. She wondered, although briefly, if her clothes would always stink of smoke.

As she carefully unfolded the messages, she realized that the papers were damp and the writing was beginning to smear. *Foolish of me to carry them in my pocket.* She placed them on her cot to dry, resolving to store them in an empty tea tin.

Refusing to succumb to the somberness that always enveloped her after visits to the cemetery, she retrieved the sewing basket that she'd borrowed from Mrs. McCreary and went to work mending her tattered clothes. She replaced buttons. Patched holes. And as she was repairing a loose seam, she heard a slosh of footsteps. She stopped and put down her needle. Rain pelted the tarp roof. Through a crack in the wall, she caught a glimpse of a dark coat. A knock on the door.

Hairs stood up on the back of her neck. Susan hesitated, unsettled by the fact that she rarely had visitors.

Another knock.

She glanced at the messages. Her pulse accelerated. She stood and opened the door, causing her heart to sink. "Mr. Wallace," she said, trying to hide her disappointment.

"Hello, Susan." Jonathan Wallace removed his hat. Rain dribbled from the elderly man's chin. "May I come in?"

Susan hesitated. "It's rather uncomfortable, I'm afraid."

"I don't do well in this weather." He turned a palm to the rain. "I raise pigeons, not ducks."

Susan's face flushed warm with embarrassment. She hated having anyone see her live like this, especially a respected mem-

ber of the National Pigeon Service and, even more, a friend of
Bertie. But she couldn't very well leave him standing in the rain,
so she stepped aside. She quickly gathered her sewing and
placed the notes inside a tea tin, then gestured for him to take a
seat on the cot.

Jonathan looked around the shelter. "How are you, Susan?"

"I'm well," she lied.

"You haven't responded to my letters."

Susan glanced at a stack of unopened mail. She struggled with
what to say and was relieved when he changed the subject.

"Your grandfather and I were quite good friends." He looked
at Susan and smiled. "Even though his racing pigeons always
seemed to outperform my own flock."

Susan tried to smile but couldn't find the energy.

"I understand that you're a cracking pigeon trainer, and that
you were studying zoology before the war."

"Second part is true," Susan said.

"I've come to offer you a job," he said. "I'm raising pigeons in
Northampton, away from the bombs. The farm is rather large, to
accommodate the training of both one-way and two-way pigeons." He paused, then wiped rain from his hat. "I'd like your
help."

Susan shook her head. "I can't leave."

Jonathan took a deep breath and sighed. "How long can you
live like this?"

The man's candidness reminded her that she had no job and
no money. She had little chance of maintaining, let alone restor-
ing, the farm. Maybe it was her stubbornness, shell shock, or perhaps even madness that enabled her to carry on living under the
Luftwaffe bombardment. But deep down, she knew there was
something else that was keeping her rooted. "Until I rebuild,"
she said.

"There's no time," he said. "The invasion could occur at any
moment."

Susan recalled the disturbing posters, illustrations of German soldiers and parachutists, presumably to help one spot the enemy, plastered over the village. The ringing of church bells had been banned months ago; they were to be rung only when the enemy invaded. Even the Home Guard, slow but spirited old men, had begun affixing armored plates to their automobiles.

"I've never forgotten how you stood up to our military at the Source Columba meeting in London," he said. "When members of the National Pigeon Service, including myself, failed to speak up on obvious errors, you had the courage to stand alone."

Susan thought of the meeting in London. A flash of Ollie coming to her aid on the train.

Jonathan sighed, then looked at Susan. "Bertie adored you."

Hearing her grandfather's name caused her eyes to water.

"He'd want you to move on."

Susan deliberated, torn between abandoning the farm and letting go of her last bit of hope. But Jonathan had shaken her core. *He's not coming back.*

"Join me," Jonathan said.

Susan wiped her face. "I have pigeons."

"We'll take them," he said. "I brought baskets. My lorry is at the end of the lane, which is too muddy to drive on, I'm afraid. We'll have to carry them."

Susan wavered. Her mind and body were drained. Her heart ached with remorse. She'd never given up on anything in her life, at least nothing that mattered. But how could she go on? Tired, hungry, and defeated, she closed her eyes and said, "Very well."

For the afternoon, under a drizzling rain, they loaded the pigeons onto Jonathan's lorry. Susan gathered her few belongings—an armful of clothes and the tea tin. She had Jonathan drive her to see Mrs. McCreary; she returned the sewing basket, kissed her on the cheek, and thanked her for all she'd done. Before departing, she gave Mrs. McCreary Jonathan's address in Northampton where she could be reached.

As they drove away, Susan's hands trembled. *Be an egg.* She buried her fear, determined to someday return to Epping, assuming Britain wasn't occupied by Hitler's army. "I'll be back after the war," she whispered to herself.

CHAPTER 55

EPPING, ENGLAND — JULY 18, 1996

"Seventeen, eighteen, nineteen," Susan counted.

"No peeking!" a small boy shouted.

"Yes, no peeking, Grandmother!" a girl called.

"Twenty-one, twenty-two, twenty-three . . ." Susan pressed her hands over her eyes. A cabinet squeaked open and abruptly closed. The screen door banged against its frame. The patter of small feet faded away. "Ninety-eight, ninety-nine, one hundred. Ready or not, here I come."

Susan lowered her hands. Her eyes squinted, adjusting to sunlight spraying through the kitchen window. She stood from her chair, hoping the pain in her knees would allow her to hold out long enough to finish the game. Last week, she had only enough stamina in her rickety legs for two rounds of hide-and-seek, disappointing her grandchildren—Hugh, age five, and Evie, seven. So today she'd chosen to use her cane, an ugly metal contraption with four miniature stubby legs. "It's for extra stability," her doctor had said. But she hated it. And rarely used it, except for when she needed extra endurance, like the days her daughter, Clover, dropped off the grandchildren.

Susan hobbled over the hardwood floor. A warm breeze blew through an open window near the fireplace, the only original part of the structure, although the stones were now in all the wrong places. She'd rebuilt the cottage five years ago, much to Clover's dismay. "Perhaps it would be more prudent to consider a retirement home," Clover had said. But although she respected Clover's opinion, it was her life. And most of her life, at least to this point, had been centered in London.

During the remainder of the war, Susan trained war pigeons in Northampton. After the war, she finished her studies and became an ornithology professor at the University of London. She got married at the overripe age of thirty-three. Raised a child. Retired. And buried a husband, Duncan, after a long and arduous battle with colon cancer. Her mark in this world, she believed, was nearly complete.

"I'm returning to Epping," Susan had told Clover as they cleaned out Duncan's closet. Clover didn't understand. How could she? Although Susan had retained the deed to the land, she'd only taken Clover, mostly as a wee child, on family picnics to the farm. The pasture had been overrun with thistle. The lofts were dilapidated. The shelter had collapsed. And Clover, not being an outdoorsy child, had refused to tinkle in the woods, let alone step foot in a spider-infested loo. The picnics were often cut short as they rushed off to a filling station with Clover's bladder about to burst.

A year after Duncan's passing, Susan began rebuilding the cottage. From memory, she worked with a local contractor to build a replica of the structure. It looked much as it did before the war, with one large exception: the cottage was one story, instead of two. "Your knees, Mother," Clover had said as they reviewed the architectural blueprints. Despite giving in to her daughter's insistence on leaving out the stairs, the cottage turned out splendidly. Susan started by spending weekends at the cottage. But within a year, she'd sold her flat in London and moved to Epping. She acquired sheep, and as their bellies fattened, the field once again turned green and fertile. And although Clover didn't fancy the farm, Susan's grandchildren had grown quite fond of their provincial retreat.

"I'm going to find you," Susan said, crossing the living room. A rustling from down the hall. Susan smiled as she made her way to a guest bedroom.

"Ahem," a wee voice whispered.

Susan turned and saw the tip of a child's shoe sticking out from under the bed.

"I wonder where you could be." Susan's cane clumped over the floor.

The foot wiggled.

Susan lowered herself, disregarding pain in her kneecaps. She plucked off the boy's shoe and tickled his foot.

"Aaaahhh!" Hugh giggled.

Susan grabbed the boy's chubby calves and slid him out from under the bed.

Hugh squeezed her. "You cheated!"

"I did no such thing," Susan said, helping Hugh put on his shoe.

"I'm it!" he proudly proclaimed.

Susan marveled at Hugh's delight in being caught. And at how much he resembled Bertie. Stocky frame. Small barrel chest. His legs, adorably bowed, like the forearms of a pug.

Hugh ran outside and shouted, "Olly olly oxen free!"

Susan, returning to the living room, looked out the window and saw Evie, a thin, wiry girl with curly chestnut hair, galloping over the rows of sea lavender. She stepped on asters, squishing their stems, and sprinted toward the porch. Susan smiled. Where a garden once grew bland cabbage and root vegetables, it now contained a variety of flowers. After the war, she'd lost her taste for homegrown food and relished buying her groceries in a store, without the necessity of a ration book.

They played two more rounds of hide-and-seek. Then Susan

made lunch—leftover lentil soup, crackers, and tall glasses of Irn-Bru.

"Mother doesn't let us drink soda," Evie said, dipping a cracker into her Irn-Bru.

Hugh took a big gulp, then burped.

"Hugh," Evie said, giving her brother an elbow.

"Sorry," Hugh said.

Susan took a drink of her soda—a sweet, citrusy orange concoction. She much preferred a glass of water or a cup of black tea. But she was glad to have made the purchase, if only to create a memory.

They spent the afternoon, as they usually did during the children's visits, with the pigeons. Along with the loo, the loft was one of the few surviving remnants on the property. Although the structure had been reduced to warped and rotted boards, Susan had had it restored by a local handyman. Except for a plastic grain barrel and the fact that there were only a dozen pigeons, the loft looked much as it did before the war.

Unlike their mother, Clover, who seemed to have an innate fear of feathered reptiles, Hugh and Evie adored pigeons. Often during the children's visits, they'd each select a pigeon, tie a color-coded ribbon around its leg, then take a road trip to Clacton-on-Sea. Without the aid of cages, there were occasional droppings on the seats and several episodes of pigeons flying freely about inside the car, which required them to keep the windows rolled up. After arriving in Clacton-on-Sea, they'd toss their respective pigeons into the air, jump back into the car, and race home. But they never knew who had won. The pigeons always arrived first. And Evie and Hugh never seemed to mind, since Susan always stopped on the way home for ice cream.

"You're lovely, Bashful," Evie said, stroking a pigeon's back.

The pigeon cooed.

Hugh plucked a rather hefty pigeon from its cubby, held it above his head like a trophy, and said, "Buzz Lightyear is faster."

Susan chuckled. Most of the pigeons were named after the Seven Dwarfs, the remainder after various animated movie characters. Susan thought of her grandfather. Bertie, fond of naming all his racing pigeons after remote Scottish landmasses, none of which he had ever visited, would have been appalled of such commercialized naming. But she didn't mind the daft labels. After all, she'd once done the same thing. *A lifetime ago.*

They spent the afternoon in the loft, until a car horn sounded. Hugh and Evie tucked the pigeons they were holding back into their cubbies and ran outside. Susan stepped from the loft, purposely leaving her cane inside, and gingerly walked to Clover's shiny black sedan that was parked in the drive.

Clover checked her lipstick in the rearview mirror, then lowered the window.

"You're early." Susan stepped to the car, its engine still running.

"I have a meeting tonight, remember?"

"I must have forgotten," Susan said, noticing Clover's navy dress and pearl earrings. Her brown hair was neatly combed. Clover, a lawyer—as well as a divorced single mother raising two children—always seemed to be rushing off somewhere.

"Aw," said Evie, "can't we stay?"

"Not tonight," Clover said. "I've arranged for a sitter."

"They could stay with me," Susan offered.

"Please," begged Hugh.

"Next time," Clover said. "We need to go."

Susan hugged Evie and Hugh, then helped them into the car and buckled their seats. She stepped to the driver's door.

"Have fun?" Clover asked.

Susan nodded. She leaned in and gave her daughter a hug, careful not to smudge her makeup.

Clover reached into the passenger seat and produced a pile of mail and newspapers. "These have been collecting at the mailbox."

Susan took the stack.

"I overheard a colleague talking about a pigeon article in the newspaper," Clover said. "I've been too busy to read the papers, I'm afraid. Otherwise, I would've cut it out for you."

Susan adjusted her weight, then grimaced when she felt a twinge in her leg.

"Knees?" Clover asked.

"They're fine," she said, recalling how Clover, for the better part of two years, insistently brought up that she should have knee-replacement surgery. And she wasn't about to admit that the long walks down the lane for the mail wreaked havoc on her dodgy joints. "Perhaps you could come and stay next weekend with Evie and Hugh," Susan said, trying to change the subject.

"You could come to London," Clover said.

Susan nodded toward the loft. "Pigeons."

"Bring the pigeons!" Hugh called from the back seat.

Clover looked in the rearview mirror. "No, Grandmother *can't* bring the pigeons."

"We should build a loft," Evie added.

Clover sighed and placed her hands on the steering wheel. "I'll check my schedule," she said to Susan. "In the meantime, see if you can find someone to care for the pigeons."

Susan nodded, then watched her drive away with Evie and Hugh waving their hands. She loved Clover. And she knew that her daughter cared for her. But they were, quite simply, different people. As she made her way back to the cottage, she thought of Hugh's and Evie's designer tennis shoes, likely purchased by their mother at Harrods or Selfridges, specked with pigeon droppings. Susan grinned.

Inside, she made a cup of chamomile tea and turned on the television, trying to avoid the loneliness that always accompanied the departure of the grandchildren. Reluctantly, she began sorting through the pile of junk mail—solicitations for credit cards and mounds of coupons—which she tossed in the trash. Then she settled into her living room chair with the stack of newspapers. With her legs propped on a cushioned ottoman, she put on her readers and flipped through the oldest edition, searching for the article that Clover had mentioned. After several pages, she noticed an unusual headline and stopped.

REMAINS OF WWII HOMING PIGEON FOUND IN ROCHFORD CHIMNEY

He endured a treacherous flight over the Channel, flying many miles from Nazi-occupied Europe. The weary war pigeon, carrying a secret message inside a capsule attached to his leg, must have fluttered to a chimney in Rochford, perhaps to rest or to warm himself from a fire. Likely overwhelmed by fumes, the pigeon plummeted from his resting place and perished. His skeletal remains have gone unnoticed for over fifty years, until Niles Googins purchased the property and began renovations.

Susan sat up straight and adjusted her reading glasses.

"I was cleaning out the fireplace; the damper was clogged with rubbish," he said on Monday. "I was pulling out debris and noticed small bones. At first, I thought it was the remains of a crow, until I noticed a red capsule attached to his leg."

Mr. Googins, a retired mathematics professor, opened the capsule and discovered a coded message on a bit of paper. The message has been dispatched to curators at Bletchley Park, where efforts to break the Nazi Enigma code turned the tide of the war. The Government Communications Headquarters (GCHQ) in Cheltenham is also diligently working to decode the message.

"Poor soul," she whispered to herself. Briefly, she wondered if it could have been Duchess or one of her other pigeons, either from Bertie's farm or Northampton. But considering the military had used over 250,000 homing pigeons during the war, the chances were unlikely. She tossed the newspaper to the floor and quickly scanned the more recent editions, hoping to find an update on the story. She found what she was looking for in yesterday's paper.

BLETCHLEY PARK AND GCHQ DUMBFOUNDED BY SECRET MESSAGE!

Experts at Bletchley Park and GCHQ are baffled by the coded message of a World War II spy pigeon found earlier this week in a Rochford chimney. They believe the red capsule Mr. Googins, a retired professor, found while renovating his house, is a type used during early intelligence operations. But to date, the code is undecipherable.

Susan exhaled. Her heartbeat accelerated.

"The communication this pigeon was carrying must have been of the highest secrecy," said Alton Ross, an intelligence specialist at GCHQ. "Thousands of pigeons were used during the war, but the messages in historical records are in ordinary handwriting, not cipher. The red capsule indicates that it's an Allied pigeon, likely from 1940. The encrypted message has us perplexed. But I'm confident we'll decipher the code in short order."

Susan stood, noticing that the ache in her knees had spread to her belly. She took in several deep breaths, which did little to allay her apprehension. She dreaded reopening memories of the war, but she had to know. Slowly, she stepped to the phone, then dialed for the operator. "Can you connect me to a Niles Googins in Rochford?"

A moment later, an elderly man's voice answered.

"Mr. Googins?"

"Yes."

"My name is Susan Shepherd," she said. "I read about the remains of a pigeon you discovered."

"I've spoken to enough reporters," Googins said. "There's nothing more to tell."

"I'm not a reporter," Susan said, surprised that Googins couldn't sense the age in her voice. "I once trained pigeons for the National Pigeon Service during the war."

"Oh," Googins said. "The calls have been nonstop since the release of the first newspaper article. Reporters. Journalists. History enthusiasts. War veterans. They've all called. Even a self-proclaimed clairvoyant from Cambridge who claimed that she could decipher the pigeon's message, for a nominal fee of course."

"It sounds as if you've had quite a response from your find," Susan said.

"Indeed."

"May I ask you a few questions, Mr. Googins?" She heard the man sigh. "I promise to be brief."

"Very well," he said.

"The article referred to the pigeon as *he*. How did you know it was a male?"

"Aren't all war birds male?"

Pigeons, Susan wanted to correct but held her thought. "No, we used both male and female. Did anyone try to verify the gender?"

"No, I don't believe so," he said, sounding a little embarrassed.

"Did you happen to notice the shape of the pigeon's head? A male's head is rather round, but a hen's skull will typically have a flat area on top."

"Hold on," Googins said.

Susan heard a clunk as the receiver dropped. She grimaced at the thought of a war pigeon being stored, in all likelihood, inside a shoe box or a piece of Tupperware.

"It's a she," Googins said, picking up the phone. "You're the first person to ask about this. All the others have only been interested in the message."

Susan paused. "Speaking of the message, did it contain a series of five-letter words? No numbers."

"Yes," Googins said. "Have you seen it? Bletchley Park and GCHQ weren't supposed to release the message to the papers until after the code was broken."

"No," Susan said. "Did you happen to make a copy?"

"I did better than that," Googins said. "I have the original."

CHAPTER 56

ROCHFORD, ENGLAND

The following morning, Susan drove to Rochford, a little over an hour from Epping. In the passenger seat was a tarnished tea tin that she'd kept for over half a century. It would have done no good, she believed, to have revealed to her husband or daughter that she once had had affection for another man. So she'd kept it hidden in a keepsake box. It was, and would always be, her secret, encased inside that tea tin. And in a small, but impenetrable, compartment within her heart.

She'd barely slept. Fear of what she might find, or not find, broiled in her brain, resurrecting vile memories of the war. Sirens. Explosions. The sickening odor of expelled gunpowder. Bertie's lifeless limbs protruding from rubble. In an attempt to rid herself of the visions, she resorted to placing a record, "The Lark Ascending," by Vaughan Williams, on her vintage console stereo. She'd listened to it over and over. A penny taped to the stylus kept the needle from skipping. But the angelic music had done little to soothe the wounds of the past. Nor did it dispel the anxiety of what tomorrow might bring.

Following the directions Mr. Googins had given her, she arrived at a sand-colored brick row house with small windows and a crooked television antenna protruding from the roof. She parked the car on the street and got out. Carrying the tin, she proceeded to the front door. The pain in her legs soon reminded her that she'd forgotten her cane at home. Her joints cracked as she climbed the porch steps. She knocked. Her heartbeat quickened. A lock clicked, and the door opened.

"Susan?" A gray-haired man wearing khaki pants and a tartan shirt extended his arm. "Niles Googins."

Susan shook the man's hand.

Niles turned to a woman beside him wearing large round glasses and a blue sweater; her wrinkled, pink-hued cheeks were powdered with makeup. "My wife, Lydia."

"Pleased to meet you," Lydia said.

Susan stepped into the home, noticing stacks of crown molding on the floor. The smell of fresh paint lingered in the air.

"Don't mind the mess," Mr. Googins said. "We're remodeling." He led Susan to the living room, then pointed to a fireplace. "I found it in there."

Susan looked at an old coal-burning fireplace but noticed the items on a coffee table. A small clear-plastic display case. Inside, resting on a thin pad of foam, the remains of a pigeon. A skull. Bits of wing. And two leg bones, one with an attached red canister. With quivering hands, she stepped closer. Beside the case, a small message. Although the piece of paper had turned brown from age, she immediately recognized the code and the distinctive penmanship. Her eyes watered.

"Oh dear," Lydia said. She left and returned with a tissue.

"Thank you," Susan said, accepting the tissue. She wiped her eyes and stared at the remains inside the plastic case. "Duchess."

"Who?" Mr. Googins asked.

"My pigeon. A pet, really."

"Pet?" His forehead wrinkled with confusion. "See the capsule? It's a war pigeon."

Susan shook her head. "She was mistakenly loaded onto a

plane in the autumn of 1940. It was one of the first missions to drop homing pigeons into Nazi-occupied France to gain intelligence. The plane was shot down with an American onboard." She glanced at the coded piece of paper and thought of Ollie. Somehow, he must have managed to avoid capture long enough to relay another message. She took a deep breath, trying to contain the swells of sorrow building inside her chest. "The message is from him."

"This seems rather unusual," Mr. Googins said, crossing his arms. "The United States wasn't a participant in the war in 1940."

"Ollie was," she said.

"Ollie?" he asked.

Susan nodded. *Oliver from Maine.* She dabbed away tears.

He took a deep breath and sighed. "How do we know this is Duchess and a message from Ollie?"

"Niles," Lydia said sternly.

"I'm merely asking a question, Lydia," he said, lowering his head.

Susan lifted her tin. She popped off the lid and spread its contents—coded and deciphered messages—over the coffee table.

Lydia took one of Susan's coded messages and compared it to the one found in their chimney. Her eyes glanced back and forth between the papers. "It's the same code, Niles. And the same handwriting."

Niles examined the messages, taking more time than his wife, then nodded.

Susan noticed Lydia staring at the deciphered messages. She sensed that Lydia understood that the communication was far more than a matter of intelligence. This was confirmed when the woman touched her arm and said, "Was Ollie your husband?"

"No," Susan said. Her chest ached, as if her torso were being compressed in a vice. "He didn't make it out of France."

"I'm so sorry," Lydia said.

After a long pause, Niles turned to Susan and said, "Can you interpret the message?"

"I don't know," Susan said. "I used to have the codebook, but it was destroyed during the Blitz." She took a deep breath, then exhaled. "I suppose I could try decoding it by using the other messages."

"We'll need to inform GCHQ," Niles said.

"We'll do no such thing." Lydia glanced at the pigeon remains on the coffee table, then carefully began placing the messages back into Susan's tin, including the one found in the fireplace.

Niles's eyes widened. "Lydia."

She looked at her husband. "Are you convinced that this is Susan's pigeon and that this message was intended for her?"

Niles hesitated, then said, "Yes, but . . ."

"These belong with you, dear," Lydia said, cutting off her husband. She handed Susan the tin and plastic case.

Susan looked at Lydia. "Thank you."

"But, Lydia," Niles said.

Lydia turned to her husband. "Do you remember the letters you wrote me when you were in service?"

Niles squirmed.

"How would you like those letters posted for the world to see?"

His face flushed. Red blotches covered his neck.

Lydia patted her husband's leg. "And if you say a word about this to anyone, I'll make sure a copy of those lovely letters you sent me as a young chap end up in the hands of your golf club."

CHAPTER 57

EPPING, ENGLAND

Susan stopped twice on the drive home to clear her watery eyes. Parked on the side of the road, she stared at the bones in the passenger seat. Inside the tin, a message from Ollie. Her head and heart reeled as the past collided with the present.

She arrived home with the intent to give Duchess a proper burial. But as she carried the remains and a garden trowel to the forest, she couldn't bring herself to break the ground. The least she could do before placing her pigeon into the earth was to decipher the message. And finish what Duchess had given her life for. So she returned to the cottage and went to work.

For a month, Susan worked relentlessly on decoding the message. She spent her days and evenings scouring over the codes. Desperate to translate Ollie's note, she took little time to eat and sleep. Exhausted, she began falling asleep at the kitchen table. And she resorted to setting an egg timer to force herself to take breaks. But either her mind was failing from age, she believed, or the words that Ollie had selected were quite different. After weeks of racking her brain over the codes, she had managed to decipher only one word, *Susan*, which was consistent with the other messages. She feared that she'd never be able to decipher

Ollie's words and that Duchess would remain in purgatory, sealed in a plastic sarcophagus at the bottom of her dresser.

As she deliberated over the message, a long dormant ache began to grow. Her broken heart, pieced together by time, had once again begun to crack. And accompanying the pang in her chest, a strange sense of indiscretion. Her thoughts were on Ollie, not Duncan.

She'd met Duncan five years after the war, shortly after completing her studies and accepting a position as a professor of ornithology at the university. Duncan, an engineering professor, had courted her, despite her overt lack of interest in him. But he was persistent, well-mannered, and, according to her colleagues, a good suitor. After a year of declining his offers to join him for dinner, she finally accepted. *Ollie's gone*, she told herself as Duncan sat across from her, eating his roast chicken and peas.

She liked Duncan, despite his banal appearance and predictable nature. And who was she to be critiquing courters? After all, she was sometimes referred to as the "peculiar pigeon lady" by some of her students, when they learned she'd trained pigeons for the war. After a year of rather one-sided courtship, Duncan proposed. She accepted. Perhaps she didn't want to live her life as a hermit. Or maybe the passing of time had enabled her to give in to the rules of social expectations—get married, have children, and make one's mark in the world. But deep down, she'd simply come to accept that there was only one true love in a person's life. And her Ollie was gone.

She'd had a good life, she supposed. Also, she had Clover and her grandchildren, Evie and Hugh, reassuring her that she'd made the right decision. Over the years, Susan had grown quite fond of Duncan. He was kind, gentle, fatherly, and always bringing her fresh fruit. "Helps with your potassium," he'd routinely say, as he'd give her a bunch of bananas. By all accounts, Duncan was a good and decent man. But she never again experienced those beautiful butterflies in her tummy, the ones that had migrated away in the autumn of 1940. And never returned.

By September, Susan had succumbed to the fact that she'd never read Ollie's message. Without the codebook, it was impossible to decipher. Besides, Bletchley Park and GCHQ had likely already interpreted the message weeks ago but were too embarrassed to report the findings. But she was proven wrong when another article appeared in the newspaper. The article was similar to the previous ones, simply requoting Googins's finding in his chimney; however, this one revealed that both Bletchley and GCHQ were baffled. And pasted below the article, a copy of Ollie's coded message:

QUYTV SODLC SKDFN SKLFE ZIEPQ DJRNV
SKWNF DOIWV JLDWP AWXPD MCJKW RSUEW
WQXZX YMSQR PLNVX SQMCI QYDSX POLRT
SKFRY XVCTR LKJHG SDFGH OIUYT QWEDR
KNVDG WDCVG ZDTUO

"Good Lord!" Susan exclaimed over her buttered toast.

She read the article twice, unable to fathom that *her* message was posted for the world to see. Not only were Bletchley and GCHQ still working on deciphering the code, amateur code breakers and history buffs would likely be racing to be the first to claim that they had solved the mystery.

Susan folded the newspaper, went to the phone, and called Clover. "Could you come to Epping this evening?" She paused, struggling to find her words. "There's something rather important I need to tell you."

Clover left work early, stopping only to pick up her children from day care. As Evie and Hugh played in the pigeon loft, Susan retrieved her tin and the newspaper clippings, then joined Clover, sitting at the kitchen table.

"Are you all right?" Clover said, fumbling with her earring.

She always rubs her lobes when she's worried. "I'm fine," Susan said, trying to reassure her daughter. "I'm not dying, nor have I contracted a debilitating geriatric disease."

"Why couldn't we simply talk on the phone?"

Susan noticed a tone of concern in her daughter's voice. "I want you to learn of this from me, rather from somewhere else. Also, I need to show you something." She handed her the most recent newspaper clipping.

Clover read the article. "This has something to do with you?"

Susan nodded.

"I knew you had raised war pigeons, but you never said anything about secret messages." She glanced at the article. "Did you work at Bletchley? I thought you had raised pigeons in Northampton. I had no idea you were involved with intelligence. . . ."

Susan shook her head. "It's a personal matter, I'm afraid." Susan uncapped the tin and spread the contents over the table.

Clover's jaw dropped.

Susan looked at her daughter. "Before I met your father . . ." She handed her an aged piece of paper.

She glanced at the message, then stared at her mother.

Susan noticed how much Clover looked like her father—high cheekbones, small nose, and a swirling cowlick in her bangs. Seeing the resemblance and realizing what she was about to say caused a lump to form in her throat. She swallowed. And for the next hour, she told her everything. About Source Columba. Duchess. Bertie. And how, during the Blitz, she had communicated with an American trapped in Nazi-occupied France.

"My God, Mother." Clover gave a long sigh.

Susan expected her daughter to be upset. Confused. Perhaps even betrayed by the fact that her mother had once had feelings for another man. But Clover surprised her.

"You were quite fond of each other," Clover said, glancing at the deciphered messages.

Susan nodded.

Clover clasped her earring, as if the backing had fallen off. "Were you in love with him?"

She paused, surprised by her daughter's candidness, then nodded.

"Ollie never returned?"

Hearing his name caused Susan's belly to ache. She shook her head.

Clover held her mother's hand.

Moved by her daughter's touch, Susan's eyes welled with tears. After all, Clover wasn't a hugger. Even as a child, she had disliked being held, let alone touched. Susan squeezed her fingers. "It was a long time ago, dear."

"But you wanted me to know?"

"Yes," Susan said. "I'm tired of keeping a secret. And I wanted you to know, in the event they ever decipher the code and link the message to me. There were few women in the National Pigeon Service. I'm likely the only one named Susan."

Clover looked at the newspaper clipping. "I'm surprised that Bletchley and GCHQ haven't deciphered the code."

"My father's codebook was from the Great War," Susan said. "Perhaps they're focusing on codes from the wrong war."

"Mother, they cracked the Nazi Enigma machine, for God's sake. They'll decipher this message." Clover released her mother's hand and smiled. "They'll be shocked when they read this."

Susan chuckled, then wiped her eyes.

"Don't you want to know what this says?" Clover asked. "These messages could help them break the code."

"Yes, but I'm not about to give them *my* messages," Susan said.

"Why?"

Susan recalled her and Bertie's decision not to turn over Ollie's messages to the RAF. Even after half a century, her grandfather's words still echoed in her memories. *Our military will get their intelligence. But they will not see what is meant for you.*

"Ollie intended this to be read by me, not our government," Susan said. "More than anything, I want to know what's on that piece of paper. But my heart is telling me that I should do this on my own."

"Is there anything I can do?" Clover asked.

"You were always rather good at crosswords," Susan said, sliding the coded message to her. "Want to help me solve a puzzle?"

CHAPTER 58

EPPING, ENGLAND

The following weekend, Clover and the grandchildren stayed in Epping with Susan. During the day, mother and daughter played with Evie and Hugh, rounds of hide-and-seek and trips to Clacton-on-Sea to release pigeons. Hugh, a persistent child, had even persuaded his mother, squeamish about droppings and irrationally frightened of catching a case of the bird flu, to hold a pigeon.

Clover, her arms outstretched, squealed as the bird flapped its wings.

"You look like the queen holding a pile of poo," Susan said.

The children giggled.

In the evening, after the children were read a story and tucked into bed, she and Clover worked on the message, although they spent more time talking. To Susan, Clover seemed genuinely interested, wanting to know more about Ollie, Bertie, and her role in the National Pigeon Service. Both nights, they stayed up late drinking tea and eating sweet-meal biscuits. And by Sunday evening, they'd gotten no further than where they'd started. But Susan had, for the first time in years, truly connected with her daughter. Despite not getting any closer to deciphering the code, she cherished her time with Clover and her grandchildren.

"Mother, what do you think about hiring a cryptanalyst?" Clover asked, as she placed her luggage into her car.

Susan scratched her head.

"A code breaker." Clover buckled her children into their seats. "With the other letters, an expert might be able to decipher the message." She stepped to her mother. "Of course, I'd make sure we had a confidentiality agreement in place."

"I'll think about it," Susan said.

Clover nodded.

"I enjoyed our time together," Susan said.

Clover smiled. "Me too." She got behind the wheel and started the car.

As they drove away, Susan blew kisses to her grandchildren, then returned to the cottage. The silence was deafening. Alone, the pressure returned, as if she had been placed inside a hyperbaric chamber. Exhausted, she fell asleep in her chair.

CHAPTER 59

EPPING, ENGLAND

Susan woke with her back stiff, as if her spine had been replaced with a steel rod. She took three aspirin and stretched her vertebrae, trying to regain movement in her arthritic joints. Barely able to touch her knees, let alone her toes, she vowed to never fall asleep in a chair again.

When the pain had been reduced to a dull ache, she made her way to the pigeon loft. Because she was late with their breakfast, most of the pigeons were already waddling around the feeding tray. Out of habit, she rapped on the grain barrel with a wooden spoon, then poured feed. She watched the pigeons peck and strut. Their talons scratched over the plywood floor. The cooing and familiar musty scent of the loft was comforting. But the temporary solace quickly faded when she thought of the indecipherable message inside her old tea tin—a ghost of the past, sealed like a genie. *Perhaps Clover was right*, she thought. *Maybe I should hire a code breaker.*

As she was refilling a water bowl, she heard a car engine. Pigeons fluttered. The sound of the automobile grew, then stopped. She stretched her back and grimaced. A car door squeaked open and shut. Stepping out of the loft, she saw a parked blue car. And a gray-haired man staring at the cottage.

The spring-hinged door banged behind her. "Hello," Susan called.

The man turned.

Susan squinted, wishing she hadn't left her glasses inside the cottage. "May I help you?"

He cleared his throat. "Susan."

The sound of his voice jolted her. She froze, believing her ears must be failing, just like her knees.

He walked toward her.

Her legs remained planted, as if her feet had suddenly sprouted roots. As he stepped to her, his face slowly came into focus. Although his cheeks and forehead were heavily wrinkled, she recognized the dimpled chin. Caramel eyes, dulled from age. His once wavy brown hair now white and wispy. "Ollie?"

He nodded.

"Oh my God."

He gazed into her eyes.

Her breath stalled in her chest. *You're alive!* Part of her wanted to wrap her arms around him. Hug him. Squeeze him. But the shock of seeing him spawned a flurry of mixed emotions. Her mind raced. *Why didn't you come back? Where have you been? What happened?* She stared at him, unable to speak.

He slowly reached his hand.

She stepped back. Her heart pounded with uncertainty. *Is it really you?*

Ollie lowered his arm and paused.

You survived but didn't bother to contact me. Susan's shoulders drooped as her joy turned sour.

"May I come in?" he asked.

She hesitated. *Were your promises merely a symptom of the war? Didn't you feel the same way about me?* And she realized that her precious memories, created under the duress of Luftwaffe bombs, may have been distorted dreams. Lies. Suddenly, her elation was buried in an avalanche of heartbreak. She wanted to cry. But despite how much the truth would sting, she needed to know what had happened. "Be an egg," she whispered to herself. She took a deep breath, attempting to gather her fortitude, then led him to the cottage.

A few minutes later, they sat in the kitchen with a pot of freshly brewed tea. Susan's hand trembled as she stirred milk and sugar into his cup.

"Thank you," Ollie said. He took a sip and returned his cup to the table. "You look the same."

Susan, seated on the opposite side of the table, glanced down at her tea. The reflection of an old woman peered back at her. "I thought you were dead." The harshness of her words cut the air.

Ollie lowered his head.

Unable to bring herself to look at him, Susan fixated on a deep scratch in the tabletop.

"I saw an article in the paper," he said, breaking the silence. "I spoke with Lydia and Niles Googins. They told me where to find you."

Susan forced herself to take a sip of tea, hot and bitter. "Perhaps you should have called."

Ollie cleared his throat. "I guess I was afraid that you wouldn't want to see me."

Susan added a lump of sugar to her tea. She stirred. The spoon clanged against the cup.

Ollie glanced around the cottage, then pointed to a framed photograph on the wall. "Your family?"

Without looking up, Susan said, "My daughter, Clover, and my grandchildren, Evie and Hugh."

"They're beautiful." He took notice of another photo. "Your husband?"

Susan nodded, feeling her stomach tighten. "Duncan at his retirement party." She paused then said, "He passed away five years ago."

"I'm sorry." He gripped his cup. "Did you have a good life?"

Susan looked up. She crossed her arms and nodded.

"I'm glad," he said.

Confused about how to respond, Susan asked, "Do you have children?"

"No, unfortunately," Ollie said.

"Married?"

"Once." He paused. "Anna died from leukemia in '52."

"I'm sorry."

"It was a long time ago."

She swallowed. "You never remarried?"

Ollie shook his head.

"Where do you live?"

"Portland." He took a sip of tea. "Maine," he added.

Oliver from Maine, Bertie's voice crowed in her head.

"I retired there after working in Boston for a regional airline."

"You got to fly?" Susan asked.

Ollie nodded.

A swarm of questions buzzed in her head. She fidgeted with her spoon. Unable to contain her emotions any longer, she stood and poured her tea into the sink. With her back to him, she blurted out what she had wanted to ask since the moment she saw him. "How could you let me believe you were dead? For the past fifty years, you couldn't find the time to call or write me a letter?"

Ollie started to speak but was cut off.

"What happened?" She leaned against the counter, alleviating pain that was building in her knees.

Ollie took a deep breath. "Where do I begin?" he whispered to himself.

"Perhaps from the beginning."

Ollie ran a hand through his thin hair. After a long pause, he spoke. "In the winter of 1940, we attempted our escape from France. Crossing the Pyrenees mountain range, we encountered a Wehrmacht patrol. Our guide, Lucien, and Flight Lieutenant

Boar were killed." He rubbed his arm. "I was shot, attempting to cross a river into Spain."

Susan turned.

Ollie closed his eyes, searching through his memories. "I was saved from drowning by two boys. They plucked me out of the river and wrapped me in their coats; otherwise, I would have died from hypothermia. Instead of turning me in to the border authorities, they took me to a monastery. I spent two months recovering."

"Then you went back to the United States?"

Ollie shook his head. "Britain."

Her mouth turned dry.

"I made my way to Portugal with the help of clergy, then boarded a ship to Britain. I arrived in Epping in May 1941."

Susan covered her mouth.

He glanced around the room. "I found the cottage destroyed."

Susan thought of the bombing. A flash of her grandfather covered in debris. "Bertie was killed."

"I'm so sorry, Susan. Bertie was a wonderful man." He rubbed the rim of his cup. "I can't begin to imagine what you went through during the Blitz."

She stepped to the table and took a seat next to him.

He cleared his throat. "I traveled to Church Fenton and joined the Eagle Squadron. After the Blitz, the RAF was desperate for volunteer pilots, even an American crop-duster who could barely lift his arm high enough to pass the physical exam. I flew a Hurricane for the RAF until shortly after the Japanese bombing at Pearl Harbor. When the United States joined the war, I was transferred to the US Army Air Forces."

"Why didn't you look for me?" Susan asked. "I left word with the neighbors that I went to Northampton."

Ollie slowly reached his hand into his jacket and removed a small book, weathered and badly water-stained.

Susan's eyes widened, recognizing her father's codebook.

He lifted the cover. Inside, small yellowed pieces of paper, pressed like old garden flowers. He took the one on top and slid it to Susan. "This was the last message Duchess delivered to me."

Susan shuddered at the sound of her pigeon's name. She retrieved her reading glasses and immediately recognized that it wasn't her handwriting. And it wasn't coded. Her hands trembled as she read the message.

> *It is my painful duty to report the death of Bertie Shepherd and Susan Shepherd, National Pigeon Service, which occurred in Epping, England on the 27th of November 1940. The cause of death: bombing.*
> *Mission terminated.*
> *S. L. Williamson, Corporal, RAF*

Susan's hands quivered. She stared at the message. "You thought I was . . ."

"Yes," he said.

She squeezed the paper. A mixture of shock and anger jarred her body. "Who's Corporal Williamson? Why would he have sent this message?" She struggled to recall the names of the soldiers who were once stationed on the farm.

Ollie swallowed. "There was no Corporal Williamson."

She stared at him. Then it struck her. She quickly retrieved her tin, kept on a kitchen cart, and emptied its contents onto the table. Comparing the handwriting from a message, signed *Flight Lieutenant Clyde Boar, RAF*, she found the penmanship to be identical. "My God."

"Boar must've gotten to Duchess and switched messages," Ollie said.

"Why?" Susan's eyes blurred with tears.

"Maybe it was because he despised Americans, especially me. Or that he was jealous of us." He leaned forward. "I believe the tipping point was when he learned that he'd lost an eye. He turned bitter, realizing he'd never fly again. I suppose I became the target for his anger, and the message was initially meant to be a cruel joke, one that I'd figure out if I made it out of France." Ollie took a deep breath and exhaled. "And even more confusing, Boar saved my life on two separate occasions."

"I hate him," Susan said. "He took away our future."

He gently clasped her hands. "I spent the trip here trying to make sense of it all. I found myself regretting what I'd done, or not done. It was the longest flight of my life."

Susan sniffed. A tear dropped onto his hand, and she noticed that he made no effort to wipe it away.

"Initially, I refused to let myself believe the news that you and Bertie had been killed. I'd been away when Duchess had returned, and I'd assumed that Boar had written the message, although he adamantly denied it. But when I returned in the spring of '41, I found the farm destroyed. The field was pocked with craters. I abandoned my doubts about the validity of the message. And at that moment, and every day since, I believed that you were gone."

Susan stared at him. She noticed his lower lip tremble.

"I couldn't bring myself to stand over your grave. I had picked wildflowers from the meadow and placed them by a loft." Ollie lowered his head. "If only I had stayed in Epping, I would've found you."

"It's not your fault," Susan cried. "*He* did this to us."

Ollie drew a wavering breath. "When I learned you were alive, I was ecstatic. And at the same time devastated by the thought of what could have been."

She inched closer.

"I hate what Boar did, too. And I imagine I could spend the rest of my days as a resentful old man. But if it he hadn't harassed you on that crowded train from London, we would never have met. You would've gotten off in Epping. I would've traveled on to Church Fenton. Our paths would never have crossed." He caressed her hand. "And despite the briefness of our time together, I can't imagine my life without you."

She squeezed his fingers, sensing the time between them begin to melt away. "It wasn't enough."

He looked into her eyes. "I never stopped thinking of you."

A secret chamber of her heart, the one she'd kept closed for over half a century, began to open. "Nor I," she whispered.

"You were always with me," Ollie said.

Tears streamed down her cheeks. Waves of emotion flooded her body.

"It was your words and inspiration that gave me the strength to escape. To never give up."

Together, they wept. The dam holding back the years between them collapsed.

Ollie wiped away her tears.

Susan looked into his eyes, then gently touched his cheek. "There's something I need to show you."

CHAPTER 60

HOME

Susan and Ollie peered down at a freshly dug hole at the edge of Epping Forest. A warm breeze filtered through the woods, causing branches to sway and creak, silencing the chirping sparrows. The scent of damp earth and moss filled the air. Ollie leaned the spade against a birch tree, its bark peeling like old wallpaper. Slowly, he lowered himself to his knees.

In one hand, Susan held a plastic container with Duchess's remains; in the other, a small piece of paper.

Ollie looked up at Susan. His thin hair danced in the wind.

"She was a remarkable pigeon," Susan said, handing him the container.

"An angel."

She smiled.

Ollie lowered the remains into the hole, then filled it with soil. With his hands, he tamped the earthen mound. Then he located a flat rock, several inches in diameter, partially pushed up through the ground by the roots of a large elm. He pried up the slab and cleaned away the dirt. Too heavy to carry, he flipped the rock, end over end, until he reached the mound.

As Ollie placed the marker, Susan unfolded the deciphered message. And read it for the second time.

Susan, If there is a heaven, and I'm worthy of making it there, I promise to find you. Yours forever, Ollie

Ollie stood and wrapped his arm around her. "After all these years, she managed to bring us together."

Susan nuzzled into him. "She's home."

He held her tight. "So am I."

AUTHOR'S NOTE

While conducting research for this book, I became captivated by a 2012 British news report about the skeletal remains of a war pigeon that was found in a Surrey chimney, decades after the war. Attached to the pigeon's leg was an encrypted message, which would baffle GCHQ code breakers for years. The mystery of this war pigeon and its indecipherable message served as inspiration for writing this story.

During my fact-finding, I also became increasingly fascinated by the extent pigeons were used in World War II. The National Pigeon Service, a volunteer civilian organization in Britain, delivered some 250,000 war pigeons to British Services between 1939 and 1945. Source Columba was the actual code name for air-dropping 16,000 homing pigeons in German-occupied France and the Netherlands as a method for locals to provide intelligence to Britain, such as troop movements. I imagined Susan and Bertie to be dedicated members of the National Pigeon Service who believed that their extraordinary birds would help Britain survive.

In addition to war pigeons, I was intrigued to learn that over 200 volunteer American pilots served in the Eagle Squadrons of the Royal Air Force, prior to the United States joining the war in

December 1941. These brave men made their way to Britain,
usually through Canada, disregarding US Neutrality Acts.
Charles Sweeny, a wealthy Londoner, and Billy Bishop, a Canadian World War I air ace, played significant roles in recruiting
American volunteer pilots for the RAF. I envisioned that someone like Ollie, a crop-duster with British ancestry, would have
the skills and motivation to join the fight.

During my research—in particular on the early stage of World
War II—I discovered many compelling historical events, which I
strived to accurately weave into the timeline of this tale. For example, Epping's Sprigg's Oak Maternity Home was bombed on
October 9, 1940, killing eight expectant mothers who were seeking a safe place outside the city of London in which to deliver
their babies. The destruction that Ollie finds when he arrives in
Britain is the result of the bombings in Liverpool, specifically the
Cleveland Square shelter, which took a direct hit, resulting in the
death of at least sixteen civilians. Also, the Luftwaffe conducted
numerous raids on North Weald Airfield in 1940, one of which I
used to launch Ollie into German-occupied France. Additionally,
I attempted to accurately reflect the various types of aircraft that
were used by British and German forces during the early stage of
the war, as well as the various equipment and pigeon-raising
methods utilized by the National Pigeon Service. Any historical
inaccuracies in this story are mine and mine alone.

While several historical figures make appearances in this book,
it is important to emphasize that *The Long Flight Home* is a story of
fiction, and that I took creative liberties in writing this tale. For
example, I invented the secret meeting in London, where Susan
receives the orders for Source Columba. There would likely have
been a strict protocol for communication between the National
Pigeon Service, British Intelligence, and the Royal Air Force,
and my research found no instances of pigeon breeders of the
NPS attending meetings in the Cabinet War Rooms. Also, escape
routes through German-occupied France were less organized in

1940. Therefore, I based Ollie's escape route on a variation of the Comet line, a resistance network that operated later in the war. Also, Ollie and Boar find refuge with Madeleine and her truffle hog, Louis, in Airaines, a village in northern France. While truffle hunting is more prominent in southwestern France, I simply couldn't resist including a truffle hog.

Many books, newspaper articles, and historical publications were important to me in my research. *The Eagle Squadrons, Yanks in the RAF 1940–1942*, by Vern Haugland, was especially helpful in understanding the motivation and journey for US volunteer pilots who joined the RAF. *WW2 People's War*, an archive of World War II memories—written by the public and gathered by the BBC—was a tremendous resource for gaining insight into the fears and struggles of Londoners during the Blitz.

It was a labor of love to write this book. I will forever be inspired by the resiliency of the British people, who endured eight months of relentless bombing—from September 1940 to May 1941—which resulted in the deaths of 43,000 civilians. It is my hope that this story will honor the men, women, and children who perished in the Blitz.

This book would not have been possible without the help of many people. I'm eternally grateful to the following talented and hardworking individuals:

I am honored and humbled that John Scognamiglio selected this book for his imprint. I deeply appreciate John's editorial wisdom and enthusiasm for bringing this story to life.

Many thanks to my wonderful agent, Mark Gottlieb, for his support and guidance in finding a home for this book. I'm lucky to have Mark in my corner.

My deep thanks to Akron Writers' Group and my network of critique partners: Betty Woodlee, Becca Orchard, Ken Waters, Karl Ziellenbach, David Rais, Krissie Lynch, Dani Turos, John Stein, Sharon Jurist, Conrad Detweiler, Rocky Lewis, Suzanne Hodsden, Christine Wright, Shannon Waller, Carisa Taylor,

Cheri Passell, Anna Bialik, Kat McMullen, Kristen Weber, and Valerie Brooks. And a special heartfelt thanks to Betty—without her intuition and encouragement, this book might not have been written.

Last, but not least, this story would not have been possible without the love and support of my wife, Laurie, and our children, Catherine, Philip, Lizzy, Lauren, and Rachel. Laurie, you are—and always will be—the love of my life.

THE LONG FLIGHT HOME
ABOUT THIS GUIDE

The suggested questions are included to enhance your group's reading of Alan Hlad's *The Long Flight Home*.

1. Before reading *The Long Flight Home*, what did you know about homing pigeons used in World War II? Can you name additional animals that have served in times of war? What were the views on animal rights during World War II? After reading this book, do you feel the same about pigeons?

2. What are Susan's fears during the Blitz? Why does she believe her pigeons can help save Britain? What did you learn about the German bombing offensive against Britain in 1940 and 1941?

3. What are Ollie's motivations to disregard US neutrality and attempt to join the Royal Air Force? If Ollie's parents had not been killed in a car accident, do you think he would have embarked on a quest to join the fight? How does his encounter with an air marshal for the Royal Canadian Air Force, as well as being robbed in a train station, influence his decision to defer college and travel to Britain?

4. Describe Susan. What kind of woman is she? When Susan attends the Source Columba meeting in London, she is the only woman in the group. Describe Susan's courage, compared to other members of the National Pigeon Service, in confronting a senior military officer on the mission's errors. What is meant by the affirmation *Be an egg*? Describe her relationship with her

grandfather, Bertie. What role does Bertie play in shaping Susan's values and beliefs?

5. While working to prepare pigeons for the mission, Susan and Ollie fall in love. What brings them together? Why does their relationship develop so quickly? At what point do you think Susan realized she loved Ollie? How is the war, particularly the nightly Luftwaffe bombings, a catalyst for their affection? What are Susan and Ollie's hopes and dreams?

6. Duchess is Susan's loyal and devoted pet. What characteristics make her unique? Although Duchess is not trained to fly back and forth, she delivers messages between Susan and Ollie. Why do you think she's able to make the flights over the English Channel?

7. Describe Flight Lieutenant Clyde Boar. Why does Boar dislike Ollie? Does he have any redeeming qualities? When Boar intercepts Duchess, carrying Susan's message to Ollie, he's in a rage after learning that he's lost an eye and will never fly again. If Boar would have known the tragic outcome of deceiving Ollie and Susan, do you think he would have acted differently?

8. What are the major themes of *The Long Flight Home*?

9. Why do many readers enjoy historical fiction, in particular novels set in World War II? To what degree do you think Hlad took creative liberties with this story?

10. How do you envision what happens after the end of the book? What do you think Susan and Ollie's lives will be like?